BY THE SKIN OF THE TEETH

To my beloved mother

BY THE SKIN OF THE TEETH

G.E.M. MUNRO

Ted Munro

TAN*GENT* BOOKS, INC

Cover painting of Solania by G.E.M.M.

Printed & bound Canada

Canadian Cataloguing in Publication Data

ISBN 0-9688886-0-7

    1. Title.

PS8576.U573B87 2001   C813'.6   C2001-900763-9
PR9199.3.M814B87 2001

Tangent Books, Inc.
3120 8th Street East, #106 - 290
Saskatoon, SK
S7H 0W2

http://tangentbooks.20m.com

Foreword

Truth, it has been observed, is often stranger than fiction.

And now, G.E.M. Munro has demonstrated that fiction is capable of powerful verity. Indeed, *By The Skin Of The Teeth*, carries an abundance of powerful observations about life in urban Canada. It is worth noting that while the situations and characters portrayed in this novel are fictitious, the circumstances and angst of the personalities going about their daily business of survival in this harsh inner city environment are all too real.

It is perhaps trite to state that the relative prosperity that most Canadians are currently enjoying has not made its way through the diverse populace that comprises Canada. In fact, the essentials of life – comfortable housing, effective education and proper nutrition – are being denied many members of our community.

Adding to the disparity of circumstance and injustice of this divide, is the knowledge that the more privileged members of society – the more nefarious beings – prey on the vulnerable. So it is that the opportunistic politicians, pawnbrokers, slum landlords and religious zealots introduced in *By The Skin Of The Teeth* prosper at the expense of those at the lower end of the social and economic spectrum.

Against a backdrop of despair and misery emerges a saviour: Solania, a woman whose charisma and strength offer a measure of hope for her people.

If readers of *By The Skin Of The Teeth* encounter familiar issues and characters in this fictitious work, they should not be alarmed. The truth has found its way to the surface.

Warren Goulding
Author of Just Another Indian:
A Serial Killer and Canada's Indifference

Chapter One

Very gradually, I become aware of an irregular tapping noise. In consideration of its possible source, as my awareness rises from my nighttime stupour, hope is its counterweight, sinking to the inverse level. By degrees of wakefulness, the tapping could be:

Christine tapping on the inside of the old van window to attract the attention of a red squirrel on a nearby branch, in which case I shall hug her to me with desperate adoration, try to inhale her morning beauty by way of kisses, tell her that it is too early to awaken;

or a farmer wondering why our old van is parked in his long driveway, in which case I shall open the back door and try to mollify him with friendly explanations of how tired we were from driving, and how we could construe little of our surroundings in the dark, and thought maybe his driveway was a concession road where we could safely stop, just talk long enough for him to peer over my shoulder to Christine smiling at him as though he was an ambassador of goodwill, which, almost certainly, he will then become;

or the frustrated life inside me attempting one last halfhearted reminder that its gift to me is dwindling away uselessly;

or the faltering pulse inside my hangover head;

or Carney tapping tentatively on the window of my new van, step number one in his daily search for drink money;

or Morag in the kitchen banging thick globs of her sort of hollandaise sauce from a wooden spoon back into a pan as though she were ringing the bells of political freedom.

With reluctance and discomfort, I force my eyes open and fix them on the grey upholstered ceiling of my new minivan, typically disgusted by reality's typical insistence upon selecting the dreariest option. I am lying on the longer seat at the rear, and over its back, through the smoked rear window, I can make out the clouded image of Carney, shielding his eyes with slender scarred hands to try to peer inside.

Because I am steadily, if not gainfully, employed, Carney is convinced that I hold an endless supply of money, all of which might be devoted to the futility of his unquenchable thirst. He's out of luck this morning, though, because I manage to remember that, before I passed out last night, I counted out the last of my change in the barroom of the Inn Continent, buying one last round for me and Carney and his underage girlfriend Velvet and another older prostitute named Laura, who kept, through the lengthening evening, leaning toward me with conspiratorial familiarity to say "My boyfriend, he's gonna kill me if I give it to you for free.", until she and drunkenness reduced it to "My boyfriend, he's gonna kill me.", planting kiss after warm, flickering kiss on my passive mouth.

"Perles, you in there?" Carney asks, tapping again.

I turn my face to the back of the seat, press it into the sort of velvet/corduroy upholstery, grey with repeated little accents of black, which may actually be spots before my eyes. I can't remember. My eyes and cheekbones ache. Carney doesn't suffer from hangovers, or at least not to the extent of complaint; his hands will tremble like Chihuahuas, but his head never turns to a kettle-boiled-dry as mine does. Perhaps that's because he's a genuine alcoholic, whereas I am not; I'm wholly addicted to alcohol, through over-exposure, but I'm not an alcoholic.

Alcoholism offers fleeting pleasures, but I don't get any. Carney spends every day trying to drink, while I spend every day trying to not drink. When Carney takes his first drink, he has made his daily success; when I take my first drink, I've fallen into my daily failure. Drink can momentarily transform Carney into a cocky, optimistic, romantic bigshot, in the lies it tells him briefly allows him to escape the truth of who he is. Alcohol only grinds my kettle head against the truth of who I am so hard and hot, the sparks sear into my eyes, scorching black spots into them, and set my hair afire.

The single benefit that drink allows me is that it causes me to pass out. As I am no longer able to sleep at all, have been unable to sleep for many months, passing out has become a necessary substitute.

So if I'm drinking out, as I am increasingly lately, I often wake up in the morning on the back seat of my new minivan, which is all right, because I won't drive when drunk, and also because, just at the moment of passing out, I am sometimes able to pretend that I'm lying in the back of my old VW van with Christine in my embrace once again, clinging to her with a foresight and good sense I've never possessed.

But I drink out in the places where I am most comfortable doing so, where my companions understand drinking like mine and pass no judgment on it, which means that I'm always sticking my clean white van into this dark environ - a symbolism that no first-year Freudian psychology student could ever resist - and that I'm waking up in the neighborhood that both holds my heart and squeezes the life out of it, this when I'm least able to withstand the torturous manipulations of its circumstance.

Carney taps, and I briefly try to remember how I liberated myself from Laura's licentious generosity. I search my mind with a growing sense of a sort of weary alarm, as I have no recollection of the end of the evening, of taking my leave of the others, of climbing into my van. Black-outs have started with me only recently, and they still unsettle me, and here, apparently, is another one. This jabs at me sharply enough that I lunge up in reflex, into a sitting position. Carney detects a shadow of motion through the smoked window, and he knocks and calls my name.

Carney always avers that we're good friends; I'd like to believe that, because I have an undeniable fondness for him, but our relationship seems too unbalanced, and I never forget where an alcoholic's final loyalties lie. This morning, though, he's just an unwelcome reminder of last night's failure.

But I open the sliding side door when he comes around to it. The rising sun ricochets off his long black hair.

"Hey, bro," he says, "let's get some coffee."

"It'll have to be The Friendship," I say. "You guys cleaned me out last night."

Carney shakes his head, but in regret rather than refusal. It offends his unwarranted pride to partake of The Friendship Inn's charitably meted meals, as it does mine. It also bothers him terribly to beg on the street for drink money, an act of expedience I've never had to experience, a humiliation which Carney conceals beneath aggressive jocularity.

We totter west along 20th Street, past the government liquor store with its inexplicable red neon heart glowing above the doorway, where a few of the impatiently intemperate are already bunched like a mold culture, their faces disfigured in blotchy eruption by the explosions in their brains, and when we get to the corner of Ave. E, I look south to observe police cars parked at hasty angles of blockage, their lights glinting blue and red like the sun off Carney's hair. This isn't an unusual sight in this neighborhood, and Carney glances at the scene without curiosity or comment.

In the morning chill, old men stand in little knots around the entrance to The Friendship Inn, fragile old men of atrophied limbs and unsteady stance in filthy flapping rags like flags of surrender in the cold white wind that blew them here. Carney, who is still in his mid-twenties, passes some good-natured remark of ridicule as we step through them. I wonder once again if Carney doesn't see his own future in their battered faces, but of course the alcoholic dwells in a state of denial and avoidance I can only envy.

Across the street, in front of the grocery supermarket, a young man in a windbreaker and jeans tries to take the arm of his companion, a young woman who swivels her arm away from him in disapproval without removing her hands from the pockets of her coat. Her long hair and clothing are clean, and she stands upright, her shoulders unbowed and her feet planted firmly together. He snatches at her again, grips her arm above the shoulder, and tries to escort her across 20th St. to the doors of The Friendship. She shakes her head in a small, constrained motion, won't budge, opens her tight mouth only enough to express an obvious objection which I'm unable to hear.

He drops his hand, in frustration gestures to her, then across. She looks in silence and dismay to the gathered rag-tags there. He speaks to her, she speaks to him. I can't hear what they're saying, but I hardly need to.

Clearly, this place, this circumstance, doesn't fulfill her expectation for her life, her expectation for the capabilities of her young man and the life they would build together. For ten millennia and more, it has been his job to provide for her and for the future; for ten millennia and more, he has developed and refined the strengths and skills necessary to his responsibilities, and she has loved and esteemed him for it, has accepted his love and esteem as worthy of her. Now, on this bright, cool morning, they are having to confront that all his preparations, all her plans, have been for naught, all the apparent approval of natural process has been in error, that their strengths and skills are denied any application, that the last half-century of ten millennia has winnowed them, like some ironic head-smashed-in buffalo jump, inescapably to a trap, in which the best he can do to provide for her now is drag her, reluctant and ashamed, to a dreary dispensary of free food.

I can't imagine by what means they managed to run around, up until today, within the cinching circle of their circumstance, so they might have foolishly believed they were somehow eluding it as it tightened around them. I don't know in what fragile fantasy they now manage to be so disappointed.

He stands slumped before her, gesturing in thwarted impotence; he can't be the man they thought he was; he can't be the man he promised her he would be. Right now, in her humiliation, her respect for him begins to erode in the corrosive atmosphere of this place; maybe she loves him a little less. In this place, this inner city slum, evil grows fat feasting on the good.

I realize that she sees me watching her, so I look away, follow Carney through the front door.

Inside and upstairs, the director looks out at us through the open door of her office. I've written favourably about The Friendship Inn in my newspaper, and she probably presumes that I am here simply to soak up journalistic atmosphere. This part of the city and its issues are the beat of my column, after all. No one here begrudges the coffee, I know that; whenever I'm here the volunteer or fine option servers offer me breakfast, as well, but, on pitiful point of vestigial principle, I always refuse. I could, if I had the stomach for it, go home on such mornings to endure Morag's witty reproofs and fix my own breakfast of my own food.

Morag, being an assistant professor at the university, doesn't leave our house until ten or eleven a.m., and I can't wait that long for coffee.

The Friendship Inn isn't an inn at all, just a soup kitchen, really, consisting of a large main room with maybe twenty long plywood tables of metal legs and plastic and metal stacking chairs, a serious kitchen behind, and side offices arrayed around, and a couple of washrooms the staff can't always keep up with. Many of its customers prefer it to the Salvation Army because it doesn't require a religious service at all, although it does advance a vague atmosphere of imprecise Indian spirituality. Anyway, the Salvation Army is for bloody-minded racist raging middle-aged white men, who don't constitute the kind of company The Friendship Inn's customers wish to keep. The Friendship serves several hundred meals, morning and noon, every day, to the destitute, the dissolute, the desperate.

At one nearby table, Rose is sitting by herself. She smiles in a manner of bashful apology when she sees me, ducking her head down so that the tips of her braids dance in her breakfast, and avoiding direct contact with my eyes. I know that she cobbles together a little income by means of paper routes and flyer delivery and any other small opportunity that comes her way — in the dark early morning, she delivers the paper for which I write, making us colleagues in her mind — and could possibly afford to feed herself at her wretched tiny basement rental room; I believe she comes to the Inn for the Friendship part, though I'm not sure she finds much of that.

"Morning, Mr. Perles," she emits in her soft burp talk. I think she calls me "Mr." in deference to my more senior position with the newspaper.

"Morning, Rose," I say, and she smiles broadly and even gratefully, like a little girl, her face radiates, but twine tightens in her thin neck, stands out in straining relief, funnelling my gaze down to her tracheotomy hole.

Carney can't bear to look at Rose at all, because he

can't pull his eyes off the hole, and it, amongst all of the gross and grotesque situations and sights he invites into his life, of all things, makes him unbearably squeamish. I've seen Carney pull sutures out of an unhealed long deep gash on his leg just for the idle amusement of the exercise, but Rose's hole is too much for him.

Anyway, Carney's attention is captured by a young woman sitting at a table further in, who sits surrounded on either side and across by a number of young men and women, forming in appearance a sort of protective circle around her. Carney is, when sober, completely devoted to his little Velvet, but he stares at this other young woman as though she is something special.

In fact, she is something special; I remember her from having seen her some months ago, standing in the light of a morning quite like this, this pretty young woman, scrubbed clean and tidy, wholesome-looking even, of recent good nutrition and health, standing under the neon heart, laughing and smiling with patience and warmth as a lascivious filthy tattered drunk man twice her age gaped in loose red-mouthed laughter at his luck as he placed hammered hands all over her, anywhere, slackly sucked on her neck, and she even held him up by a hug as his atrophied legs quivered and failed in sexual agitation. "Evray bod-day rock yah bod-day," she sang mildly, meaninglessly, lovingly. She seemed to revel in her degradation, and she smiled coyly at me as I passed by, appalled. I later, in defense, wrote a column about her.

Such was the impression she made upon my jangled sensibility, I now recognize her immediately, even though I hadn't seen her since, and even though she is much changed from that morning. She has cropped her hair off very short, and her sheen of good nutrition and health is gone; she is very thin, even gaunt, her eyes large and deep, and she is no longer pretty; but she is, strangely, now beautiful, which may be what has arrested Carney's attention.

Of the group at her table, only she has a plate of food in front of her, but it looks as though she's eaten nothing but a nibble from one corner of the bland white toast.

She disregards Carney, but fixes her deep steady gaze on me, in an air of calm critical assessment. As we walk by her table, Carney grins like a goon, and she slowly holds out her hand to me, palm upward, and slowly assumes the same coy smile she'd worn before, as though we might be sharing a private joke.

"I don't have any money," I say.

"Give her twenty bucks," barks one of the young men, a burly and surly fellow named Buster who, whenever I encounter him the street, raises his chin and lowers his eyelids to me in the perfect picture of pride and pomposity.

"No money," I say.

She still smiles and quietly says "Check your pocket. Your left pocket."

"I don't need to check," I say, annoyed.

I walk on, but my progress is impeded by Carney walking sideways to gaze at the back of her head.

"Look out," I say, and Carney looks to me sharply, as though I've committed some indiscretion or sacrilege.

Carney was raised on a reservation, and prefers tea to coffee, and when we get to the serving counter, he prepares a cup while I pour myself some coffee. Carney mixes in amounts of both sugar and powdered whitener in sufficient quantities to concoct a terrible sort of thin, faintly tea-flavoured pudding.

Turning away from the counter, I realize that both Rose and the other young woman have turned in their seats to watch me. When I meet her eyes, Rose beams but looks away shyly. The other woman, though, continues to coolly, brazenly appraise me. A couple of her companions follow her eyes to me, but the others wait in apparent attendance.

Carney and I sit at the table closest to the counter. For something to do, I inspect a nearby poster that depicts a mother holding her baby. The message on the poster reads "The Strongest Tradition: Caring", and I momentarily wonder how some government bootlick was inspired to drool out such drivel, and why all the people who ever gathered here, lives bereft of all caring except for soup kitchen ekings, dregs of charitable lip service kiss off, accepted this drool as decoration.

Carney slurps at his concoction. I need to look at my hand with concentration in order to guide my cup somewhat steadily to my mouth. My kettle head is getting too heavy for me, I fear, cast iron, but I hate to display my weakness.

"Who is she?" I ask instead, for Carney is turned to look at the young woman.

"Who?"

I lower my brow to my hand as though in exasperation.

Carney chuckles and says "Her name's Solania."

"Solania?" I say. "What sort of name is that?"

"Her name," Carney says simply.

"Where's she from?" I ask.

Carney shrugs. "Not from here."

"What's the deal with all those boys hovering around her? Are they lovesick?"

"Some people, they're saying she's a prophet."

"These people find more prophets than the bingo hall," I say. "Someone comes along and predicts they'll get drunk that night, and by golly, they do, and there's another proven prophet."

"Maybe this one's different," Carney says.

"Yes, maybe," I say. "Maybe you should consult her

regarding your lovelife. What better use of gifted second sight into the eternal plans of providence could there be than a discovery of whether Velvet will love Carney? That seems to be its usual weighty and profound employment, after all."

"Maybe this one's different," says Carney.

"She looks to be very ill. What's wrong with her?"

"They say her visions really take it out of her. Leave her all weak and tired."

"Yes, well," I say, "the same can be said of alcohol, as I hardly need point out."

"Maybe she's different," Carney says yet again.

"And maybe she isn't," I say, standing up, impatience overcoming fatigue. "Simply tell you all that you're morally perfect, that all the mess you're in, all the stupid, self-indulgent things you do, are always someone else's fault— well, who but a gifted, sensitive seer psychically blessed by the Great Creator could have such profound insight into your miserably misspent meaningless little lives?"

Carney looks at me in sudden pain, and I, too, am taken a bit aback by my vitriol. I manage to smile as though I was joking.

"Then again, maybe she's different," I say by way of apology. My knees don't seem able to lock, so I get my legs moving. "See you later."

I no longer have any positive motivation in my life; I am as the last drop on the hot iron, impelled only by what I find so terribly intolerable: like a pretty young woman suddenly splattering against the wall that has always surrounded her little life, while an undeserving, selfish and smug young woman across the river prospers without effort; or a recollection of a beautiful young woman standing as an inflatable love doll to some lolling drunk while a demanding, privileged young woman across the river craftily selects from amongst her dangling dutiful suitors; or, in frustration, offending my patient and accepting friend. I build up some steam in my kettle head and propel myself down the aisle. Solania turns to mark my progress, raises her chin just slightly in the subtlest attitude of haughtiness as I come by, and slowly holds out her upturned hand again.

Her self-assurance in this circumstance strikes me as absurd, and I recklessly offer "If you see all, why don't you see that I'm broke?"

"Your left pocket," she says calmly.

"Why would I give you any money, if I had any?"

Her companions look at me with heavy, dark expressions.

"Well," she says slowly, her coy smile returning, "one day you will kneel before me as my servant, and when you rise again, it will be as my knight. But before you come to that day, you will have great suffering."

I think I must be resembling a fish she's caught and holds gasping in her hand.

I manage to say "What audacity! I bend my knee to no one."

But the danger is that I'm about to bend both knees to everyone, so I lurch out of the hall and stumble down the short stairway, and out onto the sidewalk. I glare at the feeble zombies who block my way, and they pleasingly shuffle aside. It's necessary for me to steady myself just briefly against the brown brick facade of The Friendship Inn before I continue along to my van, which now seems impossibly distant.

At Ave. E, the police are stretching their yellow plastic tape across the entrance to the back alley running behind 20th Street's two-storey stores. If I were professionally responsible, I would investigate; but then, if I were professionally responsible, I wouldn't be in this state that makes any enquiry far too strenuous an effort.

But then, "if" is a dark dog that I can chase backward through my life, all the way to where it gnaws mercilessly at, and bays over, the very instance of my weakness and cowardice that has condemned me to stumble in search of the treasure I couldn't hold, stagger in slow starvation, hunger that petrifies to black sharp shiny coal in my stomach.

I make it to my van, sit in the driver's seat and breathe deeply as though I've accomplished something.

My column is due twice a week. My midweek deadline is this morning, but I've written nothing. From under my seat, I pull a portfolio, and with fumbling fingers I unzip it, rifle through its contents, my stash of emergency backlogged columns. This stuff is pure gold, I don't think, a lazy and cynical betrayal of everyone who will read it hoping for a glimmer of the quality that my stuff was once widely deemed to contain. In this putrid pile I've got comical accounts of my ludicrous attempts to change the light bulb in the garage I don't really have, of my ludicrous attempts to humanely dispense with the mice that aren't really in our house, of my visit to the dentist, of my comic reversion to whining infancy because I have the 'flu, wry little slices of mundane life all falling under the witty witness of Morag, who is portrayed as the patient, indulgent, good-humoured helpmeet-cum-mother that she is so definitely not. Here I've got next Christmas' column already written, a generic gift list for prominent local people that doesn't hold a trace of genuine meaning or humour, but is written in a manner that suggests it does: "To our Members of Parliament: thermometers, so they can gauge their levels of hot air. To His Worship, The Mayor: a street map indicating our worst pot-holes, highlighting the one on 24th that swallowed my entire car." Chuckle, chuckle, chuckle. Guffaw, guffaw, guffaw. Somewhere, the vengeful god of wasted trees is honing an axe to hack away at the hack I am.

Struggling in my morning's addled judgment, I try to select the least offensive column. I settle listlessly on a comic account of my ludicrous attempt to gracefully and heroically play pick-up baseball with some genial nameless nonexistent neighbours, with Morag standing by to bind my inevitable injuries; I am mindful that as I siphon off the least bilious, I further concentrate the odium of the remaining pool.

I put the portfolio back under my seat, and my hand knocks a bottle of Canadian whisky that is stashed there. I pull it out and look at it a long, longing while, weighing the beneficial effect of a hair of the dog. I hate this stuff, to me its taste is surely identical to that of liquid leaking out the bottom of a garbage truck, its smell alone is enough to nauseate me. I hate the taste of all hard liquor, I hate the taste of all liqueurs, I hate beer and ale and port and sherry, and can't imagine how anyone first concluded that mead, or whatever it was that got all this fermentation and distillation started, was something that anyone should allow into his mouth. I detest Morag's endless martinis, and their foretaste of my fate. There's a wine or two I find tolerable, but not so good as to endure its such slow motion toward where I must get.

I replace the bottle with a shudder and a curse. This is no triumph of the will, for my addictive need is still somewhat sated from last night.

As I start the van, my mind wanders involuntarily back to Solania, to the impudence of her slow smile as she held her hand out to me, as though she would favour me by accepting my offering. I find myself wishing that she would do it again, just so I could see that sly smile. And then, for the briefest horrifying moment, I am the tattered, slack-mouthed and slavering drunk she supports in cooing, loving embrace. I bang my imagination with my fist as though it's an old t.v. on the fritz. I try to occupy my mind with acute attention to driving to the city's north end, to the newspaper offices.

I need to make some token attempt at tidying myself up before I get to the office, so I pull into Value Village second hand store nearby, take the portable razor, comb and toothbrush from the glove compartment, and go into the store's public washroom.

I shave and wash my face without looking, even though there is a mirror above the sink. It's when I'm washing my neck with a wet brown paper towel that I finally discover the obvious, that my tie has gone missing from around my collar. Maybe I was worried about hanging myself. Perhaps it dangled into the toxic toilet at the Inn Continent as I was vomiting. Its loss disturbs me quite a bit, and I worry that I'll awaken without shoes or pants some morning.

In the mirror, I assess the state of my suit jacket and shirt. They look better on the outside than they feel on the inside.

I brush my teeth and comb my hair, and begin to feel that I have risen to the state of recognizably primate. I stow my toiletry tools in my jacket pocket and go over to the area of men's used clothing. Many of the ties there are of a colour and pattern suggesting they've been dipped in regurgitate themselves, but I find one that's acceptable.

At the checkout, I hand it and my debit card to the young woman cashier. Her name tag says "Hi! My name is RHONDA".

She looks at the price tag stapled to the tie's label, then to my debit card.

"This tie's $2.99," she says, and then she just looks at me expectantly.

"Yes?" I say after a moment. "That's all right."

She reaches to the top of her cash register and taps a little printed sign that states firmly "No Credit Card or Debit Charges Under $5.00", and then she awaits my response.

"You know," I say, smiling and shaking my head ruefully. "I came out this morning without my money. Or my tie. Very absent-minded."

"You must be a professor," Rhonda says in gentle jest.

"My girlfriend is," I say. "I guess it's contagious."

She smiles nicely, but still waits for me to do the right thing, whatever it is.

"Help me, Rhonda," I venture, but I've gone too far.

"Wow, I've never heard that one before," she says with noticeably less patience. She exchanges a look with a woman who has joined us with a cartful of polyester.

"What you can do is charge me for two ties. How would that do?" I offer.

"You want to go get another tie?" she asks.

"No, I don't want another tie. But you can charge me for two, and that would lift the total above five dollars. All right?"

"I'm not sure," she says. "There's our inventory..."

"Well, you could let the untaken tie stand in for a shoplifted item of the same value. That would satisfy your inventory."

She regards me with uncertainty, unsure if I'm being creative, helpful, sneaky or rude. Finally, she gives a very small sniff, rings in only the $2.99, and passes me the electronic key pad. I know that she notes my trembling as I stab at the keys.

"Thank you," I say to her as we wait for her monitor's response. "I really appreciate it."

"Okay," she says, and then in confidence allows, "I really shouldn't've." She taps arythmically on the top of her monitor and looks someplace other than at me.

In a minute, she says with a sort of sorrow "Your financial institution refuses the transaction." This is a bad start to her day.

"Sometimes they get the wires crossed," she offers in limp sympathetic embarrassment.

In instinctive reaction, I reach both hands down into my pants pockets.

"If only I hadn't —," I start to say, but when my left hand comes out of its pocket, it is holding a small folded wad of twenty dollar bills.

I hold it out before me and stare at it in amazement.

"There we go," a relieved Rhonda says brightly.

I hand her one bill, and start away to the doors, still studying the money.

"Sir!" Rhonda calls. "Your change! Your tie!"

I turn back without interest.

"Wow, you really are absent-minded," she says, handing me change and plopping the tie into a small plastic bag.

I wander back to my van, tying the replacement tie. I know that I spent the last of my pocket money in the barroom last night, but I am even less confused by my possession of these twenty dollar bills than I am by Solania's insistence that I had money in my left pocket. I would more than happily conclude that she had seen the small wad outlined against a tight pocket, but these are suit pants, creased, pleated and loose at the front, and, anyway, my suit jacket was covering my pocket.

I have no patience with hocus pocus, with charlatan shamans who confound superstitious, gullible ignorami.

"Do you take me for an idiot?" I ask Solania angrily aloud, yet I have no explanation.

When I get to the newspaper offices, I enter with eyes carefully turned away from the chatty ladies at the front desk, avoid contact with everyone on my way to the back office of Robert, the editor.

Robert isn't at his desk when I go in, but rather is standing at a side table, poring over photos with a young photographer. This is problematic, for I need to ask Robert to arrange for another advance in my pay.

Robert glances over to me, then turns back to the pictures. I toss my scurvy column on his desk, and hope that he won't begin to read it in my presence. I fall into the visitor's chair and prepare some light-toned phraseology for my beggary. The publisher deeply mistrusts any newspaper writer of legitimate literary talent, and he long ago classified me as a petulant, pretentious prima donna who properly should be starving in some garret, failing to finish the great novel. Robert stands by me, 'though, and the ongoing, albeit long undeserved, popular readership of my column supports me, too.

I have three sections to that which I might ironically refer to as my life, and I've struggled to keep them each separate and self-contained: professional, personal, and addiction; the last will often masquerade as one or both of the first two, and its insistent trespasses against them are getting harder to cover up or explain away.

In the professional section, Robert is my closest approximation of a friend, would be a genuine friend, I'm sure, if I could allow him to be. He still values the quality and significance at which my work once hinted, seemingly still thinks that I'll write that great novel, is still too generous to confront the fact that my only truly demonstrated talent is for betraying all my other gifts.

The young photographer departs and Robert turns to me with a smile, notes my papers on his desk.

"Ah, 'Perles Before Swine'," he says amiably.

My column is called 'Wisdom of Perles'. Once, in one of my moments of uncontrolled sardony, I referred to it as 'Perles Before Swine", and Robert kindly repeats it as a bon mot from time to time.

"I guess you'll be doing something about this," he

says, turning back to the photographs on the table. Robert is a good newspaperman, knows that an editor should respect a columnist's independence, but he finds his ways to subtly assign.

I heave myself up and go to stand beside him.

"I can't use these, of course," Robert is saying. "I keep telling him I won't run a close-up of a corpse. These young guys have no sensitivity."

The pictures are of a dead woman, lying in an alley behind a store.

The woman is Laura, whose now-slate-grey lips were, nine hours ago, pressed lively, warm and flickering against mine.

"The second one in a month," Robert is saying.

"What?! What?!" I demand. "What second?!"

"The second murdered prostitute in a month."

It's Laura, all right, and around her neck, knotted in cruel constriction, is my missing tie.

I grab for the edge of the table, but too late; my knees have completely buckled and I sprawl backward.

Poor Robert looks at me with dismay. He surely believes that this infirmity is a result of my drinking, and he quickly, discreetly averts his eyes, saying nothing.

Chapter Two

After years of applying torture, my single act of mercy toward my crippled and emaciated last hopes was to euthanize them when it was clear that they were unable to survive without an artificial support system. And that became clear when I realized that I was someone with whom Christine could never fall in love again. Up to that point, it had been my pitiful practice to cosset myself to sleep at night, in spite of my day's collected sorrows, frustrations and furies, with an infantile fantasy that one day — one day when it rained grapes, or when walls wept hair oil, or whenever I was somehow worthy, I don't know when, the prerequisites were reassuringly imprecisely impossible — I would search this country's forbidding and forgotten remote places for the one in which Christine was surely administering her devoted compassion; I would present myself, confess that I'd been wrong, so weak and stupid, and somehow she would cease being so courageous and intelligent long enough to love me again as hard and sorely as I've never stopped loving her.

After I'd dispatched my last hopes, comforting fantasy was beyond me, and so was sleep.

Life is short, Carney will say as an excuse as he downs his first drink.

But sometimes it isn't short enough, such as when one is lying awake in the night, unable to sleep and unable to drink enough to pass out, lest one first black out and murder Morag, who is lying beside one, taking up much more than her share of the bed, snoring fleshily, almost inviting strangulation.

Upon my collapse, Robert took me out to an industrial restaurant located in a nearby strip mall, surrounded by bearing supply store, upholstery supply outlet, wire and cable supply outlet (open to the public) and other testaments to what a romantic adventure life is. Robert force-fed me at the $5.99 lunch buffet of various vaguely oriental deep-fried gelatins. I only managed about 50 cents' worth, but still it had the unhappy result of providing me with enough energy to be frantic all afternoon.

I spent the afternoon like a chicken with a van but without a head, flapping feverishly in fleeting and inexact plans of action that would have me zipping down one alphabetical avenue just to suddenly veer onto a numerical street and then back again. One plan was to find Carney, he who will always turn up beside me if I don't want him to, but he was nowhere, and another was to arrange to sort of casually encounter Morley, the beat constable who patrols this neighborhood — one cop I get along with, who doesn't take my public criticism of the force as a personal offence — and make calm enquiries of him, but everybody knows about the availability of police when they're wanted.

And another very brief befuddled plan, demonstrative of my addled state, was to find Laura and ask her how seriously she meant "My boyfriend's going to kill me."

I did find Velvet working the 19th St. rush hour in a tiny tight sweater and a tiny miniskirt. I pulled around the corner onto Ave. G, and she came sashaying in pursuit, her narrow little girl hips in exaggerated sway, her little purse swinging on her arm. She was disappointed that I wasn't a paying john when she climbed into the front seat, but then she decided to try her luck. Or maybe she was merely mocking me.

"C'mon, Perles, wouldn't you like a date?" she asked pertly.

"Why exercise yourself?" I said. "You and Carney drink up all my money, anyway. You heard about Laura?"

"Yeah," she said, looking down to inspect the frilly

tops of her white ankle socks, the dust on her scuffed, Sunday School patent-leather pumps.

"Doesn't it bother you?"

"Sure," she said. "I felt bad all morning. But life is for the living."

I had no idea what she meant by that, and probably she didn't either.

"But doesn't it bother you that there's someone out here killing prostitutes?"

She didn't deem to answer such a stupid question. I've never met a prostitute yet who, at bottom, didn't believe that she was on the street out of inescapable necessity.

"Where's Carney, do you know?"

"I dunno," she said. "Around. Wherever. I better go."

"No, wait a minute," I said, and I caught her thin arm.

"You're costing me," she said sharply.

"Oh, hush up, tough kid! Who was Laura's boyfriend?"

"She didn't have no boyfriend," Velvet said, wrenching her arm away.

"She told me she had a boyfriend. She said he was going to kill her."

"The only boyfriend she had's the same as mine."

"What d'you mean? Carney?"

"No," Velvet said derisively. "Her pimp. My pimp. The Baron."

She said it almost with pride. I watched her a moment as it sunk in.

"The Baron is your pimp?"

"Sure," she said. "And he wouldn't like you keeping me here, not paying."

"Wouldn't he?" I said with automatic contempt. "Tell him he can try billing me. Now consider this carefully, Velvet, because I want you to tell me the truth: do you think The Baron killed Laura?"

She took a cigarette from her little purse, lit it and inhaled extravagantly. Maybe she was thinking.

"Why would he kill her? He's not gonna kill his own whore. That'd just cost him." She flashed me her imitation of a winsome smile, opening the door. "Maybe see you tonight, eh, Perles?"

She stepped down to the sidewalk, then turned and stuck her head back into the car.

"Anyways," she said in conclusive argument, "they say the guy that killed Laura took her money. The Baron's not gonna kill her just to steal his own money, is he?"

She slipped away. I snatched the wad of money from my pocket as though it was ebola virus, flung it onto the dashboard and stared.

"Nothing proves anything," I said aloud.

At this point, an alcoholic would convince himself that he needed to drown his sorrows, would seek to calm himself with drink's delusions and deceptions; but I knew that, at this moment, a drink for me would be brandy thrown on the flames, flaring wild and blue, would add unbearably to my anxieties.

I decided that a more promising course of action was to beat my brow against the steering wheel, so I did that for some time, in the faint hope that it might dislodge the memory of last night from its hiding place, and in the more rewarding exercise of self abuse, until I was disturbed by a noise at my left shoulder.

It was Constable Morley, standing astride his bicycle and knocking hurriedly, worriedly at my side window. Morley himself has a broad and generous brow with which a steering wheel could do much. His face, head, actually, is at odds with his frame, would appear, by itself, in its roundness and apple-cheeked radiance, to be suitable to someone big-boned and overweight; but his body is slender, and not through determined fitness, either; his is a sort of metabolic slimness; it's as though his body and head were designed for differing constitutions, with the body's so far enforcing its own upon the head, China and Tibet. I rolled the window down.

"God, Perles, what're you doing?" he cried. "What's the matter with you?"

I stared at him much too long, failing to make my eyes less wide.

"Oh, it's just Laura, just mourning her, I guess," I said at last. "I was keeping company with her for a while last night."

"Yeah, we knew that," Morley said. He regarded me closely.

"Did you want something?" I asked.

"I just saw Velvet getting out of your van. Thought I might get to make things uncomfortable for a john. Your van's too common, Perles, you ought to give me something to recognize on it."

"Paint it some lurid colour, maybe," I suggested.

"Could you? Would you mind?" he asked in affable humour. "Say, that reminds me, I got one for you, a cop couplet: They say that no one'll ever make a rhyme for purple,/ But I bet if you ask him nice, Wyatt Earp'll." He smiled at me with proud enquiry. I congratulated him.

"You can use that, I don't mind," he said.

"If I do, I'll give you credit."

"Don't want to take the blame yourself, that's all," he said, and, to my mind ominously, as though that thought itself triggered something, he leaned against the frame of the window and said: "When can we talk with you, Perles? You may be the last person to have seen Laura alive."

"Last person but one," I quickly corrected him.

"Yeah, sure. You left the bar with her this morning, eh?"

"I don't know," I said dismissively. "I wasn't paying attention. There wasn't anything special about last night as far as I was concerned."

"Don't bother telling me," he said. "You want to stop by headquarters, or they can drop by your place."

"No, no. I'll come in."

"But soon, Perles, like right now. Anything you can think of. Any detail."

"She said her boyfriend was going to kill her," I blurted out in upsurging panic.

"Yeah, well, that's a kinda interesting detail, there, Perles. You didn't think to be forthcoming with that?"

"You know who her boyfriend is, don't you?"

"From what we're hearing today, that's you."

"I'm not her boyfriend," I spit. "She just took a shine to me last night, that's all. Her boyfriend is her pimp."

"The Baron," Morley said.

"Yes, The Baron. Check him out."

"We're checking him out."

"Well, I mean, are you close to an arrest? Has he got an alibi?"

"He'll have an alibi if he didn't do it, and he'll have an alibi if he did," Morley said dryly. "You know, you better get some ice on your forehead, there. That's some mark."

"What is it?" I muttered, shifting the van into gear. "A pentagram?"

I drove away because I was afraid that I was on the brink of impulsively asking Morely the date of the first prostitute murder, the slaying of a part time hooker, part time beggar and full time nut case named Candy who — caring being the strongest tradition — had been left to wander, bedraggled, these unforgiving streets on her own, cooing in dotty doting over the baby that only she saw nestling in a ratty blue receiving blanket in the crook of her arm. The blue would indicate that her unseen baby was a boy.

The perfect political example of the undeserving poor bringing misfortune upon themselves, Candy was found earlier this month, in an alley, in a corner where two fences met, beaten or kicked to death, in a hunched attitude suggesting that perhaps she'd sacrificed herself shielding her nonexistent infant.

I had known Candy, and I didn't want to discover from Morley that her death coincided with one of my earlier black-outs.

I drove to a much nicer neighborhood, to the nice 'character' house that I can't afford on my income alone, but which Morag can, a noted fact that ensures that, if we split up, I'll be the one who goes.

Morag wasn't yet home, which suited me as well as anything might. I dropped myself onto the sofa and closed my eyes, which was a mistake, for the addiction took the still, quiet opportunity to start whispering to me about the bottle of rye under the van seat, and I was forced to really consider the options arrayed before a possible black-out killer, all of which were terrible, because they all involved going teetotal, and the prospect threw the addiction into a panic of self-preservation, made its whispers swell to urgent, insistent commands.

So I twisted, twitched and wrestled for quite some time on the sofa, manfully resisting the addiction's tyranny, fashioned myself for a while as a doomed heroic freedom fighter. I laid my forearm over my brow tragically, like a fallen Burgher of Calais, until the dull throb turned too acute. Enfeebled by combat, I stood and tottered to the mirror inside the front door, inspected the red, swollen steering wheel wound, a raw burger of malaise.

"The mark of Cain," I said, rapping it hard with my knuckles.

Morag came in while I was standing there, may have

thought that I was there to greet her. She was toting a number of bags from the expensive little grocery just down the road.

"Hello, stranger," she said lightly. "What happened to you?"

I didn't know if she meant in general or specifically, so I didn't attempt an answer.

"You look like hell. What'd you do to your head?" she said in a chipper sort of way, brushing by me toward the kitchen.

"You're welcome," she added, to my confusion. Morag is bright and chipper only when she is uncomfortable. She had a number of reasons to be uncomfortable at that moment that I could list, including the fact that I'd been out all night again; but the likeliest probability was that she needed a pleasant way to get rid of me for the evening. Wednesday evening is the meeting at our house of one of Morag's social activism groups. I am supposed to make myself scarce without fuss or reminder.

Monday night it's Academicians For Action. The second Thursday of every month, it's the City Park School and Community Association.

Wednesday, it's The Freedom of Form Support Group, which sounds artistic, but isn't unless gluttony is art, and I guess that some people seem to believe that it is. This group began some years ago, before I met Morag, as a women's support group that collected weekly to reassure themselves of the nonexistence of feminine sin and nonexistence of masculine virtue. As, over the years, the imminent imperilling spousal assaults and workplace sexual harassments somehow failed to manifest themselves frequently enough, and professional promotions cropped up like awkward flowers in the desert of oppression, and as the membership expanded — individually, not in numbers — as the rolls swelled, so to speak, the group narrowed, so to speak, its focus, and decided to concentrate its defiance against masculine society's cruel and unattainable imposed ideals of beauty and slender fitness. Philosophically, this was more of a shift than it might first appear, for, in practical terms, the new paradigm required a new admittance of the existence of feminine sin: the pursuit or maintenance of slender fitness, as symbolized by the Archtraitor Barbie.

I once referred to the Freedom of Form group, in my column, as 'The Sounding of Very Heavy Belles' and 'a cry in the dessert', a lapse in judgment which I wish Robert had cautioned against, for it brought forth from Morag insincere exclamations of political outrage and sincere tears of hurt and humiliation. And, to the other women in the group, I was thereafter forever the would-be sugardaddy of the Archtraitor Barbie, and persona non grata.

Privately, I refer to Academicians For Action as the Doctoral Dilettantes For Chip Dip. Its members regard me, a writer for the popular press, as certainly somewhere beneath their rarefied intellectual level, beneath serious consideration and possibly insignificantly politically suspect, in that I belong to no committees or even subcommittees, ad hoc or otherwise, and maybe only cleverly disguise my intolerance behind those printed pleas on behalf of, and sympathetic portrayals of, the needy and downtrodden. I don't dress in rumpled tweed and khaki and sweaters fraying at the cuff, and I don't have a shaggy beard nesting organic, kettle fried potato chip crumbs, so I could possibly be an aspirant plutocrat.

Morag is pursuing her campaign for promotion to Professor, and would never risk her support in this circle by any politically dicey defense of me. I know that on at least one occasion, she rose before the meeting to extend an abject apology on my unbidding behalf for something I'd written, and offered no justification or excuse, threw me on the mercy of their court.

As a matter of fact, I've never encountered a group more condescendingly, quietly contemptuous of, and self-consciously superior to, the needy and downtrodden than the leftist elitists of Academicians For Action. Morag, I know, views herself as soaring on planes high above the lower orders, from which position she, with her colleagues, is positioned to best direct their course, like traffic reporters or angels. If I were to mischievously spirit Carney and some of his doorstep drinking buddies into one of their meetings, the Doctoral Dilettantes would trip over themselves in red-faced epileptic confusion, and then they'd faint from the odour.

The Freedom of Form Support Group escapes victimization by beauty and health by preparing a groaning board for each meeting, which accounted for Morag's several grocery bags.

She set her bags down in the kitchen, and immediately set about mixing herself a pitcher of vodka martinis. True alcoholic that she is, she gave herself a random selection from her standard stock of excuses: "What a hellish day!"

The pitcher in which she mixes her martinis is of exquisite Czech crystal. The glass into which she pours a martini from the pitcher is of the highest quality, and rings musically when she plucks its fine rim between her thumb and forefinger. She shops for food and imported martini olives at an expensive little grocery that calls itself a delicatessen, and she refers to the rich dishes she prepares as delicacies.

"Do you want one?" she asked me automatically, stirring the pitcher carefully with an elegant, long-handled silver spoon. The liquor shimmered almost iridescent in the pitcher. I looked at it with revulsion.

It was Morag's constant proffering of her endless martinis that turned me into an alcohol addict. I don't care what A.A. will say about no one having any responsibility for a person's drinking but that person himself. What I know is that I had no interest in alcohol throughout my life, through good times and bad, I hated the taste and its effects disgusted me, until my overexposure through Morag's insistent, needy alcoholic sharing over a long period of time finally spawned in me an addiction like a tyrannical tumour. If Morag hadn't poured the shimmering spirits from the exquisite crystal into the less and less exquisite me, in the ostensible interest of intimacy, and to delude herself by my drinking that hers was only that of a refined and silky lifestyle, I would be free of it today and wouldn't be wondering if I was a killer.

"Do you want one?" she asked again, before adding meaningfully: "Before you leave?"

"Yes, sure, why not?" I said, sinking into one of the uncomfortable, aging Danish-modern teak high-backed kitchen chairs.

Morag, I knew, would press no enquiry as to my whereabouts last night; she would assume, even hope, that I was with some other woman, thereby easing any residual guilt about her long-standing complete denial of any sexual activity. She has an aversion to sex, which I didn't create, and which she concealed until after we'd set up housekeeping together, and she is willing to accept the bargain of me finding release elsewhere, provided it siphons off any threat to her. She wouldn't want me to rub her nose in it, of course, it would be necessary for me to be discreet, and not fall in love, and she would be relieved of that carnal inconvenience. I think she has a sort of notice posted in her mind, like in a factory, '192 Days Accident-Free', except hers would read '192 Days Bedroom-Unpleasantness-Free', which might cause reassurance in one looking at it, or might generate alarm as one calculates the manifest inevitable odds. I haven't bothered to tell her that she's been safe from my advances since the day she broke the 160 pound threshold, the threshold over which I could no longer comfortably carry her. Her group can cite Peter Paul Rubens all they want, I'm strictly a Sandro Boticelli man, myself, because Christine was the breathing image of Flora in 'La Primavera'.

Morag's group maintains that men created the fallacious concept of feminine beauty as an act of cruelty to women. The briefest even-eyed survey of history's suffering would affirm that, if men created the concept of feminine beauty, it was as an act of cruelty to men. I certainly haven't bothered to tell Morag that my idea of what is attractive has been reduced by the arid heat of my thirst and hunger to an intensely concentrated, shimmering, iridescent spirit in slashingly sharp cut crystal that is my longing for Christine; Christine, who, in her beauty and slender health and courage and intelligence and self discipline and selfless commitment and compassion, is the AntiBarbie and the very woman Morag's determinedly dissolute and ruthlessly resolute group insists does not exist.

I have believed for some time that my principal sentiment toward Morag is one of pity. Unfortunately, it wasn't until I realized that I didn't really love her that I realized that I didn't like her, either.

As she carefully placed the martini beside me on the table, I appraised her steadily, wondering if my memory of the sort of sweet, bright, needy young woman she once was, and to whom my sense of her still sometimes responded, had been overwhelmed by a lurking rage against her that had been acted out, so far, against surrogates.

Or was it, maybe, rage against Christine?

I took a sip of the drink, shuddered as always, watched as Morag silently pulled items of the evening's repast from their bags.

I have no idea why Morag wants our relationship to continue; our lives scarcely connect anywhere now; but when I speak of leaving her, she cries and cries and cries enough that her women's group would cringe, makes desperate pleading promises of sex and starvation diets, will pin me back with wet kisses until I relent or set the issue aside.

So that I can wonder what my life would have been if Christine had cried and cried at that terrible pivotal moment when I squandered my life's meaning, if she hadn't simply told me in her seamless dignity and self-control that she loved me, but couldn't force me to stay, if she hadn't been so eternally generous, if only she'd required me to be generous for an instant, if only she'd smacked my face and told me to smarten up, toughen up, get a grip on myself, that all I'd ever, ever desire was already held within her beautiful heart.

I can try, late at night, in the brown smog of the Inn Continent barroom, to reach into that terrible tantalizing moment, to grab the scruffs of our necks and shake and shake, there were times when I would really reach into the fetid air and clench my fists and shake and shake, to the encouraging laughter of those sitting otherwise morosely around me. Did Laura get in the way of such when I was beyond stopping myself?

Morag drank nearly three martinis in the time it took me to finish one. She was racing with me, which she will do now, incomprehensibly, to ensure that she doesn't have to share too much of the pitcher with me. It is she, always, who mixes and pours, she who buys the vermouth and vodka, it has always been she who was in complete control of our household liquor consumption, she who insisted that I share enough, and now guards against me sharing too much. It must be a fine balance she's had to strike; delicate, even.

I know that Morag has strategically slept with her

Department Head, pretty much in the same manner she strategically slept with me in our early days, to advance her interest; I know about her Department Head, because he made an opportunity to lord it over me. He's much older than I, and loosely flabby, and I guess he wanted to make me understand that not all of him always sags downward. It seems she even gave him department head, unlike anything she'd ever given to me. Ironically enough, Morag's presumptions of my physical infidelities are false. In my heart, of course, until I snuffed my enfeebled last hopes, I never spent a faithful night, at least not one faithful to her, so I've managed no noticeable indignation over her assignation — hypocrisy, anyway, is Morag's method, not mine — but I couldn't swear that it's not contributing to a cumulative hidden rage.

My addiction requested another martini, so I stood suddenly and told Morag that I was going out. Morag came, wiping her mouth with a dish towel, and gave me a light peck on the cheek.

"Are you coming home tonight?" she asked. "They'll be gone by eleven."

"Probably," I said.

"Maybe there'll be leftovers, too," she said, perhaps trying to lure me home.

Combusting the ethers of the one martini, I went out and stalked, with a measure of rhythmic energy, the streets of this pleasant residential neighborhood. From time to time, I would pass people working their gardens in the waning light of this early spring evening, occasionally passed others on the sidewalk, out for a slow stroll; I would warn them out of my way with dark scowls, worried that an interruption in my momentum would stall me completely, leave me plopped on the sidewalk.

Before too, too long, of course, within just a few rectangular miles, my rhythm was overcome and staggered by conflicting imperatives, that of my exhaustion and that of my addiction. I tottered to a cafe that's across the street from the delicatessen at which Morag shops. The cafe is made out of a little old house, and the front yard has been set up as a patio with small circular tables and moulded vinyl chairs.

When my life is in a state of tighter control, I avoid this cafe because it is the haunt of a certain type of resident of this neighborhood who will sit at a circular table, with a tiny espresso spoon stirring circular swirls in a circular smugness that should have been chloroformed back when he was adoring himself in his Philosophy 101 class: he is perfect, ergo his lifestyle must be perfect, and his opinions must be perfect; and his perfection is proven by his perfect lifestyle and opinions. His perfection, apparently, is what allows him to drink specialty coffees that could embarrass the less-than-perfect grown-up: exquisite precious steam-milked concoctions topped with mounds of chocolate whipped cream and carefully-sprinkled cinnamon sugar, which he delicately skims with his tiny spoon, which he licks with ecstatic savour with the perfect tip of his tongue.

Being very far from perfect, I ordered a plain coffee. More desperately than stupidly, I fleetingly wondered if I might mollify my addiction, dupe it temporarily, with a shot of the non-alcoholic syrup the cafe uses to approximate Irish coffee. I paid with some of the change from the blood-money twenty-dollar bills.

The patio has a half a dozen tables, four of which were occupied. Only one of them was presently bejewelled by a ring of the perfect-type patrons, whose imposing conversation had an air of precious competitiveness to it. At another table, I spotted Rod, City Councillor for this ward. He spotted me, too, and motioned for me to join him and his two companions. I looked away, but probably too late for him to believe that I'd missed his gesture.

Anyway, I slumped in behind another table and sucked in a bit of my coffee.

Rod came bustling over. He is short, dapper in dress, and very aggressive in temperament.

"I've been wanting to talk to you," he said in a jovial way, perching down on the front edge of a vinyl chair.

"Did I write something that offended you?" I asked without concern.

"Not at all," he said. "I wanted to discuss a possible political project with you."

"Oh," I said, taking a drink of coffee. Rod plainly noticed the trembling of my hand.

"The evening's taking on a real chill," I observed casually, preemptively.

"Would you like to move inside? We can talk in there."

"This is fine here," I said.

"We were just discussing the fall elections," Rod said, motioning backward over his shoulder to where his two companions sat. "We have reason to believe that His Worship will be vacating the Mayor's seat."

"Have you?"

"It's early yet; this is off the record, of course."

"Of course."

"We have reason to believe, certain indications that he's setting his sights, well, that's speculative ... In the event that he chooses not to run again, a number of people feel that I should be taking a run at it."

"At what?"

Rod straightened up. "At being Mayor, of course."

"Oh," I said.

"I'm just at the point of exploring potential support levels, at this point. Sounding out key individuals, you know."

"Oh."

"So, well, what do you think about that?"

"Sure, why not?" I said.

"I'm very glad you feel that way," he said sincerely. "We'll need the support of people like you, if this dream is to become a reality."

"What do you mean, support?" I asked. "Or, better still, what d'you mean by people like me?"

Rod leaned forward, placed his hands, palms down, on the table.

"You know, I've never made any secret of my deep respect for your advocacy on behalf of our disadvantaged people in our core neighborhoods."

"Hm," I said. "It was hitherto a secret to me."

Rod shook his head emphatically.

"I've never made any secret of it."

"Gosh," I said, dying for another slurp of coffee, but my tremour was getting extreme enough for me keep my hands hidden beneath the table, on my knees. "Nice to know."

"Absolutely."

"Well, good luck," I said, struggling upward in a sudden need to get moving again.

"Sit down a minute, sit down," he said urgently, holding up his hands as if to block my progress.

I fell back in my seat and tried to concentrate hard on what he might further say, as if sharp focus might straighten out my wildly oscillating nervous pulse. When he spoke, only his lower lip moved, up and down, as with a ventriloquist's dummy, and my focus landed on this trait, and his words burst like bubbles before they reached me, long, long, long strings of them glistening and popping in the streetlight silver in the darkening evening.

" —cold," Rod was saying, lines of communication suddenly reconnecting. "Do you want a fresh cup?"

"No, no," I said.

"I want you to help them understand that I share their concerns," Rod continued. "I admit that there's much I don't know, but the empathy, the empathy ——"

"Rod," I interrupted, "how long have you been on Council?"

"This fall, it'll be twelve years," he said proudly.

"Throughout the time of my observation, your own advocacy for our disadvantaged people of our core neighborhoods has somehow completely escaped me."

"Well," he said, "my job was to serve the people of this ward. And I've done that to the best of my ability. If, at times, my service to the people of this ward may have appeared on the surface to be contrary to the desires of the people of other wards, then for that I am very sorry. But as Mayor, my job would be to serve all people of the city, while at the same time recognizing, of course, that we can't live without social order, can we?"

"Do you have any idea at all how much worse things are now in the inner city than they were even twelve years ago?"

"Well, I couldn't, well, some of us, some of us are getting more and more concerned ——."

"About their electoral clout?"

"Look," Rod said heatedly, "Do you think any other candidate will even nod in their direction? The inner city is the problem no one wants to tackle, you know that. They spell political failure, those people. Who wants that?"

"Well, why do you want it?" I asked.

"I told you Perles ... I share their concerns, I share their hopes ..."

"You share their hopes?" I asked. "Describe to me their hopes. Describe to me the hopes, say, of a little boy whose mother is a total alcoholic, whose useless father is rotting in some gutter on 19th, whose older brother is in the remand centre awaiting trial, whose sister has been working the streets since she was ten years old, whose school wrote off his chances and wrote him a prescription for Ritalin the moment he walked in; tell me the hopes of his teenage sister, whose little life is held in the greasy palm of a rippling mountain of thuggery known as The Baron, her pimp and pusher; describe to me the hopes of the mother, whose children, one by one, shrivel and blow away from her in your careless neglect. I'll tell you their hopes that you share, all the hopes you've left to them: for a nice little win at the bingo. Shall I tell them to support you for Mayor because you'd like to win at the bingo, too?"

Rod regarded me severely. "I resent you reinforcing negative stereotypes of those people."

"I haven't told you anything about those people," I growled. "I told you about their conditions, and if you think their conditions are too narrowly expressed, too confined in description, too exclusive of other options, why have you and your ilk made them so? Ritalin and bingo are the strictures you've instituted, the bread and circus' allowed them by your own brahmins. You blame me for recognizing the parameters you impose."

Rod peered at me.

"Honestly, I ...," he began. "Are you crying?"

"Of course not!" I said furiously, quickly and clumsily reaching up to wipe away the curious wetness on my cheeks. "Eye strain from astigmatism ... this light is so harsh! What's the matter with that streetlight, anyway?"

"What's the matter with you, more the question," Rod said, rising up. "Do you think you're the only guy with a heart?"

I surged up, myself.

"If you had a heart, it would be broken," I said.

I tottered out and down the sidewalk without a backward look, my attention being soon overtaken by the yammering of my addiction, which was not shrivelling and blowing away in my neglect.

I wandered haltingly for quite some time, until my strength seemed to be ebbing away again, and then I feebly followed my feet back to my van.

I sort of draped myself against the passenger door, panting in a torment of temptation, my gaze glued to the driver's seat, under which was the bottle of rye.

"Should a body make a body, killing through the rye?" I began to sing softly and mournfully, over and over, until it struck me as cute, and then I worriedly stopped.

My thirst became such that I either had to drink some of that which might be Dr. Jekyll's potion, or go into my house, literally no mans land by Wednesday night custom, and get myself some water.

I can't imagine what those women find to talk about, about their own courageous resistance to the temptation to be thin, for a full evening every week, but whatever they find, they lost it when they saw me standing in the entrance to the livingroom.

All eyes were on me, and I seemed to have quite a while to survey the various expressions that were directed toward me in an atmosphere in which I, for one, sensed an electric discomfort. There were about eight women; some regarded me with simple curiosity, others with hostility or condemnation, and then there was Morag, who was dismayed.

On the stereo was a tape of singing that had been 'collected' by a member of The Freedom of Form Group, who also worked at the university and who found it necessary, every winter, to absorb scant educational and social resources to go and study and, somehow, champion, indigenous peoples of coincidentally tropical climes, some of whom, she once severely declared to me, were forced to sleep in little more than huts; by this means, she was quite unable to turn her helpful attention to the indigenous people of our own society who were sleeping in little more than huts, or maybe no huts at all, through our bitter subzero winters.

The collected singing was by some old tropical indigenous crone whose memory of her childhood's traditional songs often seemed to fail her, and whose wheezey, toothlessly sibilant singing was intermittently interrupted by a truer, sustained note or phrase, the shrill, ratcheting vibrato of which cinched my nerves tighter with each strain as I stood there. This was Morag's own copy of the tape, I knew; each one of the group had been ceremoniously presented with a copy. The songs were about the fun of playing with llama dung, I think, some of them, anyway. The old woman's name is Qlxterqlxterq or some such, which is, I suspect, ancient Incan for 'Should never be allowed to sing'. Nobody in the room dared to dislike it, but played it repeatedly with reverence.

"I must have a drink of water," I announced generally.

Morag arose as quickly as she could and said "I'll get you some.", which I took to indicate that I was denied entrance into the sanctified space, even just in passage to the kitchen.

I looked right back at the staring faces, wondering what alterations would be effected in their expressions if they thought they were looking at a real ladykiller, a mortal, rather than merely venial, male sinner.

Morag appeared before me with a glass of tepid water.

"We're not finished yet," she said. "I said about eleven."

"I've got work to do upstairs," I said. "I won't disturb

you, but I won't be disturbed, either, so you must turn down that wretched caterwauling."

"What did he say?" asked one of the women.

"We'll play it as loud as we see fit!" said another.

I leaned down to Morag's ear, and whispered: "Don't trifle with me tonight. You turn off that tape, and don't disturb me. Do you understand?"

Morag was what she calls 'tipsy', which means maintenance-level drunk, and she wasn't too far gone to notice something different in my voice; she looked up at me like a great grey owl and nodded in serious assent.

As I winched myself upstairs by the baluster, the old crone was arrested in mid-squawk, and a pregnant silence fell over the livingroom — perhaps pregnant, perhaps just very stout.

I went into my tiny office at the back of the second floor — Morag has a nice big office upstairs in the half-storey of this two-and-a-half-storey house — sat at my computer and wrote a column about Laura, said how she was a woman of ordinary decency and abilities; how, in most levels of society, such a woman can expect to thereby obtain a life of ordinary decency, and rewards, reasonably good; but how Laura, locked into her social substratum, could thereby only obtain a life devoid of ordinary decency or rewards, unreasonably bad.

It wasn't a bad column, reminiscent of some of my earlier, more promising stuff; but then I destroyed it by adding a sentimental story of "the last time I saw her alive", about how she'd told me how much she liked the tie I was wearing, and how I'd whipped it off and presented it to her as a chivalrous gift; how, in stylish flamboyance, she'd draped it, the very instrument of her doom, around her own neck. O, bitter, haunting irony.

I sat and stared long at the craven lie as it flickered

back at me, thinking about a time when I believed that my words should become vessels of discovered truth.

I'm thinking about it still, as I lie in wakeful misery beside sonorous Morag.

I've made it through the day and night without getting drunk, and I may have saved some poor woman's life tonight. But if I was a person of real courage, I would be turning myself into the police, because I know that I can't, of my own volition, stay sober forever, and I can't moderate my drinking to the extent of avoiding black-outs.

I'm stayed from that course by three factors:

One is that Laura kept saying "My boyfriend, he's gonna kill me."

The second is that, if I turn myself in, the police will almost certainly accept the convenience of compiling the case that I did, indeed, do it, and that I killed pathetic Candy, too, and then I'd never be able to prove that I didn't do it.

The third is that my desperate addiction is clawing at the inside of my skull like fingernails on a blackboard, tormenting me, terrifying me with urgent self-serving scare-tactics, screeching that, if I go to prison, I won't be able to drink, won't be able to pass out, that I shall never ever sleep, that all my remaining life will be a dark, rattling, rasping, ironclad nightmare.

Chapter Three

Carney is telling me about the time he was fleeing from the RCMP up north, when he was about twelve years old, how he swam to an island in a chilly, brisk river in his flight; he thought that he'd made good his escape, so he took off his wet clothes and hung them up to dry, a mistake, as it turned out, for the cops came to the river bank and spotted the clothes waving in the wind like snitching semaphore, and soon enough they had a boat and were coming across to the island. Skinny little Carney, clad only in his underpants, climbed a spruce tree and concealed himself there. After a fruitless search, the police left, but, vindictively, they took Carney's clothes with them. Carney waited in the tree until dark, shivering and swatting the infinite multitude of marauding mosquitoes, then swam the river, then spent the cold northern night hitchhiking in his underpants back to his reserve.

Carney has told me this story before, but he wants to ensure that I get the facts of it right. Carney has told me many stories about himself, many involving his scrapes with the law, which have been very many, involving court workers, social workers, youth detention facilities, jails and prison, the whole gamut of judicial miscarriage; Carney swears that he has never done anything more culpable than being in the wrong place at the wrong time, or trusting the wrong guy, or maybe bearing an unfortunate resemblance to the real criminal. Carney's unshakeable, cheerful belief in his own innocence is his most enviable trait.

Carney tells me his tales because he's convinced himself that I'm going to write his biography, and that he'll get rich from it. He will bestow his flowing millions on the unfortunate children of the inner city, he has assured me. He ignores my information that it would be I who gets the millions, not he, except that no one wants the story of just another young man who has succumbed to his circumstances; that people, and therefore publishers, want an uplifting, inspirational tale of the extreme rarity who, by luck or genius, overcomes the situation that has been prepared for him, so that they can take reassurance that the world will somehow go right without them undertaking the troublesome task of making it go right.

We are sitting in my van, which is parked just down 20th St. from the neon heart liquor store. It is early afternoon, and I am on my fourth day of experimenting with Plan 'A', a fairly simple scheme that has me denying the requirements of my addiction every day that I can manage to, but on the days that I can't, I must start my drinking by noon, so that I will pass out well before dark; I'm assuming that, even in a black-out, I wouldn't want to murder anyone in broad daylight.

Should Plan 'A' fail, Plan 'B' is even simpler, so simple it has a compelling streamlined, elegant efficiency that's almost irresistible: kill myself.

Carney and I are sitting on the back seat of the van, behind the obscured windows, sharing one of two bottles I've just bought. Carney is in a good mood, because he doesn't look beyond his next bottle, and sitting here with two means his future is set.

We are able to watch the passing scene of the street without being seen. Most of the people we see are seeking one oblivion or another, either passing forlornly under the neon heart, or further down the street through the bar entrance at the Inn Continent, or next door at the inn's wine and beer outlet, or are huddled in hushed cryptic conversations of the drug trade.

A little girl stands under the neon heart. On this warm afternoon, she still wears a long, dirty quilted winter coat, probably obtained from the Food Bank, stands with her hands in the pockets, her shoulders straight, her head level as she looks steadily out over the top of the passing traffic. She looks out, but is entirely self-contained, her awareness occupied by some internal drama or fantasy. Around her, scarecrows and zombies hover, their rags rippling lightly over alcohol-atrophied limbs in the gentle breeze, but she acknowledges them not at all. Behind her, the store door opens and out come a woman and a man, both carrying brown paper bags. The woman turns down the side street and the man follows her; but he looks back to the little girl and barks to her. She swivels slightly in reaction to some impetus within her interior world. He calls again, but she still gives no response. The woman carries on, anxious to party, presumably, the man stops and steps back to the little girl. He leans over, bottled tears chinking in his paper bag, and tugs at her shoulder, barks again. The little girl now turns, but without registering them in any way, and follows, head level, hands in pockets, step measured, somehow displaying a decorum and a sort of nobility none of the adults around her could ever manifest. The image of her lodges itself in my mind.

In contrast, down at the corner a very drunk and pregnant prostitute, bleached blonde hair falling in oily strands before her heavily made-up face, form flagrant in aqua stretch pants and pink t-shirt, pops into the traffic stopped at the lights, hooting at the drivers and calling them honey, shimmies her belly and breasts in desperate peddling of her unappealing wares. On the sidewalk, standing astride his rusty bent bike, a little boy laughs and laughs at her, and she tearfully bawls him out between exhortations to drivers.

She chases after him at one point, but he just wheels his bike backward a few feet, and suddenly she stoops behind the garbage can on the corner, pulling her stretch pants down as she squats.

"Happy now?!" she cries. "Now I gotta take a piss!"

And on the sidewalk below her, there appears a stream that flows around her old, worn, absorbent bedroom slipper to the curb. The little boy stares.

This episode stops Carney in the middle of one of his accounts.

"Do you know her?" I ask.

"Yeah," he says. "Beth. My brother's common-law."

"Should we go and get her?"

Carney shrugs.

"She wouldn't want to come," he says.

He takes a thoughtful pull on the bottle, and I take the interruption to reintroduce the topic of my interest.

"So, what about Velvet?"

"What about her?" Carney says as a way to change the subject.

"Did you talk to her? Will she keep her ear to the ground about The Baron?"

"I guess she hears stuff without even trying."

"But will she pass it on to me?"

Carney weighs either my friendship or my ownership of the bottles for a moment before answering.

"I can ask her again, maybe," he says. "She says she knows it wasn't The Baron, anyways."

"Well, I'm hearing from people who say otherwise."

"Yeah, well, some people say things ..."

He sits up suddenly, and looks sharply out the front windshield.

Emerging from the general motion of the street is Solania, walking carefully and slowly, as though there's a risk of breakage. Carney watches her intently as she comes toward us. Just ahead, she carefully sits down on the concrete steps of the recessed entrance to the storefront 'God's Right

Hand Outreach Ministry'. This somewhat sheltered entranceway has long been a collecting point for anyone who doesn't have enough to buy a bottle, and who wishes to pool resources with others of the same circumstance.

As Solania is the only person there, she may have a long wait, and she settles herself in. She wraps her thin arms about herself as though otherwise she might fall apart.

"Gimme some money," Carney says quickly, uncharacteristically direct.

"No," I say. "Not for that."

"C'mon," he says, but I am resolute.

"You can offer her some of that," I say, indicating the bottle. "That's it."

An angry, ashen-faced middle-aged man wearing a short-sleeved white shirt and a striped tie suddenly appears at the door of the outreach ministry and, in the tones of a barking watchdog, demonstrates to Solania that God's right hand doesn't extend to her. I can't make out all that he says, but, in scolding tones, he's clearly shooing her away.

Very slowly, calmly, with a dignity that surprises and impresses me, she stands and steps away from the entrance, and turns to gaze evenly at the man.

"Go on!" he orders, flicking air with the back of his hand, but she is now on the public sidewalk, and she doesn't move again.

"Don't you look at me like that, girlie," he barks, his lips trembling and imprecise.

Solania gazes still, and the man mutters viciously and withdraws back into the storefront ministry.

Carney springs like a spaniel from the van, doesn't bother to close its door, and marches purposefully up to Solania, who turns and regards him without surprise. He takes her firmly by her fragile arm and swings her back to the ministry steps.

He sits himself down on the second step, saying loudly "Let's siddown for a while and take a load off!" And he pulls Solania down beside him.

They sit there for a while. Carney checks over his shoulder now and then, then shouts "It sure is nice sitting here on these great steps!" Solania smiles widely at him.

He looks over to me and nods happily.

After another few minutes, he stands up and steps back to the glass door. He pounds on it several times and shouts in "We sure like your steps!", before sitting down again.

He motions over to me.

"C'mon!" he cries gaily. "We got a sit-down strike going here!"

I shake my head through the van door, and Carney laughs. Solania smiles at me with quiet delight.

Of course, before too much longer, Constable Morley shows up on his bike. I stick the bottle under the seat and step out as he exchanges greetings of familiarity with Carney.

As I get to them, Carney, ever innocent, says "But how was I to know they didn't want me sittin' here? Nobody never came out and told me."

"I'm telling you," Morley says firmly.

"But I'm tired, I gotta sit somewhere when I'm tired, don't I?" He turns to Solania. "You're tired, too, right?"

Morley shakes his head and says "You're trespassing and making a nuisance of yourself, and placing yourself in breach of your parole."

"Sitting down when I'm tired is breach of parole?!" Carney cries.

"Okay," Morley says briskly, "I'm calling for a car."

But he turns to me instead.

"Perles, can you talk some sense into him?"

I look from Morley to Carney to the man standing

behind the ministry's glass door, watching stern-faced and triumphant.

"I'm not budging 'til I've had a good rest," Carney says to me.

I say to Morley, "There's one of The Baron's pushers down there on the corner. Why don't you go and make yourself really useful?"

"Damn you," Morley says, shaking his head at my betrayal, and reaching for the radio on his belt.

It's Solania who intercedes to defuse the confrontation. She stands and lifts Carney's hand.

"Ustum," she says.

"No way," Carney insists.

"Come," she says soothingly. "You've done what you can for now. You'll be of no use in prison."

And she gently caresses his head. The magnetism of this gesture draws him upward.

"At least someone here is sensible," Morley says.

"If I wasn't on parole ..." Carney says.

"We're all on parole," Solania says to him. "From the moment we're born, we're on parole. It's against the law to be who we are, and when we act like we are who we are, we're in violation of our parole, and we'll be locked away in prison. We're born criminals."

She raises her chin to Morley in just the slightest demonstration of a challenge.

"We're against the law from birth, aren't we?"

Morley appraises her momentarily, glances over to me.

"I guess it can kinda seem that way, sometimes," he allows unhappily. "But just move along, and nobody'll be in violation of anything. I mean it, I don't want you giving me a hard time. Just keep moving along."

Solania takes Carney's arm and uses it for support and

to direct him down the street while Morley dutifully watches after them.

"Great help you were," he says to me in reproach.

"Morley, look at that mean-spirited rectal rector!" I say, motioning to the man who still stands behind the ministry door. "How can you stand taking orders from the likes of him?"

"I take orders from my sergeant," he says.

I go back to my van, and Morley wheels after me, feeling fiesty.

"Like you don't ever have to follow orders, Perles?"

I slip through the sliding side door and sink onto the second seat, and my addiction directs my thoughts to the bottle below it.

"Well, yes, Morley. I'm resistant, but ultimately obedient."

"We can't live without social order, can we?"

"This social order's more like institutionalized injustice. Strip poker with a stacked deck," I spit, "that's your social order at street level."

"Your meter's expired," Morley observes casually. He props the bike and rests on its seat. "I get discouraged, too. Too much grief every day. But I think, would anyone here be better off with someone else in my place?"

"No," I agree.

"At least I like these people. That's worth something to them, isn't it? Just between us, I worry about who'd be here instead of me if I gave in and left."

"Me, too."

He nods in consideration, then cocks an eye on me as though wondering if he may have said too much.

"What's happening with Laura?" I venture.

"I guess they're burying her," he says blandly.

"You know what I mean."

"Well, it seems your tie wasn't the murder weapon, after all."

"Really?"

"One blow to the head," he says. "Killed her instantly. The tie was knotted after she was dead."

"Why would someone do that?" I wonder aloud.

"Maybe he didn't know she was already dead. Maybe a red herring, to throw us off the scent," he says. He cocks a careful eye at me. "Or maybe as a calling card, self-incriminating."

In my chill, I manage to repeat "Why would someone do that?"

"I don't know," Morley says slowly. "Some guy seeking punishment. Or say some self-destructive guy decides the booze isn't doing it fast enough for him. Maybe he gets thinking about committing suicide-by-cop."

I can't pull my wide eyes off him, which he certainly notes. "But it was my tie," I say limply.

He says: "You talk about justice. It seems to me that justice is a very subtle thing. You take this case with Laura, for instance; I'm really sorry about what happened to her, but maybe, well, maybe justice would be served by us catching the killer and putting him away; that's my intended role, here, to maintain order by enforcing the law and apprehending lawbreakers. After a while, though, I begin to wonder if my better role here wouldn't be to look for ways to limit the individual tragedies as much as I can, and that might not always coincide with enforcing the law; for instance, maybe granting this killer one last chance to get the sort of help he needs, so he could go on to lead a life of productive compensation, and never come to our attention that way again, maybe that would be the best thing all around. Of course, it would take a special person. What do you think?"

I choke out "The Baron ..."

Morley swings toward me and says "Forget The Baron. There's no evidence linking The Baron to it. And we'll proceed on the basis of the evidence."

Morley straightens his bike upright and sets his foot on the pedal.

"But, apparently, we don't have enough evidence yet."

And with that he wheels away.

I push the door closed, and take a series of rapid gulps from the bottle, as my drinking is now falling behind schedule.

Some time ago, at what I then naively believed to be a low point in my life, I investigated Alcoholics Anonymous, but decided that it would be useless for me, because its programme is geared for alcoholics, not for alcohol addicts, and because that business of surrendering your fate to a higher power is more than I could ever pretend, and because I need alcohol to pass out. And because the flimsy filmy scraps of my life aren't worth the effort of patching together again.

Both Plan 'A' and Plan 'B' are better than Plan 'A.A.' The only twelve steps I'm interested in are on an eleven-step pier.

The rye is making me unpleasantly dizzy, so I fall backward and watch the movement of the van ceiling for a while. I don't understand how Carney, or anyone else, can enjoy this. But then, I never enjoyed rides at the midway, either.

For a while, I listen to the waves of traffic on 20th, and begin to imagine it as the lapping of a lake of liquor on a planet of which I'm the only inhabitant. I close my eyes, and the reeling of the van becomes the bobbing of a boat on the lake.

This vain daydream is abruptly disrupted by pounding on the side door of the van. I sit up, startled and very dizzy. Carney is back, and I assume he's here to drink, but when I open the door, he says excitedly "Check this out!"

Thirteen or fourteen young men and women are standing in a line across the entranceway to the 'God's Right Hand Outreach Ministry'. They are attending to Solania, who stands before them, quietly and calmly giving instructions.
I step out to hear as Carney joins the end of the line. Solania comes to him, takes his forearm in her thin hand.

"So, the first person goes and walks around the block," Solania is saying. "And when he gets back, he goes to the other end of the line."

She moves to Buster, who stands beside Carney, and takes his arm.

"When the first person gets back, then the new head of the line walks around the block, and goes to the other end of the line. And so on, and so on. Do you see?"

She steps back to Carney and reaches her hand up to his cheek, barely brushing it. "You go, now."

And Carney, beaming at me, starts off up the sidewalk.

"Now everyone move along one place," Solania directs. "Keep right in front of the steps."

She comes over to me with that coy smile, and says "I'm glad you're still here. Maybe we can give you something to write about in your paper."

"I think you just might," I say.

Without invitation, she steps to the door of my van, and without a request, I assist her in. She's as light as a feather, and her little arm feels no more substantial than a robin's egg.

"This will be our war wagon," she says, settling herself into the second seat.

"It will?"

"Sure," she says. She closes her deep, dark eyes, putting the back of her tiny hand to her brow and running it upward over her short black hair. "I wish I was feeling up to standing out there, but I'm not doing too well today. We must be careful to be nice to each other today, Perles, as we have suffering in common, and we're both pretty edgy."

"What suffering do we have in common?" I ask.

She seems surprised that she has to explain.

"We're both fighting against our alcoholism right now, aren't we?"

"I'm not an alcoholic," I correct hastily.

"Whatever," she says, unconcerned, patting her cheeks lightly. "Man, I can't stop sweating. Is that happening to you, too?"

"There's a bottle of rye under that seat, if you need it."

"Oh, come, Perles, we have to stop. We're running out of time; we can't waste what we have left on being drunk and useless, can we?"

I study her carefully.

"Time for what we still have to do," she says, answering my question unasked.

I sit heavily on the floor of the van, rather at her knee, and look at the line-up of people watching down the street for Carney's completion of his circuit.

"I can't really stop drinking," I say, suddenly and inexplicably wishing to unburden myself. "I don't sleep anymore. I must drink."

"Poor Perles," she says. I look over my shoulder sharply, but there is no hint that she is mocking me. "You'll sleep when you finally find your way home again."

"You know, telling people what they obviously want to hear is a standard and shabby device of pseudo-psychics."

"Yes, I know," she says without offence. "I could tell you things you wouldn't want to hear."

"Don't bother," I say. "I put no faith in second sight or

sixth sense or seven pillars of wisdom or nine lives."

"Poor Perles, you've become so cynical. You don't believe in anything anymore, do you?"

"No," I say. "I don't."

"Is that how you were able to write such a cynical lie in your column about Laura?" she asks sympathetically. "About giving her your tie because she liked it so much, I mean."

A jolt runs through me. From the spinning contents of my mind, I attempt to pluck some appropriate response, but nothing sensible happens to swirl by.

"Don't worry, Perles," she says, soothingly now. "I won't turn you in. You're safe with me."

"But are you safe with me?" I hiss unhappily. "How dare you tempt the attention of such a dangerous man?"

"Frankly, I find such a dangerous man very exciting. Especially if he's my own dangerous man."

She takes on that slow, coy smile. Her arms are crossed in front of her thin frame, but her right hand extends out toward me as if in casual benediction. I must resist the impulse to take it in mine and kiss it.

The rather raucous cheering and applause that greets Carney's return attracts our attention. As per Solania's design, Carney joins the far end of the line, and Buster at our end takes off up the street.

"Everyone move up a place," Solania calls, and they do.

"How long are you planning to keep this going?" I ask her.

"I don't know," she says.

"You can't think that you'll close down the ministry."

"That's not my intention. The idea isn't to do anything to the ministry, it's to do something with our people. Look at this street, Perles, look at the stores up and down this street.

Bars, liquor stores, pawn shops, these storefront ministries, storefront sham counselling services, bingo halls, all of them set up to prey on our misery. What do you call them in your column? Poverty's pirates?"

"Poverty's profiteers," I say with a spark of interest.

"Poverty's profiteers, that's it. They soak up all we have, all our money, all our energy, all our direction. Up and down this street, storefront after storefront, all of them set up to capitalize on our misfortune. Up and down this long street, mile after mile, Perles, how many of these businesses are operated by our people?"

"None," I say.

"That's right, none. How many of them hire any of us to work in them, even?"

"None," I say.

"None. That grocery store over there, it's stocked with the expired produce and dented cans from their eastside stores, but they don't cut the price for us, do they? They make us pay full price for the stuff eastside people already refused to buy at a clearance discount. Our people make up eighty percent of the customers in that store, but how many of us do they hire to work there?"

"And up on 22nd, it's all the big fast food and pizza chains. Our people make up most of their customers, and they sponge up our little welfare cheques with their rubbish. How many of us get even little parttime jobs there, though?"

"None," I say.

"It's seedy, greedy gutter-level exploitation."

"You're quoting my column again," I say, impressed and a tiny bit flattered, recognizing the phrase.

"I know," she says. "I'm your devoted reader. I like the way you can put my thoughts into words."

"Your thoughts? Those are my thoughts," I say, but mildly.

"Our thoughts, then."

"Disadvantage and despair are the economic lifeblood of this neighborhood, without question," I observe. "So you're mad as hell, and aren't going to take it anymore, is that it? Is that what this is about? A simple exercise in defiance?"

She just barely touches my cheek with her hand.

"There's only so much a person can take, isn't there, Perles?" she asks slowly and meaningfully. "Eventually, you've got to lash out, just to show that you're still alive. Don't you, Perles?"

At this timely instant, Constable Morley materializes at my side door.

"Geez, Perles," he exclaims, "What are you doing?"

"I'm doing what a journalist does," I say. "I'm observing a potentially newsworthy occurrence and asking questions about it."

He surveys the component individuals of the shifting line.

"This is your work, right?" he asks me.

"You flatter me. It's of this young lady's organization, I believe."

He looks into my van, raises his eyebrows.

"Okay, Miss, are you responsible for this?"

"For what?" Solania asks, trying that smile on Morley.

"This," Morley says, waving at the line just as it shifts one place again. "What do you want to call it, a picket line?"

"It's not a picket line," she says calmly.

"What would you call it, then?"

"I'd call it passersby very slowly passing by," she says. "Is there a minimum speed on public sidewalks now?"

Morley turns to inspect the line, locks his thumbs in his heavy belt.

"I've been watching them, Morley," I offer. "They've

never stopped moving. They're not loitering, and they're not blocking anything."

"Well, they're intimidating the hell out of the people inside," he says, "if you'll excuse the expression."

"If they don't want to see our people walking by, why'd they come to our neighborhood?" Solania asks.

Carney, in about mid-line now, calls out: "Afternoon, Officer Morley.", which generates more mirth than it merits. In turn, with growing giddy giggling, the line constituents wish Morley a good afternoon.

Morley turns back to the van, leans over me to address Solania.

"Don't you people have anything better to do?"

"No, we don't," Solania says, suddenly severe. "You know that we don't."

Morley shakes his head, possibly in frustration.

In front of my van, a squad car pulls in to the curb. Two officers who are unknown to me get out and slowly and with conscious authority step onto the sidewalk. Morley goes over to them, and they confer. The two new officers shake their heads much as Morley had done, then climb back into their car and speed away.

Morley comes back to us and says to Solania "Okay, then, Miss, I expect you'll get tired of this soon enough. You'd just better make sure things don't get out of hand. I'm holding you responsible."

He takes a pen and notebook from his shirt pocket.

"What's your name, Miss?"

"Why do you need my name?"

"Because I'm holding you responsible. You call the tune, you pay the piper."

Solania nods and says "Solania."

"Is that your first or last name?"

"It's my only name," she says.

"You must have a last name."

"Not yet," she says.

"I see," he says with a sigh. "Do you have any identification, then?"

"No."

"C'mon, your health card," Morley says.

"Health card," Solania says with quiet irony. "I'm a little past that."

"What's your address, then?"

She tells Morley an address on Ave. F.

"Basement rear, the room with the crumbling concrete floor and six foot ceiling, behind the furnace room," she says. "My landlord owns that pawn shop right over there."

She points just down the street to the Silver Dollar Pawn.

"He gives me a twenty buck kick-back from my welfare rental every month," she adds blandly, "because I let him fornicate with me every Friday night."

Morley regards her evenly.

"Yes," she says eventually.

"Yes, what?" Morley says.

"Yes, I am going to make trouble. But it doesn't need to be your trouble, Constable."

"Any trouble around here is my trouble," he says, and he gives me a quizzical look as he steps back.

I just shake my head. I want him to leave; I've fallen far behind schedule in my drinking.

He goes and passes a remark to a couple of the line participants, and then, at last, he rides away.

I dive into the very back seat, reach under the second seat and pull out the rye. I lie back and drink hard.

Solania drapes her frail arm over the back of her seat.

"Aren't you ready to stop yet?"

"No," I say.

"Not even for me? Won't you stop for me?"

"I don't know what you mean. Why would I stop for you? Just who are you?"

"You know who I am," she says lightly. "Close your eyes and listen inside yourself. You know who I am."

I am quite willing to close my eyes, and I take another hard drink as I do.

"You know," I say sourly, "prostitution is the oldest profession because it's the only profession. You are another prostitute in a world of prostitutes. You're just a little prostitute."

"You're not listening carefully," she says mildly. "Listen carefully."

I drink again, and my swirling mind begins to cloud pleasingly.

"A very little prostitute. Twenty dollars from your scumbag landlord. By golly, even I'm a better-paid prostitute than that."

"Listen more carefully," she says. "Listen to your poor heart."

A ray of sunlight penetrates the clouds. It's Christine, incorporating the conclusive argument against a world of prostitutes, shaming my contention.

"You're not Christine," I mutter.

I drink urgently, eyes closed, hoping to somehow hold the image, but Christine's beautiful features begin to soften, then flow, then are sealed behind the closing clouds again. Then there comes another beam, not golden and warm, but sharp, silver and icy, like that of a streetlamp in the cold night, and the beam shortens and reforms into a single gleaming, glinting orb, bubble of a meaningless, empty message that doesn't quite reach me; but no, a crystal ball of a prophetess, perhaps; but, no, something else ... for mere moments less than eternity, I watch it float before my imagination, inspect it with fear and fascination ...

"I see ...," I manage to say as I pass out, "I see the silver apple of the moon."

When I regain consciousness, it is dark, except for the icy light of the streetlamp that shines through the windshield. I am alone, and the van is closed tightly against the night.

I sit up and rub my face, then go to the front seat and start the van. The clock in the dashboard says it's 2:17.

I try to take stock of my condition, try to ensure that I'm capable of driving safely. I know that if I feel all right, I'm still drunk.

But I don't feel all right. I'm quivering and my head is a kettle once again. I'm sobering up.

As a further test, I mentally run through the route of quiet residential streets I can take to get home without coming to the notice of the police. I manage to imagine it without getting lost or rattling around like a marble in my kettle.

So I place my shaky hands carefully on the steering wheel, giving the van a minute to warm up in this chilly night, and it is then that it gradually registers on my aching awareness that I'm wearing a cheap fake diamond bracelet on my right wrist.

I no longer enjoy the unexpected in my life, and I stare at the bracelet with absolute dread. A little voice echoing inside tells me to drive away from where I am without looking to either side, to follow my planned route like a single-minded bloodhound, and never venture out of my house again.

But instead, I start to desperately fumble with the difficult little ring latch of the bracelet, which glitters terribly in the lamplight. I can't coordinate my fingers, and I'm raising the clasp to my bone-dry mouth to bite at the thing when I unwillingly look just up the sidewalk to The God's Right Hand Outreach Ministry.

Outreaching from the recessed entranceway is not the right hand of God, but the left leg and foot of someone else, unless God wears stretch pants and bedroom slippers.

A jumble of things go through my mind as I step out of the van and approach the entranceway, none of them agreeable. It's certainly not uncommon to find someone sprawled in drunken sleep on the streets, and this figure may not mean the worst, even though I already know that it does.

"Hello," I say stupidly as I stop about five feet away. "Hello, are you okay?"

A little strangled sort of noise escapes my throat as I recognize the bleached blonde, pregnant prostitute who'd made such a spectacle of herself the past afternoon. She's bent in an awkward heap that doesn't suggest sleep.

I bend over and venture slightly closer, braced with weight on my back leg, as though I need to be ready in case she suddenly springs up at me.

The night is very cold, and shivers wrack me to my queasy core.

Glinting in the lamplight like cheap fake diamonds, shards of smashed glass lie scattered around the figure, concentrated mainly around her spilling, lank, oily tresses. One large piece suddenly springs up and stabs at me, for it holds a recognizable bit of the brand label of the rye I had been drinking.

Somehow I fight my way through the slashing attack back to the van, and I search frantically for my own empty bottle inside it, and, of course, I can't find it.

I drive home carefully through the residential streets; I drive carefully, but my attention is divided, for I am also occupied in working out the details of Plan 'B'.

Chapter Four

Two days ago, I sent Robert my column by fax. It made some sort of impression on him, because at the end of the workday, he came to see me at my house.

The column was a diatribe against a community that tolerated a circumstance wherein one of its identifiable components was isolated and maintained in westend deadlock deadend idle indignity, ignorance and penury and economic and sexual exploitation, was scorned and dismissed for obediently occupying the circumstance that the community had prepared for it, was scorned for being down when it had been knocked down. I concluded the column with a laudatory account of Solania's little protest demonstration. It wasn't a column calculated to generate any personal popularity, or to invite any sympathy for the people of whom I was writing, or to effect any change. It wasn't seeking miracles or even mercy. It was just a denunciation.

And it was penance. I am presently in a state of penance. The flaw of Plan 'B' is that I don't believe in hell after death, so dying is too good for me, I don't deserve to die yet; I must find my hell before death; and, almost unfortunately, finding hell is as easy as pie for me: all I have to do is stop drinking.

I wrote the column two days after I stopped drinking, well, drinking alcohol, that is; now I drink tea and water at all times, have done so for the last three days, in the daytime, I'm never without a mug or a glass in my hand. Sometimes I drink tea and water both at the same time, swallow of one, swallow of the other. When I gained some control of my hands, I typed my column and started playing solitaire, and I can't stop that either, only interrupt the solitaire to make or pour tea or water, or to empty myself of both. The lines of the cards, all in that order, take on a sort of inevitably, and the cards I turn up now seem more fatalistic than tarot, it's a little hard to formulate the sense of it straight in my mind, but it's as though hell is coming at me like links of fat sausage, wide in the middle and blunt at their ends, which aren't really ends but twisted constrictions, and each card is like an individual sausage, inescapably connected and sequential, but it only makes an imprecise sense, and only to me, I'm sure, no matter how compellingly. The way things must must must be.

I play the same three pieces of music over and over, in their inevitable sequence, too, first the Love-Death from Tristan und Isolde, then the third of Strauss' Four Last Songs, because all my senses wish to sink in slumber, and then Scriabin's Prometheus.

Morag was actually paying attention to me, but very worriedly keeping her distance, observing from just outside doorways and so on. At the beginning of another sequence of my music, she ventured to ask, worriedly, if it was really necessary that it be the same three pieces each time. Jessye Norman was singing the Love-Death at the time, and I accused Morag of being intolerant of and prejudicial against fat sopranos. She constantly quietly mixes and drinks her martinis, I can hear the elegant spoon ringing against the exquisite crystal every night, it sets up a resonance in my skull, tortures my addiction, which screeches like a vulture and in turn tortures me, tries to tear out my liver, which aches terribly, or maybe it's my kidneys; whichever it is, it suits me very well.

I sit crosslegged on the carpet to play solitaire, I rock back and forth until my knees and hip joints scream in pain, then I fall back until the surge of desperation propels me upward to get more tea or rewind the tape or whatever. Morag would seem to have cancelled one of the meetings at our house, and yesterday she stayed home all day, maybe it was just a day off for her, I couldn't really swear, but I think it was because she was afraid I might die. But I have a much more liberal estimation of my capacity for suffering; I'm not going to die, not yet.

It isn't so easy to play cards when you've got blood on your hands, no, it takes some dedicated effort. It doesn't matter if, by some chance, I didn't murder that poor pregnant prostitute, didn't snuff out her innocent little booze-soaked unborn baby, or if I didn't murder Laura or Candy; it's not only evil that is properly punished, but weakness, too, and the betrayal of life's gifts, and of that I am surely guilty, and more than deserving of this hell.

When Robert came calling, it came as a surprise; I flew at the door expecting one of Morag's morally superior sisters, and I wanted to send her flying away at the sight of the wild man of her worst nightmares. Pumped up as I was, to see Robert there when I tore open the door rather deflated me, and made it impossible for me to hide from him inside.

He followed me into the livingroom, and I poured him a cup of tea, as I couldn't very well drink one otherwise.

"That was some piece you sent me," he said seating himself on the sofa. "It's not often I get a submission that has no punctuation at all."

"When one doesn't sleep, one's life loses its punctuation, " I said. "I guess that sort of slipped into the piece."

"You're not sleeping?"

"No. Never will again, as far as I can see."

"When's the last time you ate?" he asked.

"About thirty seconds before the last time I puked."

He stared sadly and sympathetically at me long enough for me to rock and heave in my chair in inspection of the cards played out on the carpet, aching to put the queen of clubs on the king of diamonds where it so pressingly and unavoidably belonged.

"Cold turkey, eh?" he said with pity.

"More like burning vulture," I said, laughing acidly inside myself. "Are you going to run the column?"

"Will you quit if I don't?" he asked.

"I couldn't begin to tell you. Why don't we find out?"

"You're condemning the whole city, Perles. It's not an opinion piece, it's an harangue," Robert said. "It may well alienate your readership, you know, all the people who've wanted to feel that they were on your side in these matters. If that happens, you could find it very difficult to reach them again. What will that accomplish?"

I don't mean to accomplish anything. I know that in this city, pointing out what's wrong is considered quite a bit worse than doing what's wrong. I condemn them because they condemned me. Until I became immersed in the world that they created by their negligent tolerance of it, I managed to nurse along some hopes in my life, however faint, false and fanciful. It was the hard flinty frozen core of their own creation, that part around which they tiptoed in tacit acceptance, if not approval, that iced the heart of my hopes, starved my soul and made a remorseless monster inside me, doomed me to finally play fatal solitaire in hell until my hunger for its sausage and suffering is sated.

That's what I might have said if Scriabin hadn't been excoriating me so enthusiastically on the stereo at that moment. Robert watched the flames flaring out of the speakers.

"Why has the westside become so personally your problem, Perles?" he asked when Scriabin was catching his breath for a moment. "Why don't you give yourself a bit of a break? Why don't you focus on the positive for a little while? The suffering of those people isn't the whole world."

"It's been my world for so many years, it's my whole world, now, and all else seems applied pretense and unreality, undertakers' cosmetics," I said. "I'm linked to those people like, like sausages, heart to heart to heart ..." ... from Christine's to theirs to mine to theirs to Christine's to theirs to mine to theirs ... theirs is the linkage of mine to Christine's ... "I would like to stop loving them ... I would like to stop loving ... I would like to stop ..."

This sent him into another thoughtful pause.

"Two weeks ago, you wouldn't have written such a piece, and in another two weeks you won't," Robert reasoned, retaking the safer professional ground.

"Maybe that's what makes it valuable," I said.

"I didn't say it was without value. But we're a newspaper, Perles; you're supposed to be writing 'Wisdom of Perles', not 'Ulysses'. I tried to punctuate it, but I couldn't figure out how to do it. It's unpunctuatable."

I smiled at him. I think it was a smile, my bodily control still lacks accuracy.

"Did you get the gist of it, anyway?" I asked.

"The gist is painfully clear," he said ruefully, "with or without punctuation. It manages to give vivid insult to everyone in the city. Tell me what you hope to accomplish with such an inflammatory column, Perles."

For want of anything better to say, I said:

"Eventually, you have to lash out, just to prove that you're still alive. Don't you, Robert?"

I don't care to prove I'm still alive, of course, I have to somehow make myself worthy of death, but Robert considered me for some time, then said:

"If you let me add that sentence to your column, I'll run it."

"Okay," I said.

"But you've got let me try to punctuate it," he added.

"Okay."

Poor Robert is mistaking me for a man on a mission of

social improvement. He believes that the publication of the column is fundamentally important to me; he's an idealist, really, at heart, and that helps him to think that I must still be one, too. The writing of it was the exercise, the expressing of it; I'm past hoping for any sort of actual communication. As for whether he really ran the column, I don't know, because I can't read, because I can't settle my eyes on a line of print, so I don't open the paper.

At night, I stalk these pleasant residential streets, revelling in the agonies of my addiction, mocking it even as I meet its insistence that, no matter what else I may think about, I never for a moment stop thinking about drinking alcohol, or about the three women I probably murdered. It's quite a load to have on one's mind at one time; I am constantly haunted by three spirits and by the craving for a fourth. I prowl past the comfortable homes of women who are protected one more night from that dark demon that may dwell in me, and often I'll picture Laura or one of the others ensconced in one of those comfortable homes, how just a flick of fate's wrist might have permitted them lives of meaning and dignity and safety, and how they were executed for the trivial sin but capital crime of vulnerable availability, how one more shuffle of their deck would have laid out for their lives a deal of different inevitabilities. It besets me, actually, that consideration, and makes me itch to go home and reshuffle and redeal. But I slither and writhe like a dark snake that coils and scoots in mad spastic pain, ignoring or savouring my exhaustion. I weave through this verdant treed and bushy neighborhood like a black ribbon, or a lethal tie that winds or knots around the laurel, and one on the laurel is four-in-hand. Sometimes I stop at the sidewalk cafe and order tea and water, not the fancy candy herbal teas of the perfect precious complacent patrons, but black tea steeped with caffeine suitable to a nightstalking, high-strung, tight-sprung dangerous man; I may sit beside a table so superbly encircled by those who claim the halo of the streetlamp as their beatification, and I'll contaminate them with my hellish proximity, corrupt the geometrical perfection of their circle with the savage penetrating thrust of my black adder stare.

Last night, when I returned home to lie on the sofa and close my eyes and restoke my hellfires and listen to the desperate pleas and rants of my addiction, Morag stepped into the dark livingroom, backlit by the ceiling light of the front hall. I was aware of her for some time; she may have believed that I was asleep, and she watched me silently, until I raised my forearm to my forehead and a sigh escaped me unexpectedly.

So Morag took the chance to say "What's her name?"

I might have said Christine, of course, might have said her name has always been and always will be Christine, but I almost said Solania.

"What's whose name?" I said.

Morag suddenly burst out in weeping, shaking her shoulders where she stood.

"She must be wonderful," she sobbed, "to have done this to you."

"Morag," I said, "you're making a mistake. There's no one."

"I know a broken heart when I see it," she said, bringing herself under some control and wiping at her eyes with the balls of her hands. "I suppose she's pretty and sexy and slim and melon-breasted ..."

I rolled away from her, set my eyes on the back of the sofa.

"I could never destroy you like this," she said.

"I know, you're very kind," I said blandly, although I might have told her that she badly underestimated the destructive powers of both herself and her martinis over the long haul.

"No, you don't understand," she said, weeping again. "That's what's so painful to me, knowing that you could never be brokenhearted like this over me."

"Honestly," I said, trying to contain my impatience, "it's rather late for you to try to find passionate romance in our relationship, isn't it? You've so diligently guarded against it."

"I know," she cried, "I know. I know I have. But something's happening to me."

"Let me guess," I said, sitting up, and getting up to leave the room and the house. "You're seeking a new plateau of platonic, self-realized, self-sufficient sisterness."

She shrank from me as I approached, obviously thought that I was coming to her, not going past her.

"Go ahead, hit me," she said.

I stopped and squared to her.

"I don't want to hit you," I said. "At the risk of obviating your cherished postures of victimization, I've never wanted to hit you."

"You want to hit me right now," she insisted. "Go ahead, get it over with."

I reached over, and through her arms raised in cringe, I firmly cupped her chin in my hand, and lifted her face to meet my eyes.

"Don't be ridiculous. I wouldn't bother to hit you," I said. "I'm the one who'd outright kill you."

She grabbed my arms and pressed her face against my chest in a gust of vermouth and vodka vapours.

"These last days, this last week," she said urgently, "I realized that I've never known you before."

"So what?" I said, trying to extricate myself from her grip. "That was your good fortune. You've no reason to know me now."

"Let me know you," she cried.

Well, her timing was off by a couple of years. She might have guessed that I have no patience. I broke free from her and strode out of the house, and walked around for what seemed to be several hours. Since I've been back, I haven't seen her, and she may not even be here, I certainly haven't sought her out, she may be relating her tale of woe and pathos in the home of one of her tsk-tsking group members.

My own support group would seem to be Robert, and even that is too much for me. He asked what Morag didn't ask, if there was anything he could do for me; but, of course, he misconstrues my motives, thinks my abstinence is my attempt to redeem and renew my life.

I prefer the sleepless nights to the days, because the nights are dark and cold and haunted, with imagined indistinguishable horrors in the black corners, and the days are early Spring in an ordered and tidy neighborhood, bright and budding, and it's a nervous strain for me to protect myself against the inherent poignant optimism probing silently for some chink in my misery. Night is my natural habitat now, and I can surrender myself to it.

I keep the drapes drawn against bright optimism's stealthy beams in the day; the house lacks the jarring geometrical knife-edge shadows of the night, is really too soft in its muted dreariness, but this is the best I can do.

I am in day five. My addiction is growing hoarse in its screeching, and it's grinding its talons blunt inside me. This is no good, it may not prove to be the relentless tormentor I'd expected; I begin to wonder if it will be necessary to feed it something just to build up its vicious energies again.

I hear a little tapping, almost a small scrabble such as a mouse might make, and I dismiss it at first as just one of those noises that have been originating from within me; but there it is again, seems to be coming from the direction of the front door. If it had been a normal knock, I would have ignored it, but this tentative little noise arouses my vestigial curiosity, so I go silently to the front window, peer surreptitiously around the edge of the curtain.

Carney is on my front steps, ashen and agitated. He inspects the number beside the door carefully, then consults a small piece of paper he cups in the palm of his hand, then checks the house number again.

The tension gets to him, and he bounds like a hare to the front sidewalk, looks from my house to my van parked in front, to the neighbouring houses on both sides, then stares long at the piece of paper.

Carney isn't a big man, but I've never seen him appearing so small and slight; I realize that I've never seen him set against anything but one- and two-storey storefronts before, haven't seen him in contrast to something like, say, the tall and stout trees that line our street.

The world permitted to Carney is tiny and circumscribed, shrivelled to maybe six square blocks, and he's far out of his element here, looks like a hare in a kennel, and I take pity on him, go to the front door to rescue him from the nebulous harms and humiliations that gather behind every window.

He is relieved to see me, smiles with chin down in shy greeting and modest self-congratulation, and springs forward to the steps again.

"Hey, Bro!" he calls more loudly than is needed, perhaps as verification for all the suspicious unseen neighbours. "So this is where you live, eh?"

He steps through the front door, but resolutely refuses my invitation to the livingroom.

"So," he says.

"So," I say. "How did you find my address?"

"Solania, she give it to me," he says, and maybe as his

defense, he shows me the address on his piece of paper, written in a careful, rounded schoolgirl script that is surely Solania's.

I resist the question of how Solania came by my address, for I fear that Carney would use it to prove her powers of divination. I just nod.

"Solania, she sent me to get you."

"What for?" I ask.

Carney shrugs. "She says we need you."

He dares to look around at all that he can see from just barely inside the front door.

"So, this is your place, eh?"

"Yes. What does she mean by that?"

"Pretty good, eh?" he says, still gazing around.

"It's all right."

"They're kicking me out of my room," he says. This isn't a hint that he's hoping to stay here instead, it's just a remark he finds apt in the circumstance.

Before he started telling me his story, I'd allowed Carney's name to suggest to me a history of nomadic adventure, travelling the continent with some seedy little midway; but no, Carney's life has been almost completely contained within the socially-sanctioned constrictions: reservation, various detention facilities and jails, and the inner city ghetto, and the more insidious imposed limitations of ignorance and inclusive economic enslavement. How he got the name 'Carney' is anybody's guess: mine is that his father was favorably impressed by a can of chili.

I am torn by Solania's summons, reluctant to go, reluctant to be responsive in any way to anything, but some unbridled bit of me is undeniably drawn to her. I regard Carney critically, picture him picking his way back through these strange streets in a pall of failure. That tips the balance.

I haven't driven the van in nearly five days, and its

steering wheel feels unfamiliar in my hands. I think of the cheap bracelet that was on my right wrist the last time I was in here; I can imagine it clearly still, and I lock on it with agitation and concern.

When I pull away from the curb, Carney, sitting in the passenger seat, says: "First time I been in this when it's moving."

"I guess that's right," I say. "So, how've you been?"

"Got troubles with Velvet," he says.

I attend to traffic, but after a few moments, Carney says "Yeah.", which means he wants me to draw him out further.

"What sort of troubles, then?" I ask without enthusiasm.

"Well, Solania, she says we gotta clean out our own house first, you know. Like, we gotta do something about our own people that are hurting us. Like The Baron."

"Solania's squaring off against The Baron?" I ask.

"She's talking against him, anyways. Solania, she's not scareda nothing. So I'm telling Velvet she shouldn't be hooking for The Baron no more. Anyways, he don't give her no protection, someone's killing his hookers and he doesn't do nothing about it. I'm getting scared for Velvet, so I been telling her that she should quit The Baron, and I'll pimp for her instead, but she isn't going for it."

"Your idea of cleaning your own house first is to start pimping for your underage girlfriend?"

"I got it worked out," he says sincerely. "I wait across the street outta sight and when the trick picks her up, I write down his license plate."

He nods in satisfied conclusion as I look over at him.

"And then what?" I say.

"Then I got his license plate," says Carney as though I'm obtuse.

"So that you'll know you're chasing the right car as you run along behind it?"

"No, I don't run behind it," says Carney. "I can't run along behind it."

"Carney," I say, "what you've got is a plan for catching a murderer if he murders Velvet. It's no means of protecting her."

Carney falls silent in consideration of this possible glitch in his neat plan.

I turn onto 20th St., and as we pass the corner of the Inn Continent, there suddenly reels out from sidewalk onto the road a one-legged young man who dramatically demonstrates that alcohol makes a poor fuel for crutches. He can't find the swirling pavement with the tips of the crutches, and he spins in pirouette on his one leg, shabby disabled street ballet, with the crutches spinning upward like wild windmills or an ugly folk art whirligig, or maybe a ride of the midway at which Carney didn't work. Maybe he actually achieves a moment of lift from his flapping crutches, for it seems to take forever for him to collapse before the screeching front tires of my van.

I'm not sure how far under the van the young man has ended up.

Carney allows to escape a rare curse word, and leaps out of the van. My wish is to reverse the van and drive home, but instead, I feebly and shakily climb out.

It appears that we've done no additional damage to the young man, who is angrily trying to drag himself out from the overhang of the van's front end.

He's a diabetic amputee: he's lost his leg either to the ravages of his alcohol-induced diabetes or to the medical system's hasty impatience; this is a matter of growing debate as the limbs are lopped off more and more frequently in this subcommunity. Anyway, he's clearly unhappy about his inability to get totally blotto at the bar and then stagger along the sidewalk for the remainder of a sunny day, is unhappily confronting the limitations of his foreshortened form as he gallops drunkenly, so to speak, toward the removal of his remaining leg.

Out of consideration of the young man's drunken pride, Carney is prepared to let him drag himself to the sidewalk unassisted, but his clumsy and furious attempts are more than my tension can bear, so I grab the young man under one arm and bark to Carney, who promptly reaches under the other arm, and together we lift him to the sidewalk. The young man snarls in shame. On the evidence of his odour, more of him is rotting already. We prop him up beside the door to the Inn Continent's beer and wine outlet.

I retrieve the crutches from under the van and put them beside the young man, who is now blubbering in incoherent rage. A few dull-faced passersby step over his one extended leg. Carney and I stand at the curb and look at him.

"He'll be okay there," Carney says at last.

"He's not going to be okay anywhere," I say. "Look at him, Carney. I tell you, this place eats people alive."

Cars snake by my stopped van without protest. No horns honk, no drivers crane to glimpse some explanatory tableau; this is but another insignificant episode of this neighborhood, nothing beyond what is already expected of it.

When we get back in the van, I say "Where are we supposed to find Solania?"

""Friendship," says Carney. "Just wait'll you see."

It's some time after noon, but Solania is indeed still at the Friendship Inn, and she's not alone. When Carney and I enter the hall, Sharon, the director, is standing outside her office, surveying the situation.

Solania is sitting at a table, and ringing around her in

various postures at the tables and chairs are well over a hundred people; these are not just street indigents, but other young people and families and grandparents, people who still struggle against all the odds for lives of propriety and decency; all are listening in silent attention to Solania, who is speaking quietly, listening with open-hearted interest, as I would expect of them: with nothing left to guard, these people are the most open to reason I've ever encountered, with no pile to protect, no position to perpetuate, they regard new thoughts or presented arguments without prejudice; if all I ever had to do was write or speak to these people, I would not be as wholly frustrated as I've become; but they aren't the ones whose opinions really count anywhere, after all, so what's the good of convincing them? Solania might well wonder, but doesn't, apparently.

People on the fringes turn briefly to watch us with a cautionary aspect as we approach. Sitting beside Solania is Buster, who nods sternly at the sight of me. Carney goes to stand beside Velvet, who is off to one side.

I stop beside Rose, who stands, typically, at the periphery. She smiles broadly at me, then turns to regard Solania.

It soon appears that Solania is occasionally referring to a newspaper folded on the table in front of her, and it further evolves that she is quoting, or sometimes paraphrasing, from my column, which the honourable Robert did run. Upon introducing a phrase from the column, Solania undertakes a careful and considered enlargement upon it.

"They tell us to be patient, but only so they can ignore our problems for another hundred years.

"They pin us down for a hundred years, and scorn us because we don't get up.

"They tell us we must invest our lives' energies in a system that pays out profits to them, but never to us. They insist on our cooperation in supporting the established social structure, yet they won't share with us any benefits of its subsequent successes, and expect us to bear alone the burdens of its failures," she says, taking a bit from the middle of the column. "They require us to serve an order that serves them, but will never, in turn, serve us. Is this fair? That grocery store up the street steals our money every day, but if one of us just spits on its floor, it's the cops for us. We're supposed to have total respect for an operation that doesn't have any respect for us at all. The pawn shops steal from us every day, but we're supposed to be so careful we don't get any dirt on the floor; just let one of us spray something on a pawn shop window, and see what happens. The bingos take all our money every night, use our money to support art galleries and museums and concert halls, but just let one of us step into one of those galleries to warm up on a cold day, and see what happens: the cops come to take us back where we belong. They use bingos and lotteries and lucky pulls to take all our money so they can support summer camps where our children can never go. Think about that.

"The slumlords steal from us and screw us, and they tell us that what we need to do is keep the walls clean and don't break the windows, and then maybe they'll stop screwing us and stealing from us, if we get down on our knees and snip the grass with nail scissors, then maybe they'll fix the water heater.

"They take all our money on 22nd St. and 20th St., but they won't let us have any jobs there; the only jobs they give us are on 21 St. and 19th St., as the sex servants of their frustrated men. Whenever an eastside guy wants to act his worst, in a way that would foul his own den, he knows where to come to do it. And then they sneer at us for taking the only jobs available. And when screwing us isn't thrill enough, then they start screwing our children, and when that isn't thrill enough anymore, they start killing us, and we're supposed to just take it. Eastside johns are raping westside babies and killing westside hookers and the cops do nothing. How long do you think it would take the cops to act if a westside guy raped an eastside baby, or if a westside hooker killed an eastside john?"

I must admit that she has genuine presence in the midst of her audience; she speaks quietly and reasonably, without shyness or hesitation, appears to be completely confident of her position. She directs her dark eyes evenly at those around her. She runs through all the issues of my diatribe, skillfully weaving into it illustrations and elaborations of her own into a seamless whole that seems complete beyond dispute. The people are attentive and respectful, often nodding soberly.

She concludes the diatribe portion of her address with:

"We are denied all progressive opportunity, whether it's educational or economic; we are entirely excluded from the pageant of meaningful human existence, but are supposed to sit quietly huddled and toss our coins as it passes us by. And they tell us to be patient, don't make a fuss, and then maybe our turn will come, if we're good and when their turn is all finished. All we're allowed are the means to obediently destroy ourselves in degeneration and indignity, and then we are scorned for using them. We're born into prison, we live in prison, we die in prison, and we're supposed to be patient and polite and obedient; but if one of us rattles his tin cup on the bars, they clamp down on him even harder, and take him from medium security to maximum security, and if that doesn't keep him quiet, then they'll dump him in a deep hole and bury him.

"For a hundred years, we've been quiet, patient, polite, cooperative and obedient, and it's killing us.

Eventually, you have to lash out, just to prove you're still alive."

She folds her hands on the table and closes her eyes. I assume that she's finished, and I shift my weight and then turn to Rose to see her reaction. But Rose, and everyone else, is waiting expectantly for more.

Eyes closed, Solania slowly raises her face to the ceiling, holds this pose for what is a long straining stretch for my present taut impatience, then slowly, theatrically raises her thin arms upward, her fingers splayed. I shake my head in unease, but others appear rapt.

Suddenly, Solania's voice rings out in an energy and fervour I would have sworn was far beyond her.

"I see a two-headed firebird rising out of the dirt and concrete! I see it rise above the pain of our lives! I see it rise in flames out of the earth to burn away the bonds of our grief and despair! I see it soar upwards in flames, and one head calls to the spirits of our people, and one head tears into all the darkness that covers us! I see it fly upwards to the light, to the freedom that is our birthright! And I see the spirits of our people rising to follow it, rising above the pain of our lives! I see the spirits of our people rising like flames out of the concrete to burn away the bonds of our poverty and hopelessness! I see the spirits of our people following upwards to smash aside all that presses down on us! I see the spirits of our people following upwards to find the freedom that is our birthright! I see the daylight of our freedom at last! We are coming to our new day!"

And she smiles a beatific smile, face upraised as if in that blessed sunbeam.

This performance is better than most other evangelical ecstasies I've seen, and it electrifies the people around me, seems to galvanize nearly everyone, and their excitement itself sends a shivering thrill through the hall.

But these people are not your normal holy rollers, they don't think to thrash around and fall twitching to the floor or even suffice with a simple hallelujah; in fact, they don't seem to know what to do with their excitement beyond reaching out to touch Solania, who, eyes closed, reaches out to briefly take and squeeze each of their hands as they crowd around her. An old woman presses forward and kisses Solania's forehead, and she accepts it as heaven's rain.

Buster takes control, directing people away from her after she's taken their hands, saying repeatedly "C'mon, now, that's all today, she's tired. Come and see her tomorrow."

Leaving sounds like a good idea to me, and I turn away, but Solania calls out "No, Perles, you stay."

I turn back. Her eyes are still closed.

"Hey, Perles!" Buster barks. "Stay there!"

"I don't care to," I say, and join the exiting flow.

But Buster breaks through the remaining encroaching crowd and grasps my arm roughly, looks down at me like a puffed-up prison guard.

I glare at him. "What's this, the freedom that's our birthright?"

This punctures him immediately, and as the wind escapes it forms the words "Please, man, could you stay?"

Rose, who can't bring herself to go forward to Solania, is nonetheless moved to burp to me "O, Mr. Perles, isn't it wonderful?"

"Isn't what wonderful, Rose?" I ask, but her question was rhetorical, and she has departed with agreement assumed.

"Just wait here, please, man," Buster says. "She needs you."

I sit down at a table. Carney comes over to me with Velvet in tow.

"What'ya think of that?" Carney asks with glee.

"Of what?" I ask. "What am I supposed to have seen?"

"She's just another whore," Velvet says meanly, happening to echo my own dispirited dismissive comment of many days ago. "She's nothing but a fake and a whore."

"How can you say that?" Carney asks, clearly cut to the quick.

"'Cause it's true. Just 'cause she's got you believing some crap doesn't mean I gotta act like her fool."

The features of her little face are as sharp and sour as rancid milk, and they send my gaze around the hall in want of some refreshing water. She clicks away in her ratty patent leather pumps, with Carney at her worn heels.

Sharon, the director of the Friendship Inn, smartly coiffed and dressed in a manner that's attractive and professional and very distinct from her customers, approaches me, concerned.

"Do you have to write about these meetings?" she asks.

"I don't know," I say. "Why shouldn't I?"

"I don't know what my board's going to make of them, and I don't know what threat they would pose to our funding from the city or the government," she says, "which is much too meagre as it is. We're supposed to be nondemoninational and nonpolitical, you know, and these meetings, or sessions, or whatever they are, are definitely one or the other, and probably both."

"How many have there been?"

"This is the fourth," she says. "And they're getting bigger every day."

"Well, why don't you put a stop to them?"

"Because I can't bear to. In my years here, I've never seen anyone who could uplift these people the way that girl can. You can see how encouraged they seem to be. Yesterday, twenty or more people pledged sobriety to her. I'm going to stand up and put a stop to that? They've got no other place to gather, you know that. But if you draw attention to it, you could put me in an awkward position."

"I don't need to write about it," I say, because I don't believe I need to write about anything anymore.

"I appreciate it," she says seriously.

I like Sharon. She's one of the very few occupationally involved with these people who seems to be sincere in her concern and goodwill.

In response, all I can say is "I must get some water." But there is Buster at my elbow, handing me a large glass of water he's fetched from the kitchen.

"Solania's ready to see you now," Buster says with no apparent irony.

"Is she, indeed?" I say, my back rising, but when I look over to her table, she is smiling at me in truly appealing friendly warmth and girlish delight that I haven't seen from her before.

I drink all the water as I move toward her; Solania nods and Buster smartly takes my glass and goes to refill it.

I sit opposite Solania and say "So, how's stardom?"

"Great," she says ingenuously. "You've been gone a long time, Perles."

"Longer than I thought," I say. "You're quite the hot ticket now."

"It's all started from that protest outside 'God's Right Hand'. And then what you wrote about it, of course; that's helping a lot."

"What is it you're doing, Solania?"

"Just sharing my gift," she says lightly, then adding, as she pats the folded newspaper in front of her, "and yours."

Buster hands me the glass.

"When you finish that, maybe we can go for a walk,"

Solania says.

"Sure, why not?"

I gulp down the water, and we stand and leave; when we get out to the sidewalk, where knots of people turn to watch us, Buster takes up a position just at Solania's elbow. She turns and barely caresses his cheek with the back of her hand.

"No, dear, not this time," she says softly. "I'll be back soon."

Buster straightens himself stiffly upright and fixes me with a hard look, but then quickly looks around to see how his rebuff is being noted by the people watching.

Walking with Solania is like slow, very slow, agony, as the careful, precise pace she sets, tortuous tortoise, is so out of sync with the rhythms of my wild impatience.

"Poor Buster, he's convinced himself that he's the other head of the firebird. But he isn't," she says lightly.

I make no comment, for my attention is monopolized by the outreach ministry, which looms directly ahead of us, and by the terrible racket my pulse is making in my head. An iron gate has been installed flush with the front of the store, so that the recessed entrance is inaccessible. There is a padlock on the gate, and posted in the window is a sign advising "God's Right Hand is Closed".

"How strange," Solania observes as we pass, "that one location can mean such different things to each of us: a scene of success to me is a scene of horror to you."

I think that God's right hand is closed on me, and mercilessly. Gasping, I sort of fall sideways into the front of the store just past the ministry. My shoulder is pained, and I sharpen my focus on it to prevent my further collapse to the concrete. My face is against the window of the Silver Dollar pawn shop, and I choose that moment to itemize the collateral wares displayed in it; dream catchers, cowboy boots, a crummy Korean thirty-one day clock, a mirror mounted in a sheet of plywood jigsawed into the shape of an eagle, its edges scorched rounded and black, many good beaded moccasins and mukluks, and then behind them the row of musical instruments, and then the various electronics. Behind the glass counter of engagement and wedding rings, the fat and greasy and pasty-faced pawnshop operators, greying hair slicked back in 1960 ducktails that look like melting 45s formed and adhered to their heads, stare at me with heat and hostility sufficient to scorch plywood mirror frames. One of them is Solania's corrupt slumlord. Taped to the inside of the window is notice of a rally to demand the closure of the Friendship Inn and the food bank. It's organized by the group COIN, Clean Out Innercity Neighborhoods.

Solania takes my hand in her little birdwing hand and coos "Come, Perles, it's all right. Don't worry."

It occurs to me I've been wasting my monster, murdering innocent women who haven't done anybody any harm.

"I'll kill your landlord for you," I say shakily. "I'll make it painful."

"How gallant; but there's no need, dear Perles," she says. "Just come."

By some seeming power of levitation, like the first of Scrooge's spirits, the touch of her thin fragile hand bears me up. She steps off the curb onto 20th Street without regard for traffic, steps out into the stream of it without looking both ways like a good girl, lets the motorists worry about us, their cars bouncing nose down in sudden halt. We gain the other side by the grace of their reflexes.

Perhaps sensing an aspect of agitation in me, maybe my palm is squirting sweat, she says "Don't worry; I've seen drivers stop even faster than that when they think they'll get to screw me."

"Maybe it's different drivers," I point out.

"No, they're all the same," she says.

She leads me up Avenue G to 21st Street, and we turn and walk along the cracked sidewalk of slowly sloping and heaving plates before the tiny, ramshackle bungalows.

"This was my street," she says. "We used to live over there, and right here was my spot where I used to stand.

"My mother brought me and my sister to the city from the north just after I finished school. She'd taken up with a white guy who didn't want to live on a reservation, so we came down here. I remember when we were trying to find a place to live, my mother wanted some decent neighborhood where she thought her daughters might get half a chance, so her boyfriend, he'd go out and see some apartment or little rental house on the eastside, and everything would be fine until the landlord saw my mother, and then the apartment or house would suddenly have been rented already. Time and again, it happened, and bit by bit the landlords winnowed us over to this westside ghetto, to the slums that were set aside for us. My mother was a good woman and a good house-keeper, clean and sober, and her boyfriend was a pig, but the eastside landlords would've rented to him, but not to her, because she was from the reservation, and our people belong in the slums.

"Same thing when we went looking for jobs; her boyfriend was a drunken high school dropout, but he could always find work when he wanted to, which wasn't very often. My sister and I had our diplomas from the band school, but the diplomas and bus fare just got us a ride to nowhere. My sister got one job in a doughnut shop once, but they fired her when they found out she wasn't Greek or Turkish, whatever they'd thought she was when she'd applied. She didn't sound like she was from the reservation."

"Neither do you," I say.

"No," she says. "We got a good education, my sister and I, unlike most. But that doesn't count for anything here. We might as well not have bothered.

"My mother's boyfriend started drinking really hard, and he put my mother out here on the sidewalk first, but she was too old, she could hardly turn any tricks at all, she'd be standing out here all afternoon and night, trying to look sexy, but she just looked awful; she'd never acted in an immodest way before in her whole life, she was raised to be an old-fashioned girl. The johns would stop just to insult her, or ask if she had a daughter; sometimes one would pick her up, and wouldn't pay her after, like she should be grateful to them. First she cried and cried, then she drank and drank, which she'd never done before, either. So then her boyfriend put my sister out here, and she started getting picked up all the time, she was so pretty, ten tricks a night, but she got into hard drugs because she hated it so much. The drugs took a lot of the money, but she used some of it to send me to secretarial school, because she was determined I wasn't going to end up like her. She swore she'd keep me from ending up like her, if it was the last thing she did.

"I got my secretarial diploma, but none of my job applications got past the first interview. I even overheard one guy chewing out his current secretary for not weeding me out before I got into his office. 'How'd you let one of them in here?!' he said. The Baron took my sister, and he gave her a spot on 19th, so then she was gone and it was my turn to come out here. I remember the day my mother's boyfriend brought me out here, I felt like I was walking out to the firing squad; it was a cold afternoon in the fall, and I stood here shivering in my secretarial school clothes, trying to look as unsexy as I could. I waited out here about an hour maybe, and I wouldn't look at any of the drivers that were scouting the stroll, then I went back inside and said it wouldn't work, nobody wanted me. Well, he marched me right back here, was gripping me by the shoulders, and when we got back here he pushed down so hard on my shoulders, I said 'What are you doing, trying to plant me here?', and then he let me have it, he just yelled that I was just a slut and nothing more, for all my fancy airs and bigshot ideas about myself, and that I couldn't come back in the house until I had money, he didn't care if I had to stand out there for a year."

She suspends her account to look at the place on the sidewalk, and then over to the front window of the little house that had been hers.

"My mother sat in the window there, crying and drinking; she loved roses, and she had these plastic and silk roses all set up on the window sill, and I remember her sitting there framed by her roses, crying and drinking, watching me until I got into that first car.

"I got into drugs and alcohol heavily myself after that, and then The Baron took me. It was a bad time."

She stops and looks to me.

"But I guess you've heard a lot of stories like that."

"Yes, I have," I say. "How'd you get away from The Baron?"

"He just let me go after I —— well, he just let me go. I quit drugs and quit The Baron at the same time. Quitting the drugs was hard, but I think quitting the alcohol may be even harder. What do you think, Perles?"

"I've no basis of comparison; I've never had to quit drugs. Where's your sister now?"

"Died of an overdose," she says. "My mother's back on the reservation, but she's still crying and drinking. Her boyfriend, he's still around, though; he lost part of a leg to phlebitis or some disease like that, maybe it was flesh-eating disease that couldn't stomach his taste. He gets taken really good care of, because he spent a couple of years in the services, and he gets to get drunk at the Legion Hall, and on Remembrance Day he dresses in a uniform and goes to the memorial service at City Hall; I've even seen him sitting stiffly in his electric wheelchair, with a faraway look like he's remembering fallen comrades, and everyone sees his missing piece of leg and treats him like he's a war hero, even though he was too young for any war and I don't think he ever even left the country. I saw the Mayor shake his hand like it was an honour just to know him, and he saluted back."

"Everyone sees his missing piece of leg?" I ask, but that's the grammarian in me.

She sends me her sly smile.

"And just take a guess what group he belongs to now."

"Nothing could be more appropriate than member-ship in the Clean Out Innercity Neighborhoods group."

"You got it," she says gaily. "He's pals with my slum-lord. The circles are small."

"Do they know that they've got you as a common link?"

"I don't think so. I mean, my place in their lives isn't something they'd necessarily want to tell each other, is it? I'm the dirty secret of both of them, I guess."

We begin walking again. She is still holding my hand.

"So, Perles, do you think my mother raised me to just be the dirty secret of a bunch of pigs? Do you think the edu-cator who devoted years to giving me knowledge and litera-cy did it just so that some scumbags could squirt all over me?"

"You know what I think," I say. "But I'm not the best authority you might consult on fulfilling early potential."

We come to a large sign that someone has erected on a corner. It says 'Our Children Are Not For Sale'.

"The problem with that sign," Solania says, "is that it

isn't true. Our children are for sale, and every pervert in the city knows it."

"If it was true, they wouldn't need to put it up," I say.

The street is quite quiet, but the occasional cars that pass us do slow, middle-aged men drivers craning over steering wheels in sideways assessment before scooting on down 21st.

"What do you think about that meeting this afternoon?" she asks me.

"I don't know."

"Weren't you impressed by it?"

"Solania, one way or another, you manage to impress me," I say. "But I can't draw any conclusions or even opinions of anything about you, because I'm unable to discern any meaning."

'That's the trouble, exactly," she says eagerly. "We're getting this interest, well, it's more than interest, it's support, but what do we do with it? If we just keep on giving discussions and visions, the people will start to find that stale after a while. We need something we can apply their support to, before it just fades away."

"Let me clarify something before you say any more. Who makes up the 'we' you're talking about?"

She sort of blinks at me with surprise.

"Why, Perles, dear, you saw how it goes. Our gifts together, our thoughts together, your words, my visions and prophecies. It's a two-headed firebird, dear. That was very clear."

"Solania, if you saw my face on one of the heads, your vision has misled you," I say, dropping her hand. "I have no gift left, I dissipated it in futility and weakness. There is none left to contribute to any sort of social enterprise of yours."

"You're the one who's mistaken," Solania says in the manner of a scolding, stubborn child. "'The Wisdom of

Perles', that's what we need, your wisdom and words, combined with my gift, a gift to our people. The prophecy isn't mistaken."

"I feel that I must point out that matters have not improved here one little bit in the time that I've been writing about them, that my wisdom, worn threadbare as it is, has been no gift to anybody, that my words have never done anything to change anything. Not for the better, anyway."

"They've changed me," she says. "They've given me courage to follow my path."

"I didn't write that column for the purpose of inspiring anyone, or guiding anyone, or giving anyone courage."

"Why did you write it, then?" she demands angrily, her dark eyes hot and sparkling.

"I wrote it..." I begin, but I have no further answer for her beyond one which I don't wish to reveal.

"Exactly," she says. "You don't even know why you wrote it. You wrote it for a reason that was beyond you. You didn't write it to inspire, you wrote it because you were inspired."

"By whom? You, I suppose?"

She stares up at me, then turns away from me, puts her back to me.

"But the way you wrote about me...," she says. "The way you wrote about what I did ..." And her little shoulders fold inward in a way that I don't want to see, so I turn away from her.

"Solania, listen to me. I don't know what you thought we could do, anyway. The conditions you thought we could rise against have already defeated me, just as they defeated Carney and your mother and sister, and just about everybody else we encounter here. If they haven't defeated you yet, then I admire you very much for that, and maybe you are the one who could somehow triumph over them, but I have nothing that can help you. I'm just playing out my time."

My leaden pronouncement tumbles to the cracked sidewalk, and I survey the little houses glumly. Back down 21st Street, a girl comes out and stands on a spot very close to the one that was Solania's, or maybe it's my imagination of Solania herself.

"'Playing', you say," Solania says slowly, lightly. "Do you think Laura would call it 'playing'?"

I turn to her. She is looking up at me, her chin raised in that defiant way.

"No," I confess. "I guess she would say it was deadly serious."

"There's more left in you than you think," she says, putting her hand on my arm. "You're one of us now, Perles. You didn't choose. You were chosen, by a force beyond your comprehension. But you've declared which side you're on, right out loud and in public. Why did you do that? Why do you always come back to us? Why do you always use your strengths to defend us against our enemies, when you believe it's hopeless?"

"I don't know," I admit.

"Of course not, why would you know?" she says. "In our tradition, we don't believe for a moment that our destiny belongs to us. We belong to our destiny. You belong to your destiny, Perles, and your destiny is with us, as one of our warriors. So let's not quarrel anymore. There's no point."

"All right, let's not," I say.

She takes my hand, and we begin to retrace our route.

When we get to the young hooker, Solania says "Hey, Beryl, how's it going?"

"Hey, Solania," Beryl says, eyeing me with some curiosity.

A few steps past her, Solania reaches upward and whispers "She thinks you're very handsome."

"How do you know?" I say in dismissal.

"How d'you think?" she says. "You know, Perles dear, I've got it figured out: my mistake was in thinking that you'd suffered enough to come to me. I was just ahead of myself, that's all. Your journey of suffering hasn't led your heart to me yet. My vision is correct, it's just that my timing was off."

"I see," I say, unequal to her dogged determination.

We go along, and I find myself concentrating intently on the feeling of her hand in mine, realize that I am holding hers now more than she is holding mine.

"Whew, let's slow down," she gasps weakly, suddenly, putting her free hand to her forehead. "We're some pair, you and me; neither one of us can eat, you can't sleep, I can sleep but it just makes me more tired; I can barely walk, and you can barely stay still. We're some pair."

We proceed very slowly.

"Poor Perles, you think I'm so presumptuous," she says. "But I say I don't presume anything, I just recognize what is shown to me, what becomes known to me. What's your name?"

"I don't know, what's yours?" I say.

"No, I mean it," she smiles. "If you tell me your name is Perles, I don't think you're presumptuous, because you know your name, even if you don't remember how you know it. Do you remember your mother teaching you your name?"

"No."

"But you don't doubt your name, do you?"

"Yes, very often I do," I say, and she gives me an impossibly light little slap on my arm.

"You know what I mean. And that's how it is with me. Our Mother makes me know things. You see? I don't doubt my visions."

When we get to Avenue F, she steers down it, saying

Chapter Four / 95

"C'mon, I'll show you where I live now."

We cross 20th Street once again in a way very suitable to Plan B, and at the southern corner of 20th Buster falls into step with us, following just behind. Solania still holds my hand, and she doesn't acknowledge Buster.

At the corner of 19th, we encounter a prostitute named Layla trolling her hook in the stream of rush hour traffic. She wears a very short black polyester-satin dress, an open black coat, and knee-high shiny high-heeled boots to emphasize her long legs. Around her neck is a long black polyester-silk scarf. Her face is heavily made up with black mascara, eyeliner and lipstick; she would probably be nice-looking with a clean face, but her attempts to transform herself into the exotic glamour girl she isn't have made her into a disconcerting ghoulish grotesquery. She turns from her careful scan of each windshield and raises her bizarre mask haughtily at the sight of us.

"Hey, Perles," she says, "what're you doing with that bitch? Don't you know she's poison ivy? You wanna spend your money on me."

"Never mind, dear," Solania says to me, moving just a fraction closer to me.

"Never mind yourself, bitch," says Layla. "You're done for. C'mon, Perles, twenty bucks, special just for you. Forget that bitch."

Buster steps up, stands nose to nose with her, his lids low over cold coal eyes.

"Yeah," she derides merrily. "Think I'm ascareda you? You think The Baron doesn't know you're talking that garbage about him? Who should be ascared, eh?"

Solania guides me by, and tugs on Buster's sleeve with her other hand. Pride requires him to momentarily resist, but then he sneers in half-smile and saunters behind us.

"The Baron's gonna get you, bitch!" Layla calls with

relish. "You, too, Buster, if you don't smarten up!"

"He can't even get out of his door," Buster calls back. "How's he gonna get us?"

"You wait and see. Perles, you're gonna be writing their obituaries!"

Solania brings the traffic to a screeching halt, receiving a profane reproof for her effort, and takes me across 19th. Buster slows his gait in front of the offended driver, smirks at the honking response. "Hit 'em! Hit 'em!" Layla cries behind us.

Solania takes me two blocks south, stops in front of a two-and-a-half storey clapboard house that, on the evidence of the rusty mailboxes with little brass Arthurian knight's helmets on them, has been divided into seven suites.

"Just wait," she says. "I just need to talk to Buster."

And she leads him a distance away, speaks quietly to him, glances over to me almost as if checking that I'm not wandering away. I'm extremely thirsty, and am going nowhere until she gives me a glass or two of water. After a few moments, Buster nods in understanding, then nods at me in a way that might be construed as friendly, or perhaps comradely, and starts back up the avenue. In front of the house a few old bushes, their thin trunks straining junkfood wrappers and bubble gum funnies from the gritty spring breezes, still reach out to greet another season with tight light green tips in entreaty.

She takes me through the splintered front door, through a reeking central hall splattered and smeared with the whole spectrum of hues from the human body's paintbox. The carpet that runs down the hall and up the side staircase is ossified, hard and unyielding underfoot.

Behind one of the three doors leading off the hall, a stereo blares "Long Cool Woman", a song I've never much valued.

The door under the stairway opens to the basement steps, and Solania leads me down. In the basement, she takes me down a narrow dark dank passageway past the furnace room to a door marked, in black paint, incomprehensibly, "2".

She pushes open the ill-fitting hollow-core door and switches on her bare-bulb ceiling light.

The ceiling is barely six feet high, which makes the light bulb a hazard.

The room is musty and tiny, with two small windows just below ceiling level. The furniture consists of one single-size, neatly-made bed, and one small side table.

On one wall is an old, rust-stained porcelain sink with a tiny stilted counter around it, and a small two-burner stove, and beside that a very old rusted and damaged refrigerator. In the sink are three clean but chipped mugs, and on the counter is a teapot. There is an aluminum kettle on the stove. On another wall is a doorway that reveals a closet-size room holding a toilet. Out of the wall of this little room there extends a limed showerhead. The floor of the main room is cracked concrete. The toilet is set on a small cement pad, otherwise the floor of the little room is dirt; there's an uncovered drainpipe in the dirt, approximately under the showerhead.

Over the bed is a cheaply-framed, glass-covered high-school portrait photograph of a very pretty girl who strongly resembles Solania in her better-fed days. A bit of black ribbon is draped around the frame.

"Home, sweet home," says Solania. "Sit down, and we'll have some tea."

There is nowhere to sit but on the bed, so I perch tentatively on its foot.

"I need some water, please," I say.

"No, wait to have tea," she insists, filling the kettle at the sink and setting it on the stove.

She turns to me with a smile, leaning back against the little counter. She seems to be expecting something.

"How long have you lived here?"

"Not yet a year, I guess," she says. "You should be glad you weren't here in the winter, it was so cold. I had to keep the oven on, and weighted its door open, not that that did much good unless I sat right in front of it. I think it's even worse in the places upstairs."

Above us, the last notes of 'Long Cool Woman" disappear, but in just a moment the song begins again.

Solania goes to the refrigerator. The handle has been broken off, but she opens it by slipping her little fingers in where the seal should be but isn't.

"This doesn't work," she says, reaching into its dark interior, "but it keeps the mice out of the tea bags."

She withdraws a box of generic tea, the house brand sold at the grocery on 20th Street. I look around the floor. I don't like mice, and I like 'Long Cool Woman' even less than I'd have thought I did.

"Yeah," she says, nodding to me, "me, too. I hate it when they start their fighting at night."

I don't know if she means the mice or the upstairs neighbours. Probably she means both, so I don't bother to clarify it.

I ask her "You were able to quit drugs and now alcohol while living here?"

"Yeah," she says.

"Unaided?"

"Yeah."

"I respect that very much," I say.

"Well, I didn't say it was easy," she says shyly.

"Well, that's the very point."

My admiration seems to discomfit her, and she turns away to make the tea. I look at the bed upon which I'm sitting, conjure a picture of skinny little Solania rocking on it in withdrawal in the wintry dark and cold. It's almost beyond my conception.

"I think the alcohol's harder," she says, "because you still have to go find the drugs, but the alcohol finds you."

"I thought The Baron was a pretty aggressive pusher."

"Not to me, anyways," she says. "Maybe to others, I guess so."

"What, were you a favourite of his?"

"Hardly," she says scornfully. "I guess he decided I was more trouble than I was worth. Besides ..."

Her voice trails off, and then a flicker of shadow over a little window draws her attention.

"Be right back," she says, and she steps out into the dark passage.

She engages in a brief whispered exchange, and then she comes back in. Upstairs, 'Long Cool Woman' begins again.

"Someone up there likes that song more than I do," I say.

"They've been playing it day and night for three or four days," she says. "There were two families living in there, but a third family moved in a few days ago, and they've been playing that song ever since."

"It must drive you crazy. I can barely stand it already, myself." I give a passing thought of sympathy to Morag's suffering through my own late musical obsession.

"I don't know why the women put up with it," she says. "None of them are exactly long cool women."

"I'm going to tell them to turn it off," I say, standing.

"Don't bother," she says. "Nobody's going to answer the door, anyways. Nobody in these places answers the door, because anything they're not expecting can only be bad news, the landlord coming to evict them, or the cops coming to arrest them, or social services coming to apprehend their children. Nothing good comes knocking unexpectedly here."

"I'll shout through the door, then."

"Won't do any good. Just sit and have some tea."

She turns to the refrigerator and gets out some generic house brand coffee whitener and a bag of sugar.

"What d'you take?"

"Nothing."

"Just black?"

With irritation at the very thought of someone suffering 'Long Cool Woman' for three or four days while trying to quit drinking, I say "Clear; tea is taken clear, coffee is taken black."

"Whatever," she says mildly.

She hands me one of the chipped mugs. The tea is obviously very hot, but my thirst and impatience are getting the better of me, and I suck in combined air and tea. My inculcated courtesy is insufficient to conceal my reaction to the tea's flavour. Solania notes my grimace.

"Yes, it's the water here. I guess it's the pipes."

She sits beside me and sips hers, her featherweight scarcely impressing the bed. I assume that the taste of the water is why she refused me a glass of it. My thirst drives me on beyond the tea's bitter taste.

' ... long cool woman in a black dress on accouna tha beautifo song ...' The unbeautiful song's inane lyrics become distinct and almost disjointed as they flow between the floorboards.

"This is intolerable," I protest.

"Just relax," someone says soothingly, but I'm not quite sure if it's Solania or the girl in the photograph.

'..just one look I was a bad mess 'cause that long cool woman had it on-n-n-n ...' squeeze through a crack in Solania's ceiling, visible balloon words connected but distinct like silly surreal sausages, I can see the words.

I look to Solania, who flows in naked silvery black-shadow shimmer around me on the bed, smiling ecstatically.

"Something's wrong," I say, trying to stand, but suddenly I'm not sure in which direction I'll find the floor. My tea spills on my leg, it dissolves the lower portion of my leg as though it's melting away margarine.

"Ahh!" I say, wagging my stumpy knee.

"I guess it's the pipes," says the Mayor, leaning over to shake my hand as though it's an honour to know me. "The pipes, the pipes are galling." I jut out my chin in manly stoicism and salute him, then gaze out beyond his shoulder, faraway, as though I'm mistily remembering fallen comrades. Carney bends before me in close inspection.

"He'll be okay there," he says at last.

"He's not going to be okay anywhere," the Mayor says. "Look at him, Carney. I tell you, this place eats people alive."

"Where are my crutches?!" I demand. "I need my crutches!"

"Just sit back and relax," says the girl in the photograph, and her black ribbon reaches out, licking at my cheek with its forked tongue like a black adder. A long, cool woman flows through the ceiling crack, Botticelli's Flora, glowing golden.

"Christine," I say, "I'm crippled and I've lost my crutches; I can't get back to you. I can't sleep. My heart will never get home again."

Christine smiles inscrutably, radiant, impossibly distant.

"Your journey of suffering isn't complete yet," coos the girl in the photograph, her black snake coiling itself around my neck.

"We must be avenged," says the flowing, encircling

Solania. "Long ghoul woman in a black dress."

"Christine is taken clear," I advise. "You are taken black."

I struggle to raise myself out of Solania's inky silvery swirl.

"Be calm. You're high and dry."

"No, I'm not high and dry," I protest. "You're going to engulf me." But I should be saving my breath against her gentle deadly rising tide, billowing like a rising silky black sail that will condemn me to my oblivion, her feathery flow sweeping so sweetly, spiraling over me, I am overwhelmed, all my senses wish to sink in slumber, and then I'm over-come.

Chapter Five

When I come to my senses, I associate the maddening endless song with my maddening endless thirst for a long cool glass of water.

Solania is lying behind me on the bed, on which I am sitting, and she appears to be sleeping. By her little window, I see that it's raining black ink in the night. Rain runs in the bottom of the window, which must be right at ground level, runs down the wall behind the little counter, then runs out and collects in a puddle in the middle of her concrete floor. The sound of the rain exacerbates my thirst.

The tea mug I had used is in the sink. I step around the puddle and fill the cup with water.

It doesn't taste as bad as I was expecting, and I gulp it down and refill the mug three times. I'm feeling very feeble.

I turn with my fifth mug of water and lean back against the sink as Solania had done, and I watch her on the bed, looking so frail and pale and precious in the bare, uncaring light of the ceiling bulb.

Of course, it only takes a few minutes of her perfect stillness to send me into a panic that I've killed her.

I call her name, and she stirs and opens her eyes, shielding them against the harsh light, and I sink against the sink in relief.

"Oh, good, you're back," she says, sitting up slowly. "I was worried about you."

"Something happened to me," I say. "I was hallucinating. It was as though I'd lost my mind."

"You were on a dry high, that's all," she says calmly. "Nothing unusual."

"What's a dry high?"

"It can happen when you're drying out. Your brain goes screwy. It passes, don't worry. You're back safe, so all is well. I couldn't keep up with you, you just raced out of here."

She gazes at me warmly through sleepy eyes.

"You don't look so good, dear," she says.

"I don't feel so good, either."

"Come and lie down," she says, reclining herself in a way that leaves room for me. I step around the puddle and sit instead.

She rests her hand on my arm.

"Where did you go?"

"I have no recollection," I say.

"What's this?" she casually asks, reaching around to my front.

"My tie," I say simply, glancing down.

But no, it's not my tie. I'm not wearing a tie. It's a long black polyester-silk scarf knotted loosely around my neck.

I stand and rip it from me, which isn't easily done, as it is damp. I cast it down as a serpent, and we both stare at it.

"Oh-oh," says Solania quietly. "This isn't good."

I respond by falling back to the bed.

"I can see Layla," Solania says. "Something's happened, and it isn't good."

My heavy and spinning head falls into my hands.

"Now, don't fall apart," Solania says. She props herself on my shoulder as she arises. "I'm going to get Buster."

She goes out of her room; I can't stand to be in it alone with the scarf and the strains of that loathsome song, and I spring after her. I follow her through the dark narrow passage and up the cellar stairs.

The main floor hall is wall-to-wall sleeping men, cheek by jowl in the stark light; some are curled, some are slumped against a wall; there are a dozen, at least; I recognize most of them whose faces are exposed to me, having often seen them gathered like gleaning tattered pigeons under the neon heart or outside the barroom door. Flaccid lower lips and beaten shoulders droop down toward the petrified, unforgiving carpet.

I am brought up short by the sight, but Solania proceeds to pick her way into the pile, stops over one form, and reaches down to it.

It is Buster, and he stiffly sits up, rotating his shoulders, grimacing. His hair hangs lank over much of his face, and his jacket is darkly blotched across the shoulders.

"Buster, dear," she says softly, "we're concerned about what Perles may have, well, I mean we're concerned about Layla. Would you go out and have a look for me?"

"Yeah, okay."

She raises her little hand to her brow.

"Check the back alley between F and G, behind a garbage bin," she whispers, looking back to me.

The wail that escapes me, I must assume, is coming from whatever small part inside that my monster hasn't yet taken on or taken over, maybe a bit of human soul residue it hasn't been able to scrape off and sweep out yet. Anyway, it widens Buster's sleepy eyes, and it rouses to stirring fumbling confusion those sleepers not too drunk.

It even seems to partially blow open the door behind which the detestable 'Long Cool Woman' is playing. A small man wearing nothing but ratty red sweat pants and a failure of a moustache looks out. The Hollies blare out over the prostrate hallies.

"What the ——" he begins, but like a panther I'm leaping over a couple of frightened old men, and I'm upon him. He tries to throw the door closed, but I'm wedged between. Inside his room, men, women and children are lying on the floor like sardine varieties.

I grab his shoulders. He's terribly alarmed.

I say: "If I hear that song once more, I shall kill you. Do you understand?"

He seems pleased enough to know that there's some convenient means by which he may save himself. He nods eagerly.

"You're a stereo nazi," I hiss, "and I'll erase you."

"Okay, man," he says breathlessly. "Sorry it bothered you."

I step back, he closes the door, and in a moment, the song is cut short to a silence that allows the clanging in my head to disturb me all the more.

I look along the hall. People are watchfully awaiting my next move. Solania is smiling some secret to me. I need to get outside. My equilibrium is not what it might be, but I try to step between the dishevelled figures on the floor. I can't manage it, fall sideways into a sticky besmirched wall. In my desperation, I consider just treating the tattered men as shag carpeting, simply striding out on top of them.

But Buster is at me, blocking my way.

"No, man, please," he says. "Just go back downstairs and wait. You don't need to go. Wait and find out."

Solania is now beside me, and her guiding light touch is drawing my arm to the cellar stairs.

"Come, dear," she says. "Nothing's certain yet."

"But you're certain already," I insist. "You've already seen it."

"Let Buster go and see."

The rousable ragtag men regard me as something definitely different, watch me with shrivelled, brown-stained eyes in red and blue paisley faces; I begin to feel as a performer in Hell's cabaret; I allow pale and skeletal Solania to lead me further down into the satanic realm as Buster makes his departure.

I sit on her bed and throw my arms about myself, not for warmth or reassurance, but as a reactive attempt to contain the murderous thing inside.

"That wasn't a dry high," I say to Solania, rocking. "My monster is seizing control of me. I must turn myself into the police."

"What good would that do?" Solania asks.

"It will prevent me from killing any more innocent women!" I say.

"Why would you think Layla was an innocent woman?" she asks lightly.

"What are you talking about?" I cry. "Layla didn't deserve to die!"

"Perles, any tragedy of Layla's life happened a long time before tonight. Anyway, people like her become an obstacle to doing what needs to be done. They stop being victims of the disease and turn into the disease itself. So let's suppose you recognized that, and removed her for the sake of our community's health? People die here everyday for no reason; relatively speaking, dying for a reason is a pretty good way to go. Layla didn't deserve to die? Who says, and anyways, what does that matter? The question here is who deserves to live? Why would Layla deserve to live?"

She sits beside me and takes my hand in hers.

She says "This place was built of guilt. Any possible trivial guilt of yours would just be a bit of dust on the ground, it isn't even worth noticing. Our gifts, they have innocence. Would you kill them, too?"

"This is sophistry," I say. "I belong in prison, where I can do no more harm."

"Where you could do no more good," she says sternly. "Look at your situation, Perles, look at it realistically. The cops don't like you because of you criticizing them; there's nothing hypocrites like better than the chance to expose the hypocrisy of an enemy, and they'll more than happily sacrifice justice and you to their own pretense of virtue. How long do you think you'd last in prison? The cops will set you loose in the middle of a bunch of The Baron's henchmen, you, the guy they say killed The Baron's whores. Good luck. Your death would be useless, and so then would Layla's.

"If our high-profile, constant advocate is found to be our hypocritical killer, just think of the comfort and forgiveness that would be found by all those who kill us everyday by exploitation and discouragement."

She takes my face in her hands, and turns it to confront hers.

"You want prison? Well, look around you, what do you think this is? Welcome to our prison; at least in our prison you could do some good for the other people here. You could try, at least."

"And I could go on killing women."

"We can prevent that just as well as any other prison," she says. "I know you're a dangerous man, dear, but you couldn't harm anybody if Buster was always there to stop you. We've got any number of guys with us with nothing better to do than protect you and everybody else, night and day, from the monster you say is inside you."

"What meaning could the death of those women possibly have?" I ask.

"Maybe their deaths led your heart to me, to combine your gift with mine in service to those who deserve to live, but don't ever get the chance."

I fear that it is only my weakness and cowardice that makes this start to sound sort of sensible to me, that my judgment, deprived of sleep, nourishment and courage, is wholly unreliable, or already under the thrall of my self-serving monster. Anyway, it creates sufficient confusion to waylay my intentions from any course.

I fall back against the wall behind the bed, and Solania slips her arms around me.

"There's so much we could do together to give meaning to so many lives that have none now. Would you really throw away that chance just because something happened to some hookers whose lives were never going to have any meaning no matter what? What purpose would that serve?"

"Oh, please let me think," I say. "I need to think."

"You need to get some rest," she says, standing up. "Come, lie down here."

My burden of guilt and fatigue is more than I can carry, and I slip over sideways on the bed, curl and stare at the store-brand tea box on the tiny counter. Solania sits beside me with her hand on my upper arm.

Buster returns, says "I went over, but I couldn't get close. The cops were already there. But it was just where you said."

I cover my eyes with my hand.

Solania says "That's all right, it doesn't matter now, Buster. We're working things out. Go get some sleep. We've got a lot to do, starting tomorrow."

"Yeah," says Buster.

It occurs to me that I haven't been lying down in the presence of another man since I was a little boy. I don't like the feeling one bit, but Buster's gone before I can raise myself up.

Solania curls in with her back against me, her head on my crooked arm, and we lie there for some time, my mind reeling. I put my hand on her thin arm, I breathe in the shampoo fragrance of her shiny short black hair. Looking out over the crown of her head, my eyes focus again on the tea box. I become fascinated by it. Its lid flap is open to me, and, sideways, I look at its upside-down photograph of rich orange-red tea in a fine china cup and saucer. That was the worst tasting tea I could remember; and I begin to think of how few, if any, of that store's customers would ever own a fine cup and saucer such as the one pictured.

"Just what is it we're supposed to do with our combined gifts to serve these people?" I ask her.

She is silent for a long time, so long that I'm sure she's fallen asleep, and so I take this opportunity to kiss the back of her head.

But in another minute she answers me.

"I see our people activated in common cause, but I can't make out what it is. That's the big question," she says thoughtfully. "We find something, project or something, to focus and renew their energies. I know you'll think of something. Won't you, dear?"

"Yes, I will," I say.

I can make no attempt to come to terms with the monster inside me, to try to reconcile its ravages would be horribly inappropriate; I'm eager to exorcise it through the most arduous and agonizing means; I don't deserve any comfort or reassurance, but before I can truly consider what Solania proposes, I need the answer to what common sense insists should be an unanswerable question; even just expressing it to Solania carries me across a line toward a commitment to her and her vision of our future together, across a breach to faith in her, and devotion to her, that seems impossibly strange to me.

I close my eyes. I make one last effort to resist the temptation to ask the question. But then I put my lips to the crown of her head, my heart jerking around in a clumsy but exuberant polka, and I leap across the breach, reach the foreign ground of the other side, and I ask.

"Can you see whether I'm going to kill anyone else?"

She rolls over and takes my face in her birdwing hands.

"I can see, yes."

"And? What do you see?"

"Our people have nothing to fear from you, dear

Perles," she says. And then, after a brief moment, she adds, "But don't worry, you are still a dangerous man."

She closes her eyes, bends her head in against my chest, and soon she's breathing deeply and evenly; I can feel each warm gust through my shirt; little impact explosives, they send shivers rippling through me, almost do my breathing for me. If I had my wish of this instant, I would stay this way forever, concentrating on her breath and her fragrance until I was dust that she set to swirling about her beautiful fragile face with each precious puff.

But I'm now committed to a duty.

So I gaze over at the tea box, and my plan begins to steep, steamy bitter, in my mind.

Chapter Six

Amid the media mania, Buster can't maintain his overbearing demeanour, looks like a mastiff pushed to the edge of madness by too many conflicting commands. With each flash, with each question, he spins and stares in unnecessary and ineffectual but conscientious protective alert. Ken, my assigned warder of today, also appears beyond his comfortable depth; he's a sincere and stout-hearted fellow, but he pledged his sobriety to Solania only two or three weeks ago, and he's still jumpy.

At the centre of attention, of course, is Solania, perfectly composed, the picture of aplomb. But it has fallen to me to take control of the situation.

At the back of the main hall of the Friendship Inn, Sharon watches us with her arms crossed before her embroidered white blouse, apparently concerned, but not distraught. In times past, the media other than me has turned its condescending attention upon Sharon's facility only twice a year, Thanksgiving and Christmas, for the standard feel-good conscience-balm turkey dinner stories.

For some time, it's been necessary for us to stack the tables and chairs all up by the serving counter right after the noon meal, to allow for all the people who attend to Solania everyday.

Today, the space and proximity imperatives of the media have forced Solania's regular multitude to occupy broad, squished sidelines. Whether there is any resentment of this amongst her supporters, I am unable to discern. Most likely, they are simply stunned that anything so intrinsically theirs should attract such mainstream attention. As always these days, even more are congregated outside along the sidewalk.

In front of me, waving his pen importantly at me, is a

CBC Radio reporter who has decided he'll be the one who first debunks this phenomenon, believes he can accomplish that by rattling little frail Solania with snarled aggressive enquiry; I overlook him in favour of a CBC Television reporter, a young woman who's impressed me with her work on other stories.

"Solania," she says, "can you tell us more about how the boycott works?"

Solania sends across her disarming delighted smile.

"By its discriminatory hiring practices, the supermarket on 20th Street has always refused its responsibilities as a good community citizen," she says. "It thought it could do that because it believed it had a captive clientele. We're, in effect, liberating its clientele with this boycott. We haven't many cars here, but we're putting together those who have cars with those who don't, car pooling to another supermarket on 22nd Street, and when that can't work out, we collect shopping lists from the people who'd otherwise be shopping there, fill them at the supermarket on 22nd, and deliver the orders at the people's homes. And we'll continue to this until the store changes its hiring policies to at least start to reflect the demographic of the great majority of its former shoppers."

"What are you calling this organization of yours?"

"We don't call it anything," Solania says. "It's just our thing."

"Was this boycott in one of your visions?" asks a print reporter, one of two from the newspaper that my column isn't in.

"Perles thought of it," Solania says graciously.

This isn't what the print guys want to hear, obviously; partly because it won't neatly jibe with the auto-select-a-stock-story they'll have set up in their mental computers on the way over to cover this, where they slot Solania's name into the convenient blanks; and partly because I'm with the competition; also, more personally, one of them, a columnist, has recently been instructed, or so Robert heard, to make his column more like the lately rejuvenated 'Wisdom of Perles'. He's here under duress, and he doesn't like having his nose for news rubbed in my turf.

The CBC Radio reporter spots some weakness, wants to portray Solania as Trilby to my Svengali, and chimes hastily in with a demanding "You're telling us this boycott isn't a matter of taking direction from your visions? You're just following somebody's orders?"

Solania smiles at him so sweetly.

"The boycott was Perles' idea," she says. "Perles was my idea."

This is received with humorous appreciation amongst her supporters, and perhaps by some of the reporters. It makes me smile, too, but the CBC Radio man presses on.

"This supermarket that you're shopping at, instead, you're saying its hiring policies are fairer to your people?"

"No, not all," says Solania. "And we've already informed its manager that we'll be instituting a boycott against it just as soon as the 20th Street store begins to meet our expectations. All the stores, all the fast food places, all the doughnut shops, they're all going to have their turns.

"On 22nd, there's a doughnut shop and two convenience stores where the hookers all go to warm up or take a break. The hookers spend a lot of money in those places, and keep them busy all night long. We're going to target them next, until they each give one prostitute an honest job. That's part of our campaign to eliminate child prostitution by getting jobs for the children's older sisters."

"What makes you think a prostitute would want a job in those places?" asks the radio man. "Isn't the money a lot better on the street?"

"We'll have no trouble finding hookers who want a decent, honest job," Solania says. "I don't care what the money difference is. We want to be able to hold our heads up."

"Why didn't you let us tape you while you were having what I understand is your daily vision?" the radio man asks, taking another tack. "You're used to having them in public demonstrations, so why not let us tape one?"

I go to the radio man, stand in front of him.

"Did we ask you here?"

"Nope," he says.

"Then why are you acting as though this a news conference called to our purpose? You're here, all of you media people are here, at your request and our indulgence. The right you have here is to conduct yourselves with respect."

"The answer to your question," says Solania, "is that my vision episodes are spiritual in nature, and many of our old people still believe that spiritual ceremonies mustn't be photographed or taped. We defer to the wishes of our elders in this matter, that's all."

"Well, I've got a question for you, Perles," says the radio man. "Are you here as a member of the media, or as the instigator of a pseudo-spiritual scam?"

He ostentatiously poises his pen over his pad.

"This isn't a scam," I say.

"Oh, it's not a scam," says the columnist for the other paper. "Then, maybe you could answer this, Perles: what's your opinion of the journalistic ethic of manufacturing news, and then trying to stake out exclusive coverage of it?"

"That's an interesting question, isn't it? When did journalistic ethic become an interest of yours?" I ask. "Any of you have always been perfectly welcome to report in depth on the issues and circumstances of the inner city; the fact that most of you completely forego the chance until something suitably sensational shows up on your long-distance radar screens has nothing to do with me. For my part, I've manufactured nothing, and I welcome you to this scene where I have always been. Now, are there any intelligent questions about the actual story here, or shall we wrap this up?"

The CBC television reporter raises her pen.

"Solania, your Member of Parliament says that your boycott is an attempt to force an affirmative action programme on storeowners and managers who should be free to hire whomever they wish, by their own criteria of merit. How do you respond?"

"We're bringing to bear free market forces, aren't we? How can a free-enterprise Member of Parliament complain about that?"

"He's quoted as saying your rhetoric borders on incitement to anarchy."

"He's never been here to hear me," Solania says. "How does he know? We aren't challenging authority, we're demanding that authority meet its responsibilities to our people. Anyways, I don't like the word 'rhetoric'; what's that mean, that we're not really sincere? He can watch and see if we're sincere."

"What effect is your boycott having so far?" asks a print reporter.

"We know that the store stays almost empty everyday," says Solania. "But we can't consider it any sort of success until we see some of our people getting jobs."

The questions become innocuous, Solania handles them adroitly; the columnist for the other paper approaches me, pulls me aside with a smile that I guess is collegial.

"C'mon, Perles, what's the deal here?" he asks. "Is she for real?"

"Read my column," I suggest.

"I've been reading it," he says. "It arouses my suspicions when a jaded skeptic like you seems to lose his abilities of critical assessment."

"Impartiality isn't a requirement of a columnist, you know that."

"But tell me honestly, Perles, just for background; I need a starting point here; do you really believe that she's the prophetess of her people? Are you really convinced?"

"Look at the number of people she attracts here every day," I say. "That must mean something."

"Well, perhaps," he says. "How hard would it be to dupe these people, really?"

"How easy is it to arouse them from their sense of defeat and futility?" I ask. "How easy is it to inspire hundreds of alcoholics to take the pledge? Not at all. There is something to all of this, there's something to Solania."

"I don't doubt that they believe in her," he says, scanning the room. "What I want to know is, do you believe in her? Truly?"

I turn from him and look at Solania. She sits at her daily position, in just another molded plastic soup kitchen stacking chair; she wears her constant clothing of a clean faded flannel shirt and clean blue jeans designed for more fulsome femininity than she places in them; in the television lights, her bare face seems even more wan and fragile, for all its beauty; there is nothing about her appearance that would ever suggest extraordinary success in anything.

But here she sits, confident and calm, the city's and province's latest faddish focal point, all the world seeming to rotate out from her tiny pinpoint pivot.

It seems a long time ago, but I once settled the entire onus of my belief and faith on Christine, and I thereafter wished to believe in nothing else; like someone who dons a flannel shirt and jeans every single morning, I wanted to be free of daily decisions in that regard; and, in a way, that was the fulfillment of my vow of fidelity to her, the best I could manage, in my weakness.

I didn't wish or deserve anything to come along to test the vice-grip of my despondency and disbelief. And yet every night, as Solania sleeps beside me on her little bed, as my assigned warder snores on a mat outside the door, I sit at the little side table and poke away at my laptop computer, writing my latest column about her and her initiatives, or composing the wording of our handouts, or framing the discussion part of her next day's public session here at the Friendship Inn, or answering her increasing correspondence, or drawing up lists of activities for her scores of volunteers, until my back, neck and head ache; and then I'll stop briefly, rest my hand on her sharp hip, and in a moment I'm restored, I'm back at work, preparing for the next day of Solania being Solania.

So do I truly believe in her?

I look back at the columnist.

"Use your eyes, man," I say. "Anyone can see that she truly believes in herself. What more do you need to know?"

He shakes his head, walks away.

The radio man is asking Solania again if her undertakings are meant to serve her visions, or is she following directions from elsewhere. This is an apt place for me to call things to a conclusion. As the cameramen dismantle and pack their equipment, a reporter from an independent television station comes up, reminds Solania that she's scheduled as a guest on her channel's dinner-hour news this evening.

"Yes, I'll be there," Solania says happily. Her light-hearted self-confidence in this sort of thing makes me wonder at its source.

When the media people move away, Solania's multitude crowds in around her like a tide; in waves it laps at her little outreaching hands, in a silent ceremony that reclaims her as theirs. This island in the tide is terra cognito to Buster, and he reasssserts his command over the situation, expediting people along.

I notice that the cameraman from CBC Television has swung his camera up to his shoulder, is capturing the ceremony from the back of the hall.

Every morning, Solania and I, and Buster and whoever is my warder of the moment, maybe Carney, maybe Ken, maybe Russell, go along to the Chinese Cafe on Avenue H, where I buy breakfast for everyone, and Solania and I force feed each other. It's our one meal of the day; it seems to be doing me more good than it is her, she remains very weak and easily fatigued.

She is very tired as the throng dwindles away and out. She curls over, lowers her elbows to her knees, and rests her head in her hands. Buster fetches her a cup of tea, and we sit down with her as she rests. Sharon joins us.

"I never wrote anything about these sessions here," I say to her. "All I've written about are the things we're undertaking. I don't know what brought the media here."

"It wasn't you, I know that," says Sharon. "It was the supermarket manager and that COIN group ringing the alarms about our den of insurrection here. Anyway, it's getting pretty obvious that something unusual is going on, with all those people crowding on the sidewalk every noon hour. By the way, Morley has passed along the complaints of the storekeepers that the crowd is creating an obstruction on the sidewalk, and we're going to have to do something about it."

"What are we obstructing?" I ask. "Easy access to the liquor store or the pawn shops? Heaven forbid."

"We need another place," Solania says without raising her head. "Perles, you've got to find us some place."

"I'm looking into the possibility of the boathouse in the park," I say. "There's a central sort of hall part to it that's suffering continuous vandalism. The city would love to have a responsible tenant in there, but I'm not sure they'd consider us to be that."

"I want you to stay here," Sharon says firmly. "We can't take a backward step to COIN, that would only embolden them; they won't be satisfied until they've closed us down completely, anyway. We need to make our stand here."

"What about your board?" I ask.

"They'll support us so long as COIN's riding around on its high horse. In a way, COIN rather serves to, well, clarify their thinking."

Rose is hovering by the doorway, patiently waiting for me to take her on the afternoon grocery run. I bend over Solania and kiss the side of her head. Buster will escort her back to our tiny room where she'll take a nap. Ken hops to, for he'll be escorting me.

When Rose, Ken and I get out to the sidewalk, Carney and Velvet are awaiting us, leaning against the side of the van. I've removed the second seat, in order to make room for all the groceries, so Ken, Carney and Velvet sit in the very back seat, and Rose sits up front in the passenger seat, organizing her lists.

Rose is unusual in that Jesus once saved her; of course, many people would claim that Jesus had saved them, that there was nothing unusual about Rose at all; however, Jesus literally saved Rose one day when she happened to be drowning in the river; astutely construing that this was not some baptismal variation, He jumped into the water and, at the last viable instant, outreached God's right hand, grasped onto her fingertips and hauled her out of the threatening current to the riverbank.

Whenever she's told me of that incident, I've involuntarily wondered if it had been necessary for Jesus to apply mouth-to-tracheotomy resuscitation; I've never asked, of course, and Rose wouldn't likely care to mention it.

At any rate, Rose and Jesus sat together for a long time, shivering on the riverbank, drying themselves in the pale midautumn sun, watching the deadly green inexorable flow of the channel. Rose leaned into Jesus for warmth and comfort, and He didn't move away from her, didn't recoil in disgust in the manner she expected of all mortal men by then; and gradually she unfolded herself in display to Him, as though her body was a roadmap of her unhappy journey: she burped to Him of her esophagal cancer, of course, showed Him the dingy blue home-tattooed initials of her succession of biker-gang boyfriends decorating her arms and fingers, showed Him the multitude of scars on the bottom of her feet, inflicted with broken beer bottle by a weasly enraged boyfriend, showed Him the tracks on her arms from her years of heroin addiction. She told Him about her teenaged daughter who had abandoned her in hatred, who was now on Vancouver's streets wasting away from hepatitis, of how her sister had once remonstrated with her, "Why do you keep tattooing yourself with those guys' initials; you know you'll just end up breaking up with them.", and her answer, "I just love them so much at the time." She'd been ashamed to show Him the old swastika tattoo on her wrist; in fact, she had earlier tried, to only partial success, to gouge it out of her flesh, so that it wouldn't be found on her when her body was recovered, and it was an ugly red wound at that time, but still distinguishable despite her determined digging.

She leaned into Jesus for warmth, and He didn't draw away from her spiritous sobs. She told Him that she tried and tried, but sometimes she'd stay in her wretched little room for a week or more, unable to make herself go out and face the world. She put her head on Jesus' shoulder and asked

Him why her life had been so miserable. He told her "Because you're a good woman who's given her full, loving heart to men who aren't worthy of it." Jesus had taken off His shoes and socks, to wring out His socks and lay them to dry on a nearby peter; after He told her that, she washed His bare feet with her tears, Rose water.

She took Him by the hand, wanted to take Him to show her sister who'd just saved her, because her sister would never believe it, but He wouldn't go with her. She told Him her address, made sure several times that He'd memorized it, and pleaded with Him to come and see her.

So far, she's never seen Him again.

Rose reacted in a responsible and mature way to her Epiphany, reasoning that if Jesus wished her to remain alive, she had no right to act against Him. No more would she hold cigarettes to her tracheotomy hole, no more would she drink or do drugs, and no more would she squander her full, loving heart on men who were unworthy of it, although this last resolve had already pretty much taken care of itself; unworthy men had all found her quite resistible since her cancer.

Jesus, it seems, wears black jeans and a white shirt these days, black socks and black leather shoes, so that's what Rose wears, managing to maintain a supply of them from the Mennonite Clothes Closet resale store. This is her habit, and she strictly adheres to a life of other clean habits, is committed to living as long as Jesus wishes.

She's proven to be an invaluable volunteer to the cause of the supermarket boycott. Her morning paper route, apparently, has enabled her to develop real organizational skills, and she has taken effective charge of the grocery purchase and delivery. I just drive where she tells me, really.

Velvet's voluntarism is desultory. She's still far from convinced about Solania, and if it weren't for Carney's commitment, we wouldn't see her at all. Carney took the sobriety pledge a couple of weeks ago, and stuck with it doggedly through the next two or three hours, whereupon he decided Velvet shouldn't have to drink alone, that wouldn't be right. He's having a hard time, though, because he refuses to drink off the avails of Velvet's prostitution, and I'm no longer good for the cost of a bottle, and his devotions and duties to Solania are time consuming, so his panning has been sharply curtailed. And he's one of my warders, which requires his sobriety, so his drinking has suffered to the point of almost threatening to lower the level of his addiction. He has expressed concerns that he may end up dry in spite of himself.

As we drive along 22nd Street, the talk of the back seat is all about the excitement of the media invasion. Ken pawned his little television set last month, and now wonders how his young family will get to see him on t.v. tonight. Velvet is suddenly worried about the possibility of her being broadcast lifesized on The Baron's huge home-theatre screen.

"Jeez, he'll have a fit if he sees I was there!" she cries. "Perles, you gotta tell the t.v. guys not to put me on!"

At the store, all but Ken and I get out. Ken is a good warder, lets me sit in silence. I set my seat to a slight recline, and close my eyes for a little while, examining the red world behind my lids.

My own addiction is now no more than a windy little whimper as it dies of thirst in its own distant desert.

My warders believe that they are my bodyguards, not my guards against more bodies. My monster lurks under cover of internal infernal smoke and darkness, has done nothing to reveal itself since the slaying of Layla, has made no attempt to wrest control of me to its demonic purpose, is most patient, opportunistic, it would seem. I silently recite the names of the four murdered women, Candy, Laura, Beth, Layla, as my litany, repeat it and repeat it in my penance.

Late at night, in mental blanks between bursts of my labours, I may find myself hypnotically occupied by some small aspect of their murders, Beth's cheap bracelet on my wrist, Layla's damp black scarf around my neck, my tie around Laura's neck. I'm also obsessed with the question of how someone who arrives at a point of recklessness in response to the relentless general despair he encounters can then manifest it as one who inflicts such suffering in the specific. Is this some contradiction, or is it some perverted extrapolation? How do I end up killing the very same people for whom I feel so aggrieved?

I open my eyes, flip my sun visor down, and, in the small mirror set into it, I search my eyes for some glimmer of the beast, some fleeting flickering early warning signal that it's creeping up behind them again.

Candylaurabethlayla.

"Something in your eye?" Ken enquires solicitously.

"Not so far," I say.

Ken smiles in bemusement.

I never frame out any comments on the murders for Solania's daily discussion periods, but every day she disinters the bodies, speaks in quiet electric condemnation of the eastside johns who come across the river to thrill-kill our women. When I tell her of my discomfort, she tells me soothingly that she knows what she's doing; she has also said that she's never seen any vision of my guilt, that she believes the atmosphere of guilt that she absorbs is originating with me, and neither it nor the physical evidence provides sufficient proof to her. "Killer johns is the most useful explanation, to my mind," she said simply.

Solania has no part in the practical application of our community initiative; she has neither the energy nor the inclination, and probably not the talent for it. She tells people - most often me - what she would like to be done, and leaves

all utility to them. Nobody resents her regal style of delegation because it's tempered with her personal warmth, her
undeniable magnetism, and because she is so very, very good
at what she does. We have more volunteers than we can possibly use, and Solania is always after me to devise new projects to keep them all actively involved, a task at which I've
yet to be very successful. She's right, of course; I've always
said that the biggest single problem of the inner city isn't
poverty, it's the individual's lack of enough worthwhile
things to do, of some meaningful focus for his day's energies.
If we can't furnish that sort of opportunity to Solania's multitude, we'll lose them again to personal projects like active
alcoholism, neighborhood feuds, diabetes, eating every potato chip ever fried, blowing welfare cheques on bingo and
lucky pulls, watching every enervating bit of rubbish on daytime t.v.

There is much to occupy my mind, too much, really,
too many reasons to not think Candylaurabethlayla, too
many invitations to encouragement, to optimism, my addiction can muster no further torments, my sleepless nights are
too easily passed, there is too much that isn't hellish in my
life. My business in these matters is to be atonement, nothing
more, and it's necessary for me to be vigilant on hell's ram-
parts.

I rest my eyes again, recite my litany, worry logistical
problems like a dog and bone, until I'm roused by the rattling
carts of Rose's return.

Ken hops out to help the other three load bulging
plastic bags into the central part of the van. Ken takes the
front passenger seat when this done, and Rose organizes and
labels bags with Carney and Velvet in the back while I drive
around to the addresses Rose tells me. Ken and Carney take
turns carrying the bags to the doors.

When I'm done with this chore, I deliver Rose and

Carney and Velvet where they want to go, and then Ken and I go to the house of Solania's room.

Buster is sitting on the rotting front steps when we arrive. His early haughtiness toward me is no longer in any evidence, and he treats me respectfully. There's no question that he's in love with Solania, but so complete is his faith in her, he accepts my more favoured place in her affections without visible rancour. He acknowledges me in a friendly way as I enter past him. Ken joins him on the steps.

I go downstairs to our room. She's sleeping. I spend a lot of time watching her sleep, which she does very beautifully, and I take some time to breathe in her fragrant essences now.

The first Friday night that I was here, I was sitting working at the little table while Solania slept, when suddenly her slumlord burst his quivering walrus bulk through her ill-fitting, feeble door. His initial shock at the sight of me was quickly concealed behind red and grey shaking jowls and narrowing little pale porcine peepers.

"Who the hell are you?" he snarled at me, as though he didn't know. As a stalwart pillar of COIN, he was surely well aware of his print foe.

"What are you doing here?" I asked, standing.

"I own the place," he said. "I gotta right to be here."

"You've got a right to be here after forty-eight hours' notice," I said. "Can it be that you're unfamiliar with the Landlord and Tenant Act?"

Solania was stirring on the bed.

"I come to see her," he said, gesturing at her aggressively.

"Me, too," I said. "She told me that, if I came every Friday night, I'd see something interesting for my newspaper column."

His face assumed a dangerous level of colour.

"I thought her window was busted," he said. "But I guess it's okay."

And he heaved himself out again. Solania was rather happily worried that I'd precipitated her eviction, but I forecast that she'd never see him here again, and my powers of precognition, in this instance, have so far proven to be superior to hers.

I kiss her on her forehead, and she awakens with a smile for me, as usual. She takes my hand and pulls herself up.

"Are you feeling strong enough for our walk?" I ask.

"Oh, yes," she says, swinging her slender feet into her little running shoes.

We go out of the house. Ken and Buster follow us at a short distance. She slips her hand into the crook of my arm for support and intimacy.

We slowly walk south on Avenue F, to the park that runs along the side of the river. This is the nicest feature of the innercity, this park, but it, too, suffers in the despair of the area; at night the junkies and sniffers and drunks haunt it, it is a nest for The Baron's pushers. Buyers and johns cruise through its winding roadway all night, and its paved paths are treacherous with broken bottles and punctured aerosol cans.

We are barely into the park before we're accosted by a reeling, mindlessly, incoherently challenging sniffer, blocking our way like a toll taker, his fingers smeared with gold spray paint, his flaccid face also smeared where he's touched himself, a mendicant Midas. He lurches toward us, but is quickly intercepted by Buster and Ken, acting decisively but without abuse, and bundled out of our way. They set him down under a nearby tree, order him firmly to stay put, then fall in behind us again, proud of themselves and jocular.

From our position at the top of the park's rolling,

springtime green descent to the river, I am able to see many children scooting or dawdling about.

"You didn't speak about education today," I say to Solania.

"Yeah," she says with a sigh of reluctance.

"It's an issue we've got to confront," I scold. "We've got a thousand children here who never attend school, obviously to no official concern. And those of our children who do attend school are dismissed out of hand as unteachable, consigned by lazy, untalented and dispirited teachers and careless principals to a Ritalin-doped pedagogical purgatory. The schools are little more than self-congratulatory glorified day-care centres, where they compose their highminded, highwinded mission statements, but success is really measured by how easily the teacher's day slips by. Those few children who stick with it to graduation are spewed out with meaningless diplomas that they probably can't quite read, unprepared to function in any worthwhile job, and certainly unprepared for higher education.

"We can call for improvements in employment levels all we want, but we'll be forever vulnerable if we can't justify our demands with capable potential employees."

"I know," Solania sighs.

I have noticed in Solania an aversion to addressing issues that will be slow and long-term in their correction.

"The children of our neighborhoods are statistically far more likely to go to prison than to university, you know," I say.

"I know."

"So you've got to talk about education."

"It just never occurs to me at the time," she says.

"Well, how can that be? You've got the talking points right in front of you every day."

"I know," she says. "I'll try tomorrow."

"Okay. We should talk about your appearance on the supper news hour."

She squeezes my arm and says, "It's a lovely afternoon, let's just walk for a while, just enjoy being together, for a change."

So we stroll slowly along. Solania sees that one of her shoelaces has come undone. She begins to bend to it, but her strength and balance aren't up to it, she grasps my arm again, straightens and sways, putting her free hand to her pale cheek.

"Oh, dear," she says.

"It's all right, I'll tie it."

I bend my knee before her, stoop and tie her lace, and as I do, she bends slightly to support herself with her hands on my shoulders. Light as her burden is, it calls again to my mind the years where Morag treated my moderate masculine strength as a brutish straining weapon, like a primitive loaded catapult, threatening to uncoil, smash out in wanton cruelty. That Solania treats it as her own support and reliable benefit stabs a thrill through me, and I extend the exquisite moment, tarry in pursuit of knot-tying perfection.

I look up at her from bended knee, and she smiles serenely down on me, touches my shoulders in turn.

"Arise, Sir Knight," she says.

I can't mask the intensity of my emotion, and it sparks a change in her smile, from serene to delighted.

I arise, and clasp her in my arms, grasping and gasping in a world that suddenly flashes into a black vortex that absorbs all, spins all into the single sparkling prism that's Solania.

"I pledge all my life's energies to you," I say, as though I have a choice.

"I know," she says, laying the side of her face against my chest, her arms under mine, her hands reaching up my back to my shoulders. "I accept your devotion."

Ken and Buster look elsewhere, with Ken making a big grinning show of it, and Buster more seriously casting his gaze down the curving course of the wide river.

She pulls away from me with a kiss on the centre of my chest, steers me along the park path, perhaps correctly detecting that I'm at this moment disoriented as to our place and purpose; her hand rests naturally again in the crook of my arm. I hold it there with my other hand, and we walk slowly along; I struggle with my need to stare at her so long and hard, her beautiful image is burned permanently into my vision.

Ahead of us, a tall, worn old man holds himself up with his lumpy and bent hands around the trunk of a small tree. His yellowing long grey ponytail pokes out from under a grimy baseball cap that barely holds to the top of his head. He wears dirty denims, jacket and jeans, and he seems to totter in imprecise inspection of something on the tree trunk. He's urinating, showing no more concern about what he's doing or the fact that he's in plain view than a horse would. He splashes his curled, pointed, high-heeled boot.

I avert my eyes quickly, look down to Solania. She calmly observes the old man as we go past, looking at his sad, sagging face.

The sight triggers a memory for her.

"A while after we moved to the city, my grandfather came to stay with us for a while," she says. "One day, he went out walking and got himself lost. Somehow, he ended up across the river at the Buffalo Head Mall. We got this call from the mall security, they said that if someone didn't come and get him right away, they were going to turn him over to the police. My grandfather always tried to be a good man, and he tried to raise his family to be upright people. There's no way he'd ever have done anything improper in that mall, but I guess him just being there was more than they could stand, they just assumed he was a vagrant drunk. So I ran over there as fast as I could to get him. We had to walk back through those eastside residential areas, and the poor old man, he was all tired out, so he was leaning on me, and I had my arm around him, I was sort of holding him up. I could feel the anger and hatred of people we passed, people looking out their windows or doors. All we were doing was what they wanted us to, just getting out of their part of town as quietly and quickly as we could, but that wasn't good enough for them; they didn't even want us to exist, I swear I could feel it; it made me hate my grandfather right there, that he was causing me to go through that humiliation.

"Then I realized, then and there, that there was never going to be any way that we could do what was right by those people, that everything we could do would always be wrong, and that there was no way that they were ever going to make any room for us in the world, that they were never going to share anything with us, no matter what.

"So something snapped inside me, and before I'd got him back westside, I'd gotten so I just loved being hated by them, I revelled in it, every suspicious or scowling face or hard look, I wore their hatred like an eagle feather.

"I still love it. It gives me a kick."

She squeezes my arm.

"Now it's me leaning on you, and you're holding me up," she says warmly. "And so now they'll hate you, too."

"Maybe," I say.

"Oh, yes, they will," she says. "You just wait and see. We could go over to 19th right now and watch the reaction of the johns to you walking arm and arm in love with me. Hatred, that's what, and it will be no different in the eastside livingrooms tonight when they see you with me on t.v. It might be different if you were some low trash, but you're not, so you're a traitor to your class. What you need to do is learn to relish their hatred, too, squaw man. It's better than a good meal, once you learn to enjoy it."

"I'll try," I say. "It suits me."

"When we were living on the reservation, we could tell ourselves that it was a big bad system of wicked government protecting itself from the blame of historical wrongs that made our situation so miserable. You get to the city, though, and you see that it's the accumulated little mundane wrongs that keep us in misery, it's the little day-to-day sins of individuals that cripple and poison us, sins of petty greed, sins of petty exploitation, sins of carelessness, minor refusals of brotherhood, trivial refusals of generosity, and, most importantly, little sins of inaction, of unimportant people who so easily forget them; that's what condemns us here in the city."

"Yes," I say.

"Our prison is built of accumulated tiny pebbles," she says. "And our lives are defined by accumulated tiny humiliations."

We go down the slope to a lower pathway that follows the river. Ahead of us, on the slopes, two city employees in coveralls ignite what appear to be small flares and shoot them down gopher holes, plugging the holes behind the gas bombs.

We watch as we approach, then Solania says "The bosses' final solution to the ground squirrel overpopulation. Final solutions never seem to change."

But further ahead, a group of raggedy young truants are playing a particularly nasty form of hookey, poised in cruel anticipation over another gopher hole, with a string noose positioned around the opening; it is a common pastime in the park, snaring emerging gophers and smashing them to smithereens on the ground with the string or cord.

"How does that jibe with your symbolism?" I ask, motioning toward the lethal, hunched circle of children.

"Yeah, well," says Solania, "my mistake; there's the real final solution: just give us enough rope to hang ourselves. We've become very good at that."

We depart from the path to go to the shabby boys, who are so intent upon their objective, they don't notice our approach until we are almost upon them. They straighten up, prepare their little faces for their hard careless expressions, which are then overridden in wide-eyed recognition of Solania. They obviously weigh the option of flight.

"Which one of you is Ryan?" Solania asks.

One little boy seems suddenly startled, and the three other boys immediately point to him.

"Come to me, Ryan," she says.

Ryan won't budge on his own, but his turncoat companions push him to Solania.

"Quit it," he hisses, but it's too late, he's delivered to her feet.

She takes his face in her hands.

"Ryan, didn't your grandfather tell you that senseless cruelty will harm your spirit?"

Ryan quickly checks with the other boys, but somehow they've immediately aligned themselves with Solania, gaze steadily at him with reproach.

"Nohenever," Ryan says, grasping at a possible excuse.

"Yes, he did," Solania says. "He told you, just as his grandfather told him. You were watching wrestling on television at the time, so maybe you ignored him."

Unable to divine the correct response, Ryan's eyes wander absently away to nothing.

"T.v. wrestling can't save a boy's spirit from harm, can it?" Solania asks.

Ryan the scapegoat looks away.

"No?" a friend prompts tentatively.

"No," confirms Solania. "But a grandfather might. A smart boy will figure out what he should be paying attention to, won't he?"

Ryan puzzles this out for a moment; then, because he believes he has the answer, he returns his eyes to Solania.

"Yeah?" he suggests.

"Yes," she says. "Now, here's what your grandfather told you, and a smart boy will listen this time: senseless cruelty will harm your spirit. Hurting a gopher for no reason will hurt your spirit."

She looks around to all the little faces.

"Sometimes we need to kill things, don't we? That doesn't harm our spirits, if we kill only when we need to, does it?"

"No," agree the boys.

"But hurting or killing when we don't need to, that harms our spirits. One day, when your body is all worn out and falling apart, your spirit is all you'll have left. So should you be harming it today? Should you be hunting gophers like this?"

"Jason, he told me," Ryan says, his finger reaffixing the blame on a boy to his left.

"What really matters is what you do from now on, isn't it?" Solania says.

"Them guys, they're killing gophers," Jason says in justification, pointing back to the busy city workers.

Solania looks along to the gassers for a long moment.

"Maybe they don't have spirits to look after," she says. "But you do."

Up on Spadina Road running along the edge of the park, a large sedan suddenly stops, and two men get out, start down the slope to us. The men are both wearing leather

jackets. The boys engage in a quick, hushed exchange, and
hastily withdraw to some distance, where they stop, turn and
watch in a way that suggests they expect something even
more interesting than gopher-bashing.

Buster, standing nearby, grunts at Ken, and they step
forward, clench–jawed, to intercept the course of the other
men, whose rapid approach may mean urgency or merely
the momentum of their descent.

"Who are they?" I ask Solania.

"The Baron's boys," she says, taking my arm again.

Buster plants himself, wide-stanced and threatening,
for battle, while Ken looks on uncertainly, but The Baron's
boys wave their hands in front of them. They stop and speak
to Buster, motioning toward us. In a moment, Ken comes
back to us. The men start to follow, but Buster firmly places
his palm against the chest of the first.

"They been looking for you," Ken reports. "The
Baron, he wants a parley."

Solania looks up to me.

"You've got no reason to talk to The Baron," I advise
her. "We can't be associated with him in any way."

Solania nods, and Ken goes forward with the message.

One of the other men says something, Buster shakes
his head decisively, then the man reaches under his jacket,
pulls out something I'm unable to discern. He hands it to
Ken, motions toward us once again. Ken trots back. He's
holding three cigarettes, which he gives to Solania.

She looks at them lying in her hand.

"Well, now I have no choice," she says.

"I know," I say. "Ken, tell them that The Baron may
come and see Solania tomorrow afternoon, at the
Friendship." From all that I've heard of The Baron, this
would be an almost literal case of the mountain coming to

Mohammed.

"They say now, we go to The Baron's," Ken says.

"We all go?" Solania asks.

"Yeah, I think so," Ken says. He's clearly nervous.

I go forward to the men, Ken close at my heels, Solania slowly coming up behind.

"We take that tobacco as The Baron's guarantee of our safety," I say sternly.

"Sure," says the leading delegate, tough and casual.

"And we all go," I specify.

The man shrugs and makes a small gesture up toward the car.

"It's just a parley, man, what's the big deal?" the second man says, and then he appends a sharp curse word. This offends his pride, having to make a tobacco supplication to a little girl who used to be one of The Baron's hookers.

"Watch your language in the presence of a lady," I snap, rubbing it in. "The Baron sends you to honour this lady, and you dishonour her with your language?"

"Yeah, yeah," the man says dismissively, and they both start back up the hill.

Buster allows just the slightest flicker of amusement to cross his stoney face. We follow up the hill, which is taxing on Solania, and she gasps lightly beside me.

At the big car, our quartet crowds into the back seat, and The Baron's boys sit silent and steadfastly forward-looking in the front. The trip isn't long, The Baron lives quite close by.

The car draws to the curb before a typical two-storey house that's maybe somewhat less rundown than its neighbours; The Baron doesn't seem to be living in very grand style for all his ill-gotten gains. His henchmen sit unmoving in the front of the car.

Buster gets out and scans the house. A hugely obese

man appears behind the screen door, beckoning impatiently to us.

"Is that him?" I ask.

"Yep," Solania says.

"Wow," I say. "So that's why we have to come to him. He really can't get out of his house."

"Yes, he can," she says. "I've seen him squeeze out."

"So I guess you boys do a lot of pretty heavy grocery runs, yourselves, eh?" I say to the men in the front. "Just think, Solania, all this time we could have been consulting real experts, maybe borrow their delivery truck."

The driver slowly turns to face me. He's grinning.

"Wait'll you see the missus," he says.

"Yeah, just wait," Solania agrees.

We get out of the car, and Solania pauses to look up at the little upper windows.

"I used to stay here," she says to me. "He keeps his young, pretty girls close by."

And as we start up the walk to his door, a round, plump girl of very early adolescence steps out the door, and is followed by a tiny girl, no more than ten years old, attired in a frilly little girl's dress, carrying a little purse.

"You say 19th?!" the hefty girl calls back into the house.

"Try her at 13th and H!" comes a thick, gravelly, wheezily laboured woman's voice.

The two girls come by us. The tiny one walks with precise little girl steps in her little white pumps, little frilly socks, and casts her eyes up at me. Perhaps I'm projecting onto them, but I believe that in them I see some plea for mercy. Something about her is sharply reminiscent; suddenly I recollect her as the little girl I'd observed weeks before, standing with inexplicable decorum and dignity in her long, dirty quilted coat outside the neon heart liquor store, somehow rising above the ragtags and rubble that collect there, standing like some miraculous upright pure white dove amid the dingy downward-pecking pigeons. I could guess that this is the first time she's ever worn a pretty little dress like this, first time she's had a little purse. I look with horror to Solania, who watches her in a sort of placid sadness. She pulls me gently, but I'm rooted through the concrete.

"Stop!" I command the girls.

They do, and the older girl looks at me quizzically.

"Come, dear," Solania says.

'This is intolerable," I say.

"There's nothing we can do."

"You, little girl, stop!" I blurt out. "What's your name?"

"Angela," she answers reluctantly.

"Angela, I want you to come with me."

The henchmen observe from inside the car. Ken stands, confused, by the gate. The hefty girl sizes me up, steps toward me.

"She's a hundred bucks," she says.

"For how long?" I say.

"Whaddya mean?"

"A hundred dollars for how long? All night?" I ask.

"You wish!" the hefty girl derides. "Hundred bucks for a b-job."

"Come on, dear," Solania insists quietly, pulling me away. "There are hundreds of children like her. Are you going to try to buy them all?"

"But I think this is her first time out," I say urgently. "We could still save her."

"Not that way, it's too late," Solania says, and she pulls me toward the front door.

The girls start down the sidewalk, the hefty girl placing a proprietary hand on the tiny Angela's shoulder. I tear my eyes from them. The Baron stands behind the aluminum screen door, waiting, watching. It occurs to me that I'm about to encounter someone even more loathsome and monstrous than I, and I take this opportunity to allow my acid contempt to reboil freely, hissing over his spirit burner.

Buster goes through the door first.

I barge through injudiciously, stalking through the small front hall, glaring around the livingroom inside. It is sparsely furnished. On the far wall is the giant tv, and on the near wall, just inside the door, is a long sofa, new but of a dated black leather and chrome fashion, and on which The Baron is now sitting, taking up half of it, like the Anti-Buddha. The sofa is far enough away from the tv screen to make one think that a better economy would have been a smaller screen and closer sofa. In the other corner of this near wall, on the other side of the door, is a matching black leather chair, which is unoccupied. The room is carpeted wall-to-wall in new grey broadloom. No pictures grace the walls. There are four tough men sitting on the floor or standing around the edges of the room. Buster assesses them darkly. In the very middle of the floor is an enormous black mound, like some great bean bag, and three little children, toddlers, crawl over it, bounce on it, lounge against it.

The t.v. displays some teary-eyed, tease-haired, bleach-blonde, twang-voiced southern ignoramus who actually thinks that it's of some international importance that her jerky layabout boyfriend slept with her very own equally-unattractive sister. A studio audience howls in mock moral outrage, but no one in this room seems to care.

The Baron is trying to grow a goatee, which makes his huge face rather resemble a big bowl of pudding into which someone has stubbed a cigarette. His hair has been permed into a swarm of greasy little black worms. He wears a loose Hawaiian shirt and giant grey stretch pants tested to their limits. His lap cradles his giant gut.

Solania follows me into the livingroom. The Baron imperiously motions with a massive mitt to the empty seat, and she sits down. I stand beside her.

The huge black mound that dominates the centre of the room suddenly moves of its own motivation, heaves, quivers and wheezes in volcanic eruption. The children aren't alarmed, but I am. The wheezing eruption evolves into a gravelling cackling laughter, one peak of its radiating ranges rises up slightly, and on top of it, where the snowcap should be, is a deeply dimpled, fat-fingered hand. A grotesque great harvest moon rises partially behind the mountains, pocked and cratered, and now creased and channeled in terrible laughter.

The mound is the fattest person I've ever seen outside of a grocery tabloid cover photo, the fattest person I've ever seen in the extremely excessive flesh. It lies on the floor like a beached whale spouting its last. Be it man or woman, it's half again the size of the horribly obese Baron. It makes Morag's group look like famine victims.

I'm dumbfounded, but the mountain speaks, in what might be a woman's voice.

"You don't look so good, baby," it cackles thickly. "Him there don't take care of you good like we did."

I've no idea who the mound is addressing, but Solania raises her chin just a bit, so I presume that it's her. The mound would seem to be The Baroness.

"Shuddup," The Baron wheezes, and the mound gurgles and ripples in apparent merriment.

"Don't pay no attention to her," The Baron says to Solania, hefting a ham hand up in casual dismissal.

Solania confronts The Baron frankly, and he settles his hands, links his sausage fingers atop that which, on a much lesser man, would be called his stomach. He sets his little peering eyes on the wall behind Solania, and he sits like that for a long minute.

Finally, he drops his eyes to the carpet.

"So, you been talking against me, honey."

"Yes," says Solania.

"Some people, I hear they been listening to you, too."

"Lots and lots of people," Solania says, in that imperturbable confidence of hers.

"Yeah," The Baron says thoughtfully. "So why you wanna do that, honey? We been good to you, ain't we?"

"No."

"We been good to you!" The Baroness wheezes.

"No," Solania says. "You're a cancer in this community, and we're going to cut you out."

The Baron nods and the mound heaves under the toddlers.

"You gonna close down the world's oldest profession?" he says. "I don't think so."

"We're going to close you down," she says.

The Baron sighs deeply. "See, there's a problem. Our stuff here, this stuff we do, we gotta a problem right now; you know that biker gang's trying to take over our operation. Why take it out of our hands, just to give it to them bikers? Why would you wanna take it away from our own people, just to give it to outsiders? Think about it."

"Then we'll close them down, too," Solania says.

The Baron snorts.

"You can't stoppem, honey. Only us, we can holdem off. Not you, never. They'd just squash you like a bug."

He clears his throat and falls into a thoughtful silence.

"That guy there," he says suddenly, pointing an accusatory sausage at me, "he writes in that paper, why don't the cops do nothing about The Baron? All the time. That's no good. Why don't he write about the bikers? Otherwise, don't get the cops excited, that's no good. We gotta workable situation here, why mess it up? Girls want money, so we helpem get it. Where's the harm?"

"Yours is not a passive operation," I say. "You actively recruit girls, you force your little girls to bring in their little friends, you hook them on drugs and booze; you shackle them to your operation. You take their money, and you enslave them, you enforce your mastery over them with your thugs: there's the harm."

"We can't live without social order, can we?" rattles The Baroness.

"You been telling our girls they'd do better with you than with us," The Baron says. "How can you? What you gotta offerem? Nothing. Nothing. They say you gonna gettem real jobs. How many jobs you gottem so far? None. You gotta stop these lies, they're just messinem up, makinem forget what they owe me."

He motions to one of the thugs sitting by the wall, who stands up with a blanket that had been folded on the floor beside him. Like he's throwing a medicine ball, The Baron stands himself up, takes the blanket, unfolds it as he steps over to Solania. Panting, he spreads the blanket over her shoulders and lap.

"We need a truce," he says. "I gotta fight off these bikers, I gotta find out who's killing my whores, you and me fighting, what good's that gonna do?"

He clenches his fat fist, shakes it momentarily under Solania's nose.

"You and me, truce," he says firmly. "No more making my whores wanna go, no more stories getting the cops nervous, no more getting our people stirred up against me. We can't live without social order, can we?"

"Just out of idle interest," I say, "what would Solania gain from a truce? What are you offering?"

"Me?" The Baron says, regarding me coldly. "Me, maybe I don't kill you guys. That's my offer."

Solania smiles. "You chose a weak bargaining position, there. You're talking to two people who couldn't care less."

"My guess," I say, "is that if you dared kill us, you'd have done it by now. You know very well what force would be unleashed against you if you harmed Solania, don't you?"

Grunting horribly, The Baroness manages to raise herself up on her elbows; little children roll off her like avalanches.

"Solania, honey," she pants, "which one o' these little suckers is yours, honey?"

"None of them," Solania says. "I haven't had any children."

"Huh," The Baroness puffs. "I thought one of 'em was yours, maybe."

With that, she collapses backward again. The floor shakes, the giant t.v. bounces a bit.

Solania says to The Baron, "You've got nothing for us, and we've got nothing for you. We can't bargain. I tell the people what I see, that's all I do; what you do doesn't fit in with what I see."

The Baron shakes his oily worms.

"You gotta think about a truce, anyways, or innocent people gonna get hurt."

Solania laughs, covers her mouth with her hand.

"Well, we mustn't let that happen," she says, taking my hand.

She pulls herself up, allowing the blanket to fall to the floor. She steps over it to the door, towing me. The Baron struggles to stand, but we are gone before he is able.

When we're outside The Baron's gate, we start up the sidewalk with Ken and Buster following. In a moment, though, The Baron's big sedan has pulled even with us, being driven by the henchman who delivered us.

"Get in," says the driver, leaning to the passenger's window. "I'll take you home."

"We'll walk," I say.

"C'mon, get in," he insists genially. "It's only right I take you home."

The fact is that time is beginning to press. Solania is due up at the SITV studio soon.

"Okay," I say, pulling the door open. I tell him the address.

"Oh, I know where you stay," he says.

Ken gets into the back seat with us, Buster gets in the front seat with the driver.

"What's your name?" I ask the driver.

"Alexi," he says.

"Alexi, what are you doing, working for a cesspool like The Baron?"

"Who else is gonna hire me?" he asks simply. "I gotta have money. So I gotta just plug my nose sometimes."

On our way, we pass the corner of 13th and H, and standing there is tiny Angela, her eyes high and distant; she swivels slightly on her spot, absently swinging her little purse.

"Any minute now, she'll be pressing her little cheek against the loose paunch of some eastside grandpa," I say furiously. I look away from her, and glimpse Alexi making note of me in the rear view mirror. "You hold your nose long enough to escape the stench of that, Alexi, you'll suffocate yourself."

"Listen, man," he says, "I don't bring home some money, won't my own daughter end up out there, maybe?"

I throw myself back into the seat, and Alexi shakes his head in a slow, small movement that might be regret.

When we arrive at the house, Alexi turns around and asks us, "You really gonna get some jobs opening up for the people?"

"We don't know yet," says Solania.

"Don't they say you can see what's going to happen?"

"So far, all I can see is our struggle."

"Can you see what's going to happen with me, in my future?"

"Oh, yes," she says.

Alexi grins self-consciously. "So?"

"So, you'll need to stay quick on your feet," Solania says, smiling. "Oh, and next time I see you, you'll be bringing us a gift."

We four transfer to my van, and drive to the northern, industrial part of the city, to the SITV studio.

It's a small station, but it has a significant local audience for its news. We are met with warm relief by a smart young woman who seems to have been waiting in the reception lounge just for Solania. She greets both Solania and me by name, then whisks Solania away from us.

I'm somewhat troubled by the fact that Solania and I haven't discussed what points she should stress about our initiatives, only to a certain extent: she seemed so small as she was led away from us.

Another young woman, one who sits behind a counter, invites us to sit and watch the programme on a monitor in the reception area. This obviously disappoints Ken, but Buster, a study in nonchalance, shrugs and sits down.

We haven't too long to wait. Quite soon, the vapid game show gives way to vapid advertisements, which then yield to hyperactive synthesized music and bright, swirling computer graphics that coalesce into the message "City News Hour". "Tonight!" deeply intones an urgent male voice-over, as a scene from the Friendship Inn appears onscreen. "The Solania phenomenon: the new spirituality and social activism of the inner city!" The screen cuts to a scene of our information picket line outside the supermarket, calmly incongruous to the pulsing music under it. "Solania threatens expanded boycott: who's next on the hit list?!" The scene then cuts to a shot of our Member of Parliament stabbing the air with his finger as he speaks angrily into an array of microphones. "Standing up for the little guy: Billy Aiken defends the rights of the small businessman!" The thundering tone of the voice-over is followed by a more sedate one saying "City News Hour, with Chris Kiegan."

Chris, a dapper man, looks studiously at a sheet of paper in a bureau sort of counter before him, noting something with a pen.

He looks up suddenly, incisively, into the camera.

"Good Evening. Our top story tonight: The Solania storm in our inner city: is it a spiritual awakening, civil breakdown, or just another medicine show?"

There follows an account of our noon meetings, which seems to subtly imply by its tone that any situation wherein so many of our people were gathered together in enthusiastic common cause or belief was intrinsically incipiently perilous to the larger society. As if in illustration, the story then focusses on our boycott of the grocery, and shows Solania at The Friendship warning of its expansion to other exploitive businesses. This is followed by the story of our M.P.'s heroic opposition to our call for fair hiring practices, presumably preferring fair-haired hiring practices. He gets a long blurb in which he portrays himself as freedom's champion and Solania as some weird communist/fascist hybrid, concluding with:

"Threats and bullying and forcing one's will against honest, hardworking small businessmen is no way to accomplish anything. This is a call to anarchy. We can't live without social order, can we?"

Chris the anchorman reappears. "With us tonight in our studio is the young lady at the centre of all this controversy. Bev is with Solania now. Bev?"

Bev is yet another smartly dressed young woman, and she sits with Solania in matching kitty-corner armchairs. Solania appears very small and wan in hers, and she holds her arms clasped in front of her. She is smiling beautifully, though, and Bev smiles back at her.

Ken lets out a little whoop of excitement at the sight of Solania.

Bev says "Welcome, Solania."

"Thank you. It's a pleasure to be here." If Solania is at all nervous, she's hiding it very well.

"So, what do you have to say to Mr. Aiken's charge that you're attempting to force unfair hiring practices on employers who should be free to hire on the basis of their own criteria? He states that all jobs should be filled on the basis of qualifications and experience. Doesn't that sound fair to you?"

Without hesitation, Solania says:

"That's like him saying that a mile-long race is perfectly fair if everybody starts at the same whistle, and everybody has to cross the same finish line; he ignores the fact that my people have been held so far back, we're starting five miles behind everybody else. If he really wants complete openness in the competition for jobs, which I doubt, he should at least wait until we catch up to everyone else's starting line.

"Anyway, I'm always impressed by the those who are completely silent for a hundred years when discrimination acts against my people, but who suddenly, today, become vociferous egalitarians the moment they fear that discrimination might, for once, serve my people."

Bev smiles brightly. "Pastor Enos of God's Right Hand, an inner city outreach ministry, has said that the phenomenal growth of support for what you call your 'practical spirituality' is actually just a crude appeal to paganism and superstition. How do you respond to that?"

"I just tell people what I see. Pastor Enos has offered my people the path of obedience in this life that leads to the chance for obedience in the next life. My people are fed up with servitude that only leads to further servitude. Let's not forget that he's been talking a lot longer than I have; why do my people choose to believe what I see over what he's been told to say? Is it paganism to stand up for ourselves for a change, to take a path that might lead to our emancipation? Why does what I say strike such a chord with the people who hear it? Maybe my people are simply responding to the power of the truth."

"Throughout your boycott, you've been stressing the critical need for what you're calling 'jobs for older sisters'. Could you explain what you mean by that?"

"We're particularly concerned about children caught up in prostitution. We've got a hundred children or more out hooking on our streets. When they see their older sisters hooking at sixteen, when they believe that all that awaits them is hooking at sixteen, they see no reason to wait, if they can make the same money at ten. What are they supposed to be saving themselves for? It's the absence of hope for anything better that takes little children out to the stroll. If their older sisters could get legitimate jobs with local businesses, little sisters would have reason to hope for the same, would have some reason to save themselves, and fewer little sisters would be on the streets. If you want to eliminate child prostitution, get the older sisters jobs."

"Interesting," Bev says, leaning forward in an engaging way. "Solania, what advice or words of encouragement

do you, a young woman who fought her way out of prostitution, have for girls who may be —"

"I didn't fight my way out of prostitution," Solania
interrupts.

"Oh," says a flustered Bev. "I'm so sorry, I somehow
understood that you'd been a, um, I guess I got ..."

"I'm still a prostitute," says Solania.

"Oh, I see," says Bev.

"Fought my way out of prostitution, how am I supposed to have done that?" Solania says. "Nobody's offered
me any job, and being a ghetto prophetess isn't exactly a paying vocation, you know."

"No, I don't suppose ..."

"But I'd love to fight my way out of prostitution, I
really would; if any of your viewers have any honest work
for me, they can find me on 19th St. most nights. But, of
course, many, many of your male viewers already knew
that."

Chapter Seven

O ne day, I'll hold your poor heart in my loving embrace," Solania says to me, "just the way you're holding me now. I'll take it with me to some place where all we need to do is love each other. I'll find our home somewhere, and I'll carry your heart to it, wherever it is. Then you'll sleep, I promise you."

"Okay," I say. I smile down at her. I'm not altogether comfortable, sitting on Solania's blanket in the park, leaning back against a tree.

But her head is nestled in my lap, and her dreamy little smile is so sublime as I stroke her forehead and cheek, trace the outline of her face, trace the course of her smile to its hidden corners, so what complaint have I? I might be floating in ether.

"And when you sleep, you'll always dream of me."

"There's no doubt about that," I say.

She looks up through the limbs and new little leaves to the cerulean sky, seems to drift away in her own reverie.

Farther along the river bank, at a discreet distance, Buster and Russell sit silhouetted against the water's diamond sparkle, watching us with intermittent sideways glances.

I might enjoy the day, but all I can do is enjoy the day as it makes contact with beautiful Solania, and surely this is why the sun burst into light a trillion years ago, solely so that it might dapple through leaves onto her impossibly perfect face this afternoon, why trees evolved and grew leaves, why grass grew, why air formed and stirred to a breeze, just so that, this afternoon, it might flutter the leaves, sparkle the water, and whisper caresses across Solania's face.

Right now, all the world has existed only to, at this very instant, reveal its treasure so exquisite, so fragile and precious and glowing and jewelled, to make all Faberge's efforts failures.

"I'll carry your heart to a place where all our cares and troubles can't reach it, I know it," she says dreamily.

"Okay."

She directs her eyes back to mine.

"I've never been in love before," she says. "Just so you know."

This may be reassurance of how exceptional is our relationship, or maybe unnecessary preemptive apology for any misstep; my own experience of being in love is grossly disproportionately distantly retroactive; Solania could be no more awkward and unpractised in active responsive romance than I. To me, love has been the lingering pain, its beauty barely a memory. So what complaint have I? She's redefining its grace to me.

Solania loves telling me that we're in love, says it with animation and wonder whenever she can. Loving her may conform appropriately to my penance, but having her in love with me seems like the unmerited remittance, like an erroneously inflated cheque arriving unexpectedly in the mail, with the omitted decimal point that I should properly report to somebody.

I'd say that she's never prepared a picnic before, either. Spam on white with sweet relish and hard orange margarine, ketchup-flavoured potato chips, a thermos of cold soup concocted of canned corn and condensed milk, a big plastic bottle of berry drink from powder, but all planned and prepared just for me, for our surprise stolen moment together when dirt and rasping grit, distempers and desperation, burdens of grief or guilt are to be overlooked here on a blanket in the midst of our incongrous island of green and pleasant park. So what complaint have I? Corn soup might be ambrosia.

I augment the breeze, blow lightly into my darling's glistening black hair.

Overhead, a pair of Canada geese wing by as if summoned, calling to us to notice, flying as one.

"Oh, look, sweetheart," Solania says with delight. "There we are."

"There we are."

"Joined together forever, following spring and beauty together forever," she says. "That's us, when we're finished with all of this. No more crawling through the filth for us, we'll forever fly up where it's clean and pure."

But, along from us, Buster falls back and raises an invisible shotgun to his shoulder, fires at the geese with "pochhh, pochhh" noises like a little boy.

"People shoot geese," I observe. "People knock them from the sky just for the cruel fun of watching them flutter and fall."

She reaches her hand up to my cheek.

"Maybe," she says. "But that's not what mated geese are thinking about when they're flying together."

"No?" I say. "What are they thinking about?"

"They're thinking about flying together. That's all. How could they possibly think of anything else?"

"They couldn't possibly," I say. "It sounds wonderful."

With my fingertips, I polish my perfect luminous jewel as she watches the geese fly away up the river.

"It will be," she says.

.

Chapter Eight

Solania spoke with vigour about the failure of our neighborhood schools, about how the withholding of normal educational opportunity holds our people down within the substrata that's been prepared for them. "When our ignorance is the tool of our oppressors," she said, "education becomes our act of rebellion."

However, she now speaks with less vitality about the plan I've concocted to confront the problem. She glances over to me from time to time with an expression of compliant concession. She holds the attention of the shoehorned crowd, however, as they are hoping for a vision.

With difficulty, Rod, the city councillor who would be mayor, circulates slowly through the assembled sardines like oil, ostentatiously presenting himself as the one fisherman who truly understands them. Somewhere, he's come up with a beaded jacket and a beaded amulet which he wears without embarrassment. His smile of sincere sympathy and concern is frozen on his face as he quietly presses folded brochures into the hands of people who'd rather attend to Solania. I think he's encouraged incorrectly by their typical courtesy.

The school plan is simple enough: although the education system doesn't have an obviously vulnerable profit imperative the way a store has, it does have financial susceptibilities that can be threatened. In this province, the annual funding for an individual school is established according to its registered enrolment on September 30th. By threatening a mass temporary deregistration leading up to that date, we might force the schools to address our issues. Furthermore, many of our students are covered by treaties with the federal government that include the promise of elementary and secondary education; bringing suit against the federal government for its failure to meet its treaty obligation could result in serious pressure on the provincial government, which then would be reapplied to the nonperforming school. One difficulty of this is proving that the schools are failing to teach our children; somehow, teachers have succeeded in convincing the public that province-wide or nation-wide comparison testing is a heinously unfair test of the performance of our children, where it's actually an utterly necessary test of the performance of our teachers and schools.

We are also considering bringing suit against the provincial government for its failure to enforce its own laws requiring compulsory school attendance of children under the age of sixteen. This is scrupulously enforced on the eastside, of course, and doesn't even get lip service over here.

Litigation became an option for us when one of the top lawyers in the city, Richard Douglas, broke eastside ranks and offered the potent force of his firm in support of our efforts.

Many of those packing the hall are children who should be in school right at this moment. Solania's recitation of our plan is pro forma, but this topic is of greater concern to many of the people here than obviously it is to her, and there are several considered nods I can see.

Carney is my warder of the day, but he sits slumped at a table near me; he is in bad shape, his face bruised blue, scuffed and swollen, and his shoulders and arms are sore and stiff. He is carefully fussing with a deep split in his swollen lower lip.

Solania, I know, is much more interested at the moment in squaring off against the pawn shops, particularly the COIN-operated ones. We are assailed on all sides these days, and COIN, the association of slumlords, pawnbrokers, and other storekeepers, is riding very high on the crest of this wave against us, which excites Solania. My problem is that

I'm not sure how we're to provide an alternative service as we do for groceries, not that pawn shops can be described as providing a service; but people who go to them only do so because they're desperate for some ready cash, and we've no means of providing ready cash to those who join our boycott. Solania is chafing, in her sweet way, impatient with my inability to draw up a scheme of retaliation against COIN. I'd like to solicit suggestions from her supporters, but on this point she adamantly insists that it's our job to offer direction, not request it.

COIN and the M.P. Billy Aiken and several fundamentalist churches have mounted a counter-initiative, modelled closely on ours, that brings eager people and grocery lists from across the city to shop at our beleaguered boycotted supermarket; Aiken holds daily pep-rallies in the parking lot, invoking the enterprising spirit of the pioneers that made this great land, and Pastor Enos gives blessings and prayers that goodness may triumph at last over our wickedness, both acting in jeering, leering mockery of Solania, and drivers seem to try to hit our picketers just for sport as they enter the parking lot. I'm not sure, but it's possible that the supermarket is enjoying more business than ever before.

A reporter for the other newspaper in the city had the journalistic acuity to ask some poor mental patient outside The Friendship if he thought that Solania was employing methods of cultish mind control on the people here, and the poor guy dutifully said "Yeah, maybe she is.", so the big headline next day read 'Solania Brainwashing Fears Arise', and the man wasn't identified as patently unbalanced, but was described as living in terror of Solania. And my columnist counterpart wrote of the 'Solania Hysteria', but mainly focussed his recriminations against me in a column headed "The Very Public Unravelling of a Once-Respected

Journalist", wherein he indicated that this hysteria was of my manufacture, in my dissipated, dissolute desperation to reclaim relinquished journalistic authority. He seemed to suggest that Solania is my sex slave, which notion I take as a figment of his fevered envy. And a brand new organization called 'Christians for Decency in Broadcasting' set up a picket of its own at the offices of SITV, demanding that the station air an apology for featuring a prostitute on its evening news hour; its picket line featured plump eastside mothers weeping into the sweatshirts of their defiled children for SITV's own cameras; and the station abjectly complied. The group's new focus, I understand, is to be the studio of CBC Television, whose reporter has been sympathetic to our effort, even though its video of Solania's meeting-ending hand-touching ritual seems to have contributed to the sensational opposition to us.

A spokesman for the police association said that its officers are overwhelmed by the sudden influx of hundreds of penniless rural people into the city, seeking spiritual solace as Solania's pilgrims, and that the seams of social order are straining dangerously, and when will the city fathers act to contain the chaotic, upswelling atmosphere of insurrection?

The board of The Friendship Inn is becoming agitated over anticipated threats to its public funding, but so far Sharon is steadfast in defense of Solania's meetings here, even at the risk of her own job.

Solania is, of course, completely undaunted, is energized by the opposition, and is, hence, particularly eager to get past my plodding practical plans for sober discussion with the Director or Minister of Education; she wants to tear into the meat of the immediate matters. She sends me a what-a-good-girl-am-I smile as she concludes her listless little speech about education.

She closes her eyes and waits for a long time, as complete silence descends upon the hall. Even Rod detects the etiquette at hand, ceases his electioneering, stands stock still.

The longer her silence, the more palpable the air of tense excitement in the hall.

Finally, she raises her face and hands upward to the ceiling. She speaks in a soft low tone that soon has people leaning slightly forward, as the press of them will permit, and cocking an ear to her.

"I see a big grey tree," she says. "This tree, it's armoured in thick hard bark, it grows no leaves, and it will bear no fruit. It offers neither shade nor food. By its stretching roots, it poisons the land in which it stands, so the earth is hard and barren all around it.

"The tips of some of its bare branches are snakes that coil and strike, and other branches are tipped by shiny steel swords, and other branches have thick worms. On all the other branches, I see children hanging by their necks, crying, choking, strangulated on the branches, as snakes strike at them, as swords slash at them, and as worms burrow into them, the children are weeping blood from their bulging eyes, and the snakes and swords and worms won't stop, but strike harder and deeper if the children try to resist, or try to wriggle away from the blows.

"I see the firebird flying above, crying as it circles, and it comes to perch on the top branch of the killing tree. Swords and snakes strike at its talons, but it stays atop the tree, and it calls down to the good earth that's out beyond the reach of the tree's roots, and out of the good earth I see springing the spirits of our people. I see that their fingers are like flames, and they rise up from the good earth and scorch the shiny swords, sear the writhing snakes and worms in their fires, burn through the bonds of the children and set the poisonous branches blazing. The children fall, but I see that they're caught up by the firebird, and it carries them to the good earth, and the spirits of our people set flame to the killer tree until it's nothing but a burnt-out stump that will torture the children no more."

"That's what I see," she says in conclusion, and she holds her hands aloft in the ensuing hush.

Councillor Rod stands wide-eyed in alarm and ashen, shoulder to shoulder with people entirely outside his previous experience, people who aren't wide-eyed at all but are staring at Solania in a range from wonder to wild intensity.

Then suddenly, almost in a panic, at some unseen signal, they press forward as a single body, hands reaching out to grasp Solania's hands, carried on a low, indistinct roll of thunder. Rod is carried forward, too, and he reaches out his hand urgently, and when he finally grips her hand, he waves it frantically over her head as though she's a victorious prize-fighter, and his face is flushed, and he's frantically mouthing something I can't hear. Buster takes Rod's hand and pries it from Solania's, and brusquely pushes him aside and along into the stream away from her, but Rod struggles, florid and frothing, to return to her. Without opening her eyes, Solania reaches out and lightly caresses Rod's red cheek, and then Buster shoves him away again.

Rod cries out in undirected fervour, then his wild eyes settle on me, and he thrashes over to me like a bad swimmer, grabs my lapels and cries:

"The revolution is at hand!"

"What?" I say.

"Long live the revolution!" he cries like an idiot out over the heads of the people.

A roar of approval answers him, and it goes straight to his head. He takes up a chant of "Long live the revolution!"

I grab him by his shoulders, and force him through the bathroom door, sort of throw him against the inside wall.

"What do you think you're doing?" I say. "Have you

reverted to your student-radical playtime, or what? There's no revolution going on here. This is social, perhaps spiritual, but not political, and don't you forget it. Now, you're just caught up in some sort of your own manic populism. Get yourself under control."

"Not political?!" he puffs. "Are you out of your mind? This is pure politics. This is the stuff I got into politics for, and I only now see how I've lost my way through the years. That girl, that girl —- she's opened my eyes, I tell you. She's given purpose back to my political life, I tell you."

"Or self-serving opportunity to your personal ambition," I say.

"Perles," he puffs darkly, "your jealously is in vain; it would be obvious to anyone but you, that girl doesn't belong to you, and you can't hold her or contain what she's doing. I could feel it when she touched me! I could feel it in her loving touch!"

"Feel what?"

But with that he pushes his way past me into the main hall.

I lean back against the the cracked and cemented porcelain sink, rub my face in my hands, candylaurabethlayla, and unhappily confront my personal transgression of wishing to find my own future in the future of what we've been doing here, of trying to impel and impose my will into some borderline optimistic tomorrow in which I claim some little portion of the wider redemption, somehow step around the rightful candylaurabethlayla impediment. I'm no better than Rod in seeking to exploit this situation to my own advantage, merely less gleeful.

I go back to the main hall, look to her who so obviously doesn't belong to me. Two women are slowly moving through the crowd toward Solania, pushing ahead of them a teenaged girl of disfigured face and shuffling, hesitant gait. I recognize this girl; many months ago, three of her erstwhile girlfriends waylaid her at the railway tracks, and beat her nearly to death because she refused to be their recruit into the ranks of prostitution; by some capricious happenstance, the girl was delivered to St. Paul's Hospital, where her own mother was unable to identify her, such were the injuries to her face.

The pack of people makes way for her as she's propelled forward by the two women, until she stands bashfully beside Solania, and the hall falls silent again.

Carney ceases fussing over his own wounds to watch.

Solania, eyes closed, turns slightly in her chair, then reaches over and takes the girl's scarred face in her hands.

"Dear," she says softly, "who hurt you?"

The girl's speech is slow and slurred.

"These girls, they hurt me."

"No, dear, they were only the weapons. Who really hurt you?"

The girl's brain, said to be once very sharp, can no longer deal with subtleties, and she shuffles in discomfort.

"Never mind, dear," Solania says soothingly. "I see that the spirits of our people are gathering around you in protection. No one will be able to hurt you again. Don't be afraid anymore."

The women with the girl begin to cry tearfully, and then the girl cries, too, and then the other people around them have tears flowing down their cheeks, and the electricity is conducted freely through all this water, and soon the whole hall is galvanized again.

"Who hurt this girl?!" Solania cries out, "And how much longer will we ourselves be the weapons they use against us?!"

"Never again!" cries Rod like a pretentious usurper, but his answer is taken up by many others.

The women shower Solania with liquid kisses on her head and face, and the girl appears to enter into a weeping rapture.

Buster is chanting "Never again!" with the others, and near him, Carney seems abnormally intense, sternly jutting out his torn lip. Solania smiles a little smile to herself that I'm sure only I notice, and it unnerves me, and I spin for a moment's solitude back in the washroom.

There is a framed sheet of steel that's been set up as a mirror over the sink, but it's dented, and grey in abrasion, and it sends back to me a misshapen image of myself, swollen- and scarred-seeming like a girl who won't be a whore, but that's not me, it's my intentions and situation that are swirling in such distortion that I can't affix my view to any definite reliable reality.

"Things are getting out of hand," I whisper to myself, but then I wonder whose hand I might have thought held things.

There comes a rap at the washroom door, and then Carney, perhaps remembering his warder duty, calls through:

"Perles, you in there?"

I pull the door open. Carney smiles carefully.

"Hey, bro, can we talk?"

I look beyond him to Solania, or, rather, to the spot where Solania is hidden by the milling people.

"Later," I say. "I must talk with her."

Carney shrugs, and says "But these guys ain't going too soon. Can we talk?"

"All right, all right," I say impatiently.

"Outside, maybe," Carney says, so I follow him around the edge of the crowd, outside to the sidewalk.

Once outside, Carney immediately heads down the street the short distance to my van, and automatically climbs into the passenger seat.

I get into the driver's seat, and look at him.

"Okay," I say.

"So, uh," Carney says, "you think you could get me dressed up kinda sharp?" He looks down with disapproval at his sweat pants and t-shirt.

"What for?"

"Well, y'see," he says, and he stops to thoughtfully finger the cut on the bridge of his nose as he stares out the windshield. "See, me, I guess I'm gonna propose to Velvet."

"Carney," I say, "that seems very unwise right now."

"Well, I'm gonna do it, anyways, I guess. And I gotta look sharp, I guess. I been thinking about it."

It was a similarly chivalrous impulse of two days ago that resulted eventually in the wounds he now nurses.

As he'd described it to me, the danger that the unknown killer of hookers posed to his darling Velvet increasingly preyed on his mind, to the point where he resolved to institute his plan of surveillance, in which he'd lurk unseen and make note of all of Velvet's tricks. So two afternoons ago, he went out to 19th Street, hid himself behind a bush, and waited and watched little Velvet strolling up and down on the sidewalk, smiling into cars and wagging her little bottom.

She was outfitted in Solania's standard garb of flannel shirt and loose blue jeans, and her hair was newly cropped short in Solania's style; this costume was not in tribute: ever since Solania's appearance on SITV and her declaration that she was still working 19th Street, there had been a constant heavy flow of eastside men seeking out Solania, not in response to her appeal for legitimate work, but for the purpose of sharing a little part of themselves with her. She'd become the city's first and only prostitution superstar, and the other hookers found themselves in a drought. So The

Baron, the soul of business acumen, had insisted that all his young and slender girls must present themselves on the street as the one true Solania.

It seems that Carney had never actually witnessed Velvet at work before, and must have avoided full-blown consideration of the matter, but the sight of her flagrant flirtations to the drivers caused him more and more disquiet, and then anguish.

When a driver stopped for her, a middle aged man in a big, shiny, fancy, white pick-up, when Carney saw his little Velvet climb up into that gleaming white truck, something snapped.

Springing out from his corner, Carney intercepted the truck just as it turned onto Ave. G., leapt onto the high hood, and threw himself against the big windshield, pleading through to horrified Velvet to stop. The driver, who'd been glowing red in ugly illicit carnal agitation, paled like a plug was pulled in him somewhere, but he didn't stop, he tried to drive away even as Carney clung to the roof of the cab and screamed in to Velvet, "Baby, please!".

The driver wove perilously up Ave. G to 20th St., swinging right and risking any number of lives with wild veers and sudden accelerations and screeching stops, desperately trying to dislodge Carney. The driver's nerves would not have been eased by the fact that Velvet began screaming abuse back at Carney in terms too foul for her young mouth.

The driver careened around the next corner, heading south on F, reeled onto Spadina, and then tore down the little road into the park, to its large parking lot, where he sent his truck squealing and lurching in a continuing failure to lose the tenacious clinging Carney. By then, Velvet was screaming incoherently and Carney was sobbing uncontrollably, and presumably the driver looked down to his lap and noticed that he was no longer feeling particularly licentious, for he suddenly halted his truck's gyrations, and called out in a quavering voice to Carney:

"Look, I don't want her anymore! You can have her if you'll just get off the truck and let me get out of here safely!"

"She gets out first!" sobbed Carney. "Then I get off!"

He saw the ashen-faced john ordering Velvet out, saw Velvet adamantly, furiously shaking her head in refusal. So soon both Carney and the john were shouting at her to get out, and with a string of curses for them both, she finally obeyed.

Carney leapt from the hood, the john peeled away, and Velvet began marching in sharp angry little steps away from Carney.

"Baby, wait!" he cried, catching up to her, trying to take her arm.

She snatched her arm away, cursed him anew, told him she never wanted to see him again, that he was crazy, and what was she going to tell The Baron?, and that Carney was in big trouble now!

She was so livid and hard, Carney's entreaties bounced off her enamelled surface without leaving a mark, and he finally threw himself into the grass amid dried dead gophers, in total despair as she strode away.

"It's cause I love you so much, that's why!" he cried.

"I don't love you no more!" she called back. "I hate you, Carney, don't you ever come near me again!"

Carney lay in the park for a long time, miserably gazing into the sky and keening for Velvet, until, of course, it seemed to him that a lot of booze would help him to feel wretched very effectively, so he picked himself up and started along the park road in pursuit of drink money. If he hadn't been so downcast with his sorrows, he might have spotted the car full of The Baron's boys in time to hide himself, but they spilled out upon him before he knew what was hitting him.

Carney's a lover, not a fighter, and he managed no sort of resistance, even by his own account; they whaled away on him until their arms were too weary, then, with a cautionary note about interfering with The Baron's commercial interests, they let him drop to the sod, got back into the car and drove off.

So Carney lay on the grass yet longer, miserably gazing into the sky and keening for Velvet, until one eye was swollen almost shut and a mouthful of blood reminded him that he was thirsty.

He crawled to the road, began to crawl along it, but was soon met by two cops in a cruiser, on their regular patrol through the park. Carney waved blearily at them, tried to smile good-naturedly, but they stared stonily down on him, pulled on latex gloves, picked him up and roughly threw him into the back seat of the cruiser.

"Maybe the hospital," Carney managed to say through the holes in the plastic screen.

The passenger cop turned and spoke to Carney in a way that was no kinder or more refined than the manner Velvet had employed earlier.

They drove him south of the city, out past the power station, and they yanked him out of the cruiser and threw him down into a field of rough stubble.

"Stay out of our town," they advised him sternly.

"Hey, man," Carney choked out in an attempted jocular tone, "don't you remember whose land your town's on?"

Carney crawled back toward the city until his hands and knees were scuffed and raw, until the sun was down and the night was turning cold. The lower temperature seemed to invigorate him, and he found that he was able to stand and stagger. By morning, he was sleeping in the hallway of the house we stay in.

"What do you consider to be looking sharp?" I ask him.

"Like you, bro," Carney says. "That'll do."

"None of my clothes will fit you, Carney," I say. "You won't look sharp, you'll look dopey."

"Well, I can't propose to her like this, can I?" he asks, gesturing simply to his clothes.

"You shouldn't be proposing to her at all," I say. "Give her more time to miss you, if she's ever going to. See if she'll come to you."

"No way," he insists. "If I don't show her I love her, she'll forget about me."

"Then you'd better let her forget about you, if her affection is so inconstant."

This reasoning is quite beyond his scheme of things, and he dismisses it as ludicrous.

"You gotta help me, bro," he says.

"If I don't help you, what will you do?" I ask.

"Just have to do it by myself," he says.

I start the van with my key and a sigh, and I drive to Ave. H, and down Ave. H to the Mennonite Clothes Closet resale store.

"Let's look in here."

When we enter, we're greeted by Della, the genial, matronly manageress. Carney picks his way through the racks of used clothing, to the back corner where the mens suits hang. He's immediately attracted to a pale blue tuxedo.

"This looks pretty good," he says.

"I thought you wanted to look sharp like me."

I riffle through until I come upon a grey pinstripe that appears to be the approximate size for him. I pull it off the rack, hold it up to him.

"Yeah," says Carney.

"Could be," I say. "Go and try it on."

Carney looks to the curtained doorway in the back corner.

"Naw," he says. "That's okay. Let's just get it." He studies the price tag stapled to the sleeve.

"Try it on," I say, pushing him to the curtain. He ducks behind it as though this is a bank heist, and I go to the rack of shirts, happen to find a white shirt with a grey pinstripe. I take it over, drape it over the curtain rod, and tell Carney to try it, too.

As I'm looking through the ties, I notice a tall woman by the cash counter; she holds a red dress that's obviously too small for her, presses it up against herself, folds upward the skirt hem that's already too short.

"Gotta be sexier than that damn Solania," the woman is saying to Della. "Whattya think, if I hem it up here, d'you think it'd be sexy enough?"

"I'm sure I don't know, dear," Della says patiently. "I'm sure I'm not the person you should be asking."

The woman laughs lightly, then spies me.

"Okay, I'll ask this guy. Maybe he's an expert," she says. "Whattya think, sweetie, does this turn you on?"

And she laughs at me as she holds the dress to her, but then there's an abrupt signal of recognition that stops her cold. She turns back to Della.

"Jeez, is that really Perles? Is that him?" she gasps.

"Yep, that's him," says Della with apparent pleasure.

The woman throws her free hand to the front of her face. "Oh, jeez, d'you think he heard what I said about Solania?"

"I would guess he did," Della says.

"Oh, jeez."

The woman hurries over to me.

"Listen, Perles, I didn't mean anything about Solania,

really. I think she's great."

"That's fine," I say.

"I mean it, I love Solania," she says fervently. "And you can tell her I said so. All those damn tricks are looking for her, but that's not her fault. I love Solania."

I am disturbed that this woman is so disturbed. I search her expression, which is fleet and active to my frustration, for any clue: is she afraid of me, and if so, why? What could she possibly know? Was she a witness from a dark doorway, or has she heard a general rumour? Her features won't settle enough to indicate anything.

"I'll tell her," I say. "She'll be happy to know it."

"Don't tell her what I said."

"Okay," I say, turning back to the tie rack.

The woman bustles back to the counter.

"I really love Solania," she assures Della. "I think she's great."

"I can tell," says Della.

The woman pays for the dress and departs.

Carney steps out from behind the curtain in the suit and shirt.

"Wow," I say. "You do look sharp."

Carney smiles with the uninjured side of his mouth.

"Yeah," he says, bobbing his head a little. "Guess I do."

"Have you ever worn a suit before, Carney?" I ask.

"No, I never," he says.

"Not even for court?"

"No, never."

On the wall between the racks is a mirror, and Carney spends some time admiring himself. He insists that we go to search out Velvet then and there, so I start to tie a tie on him, scouring my mind, while I'm at it, for any memory of having done the same thing to Laura, of course.

"Turn around," I say. "I can't tie this backwards."

I swing him to face away from me, reach around his shoulders to his neck.

"I use a windsor knot," I say. "It's more complicated to tie than a four-in-hand, but the result looks much better."

We can't find any worthwhile shoes in Carney's approximate size, so he's going to have to make do with his ratty runners. The pants are a bit long, so they drape over all but the toes, anyway.

When I pay the pittance for the clothing, Della says to me: "You know, I really love Solania, too. I don't believe any of that witchcraft talk. God bless her."

Carney steps out onto the sidewalk of Avenue H as though he's a new man, he just about struts to the van, to some vague rhythm he's set up in his battered head.

In the passenger seat, he appears to lean especially close to the open window, perhaps so that he might be better seen by those we pass.

We drive along 19th Street. On the sidewalk up ahead of us, I see a slim young girl in Solania costume, working the afternoon traffic.

"There's Velvet," I say, and Carney gives a nervous start, swallows and pales. This is no lark for him.

But I'm mistaken, the young girl is only a Solania-look-alike-Velvet-look-alike who is out trolling in tandem with another hooker, a 35 year old woman who is obviously the young girl's mother. The mother doesn't attempt the Solania imitation, is too dumpy and frumpy for it, baits her hook with too much exposed flesh, instead, flouncing in exaggeration beside her daughter partner, who stands rather demurely, casting sideways looks to her mother's desperate antics.

Velvet is not on her afternoon parade. We turn onto 20th, and Carney starts chewing on his thumbnail in consternation.

"Say, bro," he ventures, "you'n'me, let's us get a bottle."

"Not a chance," I say. "You're supposed to be on duty, aren't you?"

"I gotta have a drink before I see Velvet, I can't handle her otherwise. Just one, bro, I swear."

"If you need a drink to ask a girl to marry you, you're making a mistake," I say.

"It ain't just that, bro," he says. And then he stares dolefully out his window.

"What else is it, then?" I ask after a moment.

Carney sighs, then says, "Y'see, it's them guys at the neon heart. I'd like to go in looking like this, buy a good bottle and have 'em treat me like maybe I wasn't dirt for a change. They'd have to treat me like a gentleman if I went in looking like this, wouldn't they?"

"I don't know."

"Yeah, they would."

Carney chews on his thumbnail again. Already, he's developing the fingernails of the chronic alcoholic, nails that seem to sit like plastic ovals atop the tips of his fingers, so that his chewing now would seem enough to peel the whole nail right off, like peeling a shrimp.

As with almost everything else these days, the morally correct course is unclear to me. I do know that I'm not about to cure his alcoholism at this very moment; and even I, in days past, have been subjected in small measure to the hypocritical scorn of the neon heart cashiers as I accepted the warm welcome extended by their store's cozy, inviting exterior. And I know that, if I stand my ground, at some point later today, Carney will be out begging in his spiffy new duds, and the caustic image erodes any resolution.

Across 20th from the liquor store is its parking lot, its low fence decorated with medallions cutely painted by neighborhood children, many of whom suffered daily in their parent's alcoholism, painted during the course of a contest of a few years ago, enough to warm one's heart to a neon red glow, really, in its wholesomeness. I pull into this parking lot, and give Carney some money.

"This is the only time, and I mean it, so don't even think of asking again," I say.

Carney slips the money into his jacket pocket, then smooths his lapels and tie as though he's a born dandy. He gets out of the van, adjusts himself sleekly, looks around for whomever might be looking at him, and then with a jaunty step and swinging arms, he saunters across the road to the neon heart. He pauses, poses and pirouettes grandly for the windblown men collected in eddy on the corner there, before disappearing through the glass door.

From the parking lot, I can look down to the corner of 19th, where the mother and daughter pair still try their luck. As I watch, a car containing at least two men pulls around the corner and idles as the two women turn and trot after it. The mother is in the lead, and she sashays sexily toward the front passenger window, bends in smiling enquiry, but then is apparently rebuffed, straightens up sharply, puts her hands on her hips and swivels to look at her approaching daughter. After a moment's consideration, the mother gestures to herself, her daughter and then toward the car, in an attitude of reasonable argument. Inside the car, the two men in the front seat gesture themselves, and the driver speaks, nodding in emphasis.

The mother shakes her head, the daughter shakes her head and steps away, and the driver speaks again, waving his hands before him. The mother sinks into a small slump, puts her head to one side, and looks over to her daughter. The daughter shakes her head again, but the mother speaks, motions with one hand toward the car. The daughter slings a hip out in refusal, puts her hands on her hip, looks from her mother to the car and back again. Then suddenly she throws her hands up and climbs into the back of the car.

The car roars up toward our corner. On the sidewalk, the mother, rejected and dejected, momentarily recedes into the shy, modest woman she is by her nature, by the nature of her people, the woman she is when she's not on the stroll. Her haltered breast sinks inward in repeat mundane defeat.

The car turns onto 20th St. in front of me; there are four young men in the car, two in the front, two in the back. I can't see the girl, which means she's already down, busy at her work.

I try to suppress all reaction, subdue my pity, I look away from the unhappy mother, for there is in my mind a germ of the truly unthinkable idea dividing and multiplying and enlarging that, if true, will ensure my own grotesque, ravaged doom and the fates of many around me if I can't somehow starve it where it grows. I groan even in this briefest consideration of it.

I want to honk, get driving, redirect my attention. Carney is taking forever, probably protracting the process to his fullest possible enjoyment.

Russell passes in front of me, likely heading to our boycott picket line up 20th St., which is obscured from my vantage point. Russell is one of my warders, is Buster's older brother, is by his manner even harder, sterner and more self-contained than Buster. He walks, slow and straight, his hair pulled severely into a long ponytail that betrays no bounce or sway, and he glances through my windshield as if in inspection. I acknowledge him with a nod, which he recognizes with the merest inclination of his head in my direction, before returning his iron eyes up the street again. When accompanying me, he is utterly silent, will sometimes deign to answer a question or comment of mine, but only with some slight alteration of his expression or attitude. I like his self-importance, value its survival in someone who has certainly been told, by trivializing treatment, that nothing about his self is of any importance. He's an imposing and intimidating figure, and when he's on the picket line, M.P. Aiken and Pastor Enos moderate their mockery or fall silent altogether, even with the constant police protection at their daily rallies. I wonder for an impulsive instant if, should I leap out of my van now and challenge him, he might kill me quickly. Of course, I do nothing.

Finally, Carney emerges out from under the neon heart, a paper bag cradled in the crook of his arm. He bounces across the street and gets into the van.

"Well, was that as enjoyable as you'd hoped?" I ask. "Did anyone comment?"

"Nope," says Carney. "But I could see 'em looking at me."

He hoists his bottle, of the rye I used to drink, up to the top of the bag, twists off the cap and takes a long pull.

"I can't stand you drunk in here," I say. "You said just one drink."

"That wasn't one drink."

"No, it was two," I say.

"Just a bit more," he says, gulping quickly.

"Put it away," I say firmly.

"I'm okay now," he says. "That'll do me."

He recaps the bottle and stows it beneath his seat, then sits back to await its effects. I drive down to 19th. The mother waves at me saucily.

Velvet is nowhere to be found.

"She must be still hiding out at The Baron's," Carney offers. "Let's us head over there."

"How could you have such a foolish idea, Carney?" I say. I shift the rear-view mirror in his direction. "Do you really need another look at The Baron's response to your love for Velvet?"

Carney regards himself sadly.

"I don't care what happens to me, I can't live without my Velvet. That Baron, he'll turn her heart against me," he says. "We can't just leave her there, to forget about me."

I drive to the house where we stay, and park the van.

"There," I say. "I just saved what's left of your face. You should thank me."

"Okay," Carney says, nodding seriously. "Guess I'll go by myself."

I remonstrate with him, but he's adamant.

"My poor Velvet, she can't stay there with those guys, what's gonna happen to her over there? She needs me."

"You need a psychiatrist."

"I need my sweet Velvet, and I gotta go rescue her."

He gets set to climb out of the van.

"Wait a second," I say. "Let me see if I can get Buster and Russell or Ken to go with us, at least."

I go into the house, but find no one of any immediate use. When I come out, Carney has already started down the sidewalk, is turning onto Spadina.

I catch up with him in the van.

"Why won't you wait?" I cry with annoyance.

"Yeah, like what's she gonna think about me if I can't stand up for myself?" he spits. "Like she's gonna love a wimp hiding behind Buster."

"All right, let me go with you, at least," I say. "No one will think you're hiding behind me. Maybe he'll be more circumspect in his retaliation if I'm there."

Carney climbs back into the van with a show of reluctance, as though this wasn't what he wanted in the first place. He takes the bottle and drains another snort from it. With ever mounting apprehension, I drive to The Baron's two–storey house.

When I park, I take Carney's arm.

"I don't like this one bit, and I've no wish to see you beaten up again. If things get dicey, we step back and try another day, right?"

Carney pulls away, climbs out, and strides up the walk to the front door, where he stops and turns back to me.

"We're supposed to bring flowers," he says.

"What?"

"Flowers. And a ring."

"Carney," I begin, but then one of The Baron's toughs is at the screen door.

"Get lost," he says.

"I come for my Velvet," Carney says. "You tell her I'm here."

The thug laughs and says, "Get outta here while you still can."

"Velvet!" Carney calls suddenly. "I'm here for you, baby! C'mon out!"

"She's not here, fool," says the thug, and he swings the inner door closed.

Carney attempts to push it open, but it's already locked. Carney pounds on it briefly, then comes back along the walk, looks up to the upper windows.

"Velvet, I know you're there, baby!" he cries. "C'mon, baby, you know we belong together!"

The Baron appears in the livingroom window shaking his huge hanging jowls in ominous warning to Carney.

"You go to hell!" Carney shouts at him. "You let my Velvet out here!"

I try to take his arm, but he's worked himself up, the booze and adrenaline urge each other on in his system. He steps roughly from me, reaches down and digs a stone out of the earth under a bush by the house, steps back and flings it at the window. The window cracks loudly, but doesn't shatter.

"Velvet!" he calls, bending to find another stone. "It's me, baby! I come for you!"

"Carney, you must calm down," I order him.

The front door opens to reveal The Baron.

Carney straightens and puffs in confrontation.

"You got my Velvet, I know it," he says. "She's mine, she's not yours. Send her out to me."

"You got guts, I'll give you that," says The Baron. "But you got one minute to get outta here, or you'll be sorry."

And he swings the door closed again.

Four or five little children, grimy of face and threadbare garb, have gathered in silent witness on the public walk beside my van.

"C'mon, Carney," I say. "If Velvet is in there, she's seen that you love her. If she loves you, too, she'll find a way to come to you later."

"No," Carney gasps. "He'll keep her from me. I gotta get her out now."

"But how?"

"Velvet, baby!" he calls again. "Come to your Carney!"

And then I see in the livingroom window, rising horribly, the cackling, wheezing red moon that is The Baroness' face. It immediately occurs to me that, if she has gone to the tremendous effort of being raised up to look out at us, it is certainly in anticipation of something much more interesting than we would wish.

"Carney," I say, chilled, latching an icy grip onto his arm without courtesy, "we've got to go."

I start to drag him along the walk.

The door opens, and The Baron's thug, now pale and terribly intense, rushes toward us. Carney turns to meet him squarely, holds up his free hand defensively. Under it flashes the blade in the thug's hand, just a glint in the afternoon sun, and Carney bends suddenly forward.

The thug, possibly overcome by the true enormity of this action, steps back, swallowing hard, staring at the reddened dagger.

Carney takes a backward step, grips my forearm for support.

"Hey, man," he says to his attacker, "is that the best you can do? I can take that."

But this is empty bravado. Almost immediately, he wavers and sinks back into my arms.

"Oh," he says. "Look at my new shirt."

Over his shoulder, I see The Baroness puff so hot and red, volcanic in orgasmic eruption, and, in the door, The Baron is ordering me to drop Carney, they'll deal with him.

I step back, dragging Carney, and The Baron barks at his thug to stop me, and the thug steps threateningly forward, but I can see in his face that his heart's gone out of this killing business, and I carry on toward my van.

The Baron is shouting at his thug, who stands with the dagger loose in his limp hand, and suddenly Velvet squirts out through the door like a shiny bead of quicksilver, and she flies past the thug, screaming Carney's name, throws herself on him, screaming his name in loving hysterical grief, so that now I'm dragging the weight of them both.

"Oh, baby," Carney says feebly.

"Velvet," I command, "open the sliding door! Open the sliding door!"

But she's beyond instruction, clinging to Carney, lurching and wailing.

"Open the sliding door!" I say, struggling to keep us all upright.

Behind me, I can hear the distinctive sound of the

door sliding open. A serious little boy from the group of spectator children has responded to the emergency, and has somehow opened the door. I drag my burden into the central part of the van, where the second seat was removed for the grocery run. I dump Carney there, and he's draped in Velvet kisses and tears.

I step out again, push the door closed with the unnecessary but conscientious help of the little boy. I turn just for an instant to the house. The assailant is a snowman, frozen and white, on the walk. The Baron lowers as dark as thunder behind the door, and his gargantuan wife quakes, seismically significant, behind the cracked window.

I race into the driver's seat and start the van.

Velvet is atop Carney, but beside herself.

"Maybe the hospital," Carney manages to say through the howls and her spastic screams.

I've started the van. We are actually close to St. Paul's hospital, but in Velvet's demanding din, I can't quite recollect how to operate the van's controls.

"Velvet, be quiet!" I cry, watching Alexi step out through The Baron's door. "I can't even think to drive!"

Beyond my expectations, Velvet's volume drops almost immediately, and I instantly become a driver again, squealing away from the curb and up the avenue to 20th St.

"Oh, baby," Velvet is sobbing, "it's all my fault."

I can see The Baron's big sedan following some distance behind us.

"Hey, bro," Carney says weakly, "can you get the blood outta my new suit before they bury me?"

I've heard that the city simply cremates a dispossessed street rummy like Carney, and that he would burn readily with a bright blue, blazing flame.

"Blood's hard to get out," I say, wheeling onto 20th. "You'd better stop bleeding."

There's a lot of traffic, but it's moving; nonetheless, the few blocks to the hospital seem to elongate ahead of us. Behind us, The Baron's car swings onto 20th.

"Oh, God!" Velvet cries suddenly, "He's dead, he's dead! Oh, baby, I'm so sorry! I'm so sorry!"

And she buries her little face into his sanguine shirt, smearing herself, sobbing:

"... I'm so sorry, baby, please forgive me, baby, I'm so sorry, baby, please forgive me, baby ..."

Ahead of me, the light is turning red, but I barrel through the intersection at Ave. P, turn sharply right to St. Paul's emergency entrance. I pull Velvet off Carney.

"Open the door," I say, lifting him into my arms like a big baby. This time, Velvet obeys, and in a moment, I'm through the automatic sliding doors. Carney feels very thin, barely weighs anything, it seems, and I'm able to move quickly. It may be wishful imagination, but I believe that I detect tiny shallow pants coming from him. Or maybe it's Velvet, who's just behind my ear. I'm pretty sure it's not me, for I believe I suspended my breathing back at The Baron's.

"Help us!" she broadcasts into the emergency reception area. "Help us!"

We don't represent an exceptional event to this hospital. In quick order, they've unburdened me, whisking Carney on a gurney though some other double doors; a woman in an unflattering, almost see-through pale green uniform is telling us to join a line-up to any one of three partitioned desks, and, almost simultaneously, a security guard is instructing me to move my van.

Red Velvet looks like a terrified six-year-old, but I leave her in the line, go out to the van.

There is no blood to be seen in the van; Carney's new used suit and Velvet must have absorbed it all. I look down to my chest. I've a lot of blood on me, my shirt and tie are soaked with it.

I get into my van, manage, despite shaking arms and hands, to drive into the paid parking lot. It's a small lot, but there are a few empty spaces; I think much of the hospital's business is walk-in or delivered by ambulance. As I straighten in a space, The Baron's sedan suddenly draws up behind the van.

I wait for a moment, scan out the windshield for any options or opportunities, but see none except for the dawning glimmer that a hospital parking lot is probably one of the best sites in which to be stabbed or shot, so I get out of the van, go past the sedan and start across the lot to the emergency doors. Alexi springs from the car, but I'm too unhappy and discouraged to increase my speed.

He catches up to me quickly.

"Wait up," he says.

"No, " I say. "I'm in a hurry. Just knife me and let me get on my way."

"Geez, Perles, you are a funny guy," he says.

"Yes, I always keep myself in stitches. But I suppose that's what you've come to do."

"Your bud, there, did he croak?"

"I don't know yet," I say.

"Too bad for him the neighbours were looking on, so The Baron had to make an example of him."

"He had Carney stabbed just to impress a handful of little children?"

"He's got his reputation to worry about, I guess. If Tommy wouldn't've lost his nerve like that, he'd've done you, too. That's what The Baron wanted. You're lucky to be alive."

"I'm not feeling very lucky."

"Yeah, well, you're lucky, 'cause The Baron, he sent me to finish you," Alexi says conversationally. "He coulda sent some guy'd be happy to do the job, but he sent me, and me, I don't see that it's necessary, maybe."

I stop and confront him.

"How many people have you murdered, Alexi?"

Alexi assesses me for a moment, then slowly smiles.

"Yeah, well, guess I don't wanna start now, neither."

I turn away from him again.

"Good, I guess," I say. "See you later."

"Just don't talk to the cops," Alexi cautions seriously. "Those cops, they don't want to be bothered with our stuff, anyways. They'd just pick up Tommy, and leave it at that. You don't got nothing on The Baron, anyways."

"But you do," I say in an upsurge anger. "You heard The Baron tell Tommy to kill Carney and me, didn't you?"

Alexi, to his credit, appears to entertain a moment's consideration.

"Yeah, like I'd put a gun to the head of my wife and little daughter," he says. "I'm going to kill them so we can get The Baron?"

He steps up very close to me.

"I'm supposed to finish you and Velvet," he says. "But I'm letting you go. That means, if you make trouble for The Baron, you make trouble for me. So listen, Perles: you make trouble, I won't just come and kill you two, I'll stiff that little kid, Angela, you're so worried about, too. I kinda like you, but I like my daughter better. You got it?"

I search his eyes, and find no reason to doubt that he means it.

"I've got it," I say.

"And if you don't make no trouble, I'll look out for that girl for you, how's that?" he says reasonably. "Keep her outta trouble, maybe."

"Okay," I say.

When I get back into the hospital, Velvet is sitting in a

chair, sipping water weakly from a paper cup. A police constable is looming over her. She doesn't look at him, looks past his elbow or down at her cup.

But she tells him that she didn't see what happened to Carney.

Then I tell him that I didn't see what happened to Carney. Velvet is basically telling the truth, and I'm completely lying, but the policeman demonstrates that he believes me, and doesn't believe Velvet.

We sit side by side in the waiting area, for minutes stretching into an hour and then two; crushed Velvet dissolves into tears frequently, will accept no comfort from me, not that I have much of any value to offer, seems to reject my little attempts impatiently. She still blames herself for Carney's stabbing, but by questions like "Why'd you even let him come?!", I sense that she's winding herself up to catapult some of that burden over to me.

Across from us, a middle aged woman holds a tissue under her nose as she paces to and fro, waiting to learn the condition of her husband, who's suffered a heart attack. Standing excitedly in the line to the admittance desks are a young woman and her husband; she's in labour, and advises her husband as he times intervals and durations on his watch. This is a place that spins small worlds around like a juggler.

At last, a young doctor comes out, enquires at the desk, and her attention is directed over to us. She appears very drawn and serious as she comes to us, and Velvet bursts out crying again. I can't decide if I should stand or stay sitting, so I stand.

"He's dead, isn't he?" Velvet sobs to the doctor.

"We had to do a lot of patching up inside," the doctor says to me, with what may be disapproval and without answering the pressing question, and I momentarily wonder if this is deliberately suspenseful, prolonging our punishment.

"Is he alive?" I ask sternly.

Slowly, she says "Yes, but in critical condition. He won't be out of danger for quite some time."

"How long is quite some time?"

"That will depend on his progress," she says.

"Well, let's say his progress is as could be expected, how long will quite some time be in that case?"

"That depends," she says. "He'd do better if his general state of health was better to begin with. He's in poor shape for a young man."

"Can I see him?" asks teary Velvet.

"Not now, Solania," the doctor says. "He's still under in our I.C.U. Come tomorrow morning."

Velvet whispers to me "Did she say 'I see you come tomorrow morning?'"

I look at Velvet and am suddenly filled with an additional horror and strange urgency. The doctor starts away, but I call after her.

"What about her?" I demand, motioning to Velvet. "Won't you do something for her?"

The doctor turns and regards Velvet.

"What's the matter with her?"

"Well, can't you see? She's bleeding profusely from her nose and mouth," I say sharply.

The doctor looks more closely at Velvet; Velvet puts her head to one side, touches her ruddy face.

"What's with you, Perles?" she says. "That's Carney's blood, not mine."

"What?" I say. I'm very confused.

"I'm not bleeding," Velvet says, and the doctor appraises me with a professional eye.

"No, of course not," I say. "Of course not."

"Are you okay?" asks Velvet.

"It's just all this blood that's all over us," I say, looking down with new horror at my own clothes. "We've got to get this blood off us."

I grab Velvet's hand.

"Come on, we've got to go."

I pull her out of the hospital and to the van, too fast for her comfortable pace, which may have slowed through the custom of her occupation, and she resists silently all the way, but I'm headstrong.

Only when it becomes obvious that we are departing the inner city does she enquire where we're going.

"Some place where we can get clean," I say.

I drive to Morag's house, park in front of it.

"Come in," I order Velvet.

"Whose place is this?" she asks as I unlock the front door.

"Mine, sort of. Partly mine."

I haven't been back for several weeks, and the interior is almost as strange and fresh to me as it is to Velvet. The place is clean, which is possibly what drew me to it at this moment, very unlike any environment of my recent weeks, but it's also sterile, undecorated except in ways that will display its inhabitant's correctness: an ugly squat fat little imitation primitive fertility goddess sits on the glass-topped end table, intellectual minimalist graphic art in crafty matting and simple frames fail to emanate any intrinsic meaning from the walls, academic journal and glossy book of folk art crafts on the glass-topped coffee table over the lumpy, home-spunny woven nature-tones area rug over the neutral beige hard-twist carpeting, even the Missa Luba and Holly Cole cds set out in calculated casualness on the stereo cabinet, beside the small collection of various-shaped crystal prisms, all of them where they are to express nothing of Morag but her desire to properly impress those who might see them, and all of them, of course, saying absolutely nothing about me. It has all the character of a realty developer's show-home.

I call out for Morag, and, to my relief, receive no answer.

Velvet looks around, then regards me quizzically.

"You stay at Solania's when you could stay here?" she asks, incredulous.

This is the opportunistic practical prostitute part of her, which first and foremost sizes up everyone and everything for its manipulation and exploitation potential, distorts her relationship to the world around her, the gnarled and ugly branch of her that's grown of the wrongly bent twig.

"Yes," I say, "just as you fled The Baron's house for Carney."

She sighs and nods simply. I remove my tie and tell her to take off her shirt, and at first, of course, she misconstrues my intention, is somewhat offended by the inappropriate timing, but doesn't seem all that surprised and apparently holds the question open. When she understands that I mean to launder it, she becomes, in this context, all shy and self-conscious. However, in my impatience she sighs, looks at the ceiling and quickly removes both her shirt and jeans and tosses them to me. Her underpants and little brassiere are dull grey and safely unsexy. I direct her to the kitchen sink to wash herself.

I go to the basement and put her jeans and our shirts in the washer, heap in enough detergent powder to bleach an environmentalist to chalk white shock. My tie is the one I bought the morning after Laura's murder, so it's now doubly blood-stained in my mind, and it's a relief, really, to throw it out. At the concrete sink in the basement, I scrub my stomach and chest hard, though I can't see any blood on it. There is no towel, so I go to the main bathroom on the second floor for one, and then I get two of my shirts from the master bedroom. I don one and take the other for Velvet to borrow.

By the time I get to the kitchen, Velvet has finished washing and has found Morag's vermouth. She sits with a cut crystal tumbler full of it at the diningroom table. I hand her the shirt, snatch the bottle from in front of her and take it back to the kitchen.

"I don't care, anyways," she says, taking another swig from her glass. "This stuff tastes like cat pee."

"And when did you find out what cat pee tastes like?" I say. "That must have been a desperate night."

She lets out a little girl giggle, but then sinks down onto the table, her head on her folded arms, her hand slowly twirling the glass.

"What if he doesn't get better?" she says.

"What if he does?" I say. "What are you, Velvet, fifteen or sixteen years old, and what's Carney, maybe twenty-three or four? You're both little more than babies. If Carney survives, what will it be for? So you can merely go on being a street walker, so Carney can merely go on being a doorstep drunk? Is that what we should be hoping and praying for? Some elongated death dance in hell?

"You two always talk as though you've found some simple secret, live for the day, live for the day, like it's some tribal wisdom overlooked by all those suckers caught up in the confusion of overwrought civilization, except that it's not the day you live for, but the drink, or the drug, and you don't live for it, you die for it; every crummy day, you die for the crummy day.

"So, what if he doesn't die? What are you going to do?"

"Shut up, Perles!" Velvet cries angrily, rising up in recrimination. "You don't even care if Carney lives or dies!"

"I care if he lives," I say in frustration. "But how am I supposed to care if he dies quickly over the next five hours or slowly over the next five years?"

"You don't even care!" she says gulping down more vermouth.

This is a useless exercise for me to have entered into.

"That isn't it," I say.

I go downstairs and take the clothes out of the washer. It seems that the detergent has lived up to the claims emblazoned on its box. The blood is gone. I put the clothes in the dryer and go upstairs.

Velvet has refilled her glass, but has left the bottle in the kitchen this time. The shirt I lent her lies on the floor, perhaps in fidelity to Carney, a refusal to accept any consideration from his callous betrayer.

I collect my mail from the little table in the front hall, take it to the livingroom, sit on the sofa and sort through it. Most of it is boring rubbish. Robert has told me that I've got a pile of letters sent care of the newspaper office, but I can't make time to go up and get it.

In this pile, however, is an unstamped envelope with just my name, in Morag's handwriting. Inside is a greeting card showing a uniformed Claude Rains and a trench-coated Humphrey Bogart wandering into the fog of the Casablanca runway. Inside is the message "This could be the start of a beautiful friendship...", to which Morag has added "When can we get together to talk about things?"

Velvet watches me surreptitiously from the dining table. Finally, she takes a deep breath, and says, as though the conversation was never broken: "So what's your big idea, then? What're we supposed to do?" She says it in a sort of accusatory anger, but still indicates, to my amazement, that she's actually been thinking about what I said. Then, for good belligerent measure, she adds: "You got no reason to be so high and mighty, just 'cause maybe you quit drinking; I mean, your girlfriend's a whore, too, remember, so what makes you think you got the answer?"

"Perhaps I don't have any answer," I say. "I know that the first step to finding the right answer is identifying and asking the right question. And I know that if Carney makes it, you two have to apply your lives to some positive direction. To surrender the course of your lives to blind chance anymore will seal your doom."

This pontifical pronouncement, of course, ignores the fact that it was Carney's belated attempt to take control of his circumstance that's possibly cost him his life.

And as if to assert its powers, blind chance has arranged for Morag to enter the house at that moment.

"The prodigal has returned!" she says, nervously chipper and bright.

But then her eyes fall on Velvet, who has sprung to her feet and is trying to cover her torso with my shirt. Morag's smile flickers very briefly, but sets itself again.

"And with your famous friend Solania!" she says with aplomb, but within her air of academic condescension, too. "Perles, won't you introduce us?"

"Morag, this is Carney's girlfriend, Velvet," I say, to Morag's obvious brief embarrassment. "She's a damsel in distress Carney and I rescued from a very large and dangerous dragon this afternoon."

"My gawd, what an exciting life you lead these days," Morag says with an enthusiasm I'm expected to recognize as false. "Who would've ever guessed you were capable of such courageous and romantic behaviour?"

"Certainly, you've had no reason to suspect it," I say. "Anyway, there's a difference between courageous and reckless."

"Reckless being, say, rutting with Carney's child girlfriend in our livingroom?" she says in a lofty disapproval, as though sex aversion isn't sex perversion, itself.

I explain to her about Carney and our clothes, and she's suitably shaken by the account.

I would have been pleased enough with Velvet's undressed presence even without the handy explanation, for it prevents me having to discuss the future with Morag as though I have one.

Morag fixes herself a martini, which Velvet takes as permission to finish off her tumbler of vermouth. Morag tells me that the Academicians for Armchairs have applied to her to arrange for Solania to address their group, maybe give a lecture at the university; it would seem that Morag's connection to Solania, the meticulously unmentioned me, has elevated her professional status. She shows me an example of buttons that her group has produced and are distributing throughout the academic community: 'Solania Solidarity!' the message reads. She shows it to me as a badge of merit, proof that they're doing their part in our struggle; even so, Morag can't conceal her constant condescension, as though this phenomenon is some laughable little fluke that she certainly sees right through, as a martini, for instance.

Velvet is becoming pouty in this attention to Solania, sighs aggressively, hunches her shoulders and slings her head sullenly and in the effects of her inebriation.

Morag doesn't notice, talks about me asking Solania, and related matters, until Velvet can't bear it.

"Doesn't anybody here care about Carney?!" she cries, meaning 'Doesn't anybody care about Carney's grieving girlfriend?' After all, tragedy is a total waste if it doesn't at least attract attentive pity.

Morag misunderstands the message of the question, goes to telephone the hospital to get an update on Carney's condition, which is reported as unchanged.

I get the clothes from the basement. Velvet's jeans are still slightly damp, but my restlessness has returned, and I take them up to her. She puts them on without complaint.

At the door, Morag stretches up and kisses me, squeezes my upper arms in reassurance or familiarity.

"I can never get in touch with you these days," she says.

"I'm so very busy," I say in meaningless avoidance.

"I know," she says warmly. "Call me soon, though."

"I'll try."

In the van, Velvet tells me that she needs to get to 19th Street.

"What for?" I ask.

"I gotta work my corner, of course," she says. "Or some girl'll take it."

This is the equivalent of a farmer having to get out to his fields, to take off his crop according to its timetable, whether or not his wife lays dying at home; Velvet's an industrious girl conscientiously confronting the unyielding realities of the only industry available to her.

But I tell her:

"I think you'd better render unto Caesar what is Caesar's tonight. The Baron is very displeased with you, to the extent that you may need our protection."

Velvet chews hard and fast on her lower lip.

"You mean I can't hook tonight?"

"Not if you value your life."

She ponders this a moment, then says "Take me over there, anyways. If some bitch's gonna steal my corner, I wanna know who it is."

She's such a cocky kid. The first time I encountered Velvet, I was parking my van on G, when she hopped into the front seat, thinking that I'd stopped for her. While I explained that she was mistaken, she recognized me.

"I know, you're the guy who writes about the people here," she said.

"Yes," I said, rather surprised. "Do you read my column?"

"No," she said carelessly. "Some people, they say you're trying to help the people. Is that right?"

"I guess so, if I can."

"Well, if you're trying to help the people, gimme fifty bucks."

"No."

"C'mon, man, I gotta have fifty bucks," she insisted. "I gotta, I gotta pay somebody, or they're gonna take my baby away from me."

'What are you talking about?" I scoffed.

"I mean it, man!" she cried. "These guys, they're gonna —- okay, okay, make it twenty!"

"Not a chance," I said.

"What about my baby?!" she cried, aghast at my cruelty.

"You don't have a baby," I said. "You're a baby yourself."

She pushed the passenger door open with a livid curse, and at the same time spit richly against the inside of the passenger window.

The next time I saw her, I was with Carney, whom she didn't yet know well. She laughed about our earlier exchange. She remembered it as funny.

Now, she wants me to take her to her corner, but first she wants me to take her to the drive-through window of a fast fatburger place on 22nd.

"That's the restaurant we're boycotting," I remind her.

"Yeah, but they got the best fries," she says blithely. "And I'm starved."

I take her to our designated temporary alternative,

which she accepts grudgingly. She eats a cheeseburger and pale french fried sticks that may once have been potatoes, and slurps at a milkshake, without conscious delicacy as we go along to 19th. There is no one to be seen at her corner when we pass.

The lamplit streets crawl, however, with little children, booze- and bingo-orphans, tiny, dirty ragamuffins in knots of three or four, who spend their lives being where they shouldn't be, lying at home when they should be in school, and roaming the dark, depraved, dangerous streets when they should be lying at home.

As we approach 19th and C, I catch sight of a figure lying in the back alley running between D and C, behind the Salvation Army mission. I quickly turn into the alley, shine the van's headlights onto the prostrate form. It's a young woman.

I can't tell, from the van, if she's dead, or merely passed out. What I can tell, unfortunately, is that some section of my sequential sausages of speculation here now holds the hope that she is dead;

hopes that she has been murdered in the manner of the other murdered women;

because I know for sure that I didn't murder her;

so then maybe I didn't murder the others, either.

So some part of me, as I shakily step from the van, wants her dead so I can get off the hook. And that's the little inescapable means by which the monster that lurks inside me will recreate me in its own image.

Velvet watches me with some interest, as she continues with her unhappy meal.

I bend over the woman. She's lying on her back, her arms and legs fanned out. She's wearing a clean t-shirt and clean jeans, insufficient as the night cold takes hold. She looks familiar to me, but I can't precisely place her. I am still unable to tell if she's breathing, and with my own breath held tightly, I lean my ear to her mouth. I still can't hear, so I take her wrist in my fingers. Her arm is cold, but not necessarily death-like. I turn her arm over to try for her pulse; running across her inner arm are seven or eight raised scars, roughly parallel. I reach over her for her other arm. It bears a similar pattern.

I press my fingers against the scars of the first wrist, feeling as though I'm prying into the privacy of her despairing diary by touching those suicidal welts. I can't find a pulse, but I'm inexpert in this, and the pulse may be hidden beneath the tough tissue of the scars.

I lean down again, put my ear right by her mouth, and then I can hear very rapid, very shallow breathing, as you'd expect from something like a baby bunny.

Most of me is relieved.

I slap her hand. "Can you hear me? Can you sit up?"

I sniff at her mouth. I can't smell alcohol.

What I can smell is cigarette smoke, but not coming from her. I look back to the van to see if Velvet is smoking; only then do I see a small, grey-haired man standing by the chain-link fence of the Salvation Army yard. He's wearing a white apron over his other clothes, and he's quietly and calmly smoking a cigarette, watching me.

"She's passed out," I say to him.

"Yeah," he says.

"I'm not sure she's drunk," I say. "I can't smell alcohol, her breathing is extremely shallow, and she has a history of attempted suicide. This may be serious."

"You a doctor?" he asks.

"No," I say. "Do you have a bed free in the Sally Ann?"

"We got no facilities for someone like her," he says emphatically. "Nothin'."

"Just for the moment, until we can get her some help."

"Uh-uh," he firmly shakes his head.

"Then help me get her into my van, I'll take her to the hospital," I say. I should just paint a red cross on my van.

"You don't wanna do that," he offers. "Something happens to her on the way, you'll be criminally responsible."

"That's not right."

"That's the law," he says calmly, drawing on his smoke. "You wanna call the cops."

He is joined by a larger and younger man who's also wearing an apron. I appeal to him.

"Give me a hand with her," I say. "I'm worried that she may be dying."

"She's not dying," the second man snorts. "She's been lying out here since early this afternoon."

The older man nods in agreement.

I straighten up to survey these two afresh.

"I see," I say. "And so, on your smoke breaks, you've been coming back here to, well, what? See if she's still here? Poke her? Feel her up?"

The two men look at me without reaction.

I have in my mind an image of mangy dogs which are too deficient in natural requirements to hunt, but which will opportunistically tear at the living flesh of a rabbit downed by disease.

It begins to rain. Drops splash out of the dark sky into the young woman's eyes, but this doesn't begin to rouse her.

"Velvet," I call, "bring me some papers from the van."

I look at the woman again, wonder from whence I recognize her. I realize that I don't know her, but that she looks very much like a little girl I used to know, a little girl who could run like a rabbit, easily outrunning any of her schoolmates on the makeshift track in the rough field outside her northern school; a girl who would carefully consider her answer when, in her class, she was asked to write about what she would be when she grew up, like her classmates, weighing the options and their benefits until arriving at the modest aspiration of nurse, or teacher, like her classmates, weighing the question with heartbreaking sincerity; a girl who wouldn't have answered 'When I'm grown up, I'll be an addict who's discovered that all my life's apparent choices were illusory, an addict who'll squander my energies in attempts to escape the prescribed reality of my life; when I'm grown up, I'll collapse in back alleys to be ogled, sniffed around and pawed by wasted kitchen hands from the mens shelter.", the answer that I now know would deserve full marks.

Velvet is standing beside me, extending some of our information sheets with one hand, wiping her mouth with the other.

"Hold the papers over her face," I instruct her. "Keep the rain off her face."

Velvet complies. She doesn't look at the woman, though, she's busy in critical assessment of the two apronned men.

"I'm going to call the police," I say to her. "You wait here. I don't trust these men with her."

Velvet looks as though she doesn't trust them with herself, either. They stand impassively, past shame or insult, it would seem.

Across the street from the Salvation Army building, by the edge of an empty lot, is a public telephone. On the surface of it, it's an odd place for a phone, promising little function. But, as a matter of fact, it's in frequent use by prostitutes and pushers. I've never had to use it before, myself, and I'd rather not have to now; I'd quite like to disinfect it first, but I don't even have a tissue with me.

I hold the mouthpiece as far from me as I can.

When I report the woman to the police station, the

bored woman on the other end of the line asks me: "What race is she?"

"What does that have to do with anything?" I ask.

"We like to know what race," the woman says again.

"I don't know," I say.

But we wait forty-five minutes for the police paddy-wagon to arrive, so they've deduced their answer by the location. By then, the aproned men have disappeared inside the back door of the Sally Ann, and Velvet is flaked out on the back seat of my van. The young woman hasn't so much as twitched in that time. The two cops who come are the ones who showed up at Solania's first little protest, outside the God's Right Hand ministry. They snap on their latex gloves as they saunter to the woman.

One of the cops crouches down and slaps the woman's face, saying "Honey, I'm home, how was your day?" His partner opens the side door of their wagon.

The woman shows no sign. The cop pulls a metallic pen from his pocket, takes her hand, and presses the barrel of the pen hard against her fingers between the first and second knuckles, rolling it back and forth, bears down on it until the woman finally whimpers in response.

"What are you doing there?" I ask.

"I'm not doing anything," he says defensively. "I'm just holding my new girlfriend's hand. You're my new girlfriend, aren't you, baby?"

As he continues to roll the pen, the woman ineffectually, awkwardly attempts to crawl away. The two cops scoop her up.

"Whoa, baby," says the first. "You aren't forgetting our date, are you?"

But she's passed out again, almost immediately, so they drag her to the door of the wagon and pretty much throw her in to sprawl on its steel floor, and lock the door after her.

The first cop looks at me with a smirk and shake of the head as he pulls off his gloves, as if to say he's seen it all before.

"The problem," I find myself saying to him, "is that you haven't seen it all; you've seen one tiny aspect of it over and over again, but you haven't seen her as a little girl studiously writing down her hopeless unassuming hopes for her future, you haven't seen her, with all her birthright energetic elan, race around a scrubby track as though she was winning the Olympics. You haven't seen it all; all you've seen is what's left over when we get through with her. You've scarcely seen anything, and that's your problem."

He looks at me, and his smirk transforms to scowl.

"You're the one with the problem," he says, getting into the passenger seat.

In another moment, they're gone.

"They didn't see me, did they?" Velvet calls from my van.

"No," I say, climbing in.

I start the van and drive the short distance to Solania's house, and tell Velvet to come in with me.

It being a rainy night, the front hall is crowded with otherwise homeless people, and we pick our way through them, and downstairs to Solania's tiny apartment.

Buster is sitting on the mat in the narrow passageway leading to her door. At the sight of me, he springs up, waving his hands before him.

"Hey, Perles," he says, strangely agitated. "How about you take a walk around the block or something?"

"What?"

"Cool it for a little while, could you, man? She says she doesn't want to be disturbed for a while."

"I want to talk with her," I say firmly.

But he is adamant, and won't move to allow me to pass.

"What's going on, Buster?" I say.

"Geez, man," he says apologetically, "just give it five minutes, will you? Just take a nice walk around the block."

"Geez, Perles," opines Velvet, "does he need to draw you a picture?"

I lean against the damp, cool concrete wall, look down at my feet and try to quell my stomach.

"C'mon, man," Buster says kindly. "Why don't you make it easier for yourself?"

"Why should I make it easier for her?" I ask.

"You know how she is," he offers.

"I guess I don't," I say. "Or, rather, I didn't."

The moldy atmosphere is contributing to my nausea, and a walk in the rain actually appeals to me as much as anything could, and I would start back out the passage, but Velvet is in my way, and she's confused about what it is I intend, and I'm caught in an instant of inarticulation.

And then behind me, from behind Solania's thin door, there comes a loud smack, a cry of panic and pain, and a man's voice yells "You dirty bitch, you cut me!"

I turn, and Buster bursts through the flimsy door, stands in the briefest scan of the room, which is long enough for me to see red-faced and red-handed Rod, the city councillor, standing, bent slightly in hasty readjustment at the crotch of his trousers, over sprawled Solania. Rod looks up just in time to see Buster plummeting at him, and he screams like a little girl, kicks, wrenches and scratches as Buster takes him in a hammerlock down to the bed.

I step through the door.

Rod is screaming, and Solania is smiling, but she's bleeding profusely from her nose and mouth. I bend to her immediately, but her expression changes to alarm, and she tries to scrabble away from me, until she's backed against her little sink.

"Stay away from me!" she cries. "Don't touch me!"

"I'm not going to hurt you," I say.

"Stay away, please, dear!" she says, cupping her hands under her chin, collecting the flow. She rises up quickly, if unsteadily, bends over the sink and runs the water over her hands and face.

Rod is gurgling in Buster's hold as though he might die. He looks to me beseechingly, eyes bulging.

"Perles," he gags out.

"What?" I say.

"Help me," he gags.

"Kill him, Buster," I say.

Rod squeezes out a little mangled cry, he struggles uselessly, and tears overflow his eyes.

"Oh, wait, I meant don't kill him, Buster," I say.

Buster relaxes his hold minimally. Rod starts to sob and gasp most annoyingly.

"Take him out to the hall. But don't let him go."

Buster jerks him up and drags him out. On the bed sit five twenty dollar bills. I shoo Velvet out to the hall and close the door.

"Let me see you," I say to Solania.

"Don't touch me," she says again.

"I won't, but let me see you."

She raises her face to me. Her lower lip is split and is starting to swell, but is no longer bleeding badly. Her nose still flows, and she tips her head back.

"Don't do that, you can choke or breathe blood into your lungs," I say.

I take a paper towel and run it under the water, fold it into a rectangle and place it over her nose.

"Now pinch your nostrils, to constrict the blood vessels."

"Okay," she says, batting big teary eyes up at me. "Thank you, sweetheart."

"Don't stop until I get back and check it," I tell her.

"Yes, dear."

She steps weakly to the bed. Before she sits down on it, she carefully picks up the bills with her free hand and puts them into her pocket.

Out in the little passage, Buster holds Rod in something that might be a full nelson; I've forgotten much about childhood wrestling. Velvet looks on with interest. Rod hangs like rag doll, has forsaken his struggle.

He returns my contemptuous stare with an appeal to our fellowship.

"Perles," he mews in self-justification, "she cut me."

"You don't look cut to me," I say. "Where did she cut you?"

He casts his eyes meaningfully down to his open fly.

"She had something sharp in her mouth," he sobs, as though me hearing that will help his case somehow.

"Well, let's examine the wound," I say for the cruel fun of it, and Rod whimpers and squirms pleasingly.

"Let's beat the snot out of him," says Buster, clenching his teeth in savour.

"So he can publically portray himself as the innocent victim of our random violence? No, thanks," I say. "We need a more subtle punishment."

"Just let me go, for gawdsake. It's all a stupid mistake," Rod cries. "Okay, I was wrong, I admit it. I've learned my lesson, Perles, I swear."

"One more word," I hiss, "and I'll line up all those people upstairs, and give them the chance, one by one, to take out all their frustrations on a real city councillor. One more word."

Rod regards me with bug-eyed terror, and I'd allow

the minutes to stretch out in my miserable enjoyment of it all, but Buster is growing weary and impatient.

"Velvet," I say, "give this guy a big purple hickey."

"What?" she says. "Are you kidding?"

"A big purple one, on his neck, right under his jaw-line, where his collar won't cover it."

Buster holds Rod more tightly, and Velvet rolls her eyes.

"Okay," she says with a shrug. She leans into his neck like a vampire, and Rod, wild-eyed, jerks and sputters, then screams.

"Come, come, Councillor, just let those eastside fantasies flood back into your fevered brain. A pretty, young westside girl is sucking on you. Lean back and revel in it."

"I'll kill you, Perles, I swear!" he cries frantically.

"By golly, I hear that a lot these days," I say.

It soon evolves that Velvet is amazingly adept at applying a hickey. The thing that she leaves on Rod's neck looks like it could start talking at any moment.

"There, now," I say. "How are you going to explain that at home, Rod?"

Buster erupts in a guffaw of delight.

Rod glares at me, his eyes so hot with hatred, his tears boil. I tell Buster to take him upstairs and deposit him outside.

I return to Solania's room. She's standing at the sink, stripped to the waist, holding her nose with one hand, and washing her shirt with the other. My life is becoming repetitious in the worst ways.

Solania is impossibly thin. Every fine bone, every sinew and every striation of every slender muscle shows as though she's an anatomy lesson, as though Leonardo drew her as a silverpoint study. She's impossibly beautiful.

I sit on the bed and watch her a long time.

"How's your nose?" I ask at last.

She carefully removes the paper towel.

"It's stopped bleeding, but it sure is sore."

"You can't blow it, no matter how badly you want to. All right?"

"All right.'

"He says you put something sharp in your mouth, to cut him."

She looks down to her shirt, squeezes and rinses it again and again.

"Is that true?" I ask eventually. "Would you do that?"

She sighs, and looks up to the dark little window.

"I have a tooth, a molar with a sharp edge on it," she says.

"I see," I say. "Is it decayed?"

"No."

"Then why does it have a sharp edge on it?"

She turns to me, inspects me closely. My own heart begins to pound in the rhythm of her breathing.

"Wait, I don't want to know," I say suddenly.

"I filed it," she says, watching me still.

I breathe deeply several times.

"You filed it," I say slowly. "As with a nail file, you mean?"

"A nail file didn't work properly," she says in a hushed voice. "I had to get a little metal file."

"Oh," I say. "I wouldn't have thought that would be necessary."

"Yes," she says. "My teeth are very hard."

"Yes, I guess so. Of course, the question remains," I say, but I don't think I want to give sound to the question. I stare at her in silence.

"The question remains," Solania says, her coy smile slowly creeping across her swelling mouth, "why would I file my tooth?"

"Yes."

"I filed my tooth," she says very slowly, "so that it would be very sharp ... so that I could cut anything a man puts into my mouth."

She smiles at me, and I look at her. I don't smile back.

"Oh," I say. "I see."

She stops smiling.

"I can't expect you to understand."

"If you don't expect me to understand, why did you tell me?" I ask. "To drive me away?"

"I told you——," she says, faltering slightly. "I told you because telling you such a thing is the only form of intimacy that's been left to me."

Putting this into words brings an upwelling of tears to her, which I can't bear to see, so I look away, to the black-ribboned school photograph of her sister, which doesn't help, then to the cement floor.

She steps over to me, cradles my head against her narrow naked chest, and I can hear her heart and her light, whispery sobbing.

She says "But all I've done is make you hate me."

I close my eyes, listen to her interior workings.

"I don't hate you. I love you."

I take her arms and steer her to sit beside me.

She blinks bravely.

"I love you. I could never stop loving you," I say. "But I don't think I can stand anymore. I see that hell just keeps spiralling downward, and I've slid into it farther than I can endure."

She takes my arm and hugs it to her.

"Maybe you can endure more than you think," she suggests.

I shake my head and stand up before her, then bend

and kiss her forehead.

"See you," I say.

"When will you be back?"

"I don't know."

"Will you be back?"

"I don't know," I say.

I go to the door.

"How am I supposed to not blow my nose, if you're going to make me cry?" she says.

I close the door behind me and go upstairs.

On the stairs leading to the second floor, Velvet and Buster sit talking.

"Hey, man," Buster calls as I go by. He hops down to catch me. "Velvet, she's been telling me about Carney. She says you saved his life."

I glance over to Velvet.

"I haven't saved anybody's life," I say to Buster.

"What're we going to do about The Baron?" he asks darkly.

"What do you mean?"

"We can't just take that lying down, man. Carney, he's one of our own."

"What's your thinking, Buster?" I ask. I sweep my hand toward the feeble raggedy men slumped around the hall. "Shall we send some of our tottering scarecrows to go over and rough up The Baron's thugs? Or how about we send over some picketers? The Baron's boys can pick them off one by one as they march past, like at the midway."

"We gotta do something," Buster insists.

"Ours is a social activism group, if it's even that," I tell him. "It's not a gang, it's not an army, and we're in no position to mount a campaign of either aggression or retribution. When we go to the mattresses, it's just so some eastsider can screw us for a few bucks. So put your militant daydreams away."

I walk out through the rain, which is now falling heavily, to my van, and I drive away without confronting the fact that I've nowhere to go. I drive through these streets, through the rain that could teem and teem and still not clean them, until, with incoherent cries of exasperation, I park on 20th St. and watch the rain run down the fogging windshield.

Once, when I was a boy, when I was in a field that was far from here, my attention was caught by panicked squeaking near my feet; I peered down through the grass, and there went scooting by a garter snake with a baby mouse in its mouth; I've heard that snakes eat their prey head first, but this snake was eating the mouse backward, tail first, and the mouse's front legs and head were still outside the snake's maw as it slithered by, and the baby was squeaking, high pitched and desperate, and there, chasing right on the snake's tail was the mother mouse, darting forward and biting the tail of the snake.

Being a soft-hearted boy, I ran after them, wanting to help the baby and its valiant mother somehow. The snake stopped and turned on the mother in feint, and she darted forward, overcoming every impulse toward her own survival, and attacked the snake time and again as the snake slowly swallowed the squeaking baby. Eventually, the mother became aware of my looming presence, and that was too much for her; it was I who finally sent her scurrying away in defeat.

Obviously, I've always remembered that event as somehow significant, but I never anticipated that it would become the recurrent defining image of these days of my descent, of snakes preying on helpless babies as their mothers protest uselessly and I interfere in futility.

I lower my spinning, aching head to the steering wheel, rest it the for some time, watching the shadows and reflections of the rivulets on the window projected onto the passenger seat.

There, below the seat, peeping out like a mouse but hissing like a snake, is the neck of the bottle Carney bought earlier that day. I reach down for it, lift it to my lap. It's nearly full.

The main problem with never sleeping is that one doesn't get to awaken from one's nightmares.

I weigh Plans A and B, balance them one against the other over the fulcrum of this bottle's mouth; pursuit of either will require its contents, either for the temporary oblivion of Plan A, or for the reckless nerve for the permanent oblivion of Plan B.

I remove the cap, take a big gulp that crashes like a frothy breaker inside my brain, and as it washes out again, it reveals a rabbit near-drowned in the sand, and two scabrous dripping dogs tearing at its living flesh; another long swallow, and another crashing wave which recedes to reveal Carney lying dying, sodden in red tide flowing from his first suit. Another pull, another wave, racing out to reveal a ribbon of black velvet tied to a hook, cast out into the roaring surf to catch sharks and barracudas and stingrays and eels.

I gulp and gulp and gulp, it's a tidal wave smashing my beachhead to brine damage, I'm swirling breathless in its undertow; it tumbles wildly out again, and there, beached, out of her element, is my beautiful Solania, sprawled, stranded on the strand, naked from the waist up like a mermaid, smiling but flipping and gasping and bleeding profusely from the mouth, but from what? from another hook? from an easterly blow? or is it the blood of what she's been eating?

This stuff is hitting me harder than I ever remember it, and choices of either A or B are already now as governable as a game of spin the bottle.

Anyway, I've named my poison, and I suck at it again. I loudly toast Carney, who's toast, as they say, I say with a rye smile. My sharp tooth of the ungrateful chide of Solania, my sharp serpent tooth is lacerating my lashing, flicking forked tongue, faithless in its pledge to my beautiful Solania, so I anaesthetize it and disinfect it simultaneously, this is marvelous stuff, when you consider all it might do.

I pull and pull again. I stumble to the back seat and collapse onto it, and pull again. I close my eyes and try to spin the bottle in the direction of radiant golden Christine, but I can't find her anywhere, just as I won't find my shimmering silver Solania soon enough, because, in the hard weather, I'm the night rain on the windshield, black and refractory as I run away.

*   *   *

Into my cold damp clouds there wafts a misty fragrance of roses, like a child's first cheap toilet water, sweet and unsophisticated. My neck is aching sharply, I'm lying awkwardly beside someone whom I dimly assume to be Solania, except the fragrance is contradictory, and in a slowly surfacing curiosity, I pry open my sore eyes, and the sight for them is Rose's face right at mine, just about nose to nose.

My heart starts, I stare at her in alarm, and my kettle head rings and cracks like the libertine bell as I become aware that she's not breathing. There's no question: she's not breathing.

I cry out in terror, roll right off the back seat of my van, roll about on poor Rose's grocery-sorting platform, I'm gasping uselessly in wrenching convulsion, o! poor poor Rose who never harmed or offended anyone, who never generated anything inside me of which I was aware but sympathy and appreciation.

I can't stand the blast of this gun-metal morning. I writhe like a crushed cat, forward to the driver's seat, with shallow stacatto sobs I pull myself up into it. I claw at my brow and eyes.

Why do I spare the despicable and kill those who've aroused my sympathy? Candylaurabethlaylarose, Candylaurabethlaylarose, Candylaurabethlaylarose has never done anything but generate sorrow and kindness in me.

This is the recognition that I have so awfully avoided, and it swells and explodes in my head right now.

My worst cancerous fear is confirmed, that it's not some other, separate part inside me, a distinct monster of vicious hatred that is murdering these women, which might somehow be suppressed by vigilance and love, but a monster of misdirected pity and love relieving the forlorn of their suffering; what I've always failed to do in my life, try as I might, is place any controls or limitations upon my pity and love. That is every bit of me, and so my mania is all that I am, I am grotesque, perverted in distortion to the very bone, and without remedy.

I am the monster that screams with love.

I scream with love into my monster hands now.

Through the windshield, I see the gaping grey maw of my future, my very very short future. I shall drive my careening van into it, I shall test the new iron railings of the University Bridge, and as I plunge downward into the grey funnel, I shall somehow clasp the pressed Rose to me and beg her forgiveness.

Hand palsies down to pants pocket.

My car key isn't there.

I check the ignition. The key isn't there, either.

Desperately, I wrack what's left of my addled brain.

Somehow, I adjust the rearview mirror to fix on the corpse of Rose. The possibility looms that the key slid from my pocket as I ghoulishly lay beside her. I can't see it from here; it may have slipped beneath her.

For someone who plans to clasp her to me at the ultimate moment, I'm having real difficulty in steeling myself to go back and root underneath her for the key.

I sit slumped for a little while, mainly looking out the windshield, telling myself that I've surrendered any right to indulge squeamish sensitivities.

Then I rise up and totter to the rear seat.

I bend down.

"I'm sorry, Rose," I say for this latest indignity.

I plunge my hand under her.

And Rose shoots up in silent surprise.

I cry out horribly, and collapse backward, between the front seats.

We stare at each other.

Well, of course, it's Rose, of course she wasn't breathing, at least not through her nose or mouth. I ejaculate a sort of dreadful laugh-cry.

She gulps at the the grey early-morning air, but communicates through her expression of deepest regret and apology. She starts up to flee, but I manage to snag her arm.

"Don't go, Rose, don't go," I say, crawling up to sit beside her on the seat. "I was startled, I didn't know that you were still —- here. O! Rose!"

"I'm sorry," she burps, with a pleading sort of smile. "You were so cold, I tried to warm you."

"O! Rose!"

I still hold her arm, and it does feel lovely and warm in my icy hand, as I shiver beside her. She wears her usual black jeans and white shirt, but a lined raincoat drapes her far shoulder. It would seem that it had been our blanket.

"Sorry," she burps.

"Don't be sorry, you were very kind. I'm grateful to you."

"I should go."

"No," I say, "I'd like you to stay, please."

She nods simply, bobs the ends of her braids against her shirtfront, leans into me lightly to share her warmth as I tremble, and she looks out the windshield in some concealed contemplation as, for breakfast, I spoon through my scrambled brains.

"How did we happen to be together?" I ask eventually.

"I came to the corner for my papers," she says. "Saw your door open here. You were sitting here," and she motions to the side doorway, "getting wet in the rain. You said you were enjoying the seaside."

She smiles widely, as though this was either comical or quizzical.

"I suppose I was drinking."

She nods.

"Sorry," she says. "I took it away from you. Sorry."

"That's all right. I'm glad you did."

"I took your car keys, too, just to be on the safe side."

"Oh. Good, good."

She nods again.

"You were so cold."

"Was I ... did I behave properly toward you?" I ask hesitantly.

"Oh, yes, Mr. Perles," she says seriously. "You're always a gentleman when you're drinking. Don't worry."

"I am?"

She nods her considered approval. "Always a gentleman."

"But how many times can you have you seen me when I'm drinking?" I ask.

"Some times. I see a lot on my deliveries, late night, early morning." She holds her hands up as though it's obvious.

Rose's necessity of gulping air to speak causes her to pause at unusual intervals; the effect of this is to impart an import and air of careful thought to what she says.

"Always a gentleman?" I ask.

She nods. "And always so sad. Why are you so sad, Mr. Perles?"

Actually, I'd have said that I was so full of horror, disgust and tortured love, anything as passive as sadness wouldn't find a spot in me on which to settle. For a moment, I'm about to give her some answer that's elusive, such as "Because I'm too tired to be crazy.", but automatic slippery flippancy never strikes me as being appropriate to Rose, somehow, and never less so than right now. And suddenly, instead, I find myself telling her about Christine, something I've never done with anyone else.

I tell her how Christine and I, desperately in love, and fresh from university in the east, drove across the country in my old van with the mattress in the back, camping through the late summer, travelling to our first teaching jobs in an isolated, far northern community; how blighted and benighted we found the community to be when we got there, how it laid me low in the face of our professional impossibility; how it brought out the despair in me, but the best in Christine, how she rose with courage and intelligence and dedication to all its challenges; how the example of Christine's commitment and compassion was the wellspring source of my small successes there; how Christine's own considerably more significant successes renewed her commitment everyday, but after two years of grim struggle, the pall of the place became more than I wanted to bear any longer; how I convinced myself that my artistic literary calling and its fragile sensibilities required a more congenial, colourful environment to become productive; how much for granted I came to take Christine's love for me; how I convinced myself that she would respond in my favour to the ultimatum I placed before her, and then, when she responded in the interest of the other people she'd come to also love, I idiotically convinced myself that there would be another Christine for me wherever I went, Toronto, New York, Paris, in pursuit of my creative muse.

"I never got to Toronto or New York or Paris, of course," I tell Rose, "and my creative muse lacked any fidelity, and then, in irony, I end up immersed in a neighborhood no more favoured than the community I abandoned so many years ago, only this time I confront it without Christine's strength and comforts.

"I'm so sad because, for years, my soul has stumbled in the darkness in forlorn search of the inspiration that provided all the light of my life. Instead of emulating her strength and selflessness and courage, I succumbed to my weakness and vanity and cowardice. And in doing so, I surrendered all meaning and significance.

"I used to sustain myself with stupid hopes that one day I might be redeemed by our reunion, but finally I came to realize that I was no longer a person whom she could love. Some sins are mortal, Rose, some self-inflicted wounds are beyond recovery."

Rose nods in silent sympathy, absently fingers the remnant nazi tattoo on her wrist. She rummages in the pocket of her raincoat, and pulls out my key, but also a battered man's wallet, which she opens and from which she draws a small school photograph. She hands it to me. It's of a teenaged girl who smiles brightly, and resembles Rose.

"Is this your daughter?" I ask.

Rose nods, smiles like her daughter.

"She's as pretty as you are," I say. "Have you heard from her lately?"

Rose's smile flies away, and she shakes her head.

"You see," she says, "we both long for someone who deserved better from us."

She takes the photo and looks at it lovingly before returning it to her wallet.

"But we can recover from our wounds, Mr. Perles," she says. "Jesus found me, and now you've got Solania."

"Have I? I'm not sure at all that I've got her. And Jesus never came back to you, Rose," I say, but not contentiously.

"I just wait," she says. "One day he'll show me why he saved me. I know it must have been for some good reason."

She looks out to the lightening morning sky, sits that way for a while in apparent contemplation of the better day to come, when His plan is revealed to her, that which makes sense of her latterday toil and loneliness.

"My papers," she says suddenly. "I still gotta do my papers!"

She smiles at me as if to say 'Where's my head?' as she springs up to the sliding side door. She's very familiar with this van by now, and she opens it slickly.

I take her arm again as she steps out.

"Rose," I say, on impulse, "do you ever wonder why He didn't heal you, make you whole while He had the handy opportunity?"

Rose regards me steadily, weighing her answer.

"I guess He likes me the way I am," she burps.

"Yes, I guess so," I say.

I step out to the sidewalk and watch her hurrying away, pulling on her raincoat as she goes. Up on the next corner, I see the pile of her newspapers, wrapped in plastic against the rain, which has now stopped.

Everything about 20th St. is grey, clammy and dispiriting. Beside me, limp, torn and faded notices for tedious events that are long over with, anyway, hang from a lamp post, notices for special bingos or fifth-rate wrestling matches or tenth-rate singer-guitarists, or other little nozzles to suck up the last available pennies of the undiscriminating, undeserving underclass.

I turn to close the sliding door, but my eye catches sight of a corner of something sticking out from under the rear seat. I don't know what it can be, think it must be Rose's, so I reach for it quickly. It's a small ratty old blue receiving blanket. I hold its corners, let it fall open before me.

"I recognize this," I say aloud. "This isn't Rose's, is it?"

I cock my head to peer under the back seat.

"Who knows how long it's been under there?" I say.

I shake it out absently, it flaps limply like an old out-dated notice of scheming misrepresentation and manipulation for an event long passed; then I fold it neatly, and place it back under the seat.

"Possibly ever since Candy had to let go of it," I answer myself.

I shiver again in this atmosphere, then I get behind the wheel, drive my van to the house where Solania stays.

I find Buster on the pad outside her door, sleeping, but he awakens at my approach, watches me silently as I step by him.

I push her door open quietly and enter into the concrete gloom of her room. She lies small and precious on her bed. Her lips are badly swollen now, but this does almost nothing to diminish her beauty, and does nothing at all to lessen my longing to hold her in my arms.

I lie down beside her, slide my arm under her head.

She stirs, grips the front of my shirt and pulls herself into my chest.

"Oh, my darling," she whispers. "I knew you'd come back to me."

"How much do you love me? Answer me truthfully."

"I love you without reservation. I love you completely, with all my heart, and I always will."

I sigh through her short black hair.

"Nothing else is as I want it to be," I say.

"Oh, I know, I know," she coos softly. "But, darling, that's why you're here."

Chapter Nine

There he is, the new king pimp with his Jezebel whores!" cries Rod the Councillor, his voice ringing through the megaphone with all the fervour he once displayed in hailing the coming revolution. It echoes across 20th St. from the podium set up on the tail of the shiny new pick-up truck in the supermarket parking lot.

I am just stepping out of The Friendship Inn, and Rod is in the middle of his repeated harangue in which he promises to put forward a motion to suspend all city funding of The Friendship at the next Council Meeting. He stands flanked by his new brothers-in-arms, M.P. Aiken, Pastor Enos, and the president of COIN. I am accompanied by Ken, Velvet, Rose and little Angela, so I suppose that Velvet and Angela are the Jezebel whores to whom he's referring. The new king pimp, I know, is supposed to be me. Relatively speaking, of course, it's preferable to the other possibilities I've been confronting.

Rod knows no caution. Buster's brother, the tall, hard Russell stands right before him, unperturbedly surrounded by congregated opponents of our initiatives, his arms folded, watching Rod's performance from behind reflective sunglasses, but Rod, unlike Aiken or Enos, doesn't find Russell's presence to be any cause for more circumspect rhetoric, any more than the thing under that bandage on his neck causes him to reconsider denouncing Velvet.

Actually, Rod is nursing many apparent areas of pulsing florid discolour in his neck and brow as he fulminates about our ruthless assault upon all things decent in the larger society, our flagrant flouting of the very foundations that made this city, this province and this country great.

"We can't live without social order, can we?" Rod cries, and Enos cries amen! and Aiken cries hear! hear! and the president of COIN grunts in applause of Rod's perceptive insight.

His depiction of me comes as no surprise, for in the other newspaper last week, my counterpart columnist described me thusly in an item headed 'Strings of Perles: Puppetmaster Becomes Pimpmaster, Says Insider.' The quoted unidentified insider, who related having witnessed me ordering a young girl to enter into a sexual activity merely to prove my new iron-fisted command, is surely none other than Rod, and now Rod quotes the columnist quoting him.

The fact is, I do have an awful lot of prostitutes around me these days, or former prostitutes, actually, mostly bewildered refugees to our camp after the recent very messy matter of The Baron left them feeling vulnerable and threatened, and who often approached us on the advice of Alexi, one of the few survivors of the attack and someone The Baron's prostitutes had come to trust.

And we have a great many of bewildered refugees from the boycotted bingo halls, purple dabber junkies who are just now reattaching their adrenaline addictions to Solania's sessions and visions. The bingo boycotts are proving to be successful, as is the pawnshop boycott. While Aiken and Enos and the religious right continue to bring in eastside customers for the supermarket, and the grocery boycott must be regarded as a failure so far, the Knights of Columbus have been less effective in filling their bingo palace with eastside suckers, and COIN has, strangely, encountered a complete failure to bring in eastsiders to take up the slack in their usury pawnshops.

With the pawnshops out of bounds and the prostitutes out of business, cash is getting scarce - though the erstwhile bingo junkies are relatively to the good - and with the steady influx of rural pilgrims, the burden on The Friendship Inn has risen by a couple of thousand meals a day. The Roman

Catholic Church and the United Church are organizing emergency donations, demonstrating that a bit of what The Lord taketh away through bingos, He sometimes giveth through the soup kitchen.

The Freedom of Form Support Group, perhaps having resolved in subcommittee that Solania is as thin as she is through either male-manipulated anorexia or poverty-enforced starvation, have volunteered en masse, so to speak, as cooks and servers for the noontime meal at The Friendship, showing up with their hair close-cropped and wearing very large flannel shirts and capacious jeans. This evinces an imprecise understanding of our objectives: our point is that our people need meaningful things to do, need the opportunity for useful employment; we are, just as a beginning, more than able to cook for and serve ourselves.

Sharon has nothing for the Freedom of Form women to do, so she turned the problem of them over to me.

I suggested to Morag, to whom an imitation of Solania is quite unbecoming, that her group would be more useful to us out on 20th St., augmenting our now numerous picket lines and showing support from outside the inner city. They liked this idea even better, and they arrive promptly everyday for Solania's sessions and then their picket duty.

We've had to set up loudspeakers outside The Friendship, and our adversaries across the street conduct bizarre amplified debates, mockeries and running refutations which we can't hear inside, but which make for clouds of confusing cacophony for Solania's hordes of supporters crowded on the sidewalk.

How Perles went from Puppetmaster to Pimpmaster:

The day after Carney's stabbing, two men in a stolen slummobile drove to the outskirts of the city, to the clubhouse of the biker gang that had been greedily eyeing The Baron's entrepreneurial holdings. The two men, whose faces were concealed behind bandanas worn bandit-style, but who were reported by a witness to resemble The Baron's type of thug, stepped from the rumbling car with two rifles and promptly set about shooting out the windows of the club-house. Then they leapt back into the car and roared away.

Aside from the windows and walls, nothing was hurt in the clubhouse but biker pride, and war was declared.

Alexi insists that the two attackers weren't The Baron's boys, that they were all oblivious to and unprepared for any war with the bikers. However, when, early the next day, three hogs on hawgs thundered up The Baron's residential street, the slummobile was parked nearby, and that would seem to have been adequate evidence in their miniscule minds, and their retribution was swift.

Taking their own weapons from hawg holsters, they shot to shards the window that Carney had cracked with the rock. And then, to up the antagonistic ante, they threw a small bundle of dynamite sticks through the window frame into the front room.

According to Alexi, at the time of the attack, The Baron's household was lounged about the front room, occupied in the innocent amusement of a t.v. programme wherein an aggregate of ugly, inarticulate teenaged husbands were, one by one, confronting their doughy child brides with the information that they'd recently impregnated the brides' mothers.

When the glass started flying, the more mobile members of the household dove for the protection of corners; The Baroness, of course, was beached in the centre of the room, and was, aside from some futile rolling ripples and savage screeches, helpless under the onslaught. In the brief period of calm after the shooting, The Baron ordered a thug or two to crawl over the broken glass to see if The Baroness' screeches were of agony or fury; just as they were expressing that this seemed an unappealing assignment to them, the bundle flew through the window opening. By his good fortune, Alexi spied it for what it was before the bundle buried itself in one of the hidden valleys of The Baroness Range. And, as quick on his feet as Solania had warned him he would need to be, he grabbed little Angela by her stick arm and flew out the front room doorway. He was closely followed by The Baron himself, who also seems to have recognized the explosives. His massive girth, however, became lodged in the doorway, and, despite panicked pushing from the other side, he effectively sealed the doom of those remaining in the room. At the instant of the explosion, Alexi was shielding Angela beneath him in the corner of the front hall by the front door, The Baroness was squealing like a careless abattoir, and the red-faced Baron, Alexi said, was squirting tears out like a water pistol in his self-pity. A desperate thug was attempting to scale him.

The Baron, albeit inadvertently, saved Alexi's life, his lodged enormity protecting Alexi from the effects of the blast.

Alexi wasn't too, too graphic in his description, but he suggested that there was sufficient Baroness to thickly coat the whole first floor of the house, walls and ceilings, and much of the front yard. The concussion killed The Baron and everyone else trapped in the room.

Angela was typically silent and self-possessed throughout all this. Sitting stock still in the front seat of The Baron's big sedan as Alexi careened it away, she steadfastly refused to be returned to the mother and stepfather who'd drunkenly surrendered her to The Baron's designs for her, wouldn't reveal their address.

So Alexi drove around through the strident siren songs until he thought of Solania's words to him. He pulled up in front of our house just as Solania and I were returning from our Chinese cafe breakfast.

He led Angela from the car to where we stood waiting.

"Here's your gift," he said to Solania.

Solania reached down and stroked the girl's black hair.

"The Baron," she said slowly. "He's dead?"

"Yeah," Alexi said without obvious surprise. "He's dead, all right."

Solania gripped my arm more tightly.

"Are you sure?"

"He's dead, all right," Alexi confirmed. "The missus, too."

Solania began to sway lightly on my arm, and I looked to her in concern. Her eyes were closed, and she wore a small, but ecstatic, smile.

"Wait here," she whispered after a moment. "I'll be out in just a minute."

She went inside the house. I sat on the front step, mulling things over, and looking at little Angela.

"See," said Alexi, sitting down next to me. "I kept my word to you, too."

"You would seem to be a man of honour."

Angela rocked lightly, withdrew into herself under my scrutiny. Alexi gave me a first brief account of the morning's event.

"It was the bikers. I saw'em," he said when I questioned him more closely.

I studied Angela.

"Are you all right?" I asked her.

"Uh-huh," she said without looking at me.

"Are you frightened?"

"Mm-mm."

Maybe Angela wasn't frightened, but it proved out

over the next days that the bikers' methods were too much for most of the women and girls whose career management they'd wished to assume. Many of them sought the refuge of Solania's nebulous promise of some sort of redemption over the bikers' threats and offers of a steady drug supply, quit the street, and several even took the sobriety pledge. And they attend Solania's sessions, where they've been seen collected around me by people who don't tell how they recognize them as hookers; which is how I became the new pimp king.

Morley has confided that the bikers believe that somehow I've snookered them, concede that I am the pimpmaster, and that for the time being I'm too powerful to be challenged.

What isn't explained is why I don't have my hookers out on the street, making me money. Maybe I'm creating an artificial shortage, forcing the price up, like an oil cartel.

Solania's visions continue to arrive inside her, apparently on demand; and it's become a regular practice to conclude her sessions with the presentation to her of damaged or forlorn people, not for some miraculous cure, but for Solania's sanctification of their suffering, as if every hurt is a war wound, or a battle scar in our struggle for our freedom. "Who hurt this woman?" Solania will cry, and it's never her loutish husband who's carved out her horrible hare lip, he's only the weapon in the hands of our enemies.

It makes me cringe, every time.

Carney has been transformed in these sessions from a reckless romantic fool into a fallen freedom fighter; it's a story that inspires the prostitutes in particular, the heroic glowing gallant emerging from the grit and gloom to liberate the hostage harlot sex-slaves, with enough truth to sustain it. That Carney continues to hover between life and death is a nerve-racking circumstance that someone who isn't in love with Solania might suspect her of exploiting with cynical calculation. It goes unmentioned, of course, that his recovery would have been much expedited if he hadn't been tearing himself apart in tremendous delirium tremens.

Solania quietly, patiently tells me that the people need these presented exemplar embodiments of their own suffering in order to really personalize the impediments, prohibitives to their progress.

Today's session concluded with Alexi, who's now regarded as a sort of Gawain to Carney's Galahad, a lesser but still noble knight, pushing little Angela forward through the pressing crowd to Solania; the people, perhaps sensing something of the emotional wallop to follow, broke apart to make way for the steady little girl, receded like the Red Sea, stood in a hush of anticipation.

Solania, eyes closed, of course precisely framed Angela's little face within her feathery hands, pulled her to her and kissed her brow. She gently turned Angela to face those watching, fluttered her fingers lovingly over the child's slight form.

At last, Solania whispered, "Dear, tell us who hurt you."

Angela looked to Solania, who nodded in encouragement, and then out to all the expectant faces, the hundreds of people awaiting the answer that would verify their own pain and sorrow. Angela, in her manner of serene sadness, seemed to appraise each face individually, seemed to absorb each into the answer concealed within her self-containment.

"Tell us who hurt you, dear," whispered Solania.

Still Angela surveyed those eager eyes before her.

Then her straight little mouth opened, and her little voice rose out of her, rang like a soprano solo into the ethereal reaches of a vaulted cathedral, pierced hearts and minds in the simple purity of her answer.

"The men in the shiny cars hurt me. The men in the

shiny trucks hurt me."

And then Solania folded her into a tender embrace, said softly, "Don't worry, dear. We'll never let them hurt you again."

I had to look away, but when I did, it was to see all in the hall staring in a precious silence, as if this was a fragile rapture which none would ever rupture; Morag's group, standing in a bunch off to one side, was turned to salt at just this first glimpse into the reality of Sodom, was white, dry, threatening to crumble into a pile at a tap.

So now we step from that charged atmosphere out into the blaring hostilities of Rod, a man standing on the back of a shiny truck.

Some people really are too stupid to survive. Every year in this city, some idiot rides his snowmobile out onto the springtime river ice, crashes through and drowns. Every year, this is reported in the media as a tragedy, rather than a laudable function of natural selection.

Rod, rather than taking some cautionary lesson from his narrow escape from our midst last time, is clearly emboldened by it; braying in bravado through his bullhorn, he steers his snowmobile onto our springtime ice. It holds beneath him as he excoriates me; everyone here knows that I'm not a pimp, but they also don't view me as any sort of victim of these boys across the way, reckon that I can more than hold my own with them; a verbal attack on me doesn't excite any protective response.

However, there's a low groan as he ventures further out to vilify the Jezebel whores, a groan to which anyone with an eye on Darwin would attend when he motions at Velvet, but, unfortunately for him, in the general direction of little Angela and seems to typify the Jezebel whores as temptresses, sirens luring astray the men in the shiny cars and shiny trucks.

He puffs and pants, reels on the back of the truck, mops his brow, catches himself up in his own hyperbole, and misses the obvious hostility his rant is generating. When Solania and Buster step outside, and Rod espies them, well, he's past any moderation.

"There she is: Queen Jezebel! Harpy!" And he calls upon the people to turn away from their witch queen enchantress, to overthrow her evil hypnotic dominion over them, to come instead to the support of those who truly share their dreams and aspirations, and who will assist them through the established social order to realize their brighter day.

Rod signals urgently to an apple-cheeked young man, who smilingly steps across to our milling people and attempts to distribute new brochures. He's met with no response until he steps to a member of the Freedom of Form group, a very pugnacious woman named Birgid, into whose own cheeks the colour has now flooded back. The young man hands her a brochure. She takes it, then grabs his little stack of them, and she throws them in his face, which stops smiling.

With a savage cry, Birgid - being maybe more fervid for freedom of form than of speech - charges across the street to raging Rod, and her sisters fall in behind her in a roughly triangular pattern, so that for a moment it looks like some reverse bowling game, where a delta of heavy round balls thunders down the alley at the single pin, or the single Rod, who suddenly has the sense to gape in terror. Enos and Aiken cower into the corners of the truck box, and the COIN man throws himself over the side and runs away.

Our people surge across the street, maybe in fury, maybe just in hurried curiosity.

I hear Rod screaming briefly, think maybe I see an arm or two of his beaded jacket rising in wild flail, but my view is pretty much obscured. I step forward, start to shout for our people to stop, but this is just the sort of security crisis of dangerous disarray for which Buster and my warders have been training themselves, and they fly into active duty: Buster grabs Solania and throws her back into the corner of the entranceway to The Friendship, and shelters her there, and then Ken does the same to me, tackling me into the other corner.

I'm on the seat of my pants, sprawled under Ken's straddling protection.

"Ken! Let me up!" I call, but he's pressing down firmly on my shoulder, and ignores me, watches out over his shoulder for whatever might approach.

People are still pouring out the door of The Friendship, but through the flashing gaps between their legs, I'm able to look across to Solania, who's in roughly the same position as I, under Buster. She's laughing with glee.

Our people swarm across, mill about in agitation on the street, but out between Ken's legs I see little Angela, somehow neither knocked over or swept along, still standing on the sidewalk, arms folded before herself, pivoting slightly at her waist, swivelling back and forth, staring out above the rippling melee. Then there's Rose, smiling down on her, extending her hand. Angela openly assesses Rose for a moment, then reaches to take her hand. Rose gently and calmly leads her down the sidewalk and away from the fray.

I struggle to my feet against Ken's resistance.

Across the street, Rod, unbloodied and unbowled, is managing to keep his furious Freedom of Form attackers at bay by swinging one of our own picket signs that he's grabbed, describing an arc before him. Our people press and crowd.

The horn of the shiny truck starts a constant blare, and the truck lurches suddenly backward, sending the immediate mob scurrying from its path and Rod tumbling to the floor of its box. It would seem that our counter-campaigners are about to make a getaway, but then I see that it's Russell at the wheel, and in an instant he's shifted the truck forward again, smashing through the doors of the supermarket, has driven the truck right into the store.

A great roar erupts, and people surge over broken glass and twisted aluminum and through Russell's ragged opening.

Buster is bustling Solania back inside The Friendship, and Ken grips my shoulder with the same intention for me. But out in the centre of the street, Constable Morley is standing, sharp-eyed and intense, hand at holster, two-way radio at his feet, at the focal point of a ring of seething, coiled young men and women.

I push past Ken roughly, but grab his arm as I go.

"Come on!" I command him.

Together, we break through the circle threatening Morley, and we hurry him into The Friendship, as well. Morley races up the stairs to the main level, and Ken and I are on his heels.

He turns into Sharon's office, where Solania, Buster and Sharon stand observing the rampage through the front window. Morley grabs for the telephone on Sharon's desk, but Buster springs to him, wrenches the telephone from him and wags a warning finger. Morley reaches down to his holster once again; Buster laughs at him, then turns back to the window, still holding the telephone.

"Perles," Morley says to me in appeal.

But I uphold the judgment of the lower court, shake my head and go to watch out the window.

"They could be killing that guy," Morley protests, joining us at the window.

"Then they'd be wasting their time," Solania says lightly.

"Our people aren't the killers," I say.

As if in proof, the automatic door at the other side of the store flips open, and out scurries the staff in their green and white uniforms, and in their frantic midst are Rod, Aiken and Enos and their few supporters, and down 20th St. they flee, as though they're being hotly pursued, which they're not.

A cash register crashes through a large plate glass window at the front of the store, and shortly after that, plastic bags of groceries start to fly through the new opening to the sidewalk. People outside rush forward and snatch them up, lift the bags over their heads like trophies of the hunt. This process carries on, and in its way, it's strangely orderly, deferential and cooperative, with no competition for the plunder. Younger people carry bags to older people on the fringe of the milling mob.

We watch this for some time. Then I turn to Morley, and say "The best thing your guys can do is stand back and let this exercise play itself out."

"If you let me have the 'phone, I'll tell them just that," he says.

I gesture to Buster, and, smirking, he presents the telephone to Morley.

I look over at Solania. She stands with her hands on the window like a little girl looking into a candy shop, her mouth wide with delight.

*   *   *

The Mayor leans over me, smiling as though it's an honour to know me.

"This may be all right," he says, handing me a mug of tea. "We can't seem to make a good cuppa here. I guess it's the pipes."

"Thank you, I'm sure it'll be fine," I say. The mug is decorated with the seal of the city. Beside me, Solania places her mug on the long conference table at which we sit.

Across from us, the Chief of Police is shaking his head. The Mayor is smoothly, elegantly patrician in his manner; the Chief looks like a grandfather reading a story to his grandchildren, white-haired, red-faced, with bifocals perched precariously on the tip of his little nose. However, it's the Mayor who's extending kindly, friendly overtures. The Chief's surrounded by obvious icicles. We may assume that he's mindful of my published criticisms of his force.

"You seriously maintain that Russell was trying to rescue the men in the back of the truck?" he asks.

"Trying to drive them out of harm's way, yes. That was my interpretation of it," I say. "But then he had to veer suddenly to avoid a group of people, and that's when the truck accidently slammed into the store."

The Chief guffaws, and the Mayor chuckles as he retakes his seat beside him.

"It seems to me," I add, "that the question before you is whether you should give him a citation for careless driving or a citation for bravery."

"The question before all of us," the Mayor says, "is, how are we to prevent a recurrence of these events?"

Over our protest, both men are lumping The Baron bombing and the ransacking of the supermarket together.

"I've been raising the alarm for years about the volatile stresses developing in the inner city," I say, "which you've seen fit to ignore. Even now, you only wish to know how to contain the situation, not how to bring improvements to it. Why should we have any interest in participating in the smothering of our people's legitimate dissatisfaction?"

"Believe me, Solania, Perles," the Mayor says in a conciliatory manner, "mine is a sincere inquiry into what we can do together to address, well, what you call the stresses of the inner city. I'm looking for improvements, not containment."

"Then what's he doing here?" I ask, nodding over to the Chief.

"We need to cooperate together, all of us," says the Mayor. "We need to open and maintain lines of communication."

"Right now, our sworn enemies, those who precipitated the riot by their antagonisms, are encamped in that supermarket parking lot, mounting a circus of broadcast harassment against us, shielding themselves within the guardianship of a ruthless gang of outlaw bikers that plans to enslave our people in the skin and drug trades at its earliest opportunity. And you're calling upon us for cooperation. Call upon Aiken for cooperation. Call upon COIN."

"We're powerless to clear them out," says the Mayor. "We would if we could. But within the sphere of what's possible for us, what is it we could do? Let's find solutions."

I allow a sigh to escape me.

"Will you continue your funding of The Friendship Inn?" Solania asks.

"I should be able to, for the short term, at least. Rod's too ill for tomorrow's council meeting, apparently, and I doubt that any motion will be presented by another councillor. Though I should warn you, COIN and the God's Right Hand people have organized a whole succession of supporters to address council against you tomorrow. It's not a meeting I'm looking forward to, I don't mind saying."

"What's supposed to be wrong with Rod?" I ask. "He wasn't hurt."

"No, it's some nasty 'flu he's come down with," says the Mayor.

"We would like to see the city seriously confront the inequities in its own hiring," I say. "And I don't mean by hiring a handful of our people to push brooms on sidewalks."

The Mayor nods, but says warily, "Do you mean some sort of formal employment equity policy? Because I can tell you, the climate for any such measure is very poor, politically, just now."

"Because we've made such a hot issue of it, I suppose," I say.

"Yes, frankly."

"But if we hadn't made such a hot issue of it ..."

"Just not at present," the Mayor says. "Perhaps through some informal predisposition ..."

"Like some unenunciated intention of your own, perhaps," I say, "which can be filtered out without a trace through your muffling managerial layers."

"I tell you, I couldn't get any formal policy through council. That's just the political reality."

"Our people have absolutely no representation on either city council or the school board," I say.

"That's because your people don't vote," says the Chief.

"They don't vote because they never have anyone for whom to vote," Solania chimes in. "And with the gerrymandered setup of the ward system as it is, any candidates of ours will always be swamped."

"Well, there's certainly a possibility of a review of ward boundaries," the Mayor suggests.

"A review by whom?" Solania asks.

"We could work that out. But that, once again, isn't going to be immediate. What measures are you seeking in the immediate future to defuse the, well, the explosive ..."

"We need police protection from the bikers," I say.

Solania gives me a tiny shake of her head, a motion that is repeated more emphatically by the Chief.

"There again," he says, "the bikers aren't breaking any

laws by parking in that lot. Without a complaint against them from the supermarket owner ..."

"I don't expect you to arrest them, I want protection from them," I say. "I know that it wouldn't be popular duty."

"We don't like the bikers any better than you do," the Chief says.

"And you don't like us any better than the bikers do, I'll hazard," I say.

"Look, Mr. Perles, if the bikers undertake any action against you ...," says the Chief.

"We can take care of ourselves," Solania says firmly.

"I don't like the sound of that," the Mayor says. He raises an eyebrow at the Chief.

"Better we rely on ourselves than on reluctant cops," she says.

"Can I ask you something?" the Mayor says with a hint of frustration. "Where do you see your activism taking you? Is this to be a permanent construct of our city, or, well, where does this end?"

"It ends with our people as full, free participants in the economic, educational, political and judicial mainstream of this city, this province and this country," I say. "That's all."

"Oh, that's all," says the Mayor.

"By any means? Or at any cost?" asks the Chief. "Just so we know what to expect, I mean."

"We're not fighting for our convenience; we're fighting for our lives," I say.

"So far, all I'm hearing are your demands," the Chief says. "Where are your assurances of peace and order in the streets?"

"Look," I say, "We don't happen to enjoy the fact that it took a bombing and a riot for us to gain your official attention for our initiatives. That's a matter of great distress to us. Personally, we would have found it much more satisfying if our peaceful methods had borne fruit. But it's you, you, you, who have shown us what really generates a response around here."

"We can't live without social order, can we?" the Chief growls.

"Our people haven't found how to live with social order," Solania says.

"Well," says the Mayor, rising and holding up his hands to us in placation, "I think this serves to prove my point. We need to establish an ongoing, open and free dialogue between us."

This is the signal that our interview is over. It's done nothing but irk me, and I start for the door of the conference room straightaway; but the Mayor intercepts me, takes my arm and shakes my hand warmly.

"Good to see you again, Perles," he says. "I never miss your column."

"And," he says, turning with something of a courtly flourish to Solania, "what a pleasure to finally meet this extraordinary lady. Perles is mistaken, you know; I've been paying close attention to you all along. Good of you to come this afternoon."

He takes her hand in a gentlemanly fashion. For an instant, I think he's about to bend and kiss it.

But instead he says, "Call me at any time. Any time. And we'll be in touch."

And Solania smiles at him in a way that would dazzle the dead and buried.

We come out of City Hall, walk across its little plaza to the police cruiser waiting to return us to our house. Either by chance or by indecipherable design, the officer assigned to drive us is the one who came to take away the woman collapsed in the alley behind The Salvation Army. He sits behind the wheel, regards me with no sign of recognition.

I throw open the front passenger door.

"Step out here," I order.

He gets out, putting on his hat as he does, and looks at me with guarded curiosity.

I take Solania's hand.

"This is my new girlfriend," I say to him. "I'm holding my new girlfriend's hand. Now, you come around here and hold the door for her."

Stoically, stiffly, the officer circles around the front of his car and opens the back door for Solania, who slides into the back with the merest nod of acknowledgment. I get in after her, and the officer closes the door.

As he drives us back to our neighborhood, I turn and look at my beautiful smiling Solania for a long time.

"What?" she chirps at last.

"We can take care of ourselves?" I say. "Armed with what? Empty macaroni boxes and dried up bingo dabbers? How are we to take care of ourselves?"

Solania laughs and squeezes my arm, kisses my shoulder.

"That was great," she says gaily. "You were so great; 'full, free participants in the mainstream ... That's all.' That was so great."

"What are you so happy about? Has it escaped your notice that we've yet to open up one job for anybody, we've closed down the only grocery in our neighborhood, we've threatened the existence of the Friendship Inn and the food bank, and we've got Parliamentarians and biker gangs setting us in their gunsights, the police wish we'd die, and City Hall is a quaking pile of sludge that would suffocate us? What, exactly, are you so happy about?"

"I've got the men in the shiny cars begging me, 'Please, little girl, please don't hurt us!'" Solania says. "Why wouldn't I be happy?"

Chapter Ten

Even as Solania and I were meeting with the Mayor, a man came into The Friendship looking for Solania. The manager of a shop on 22nd St. that mainly sold doughnuts and coffee, but also some meals of standardized soup and sandwiches, he came in the spirit of goodwill, or maybe in the spirit of not wanting a truck through his doors. He failed to find Solania, but instead he found two teenaged girls, Velvet and Tawnee, working hard and effectively in a kitchen that was busier than his will ever be. He straightaway offered them jobs in his doughnut shop, which, ironically enough, wasn't intended as one of our boycott targets. The girls nervously accepted, and although they're the only members of his staff who are never allowed near the cash drawers, they represent our first employment successes.

The manager took it upon himself to alert the media to the hiring of his new employees, and television and print both made much of it, interviewed the manager, interviewed the shy girls, interviewed the other employees, who said, yeah, it was cool, they were just like any kids working there; then they solicited the comments of Billy Aiken, who roundly condemned the manager for knuckling under to scare tactics and bullyism and anarchy, and threatened to stage a boycott of the doughnut shop.

Aiken's boycott hasn't materialized, yet, as he suddenly discovered a greater moral affront for his attentions; and the shop, meantime, is enjoying a sharp increase in sales, coming from such people as Academicians for Arteriosclerosis, who recognize their duty: gobbling glazed goodies in Solania Solidarity.

And then a convenience store at 22nd and P, which was under our boycott, followed suit, met with us, hired two young women who'd once frequented the store as prostitutes seeking a soft drink or a moment's shelter from the elements or from their own recurrent sense of dread. And soon the business of the convenience store took an upswing, too, with new customers popping in for chips and huge drinks, people who went out of their way to engage in warm exchanges with any staff member who looked like a possible former hooker.

*   *   *

When Rose led little Angela to safety from the supermarket riot, she took her to her tiny basement suite, where Rose softly burped reassurances and kindnesses to the little girl, made her weak cups of tea and peanut butter sandwiches, all of which Angela accepted in silence, often staring with undisguised interest at Rose's hole.

When night fell, Angela climbed onto Rose's single cot, pressing herself against the wall to allow room for Rose. When Rose arose at four in the dark morning, Angela got up with her, followed her silently out to the streetcorner, to the piles of newspapers and advertising flyers, helped Rose load them into the shopping cart, Rose's found riot-remnant, and assisted her well through the deliveries.

After breakfast at The Friendship, Angela disappeared, and Rose sighed in assumption that she was gone for good. But later that day, just before the grocery run, Angela returned, bringing with her another girl scarcely any bigger or older than Angela, another refugee from The Baron's enterprise. Rose took them both on the grocery run, and they assisted with serious application; the next day it was three more girls, and then another two, so on, so that Rose's little suite was wall-to-wall at night with former baby hookers, ranging in age from nine to fourteen.

And when they kept coming, Rose realized that she

was going to have to make a change.

Of course, she knows of every unoccupied or abandoned house in these neighborhoods, the ones in whose mailslots or doorhandles her flyers fade, flutter, corrugate and yellow. She knew of a two-and-a-half storey house, on a corner across from the schoolyard, that had stood empty for a long time, its large diamond-shaped, dull green tar shingles peeled or ripped here and there from its outer walls and strewn with other garbage and broken bits over its neglected and unplanted property, its windows broken here and there for minor-league sport.

Being an unsophisticated sort, Rose reckoned that an empty house that was, through neglect and vandalism, breaking down into its natural elements and her new and growing brood made a good match, so she led her dozen or so over to the ratty place. With little effort, they broke into it, and then, by cigarette lighters and giddy but reasoned deduction, they collectively figured out how to throw the main breaker switch in the spooky basement, and then found the proper lever at the water meter. With brooms and mops and buckets from the Mennonite Clothes Closet, they set about to cleaning the rubble and rubbish out of the house, scrubbing its rippling linoleum and fractured walls, its six filthy toilets in the six suites into which it had been subdivided.

That evening, the girls laid down exhausted on their little coats and jackets, an accommodation not unknown to any of them, and squealed at the scrabbling and squeaking from the rodential walls and ceilings until they dropped off to sleep.

They had carried Rose's cot and mattress to the house, and Rose and Angela shared it in the frontroom of the main floor. At some point in the night, Rose awakened and found Angela sitting up, staring wide-eyed.

The top third of the front window was of leaded stained glass, and by some mistake or miracle, this exceptional decorative feature, this phantom of an earlier and better intention, hadn't attracted anyone's wanton impulse of destruction, and its little figured panes of green, purple, yellow and etched white, its bevelled diamond lozenges were all intact, and through them the streetlight was shining, setting coloured flame to them. And Angela was transfixed by it.

She had, by then, been with Rose for four days, and had yet to pass a word to her. But when Rose patted her arm, to gently break her spell, Angela opened her straight little mouth and said:

"I'm so happy, I could die."

Really, a little girl growing up in her circumstances should have known better than to irresistibly tempt fate with such an expression.

The girls spent the next several days cleaning, patching broken windows with the plastic from Rose's newspaper bundles, scrounging unwanted furniture and mattresses, and delivering newspapers and groceries, attending Solania's sessions and struggling to adhere to Rose's strict house rules of no smoking, no drinking, no drugs, no swearing and no suicides. And every morning, after the papers, Angela settled herself on the cot in the front room to watch the first rays of the rising morning sun set her window afire.

Then fate found its opportunity in the mother of one girl, a mother who sobered up enough to notice that her little daughter's prostitution pittances were no longer available to help keep her drunk, and she undertook to find out why that was. Her enquiries of neighbours eventually led her to Rose's recovery hostel, and her reaction was hostile. She demanded that her daughter return to the service of her home and habit, and the girl refused, and Rose refused to turn her over. The mother took some time on the sidewalk to be highly and loudly and descriptively critical of Rose in every way.

So then she toddled away, fuming and smacking her gums together. Rose knew enough to be concerned, but she put on a brave face for the girls, took the distraught daughter's face in her hands and smiled in reassurance; Angela stood at her arm and said, "Don't worry, dear. We'll never let them hurt you again."

It would seem that some vestige of sense kept the mother from phoning the police to complain that her little girl was being prevented from her proper calling. But it seems that, instead, as the even better idea, she phoned the city's other newspaper, where she was connected to its star columnist counterpart to me, who encouraged her to unburden herself of her maternal grief and outrage.

The headline of his next column was "The House of the Falling Daughter", in which, from behind the protective cover of his source, he nearly stated that the house was one of abducted or brainwashed underaged hookers of my operation. He dubbed it Perles' Ring, and referred to me as the most despised man in the city. He painted a very sympathetic portrait of the mother, though.

I disapprove of interpaper debates as journalistic egoistic infantilism. However, for Rose's sake, I felt that I had no choice but to refute those allegations in my next column. I pointed out that all the girls had been street urchins at urgent risk until Rose provided a home for them. Robert wrote a spunky editorial entitled "Let Lying Dogs Sleep", in which he lambasted the other columnist's position and practises, mistakenly coining the term 'Solania's Orphans' for the girls; the other media picked up on the term, and it stuck.

CBC television, in the course of an otherwise positive story on the asylum for 'Solania's Orphans', somehow discovered its location, and, infuriatingly, showed the house onscreen, with the school readily identifiable in the background. Our opponents immediately dispatched a detachment of their activists, COIN protesters, politicians, zealots and biker thugs to the front and side of its corner lot, where they marched and shouted such slogans as "Clean Community Now!"and "Not Here! Not Now!". And the girls inside screamed and wailed, and Rose came out to the front steps, gulping and failing to burp in any coherent way, waving her arms, trembling in terror, providing much fun for many, but for the bikers in particular, who ridiculed her in rough imitation, as though she was Quasimodo on the steps of Notre Dame.

"Christians for Decency in Broadcasting" promptly changed its name to "Mothers Defending Children", and showed up in time for the next days' news cameras — the very mother of the girl inmate also showed up, but, after a hasty appraisal by the protesters, was hustled out of view as potentially damaging to their righteous cause. Instead, the same pink eastside mothers paraded before the cameras, clutching the same pink eastside children desperately to them as though, at any moment, Rose would swoop out and snatch them from the maternal bosom. When the SITV reporter tried and tried again to ascertain whether their protest was in defence of or against the girls inside, the mothers were unable to sound any more intelligible than Rose.

At about the time that fifty or so of our supporters arrived on foot to crowd protectively into a buffer band and stare at those against us, a COIN operator recognized the house as belonging to one of its prominent members, Solania's slumlord, as a matter of fact. A great cheer went up in their ranks as this nugget was passed amongst them. The day was surely theirs.

A delegation went at once to the Silver Dollar Pawn,

and they burst through our picket line there with raucous laughter, apparently could barely contain their mirth as they described our idiotic blunder of squatting in a COIN house. According to our picketers, the laughter fell off sharply as the slumlord refused to call the police to oust the squatters, refused to take out an eviction action with the sheriff's office; cajole and remonstrate as they might, he was steadfast, would have none of it.

They stumbled back out, wholly at a loss to explain his obstinacy.

They weren't the first to identify the ownership of the house. Solania recognized it as soon as I took her over from the Chinese cafe to see Rose's set-up.

So we soon paid a visit to the Silver Dollar, and Solania's slumlord was very gruff in bluff as we stepped into the acrid cigarette reek of his store.

"What the hell do you want?!" he croaked at us, wincing as he did. Never very melodious, his voice was today a rough rasp.

In terms of acting tough, he was at an insurmountable disadvantage; Solania had, after all, seen him all soft and spongy with his pants down, and her eyes steadily projected that awareness to the screen of his eyes as she put on her coy little smile. He wilted immediately.

"You sound terrible," she observed without concern.

"Throat," he said. "Can't shake it. Had it for six weeks."

"Perhaps another cigarette would help," I suggested.

"We're here to strike a bargain with you," Solania said, most self-assured.

"Will it get your guys out from in fronta my store?" he croaked slowly and suspiciously.

"Oh, no," Solania said.

I began to explain to him that we were quite prepared

to prove that he's been scamming social services by claiming welfare rental payments for people who resided in his buildings in name only, that we were aware of numerous homeless people who allowed themselves to be listed as his tenants for a kickback of fifty dollars a month, while he pocketed over four hundred per name.

"Your house on Ave. H, for instance, had eight suites, but we know that you were claiming welfare rentals for at least twenty occupants," I said.

He rubbed his mouth for some time, apparently exploring his options.

Solania shook her head angrily, impatient with any possibility that he even had options to explore. She went to his door, and motioned for a young man on our picket line to come in.

She took the young man's hand and led him right up to the slumlord.

"Darwin, dear," she said, "I want you to burn down two houses tonight. Will you do that for me?"

"Okay," Darwin said. "Any two houses?"

"No, no, dear, I'll give you the addresses. And then tomorrow morning, I want you to go to the police and turn yourself in. I want you to tell them that this man hired you to burn the houses, so he could collect the insurance. We'll provide you with evidence. Will you do that for me?"

"Okay," he said, nodding sincerely.

The slumlord gaped, unbelieving.

"He'll never do it!" he sputtered. "He'd go to prison for it!"

"A prison full to bursting with our people. He'll go to prison, and he'll be treated like a king. And you'll go to prison, too," she said calmly. "But you'll be treated like a queen."

So we left the shop with a pact preserving Rose and

her waifs as his tenants.

I asked her, "Don't you have any regard for the truth?"

"Darling, we're not dealing with the truth, we're dealing with the law," she explained blithely. "The law is designed to work against us, so we must work the law to our design."

All the coverage of Rose's project attracted donations of clothes and furniture and books, and also attracted more homeless girls, and attracted the entreaty of some parents who asked that Rose take their obstreperous and defiant daughters, and of some mothers whose daughters weren't wild, but who recognized that they themselves were, by enslavement to their addictions, incapable of providing good homes.

In the event of the owner refusing to roust the girls, the protesters dug in, in a manner, parking their motorcycles and cars around the house, setting up lawn chairs on the edge of the schoolyard, and generally maintaining low grade harassment of those who came to the house, crowding around them and impeding their ingress and egress, sticking signs in their faces. The girls and Rose came and went in knitted groups, always. A few of our supporters were usually on hand.

On the morning that Alexi and I took Velvet and Carney to the house for mutual inspection, Member of Parliament Aiken was among his hired guns. We had to park some distance away, as Aiken's new truck, shining beneath the painted message "Billy Aiken, M.P. - At Your Service!", was positioned directly in front of Rose's house. As we stepped from The Baron's car, his group crossed the street to stand in front of the little gateway of the house.

I found myself face-to-face with Aiken for the first time. His dull little eyes held cunning without intelligence, like a garbage dump dog or a kitchen hand at the Sally Ann.

"Ubiquitous Mr. Aiken," I said. To my pleasure, he didn't seem to know the meaning of 'ubiquitous' and decided to take offence at it. He stood directly before me, blocking my way, clenching fists and jaw.

"You're the ones better quit," he growled lowly in answer.

His biker guards circled around us.

I said: "You've already gathered all the reactionary redneck vote you're ever going to get. Why don't you just skulk back to the little clerking duties for which we pay you?"

"I go where the people need me," he said.

"If you don't step aside, you'll have gone where the people kneed you," I said.

Neither he nor the members of his party are noted for intellectual facility, and he couldn't make anything of my little pun. He posed in a pretense of looming threat that was merely laughable, before slowly stepping aside.

But as I moved past him, he said, "You're everything that's wrong with the world."

When he'd been asked in the press about the appropriateness of bringing in a bike gang reinforcement to his quasi-political protest, he'd attested that we'd made such security measures necessary, and that we posed a greater threat to social order than the bikers. What these people call social order is nothing more than a sanctioned food chain, in which the worst of his people are preserved in depredation upon the best of ours.

Carney was in his suit, which now looked rather large on him. Velvet was wearing her store uniform. Alexi had lately assumed the habit of wearing a Clothes Closet suit, as well, with white shirts but florid ties and handkerchiefs. I expect that the girls watching our arrival from the front door found them to be an impressive trio, especially in comparison to the seamy grunge of the bikers, who slowly broke apart to let us pass.

Carney still carried himself rather precisely and weakly, and Velvet lowered her head in sideways sharp scowl as they followed me up the little walk.

But Alexi tarried a step, peered at the biker beside him with exaggerated examination; then he just touched his own nose, and with a little friendly smile said, "Say, you got a bit of slops on your snout, there." Then he laughed happily and sauntered up after us.

The girls had been hoping for Solania to come, and when they asked about her, I told them of how she was very tired lately from the demands of her activities, and needed to rest mornings. They were obviously disappointed; Solania is still far and away the highest, brightest star in their firmament, but Carney, Velvet and Alexi enjoy considerable celebrity with them, too.

The girls proudly guided their guests through the house, which was still in terrible disrepair, but at least was clean. The rooms were tidily kept, and stuffed toy collections were lined up on neatly made beds, tiny wardrobes were hanging in closets or folded in donated chests of drawers.

Angela stood beside her stained glass window, raised her hands to it in display.

"This is the most beautiful thing in the whole house," she said solemnly.

"Or it was until you walked in," I said. "Then it became the second most beautiful thing in the house."

She smiled as though some underlying muscles resisted the elastic exercise of it, a slow, small smile.

But she couldn't acknowledge my compliment, her greater loyalty was to her window.

"You can't tell now, but when light shines through it,

it's the most beautiful thing in the whole world," she stated. Then, as a conscientious afterthought, setting the whole world in its proper order, she firmly added: "Except for Solania."

Carney and Velvet are yet coming to grips with stardom, and they were unaware that the girls were eager for a word of approval after the tour. So I provided it, congratulating them on their wonderful progress. I don't know if this sufficed with the girls. I'm not a star, although I suppose I am exalted by my intimate proximity to Solania.

Anyway, little Angela took charge of things, like a proper hostess offering the guests pride of place on the hardtwist faded 1940s sofa and armchair suite, pouring them tea and inviting orderly questions of these heroic role-models from the other girls.

What's the hardest part of your job, Velvet? Not eating all the doughnuts. Much giggling. No, really, 'cause, y'know, we can get diabetes real easy.

Is your job really better than working the street? Yeah, it sure is; you know that dirty feeling when you been hooking, makes you want to just wash and wash and wash 'til your skin's just about gone? Well, I never felt like that after a shift at the doughnut shop.

Did Carney really say "You can't kill my love for Velvet." when he got knifed? I don't know, yeah, I think it was maybe something like that. Yeah, it was something like that.

Carney, Velvet and Alexi are the stuff of legend, arising just when our people were utterly out of the stuff of legend.

Solania is of the essential elements; she's the stuff of mythology.

Then Carney told the girls about his and Velvet's ongoing so-far successful struggle with alcoholism. Many of the girls there —- although not Angela, I know —- have spent a notable portion of their short lives absorbing that which is pumped through their neighborhood arteries by the neon heart, some may even be truly addicted, and all of them have seen their circumstances spoiled by the fetid flow. They nodded in serious familiarity as Carney spoke.

Members of biker gangs, of course, are not particularly introspective regarding their own drinking. Bikers swilling beer on a late night vigil against a new day can provide a convenient tool for cruel fate.

And so it was that, that same night, as Angela indulged her habit of awakening in rapt appreciation of the streetlight glistening through her precious brilliant stained glass window, she saw the glowing coloured pieces suddenly bursting inward, flying in through suddenly thrusting twisted strands of lead to fall in sickening tinkling to the bare floor.

Perhaps, at first, she may have thought that she'd broken it herself by staring at it too hard, by valuing it too highly. I know that she crept out of the cot without disturbing the sleeping Rose, and can guess that she went to the shards of her shattered jewel, tried to piece them together, when she came upon a fragment of brown glass that had no place in her window; looking over, she found the partially-broken beer bottle, picked it up by its intact neck and puzzled over it briefly, then looked through the window to the three bikers who were standing on the sidewalk outside the rickety picket fence, under the streetlight. Two were still drinking from beer bottles, one stood empty-handed. Maybe they were afraid of the dark.

Man is hobbled by his persistent inability to recognize what is of importance. The biker who finished his beer and pitched the bottle at the window of his enemies undoubtedly did it for want of any better plan, his malice was surely lightly considered and casual. He surely didn't recognize the window as being of any special significance, surely didn't recognize his cruel gesture of harassment as a critical event that would, ultimately, prove to be fatal.

With a high scream of fury that roused Rose, a high scream of steam too long pent up under too much pressure, little Angela, clad in Clothes Closet mismatched and faded pajamas, flew out the front door, down the short front walk, and flew at the empty-handed biker with the lethal remnant of his own bottle.

Alerted by her continuing scream, the biker, five times Angela's size, was ready for her as she dove at him. He grabbed the wrist of her threatening hand, grabbed the front of her pajama top, and threw her away from him, so that she landed with the small of her back on the pointed staves of the fence. Somehow, she pushed herself off the fence and flew at the biker again, to the hilarity of his companions.

He grabbed her arm once again, twisted it as he laughed down at her, her eyes tearful, brilliant and brittle like stained glass.

One of the others said: "Don't wreck the face. We want her pretty when she's working for us." Rose, who was by now racing through the door herself, heard him say it.

Gleefully, the biker twisted and twisted Angela's little stick arm until it snapped. Angela screamed, Rose writhed in anguish.

The biker picked up the little girl and, laughing in derision, tossed her at Rose as though she was a beach ball.

*   *   *

Inside The Friendship Inn, Solania is speaking to her multitude. I'm standing at the front window in the general office; I am able to look over the counter and watch Solania, and look out to see hundreds of her supporters covering the sidewalk. Across the street, Pastor Enos, as always, is delivering his counter-sermon, speaking through a microphone, standing on the back of a party pick-up. No one is listening to him; his biker guards have no respect for him, and, to his tiny credit, he's none too comfortable in their company. But he keeps on talking. He's saying, as he always does, that we willfully refuse to accept God's intentions for us, and that bridling in discontent against the position in which God has placed us is our sin. And that Solania is the devil.

To give the devil its due, I return my attention to Solania. She is recounting the incident of last night.

Angela is still in St. Paul's, silent and faraway, with Rose stroking her little forehead, her poor little arm in a cast that's still drying, dressings on her back. She's being held for observation, because the resident doctor is concerned about renal damage. He also informed Rose and me that it's his duty to flag a case such as Angela's for both the police and Social Services. He clearly considers our story of midnight bikers to be bunk, and that either Rose, who was identified by Angela as her mother, or, more probably, I inflicted the injuries. How he could remain cosseted in oblivion to the bizarre nature of these days in these environs is beyond my ken. Parental abuse is far too mundane to be a possible explanation these days, whereas what could be more plausible than a bully biker capriciously beating up a child who was trying to kill him?

No one here in the hall or out on the street has any difficulty believing it, that's clear. Even Morley couldn't seem more upset, shakes his head with all the emphatic protestant ejaculations of those around him.

"We promised our children that we'd never let these people hurt them again," Solania says. "What was our promise worth?

"In my heart, I see our children, fallen on the hard, poisoned ground, crying out under plundering vultures that rip at them, our children and the firebird are crying out to the spirits of our people. But the spirits of our people won't hear the cries, they just huddle kneeling at the base of the killing tree, begging it for the shelter it won't provide, begging pitifully for the fruit the killing tree won't ever bear.

"I see a little girl trying to fight back against the vultures, striking back at those who raid us, steal or ruin all that is good and beautiful about us just for their greed and wicked pleasure.

"Will our people merely look on as this little girl fights for us? Will she forever fight alone? Will they simply watch as she's thrown, broken, to the poisoned ground?

"How much longer will we sacrifice our children to appease false gods? How much longer will we allow this little girl to take up, alone, the fight that properly belongs to us all?

"How much longer will we beg our oppressors for the decency and generosity they don't possess? When will we fight?"

Across the street, Enos has stopped talking, is staring at our loudspeakers and our multitude leaning into them. Both Morley and Sharon in turn look to me in questioning concern.

Into the taut silence, Solania says:

"Eventually, we have to lash out, just to prove that we're still alive."

She looks severely into the eyes of those gathered around her.

"Don't we?" she says.

"Wait, Solania!" I find myself shouting from behind them. People turn to look at me. I hop up onto the counter, raise my hands. "Wait! They may not understand what you mean! Explain to them that you mean a non-violent struggle! We can't literally, physically fight, we'll be destroyed! Explain to them what you mean!"

Solania looks out over their heads to me, assesses me sternly, her eyes hard, dark and defiant.

"Please, Solania," I say. "Tell them what you really mean. Make them understand that you mean by nonviolent methods."

And then into her hard eyes there spring softening tears, which spill out and down her cheeks as she stares at me. She shakes her head in apology and regret.

"Please, darling," I say.

And she softly says: "But that's not what I mean. I mean that, eventually, we have to lash out, just to prove we're still alive. I mean that eventually is now. Our beautiful broken children cry to us to avenge them, to avenge them now."

I can feel the thrill charge through the crowd. My heart beats as though it might explode. I can't pull my eyes from my tiny beautiful Solania, and she stares at me steadily and painfully through her tears. Peripherally, I'm aware of the thundering, crying crowds storming down the flight of stairs. Morley is at the counter, shouting up at me.

Outside are war cries and Pastor Enos, perhaps less than entirely willing to accept God's immediate intentions for him, prays into his microphone for mercy. I can hear frantic kick-starts of motorcycles.

I hear war cries and cries of terror and agony, cries of rage and panic, heavy metal crashes to the concrete, and Morley is crying "No, no, no, you'll ruin all you've done! No, no, no!", but the imperative for my intense sense is Solania, who clenches her little feather hands on her lap, rocks back and forth as she returns my awful stare.

She rises up from her chair, and steps with frailty and

uncertainty through those people who remain in the hall, the old or the frightened or the confused, across the floor to where I still stand atop the office counter.

"What am I supposed to do now?!" Morley shouts to her as she comes.

And she moves past him without notice.

She wraps her little stick arms around my legs, hugs herself to me, suddenly sobs into my legs.

"Pandora," I say. "What have you done?"

She moans in pain.

But then she raises her face to look up into mine.

"Oh, my love," she whispers, "I've done what I must."

Chapter Eleven

The floor of the liquor store under the neon heart is a lethal reeking obstacle course, its floor slippery with liquid, a giant zombie drink, really, but woebetide the person who does slip in it, for the penalty is the littered shattered glass everywhere, bottles and windows swimming like ice in this drink. A lit match right now would make quite the flambé.

The liquor store was ransacked in the first wave of the rampage, and that much more of its stock was smashed than was spirited away, so to speak, is a testament to her people's fidelity to their Solania sobriety pledge, double proof, so to speak, that their motivation in its destruction was outrage more than thirst. Throughout the black hours, this remains a sober uprising, which is why it's been so awfully effective.

Down the street, firefighters still fight fire at the Inn Continent. I begin to picture a stray spark igniting the floor, immolating me in blue flame like some foul entrée. So I pick up my pace to the limit which the other perils will permit. I find two intact bottles, one of stuff that I know I hate, the other of stuff I suspect I hate, then, on wary tiptoe, I pick my way outside to relative, only relative, safety.

Actually, the very first wave swept right across the street from The Friendship to the grocery parking lot, where a few bikers, I'm told, ran away straightaway; others made the error of trying to flee on their hawgs. One or two apparently succeeded, the rest were overcome, thugs beaten to bloody gore by people who'd never beaten anything but an egg before. No one knows if any of the bikers died. Pastor Enos, no Brébeuf, was pulled shrieking from beneath the party pick-up just after it was smashed but before it was set alight. I saw him wandering in a wondering daze through the apocalypse some time later, apparently unhurt. I don't know what became of him, he was probably rescued during the first sweep of the police riot squad. The pastor of the United Church at H and 20th, though, I've seen her since, out in the smoke and grey and sparkling fragments of this street between police sweeps, seeking those who are hurt or battle-weary or shell-shocked, offering them sanctuary in her big brick church.

It's been reported to me that Buster's brother Russell led another wave over to Rose's house, where the bikers were taken by surprise. One of them shot into the onrushing crowd, and some of our people were wounded, at least, maybe one or two mortally, I've heard conflicting reports. But there's no doubt of two things: that 'Mothers Defending Children' were seen banging on Rose's door, begging for children to defend them, and Rose admitted them, and that Russell's mob set upon five bikers and killed them all, including, presumably, Angela's assailant.

Aiken was nowhere to be found, and his political supporters suffered no fatal injuries, as far as I know.

The pawn shops have always been situated here as imperial colonial outposts, fortresses in wild and possibly hostile territory, which is why their windows are all barred; as in days of old, the fortified gates are unlocked at certain times to allow for trade with the local savages, and, as in days of old, the savages get the worse of the deal by far, and are expected to immediately squander their paltry exchange for drink down here at the neon heart. It's a concise, closed system, tried and found true to its imperial design over much time.

As the liquor and pawnshops are so closely linked, it was inevitable and natural that our people would turn their destructive attentions from the neon heart to the pawnshops. Now all that remain intact of the shops are the iron bars; all that they were meant to protect is trashed, smashed or redistributed; it would be too much to expect of justice that the items were neatly restored to the people who'd hocked them in the first place. At the auto pawns, the slummobiles drift like ghostly wrecks above a gleaming glassy turquoise pellet sea, little coloured flags strung above them flapping like remnants of tattered sails.

The police formed at Idyllwyld and 20th, robotic in riot gear and sheltering behind shields, steeled against the idle wild. Spread across the breadth of 20th, up they marched, batons, pepper spray and tears gas guns at the ready, to no purpose: we aren't Korean students playing to the cameras: even as a rampaging mob, our people simply aren't confrontational in nature, and at each approach of the police line, they would merely melt into the side streets and back alleys, or into the backyards they knew like, well, their own backyards, only to reconverge on the street behind the police lines. It was very frustrating for the cops, no doubt, like trying to collect a river with a rake.

Only Morag's Freedom of Form volunteers, in odd contrast to their name, stood as a cohesive confrontational bloc against the police. I saw them after they'd been gathered up, when they were being led to the wagons; they were already yelling to the television cameras about police brutality. Morag herself was flushed, furious and viciously vituperative; I've never seen her look more alive. When she caught sight of me, just as she was being shoved into the wagon, she called out "Never give up, Perles! Never give up!", and all of her companions cheered and hooted, apparently for me.

Mainly, I move like a ghost myself through the destruction, as though I'm not really part of anything. When the police sweep through, I step into a doorway, and they neither molest nor arrest me; the rioters, of course, threaten no harm to me, but neither do they expect me to join into their devastations, so everything has taken on a sense of unreality to me, as though I've accidently stepped onstage during some wild grand opera with which I'm unfamiliar, and all the performers play out their parts around me.

At one point a police sergeant behind the line, his own voice worn out, handed me a bullhorn and told me to order my raiders in the vicinity to disperse and return to their homes. He couldn't know, of course, that I'd already appealed for peace to no effect beyond a terrible rent in my heart.

But I raised the horn to my mouth, I felt like Gabriel for a moment, so I said: "Disperse. Go to your wretched little hovel, if you have one, and if it isn't burning. Go peacefully to resume your wretched, pointless life. Go to your miserable little rat hole and wait patiently for justice to root you out there at its own convenience and pleasure and safety, to gang up on you individually, to exterminate you for aspiring to anything better and causing a moment's nervous anxiety to the social order," and by then the sergeant was trying to wrest the bullhorn away from me, but I fended him off with my free forearm, "trade your moment's outraged objection for your constant subservient subjection, peacefully return our system of justice and social order to the reassuringly pre-dictable —-"

And then the sergeant managed to grapple the bull-horn away from me.

I looked out past his shoulder.

"Nobody's dispersing," I observed. "Oh, well, I tried."

And as I stood there, a young woman ran up to me from a radio van marked "ALL NEWS RADIO" parked near some police vehicles, with an earphone head set and a remote microphone.

"Here," she said, handing me the headset, assuming my cooperation, "we're live to Carlotta Harrington on air in our studio."

I held up the ear piece. I could hear a woman on air, drooling, slavering over our story in a most unseemly fashion; after afternoon after afternoon of filling too, too much air time with too, too little news, she was gorging herself on our succulent catastrophe, I think she was slathering it all over her body, panting and slobbering orgasmically. She gave what was surely a grossly inflated number of the dead and injured, and made it sound as though the whole westside was ablaze in conflagration; she passed on without verification, allowing that it was an "unconfirmed report", that Rose's house had been razed with many of Solania's Orphans dead. Solania herself has yet to issue any public statement on —- Do we have Perles on the line? Do we have Perles? Is Perles —- yes, we have Perles? Perles, are you there?

The young woman with me, who also had a head set, nodded to me eagerly, holding up the mike.

"I'm here," I said.

"Welcome to the show," said Carlotta.

"Uh-huh."

"It's been reported that Solania explicitly incited her supporters to this riot. Do you have a comment on that?"

"No."

"No, she didn't, or no, you have no comment?"

"Yes."

"Just moments ago, on this show, Police Sergeant Crothers informed us that they will be investigating a number of possible charges against both Solania and yourself. Do you have any comment on that?"

"No."

"Tell our listeners, what's this about, Perles? What do you hope to accomplish by this sort of action?"

"Nothing," I say.

"Then why are you doing it?"

"Why not?"

"Are you suggesting that people have died to no purpose?"

"I understand that some have died to the purpose of them being dead."

"And that's all right? You condone that?"

"I didn't say that I condone it."

"But you seem very glib about the loss of life."

"Not at all. I understand that, as drug-pushing, pimping, murderous biker thugs go, they were very fine people and their deaths represent a tragic loss to our community."

"Well, maybe you can tell us what's caused this insurrection."

"You don't know what's caused it?"

"I mean, specifically, why today? What was its trigger?"

"It didn't have a trigger, it had a very long fuse, and we didn't light it."

"Who lit it, then?"

"Let's say you did."

"We're aware, of course, through your column, of your habit of placing the blame for all the misfortunes of the inner city on the larger community. Do you now expect the larger community to respond in the way you want to this violence?"

"No, I've never expected the larger community to do anything but try to ignore forever the conditions that were festering over here, and to protect its cozy oblivion. But actually, Carlotta, I meant to suggest that you lit the fuse."

"Me? You mean me, personally?"

"Sure. Why not? I blame you. I think the people blame you. They're destroying every Carlotta in the neighborhood. No, wait, that's every car lot. My mistake."

"You're not taking this seriously, I can see," she said with disapproval.

"I don't find talking to you to be worthwhile, no."

"Then talk to your people, over our show. What message do you have for your people out on the street right now, Perles?"

"This may come as a surprise to you, but our people on the street don't happen to be listening to your programme at the moment."

I handed the earpiece back to the young woman.

"Sorry," I said.

But she was already walking away, speaking into the microphone, saying "Yes, Carlotta, I'm here. Yes, I'm just going to see if I can speak with ——."

By then, the police were breaking down their thin blue line as ineffectual. Some of our people had set up road blocks on 19th and 21st and had trashed the cars and trucks of anyone who might be a john, allowing no benefit of any doubt, and there were assaults against the windows of our boycotted businesses on 22nd, there were fires springing up here and there throughout the neighborhoods, and pretty much everything that was going to be wrecked on 20th had already been.

So the structured sweeps were discontinued, and forces deployed elsewhere, and I was free to wander up 20th, kicking at the debris and strewn bits and pieces; people seeped out from the nooks and crannies and sidestreets, wandered in inspection like me or jigged and trotted and hooted and pumped raised fists in some insane celebration of our people's perseverent obedient predisposition to self-destruction.

As with all the pawnshops, the Silver Dollar was gutted, leaving the toehold security of Rose's house who-knows-where. The big bingo hall up across from the United Church had no windows left, and some of its stacking chairs and tables were scattered out into its parking lot, some newsprint pads of game sheets fluttered in the smokey pall, but there's not much to destroy at a bingo hall; it must have left its raiders rather disappointed.

That unseen missile, that lance from Solania's dark eyes that pierces my heart, twisted and tore anew as I came again to The Friendship. It was undamaged; for all its ill conception, ours is a discerning, discriminating despoliation; even our loudspeakers hadn't been knocked from their stands. I looked up to its windows. Sharon stood in one. I think she was weeping. She didn't acknowledge me, nor I her.

The iron gates of God's Right Hand had been cut open, possibly with tools seized up from the Silver Dollar, and any attendant St. Peter had fled his post. On the back wall of the entranceway, someone had spray-painted the scrawled message:

'SACRED GROUND!
SOLANIAS THROWN!
HISTORIC SITE!'

For just an instant, I caught a glimpse of her sitting there on the steps, her throne, quietly delighted, Carney raucously happy beside her.

A bunch of young men that I didn't even recognize came up to me and excitedly itemized the destructions in which they'd personally participated, as though all that we'd worked for, all of our hard-won tiny articles of success didn't lie in useless fractured bits at our feet, as though our weeks and months of arduous considered, constructive labour and organization, in which they'd not participated, had been superceded, obviated by their one afternoon of rash, unreasoned rampage. They brayed like asses, wanted my approval. I withheld it.

And as I looked into the eyes of all of the people I encountered, as I made my listless way through the broken glass and detritus, rummagers, gleaners, celebrants, I found no spark of understanding of the damage we'd done to ourselves, the new self-inflicted wound. The charcoal atmosphere on 20th St. was of, say, the world's ugliest carnival, the grittest show on earth; maybe it was understood to be unhealthy and unprogressive and wholly calculated to our loss, but it was mounted here for our freaky passing pleasure, and they were the suckers set to enjoy it.

In this complete absence of sobering reality, I made my way down to the neon heart.

And in the spirituous wreckage of the store beneath it, I've found two bottles still intact, one of stuff I know that I hate, and one of stuff I suspect I'll hate. But, given that I hate almost everything under the smoke-obscured sun at the moment, I might have expected nothing else.

I stand with my booty bottles outside in the intersection, weighing one in each hand, listening to the rising and fading sirens, the calls of people swirling around me like the smouldering reek.

Above the ruined doorway of the liquor store, the neon heart still glows red like a helpful beacon for the blind drunk, for those lost in the fog it so conscientiously created. It glows still while Angela's window lies in broken scraps on her rippled linoleum floor.

Something about that strikes me as incorrect. I look down at the bottle of the stuff I know I hate, toss it a bit in my hand.

Then I fling it at the neon heart.

I've missed it, the bottle smashes in the stucco just below it.

I make some calculations and adjustments for the trajectory and velocity of the bottle of stuff I suspect I hate.

I fling it as carelessly as a biker under a midnight streetlight.

I smash the neon heart to smithereens.

"How did that feel?" asks the voice of my love.

For a moment, I believe that she's projected her question into me from afar. But then I spin around, and there she is, standing in the street.

"Not as good as I'd hoped," I answer. "I guess I'd rather hoped it would bleed, maybe sputter spasmodically in agonized death throes. But it just went out."

"Too bad," she says.

"What are you doing out here? Come out to admire the whirlwind you whipped up?"

"I was looking for you," she says. "I've been waiting for you. I was worried about you."

"No need to worry about me. Where's Buster? Why are you out here alone?"

"There were things I needed him to do. Where have you been?" she asks. "Just going around?"

"I've been nowhere, which is just where I belong," I say. "In a world cleaved in two, I have no place in either part. I just look on in misery from nowhere, which is where I belong."

"You belong to me," Solania says.

"Yes, yes, of course, I belong to you, but I've no idea where that is. It would seem to be nowhere."

"It's up there," she says, motioning skyward. "Up past the clouds."

"I see," I say. "Well, that's not cloud, it's smoke, it's your smoke, Solania, and wherever I am, I'm utterly underneath it."

"I know that I've hurt you," she says. "I didn't want to, how I wish I could have avoided it. But you want to hurt me now, don't you?"

"Solania, we've destroyed the structures of our people's lives, without having made any real preparation for any structures to replace them. Their habitat, wretched though it was, has been reduced to our wasteland."

"You'll figure out what to do," she says. "I know you will, darling."

"Haven't you heard? I'm going to prison. So are you. We're going to be locked away from these people and from each other. What're we going to do from there?"

"Prison? Why would you go to prison?" she says, suddenly shaken.

"Oh, darling," I say, suddenly deflated, myself, "did you fly to me over the clouds, or did you walk to me through these streets, under this pall. Didn't you see what we've done? Don't you know what an opportunity we've given our enemies? We've made a hero of Aiken and a prophet of Enos, we've made COIN our innocent victims, we've maybe even made martyrs of those damn bikers. We are now political death to anyone who's even vaguely sympathetic to us. We're going to prison, and our people are about to feel the full weight of vengeful law unleashed to reestablish the social order."

"No," she says adamantly, "Our people will fight. Now that they've started, they'll never stop."

"But they weren't fighting," I say. "They were just breaking things. And now they've broken everything. So what do you think they'll do now?"

"They'll fight," she says, raising her little hands to her brow. "They'll go on fighting. They'll smash at the things that pin them down. No one can stop them, now that they've started."

She blinks rapidly and begins to sink. I catch her, pick her up into my arms.

"Are you all right?" I say to her.

"No," she gasps faintly. "Darling, I think you'd better take me home."

I'm not feeling my very most robust, but she weighs nothing.

"I'll take you home."

She curls like a baby in my arms, feebly grips my shirt front with her hand, rests her beautiful head on my shoulder.

"You musn't go to prison, darling," she whispers. "We can't allow you to go to prison."

"Okay," I say.

Solania regards hospital no more favourably than prison; we've been through it a thousand times, and I know that there's no point in raising the possibility with her now. "They treat my kind like dirt at the hospital.", is her invariable dismissive answer.

So I hug her to me and start down 20th Street to our corner, and as we go we collect ragtag raiders, from the rubble and caverns and pits and bunkers in our wasteland, they emerge to gape in silent concern over their fallen icon, and step in behind us to follow, as she whispers in warm, weak little puffs into my neck.

"I'm so scared," she gasps at one point, and that sends a shiver through me, for she's never seemed frightened before.

But I say, "I'm so sorry, darling, I shouldn't have frightened you. You know that I'll take care of everything. Don't worry."

We're a magnet for our marauders as we go along, I don't know where they're all coming from, from what crevices and seams, but they fall in behind in hushed honour of the one whom they adore.

I look down to my darling. Her eyes are closed, and her head bobs lightly in rhythm to my step.

"Look over my shoulder," I tell her.

She slowly opens her eyes, raises her head, and gazes out behind us.

She smiles and lowers her head to me again.

"Is this a victory parade?"

"Something like it," I say.

Our silent procession approaches a knot of remaining riot cops, dark steely clouds reflecting off their visors and maybe revealing the expressions behind them, and they stand poised in guarded postures. They can make nothing of this, I'll bet, these who demand fealty of our people by threat and intimidation and indignity and deprecation and midnight mystery tours, they can make nothing of she who wins and holds willing adherence through love and pity and inspiration, who can set off an uprising with merely a word, and end it merely by slipping into my arms.

They say nothing as we pass.

We turn down Ave. F, and people who've been hiding in their tiny homes from the rambunctions creep out in curiosity and then hush alarms behind their hands as we come.

Nineteenth St. is a disaster of ruined vehicles. Who knows what enduring sexual trauma may have been instilled here today, Pavlovian in reverse, where the sounding of the sledgehammer causes dog tricks to stop salivating. Up the street, a pick-up that won't pick up still burns.

I carry her down to our house, where my van is unharmed. On our rotting little front porch, I turn to look at all the people who've followed. They spread themselves out across the front of the property, out over the avenue, crowd onto the front yards across the road, and stand, watching, preparing themselves to wait. The avenue fills with them, they are coming still.

Solania looks out over them with a weary little smile.

"What should I say?" she whispers to me.

"I don't know."

"Tell them that I cherish them."

"Solania says that she cherishes you all!" I call out. "We face difficult days ahead. Solania asks that you all support each other in every way that you can."

I take her inside and down to our little bed, cover her with the blanket of our idyllic picnic. She takes my hand and kisses it, and closes her eyes, and eventually her breathing deepens, and her grip loosens, and I stroke her head as I've done so many times, I can do it all night, I know that I can, because I've done it all many nights as I sat beside her.

In a while, Buster appears at the door. He looks past me to Solania, shakes his head slowly.

"Morley's outside," he says to me. "He wants to talk to you."

Buster and I go upstairs, out to the porch. Out by the edge of the now very large crowd is Morley in mufti, and he's with a group of people who surround him in close limitation, like white blood cells around a contaminant. I send Buster to bring him safely through the collected throng.

Morley follows me into the house.

"Do you have any idea how many people will be sleeping in this hallway tonight?" I ask him.

"More than last night," Morley says. "If you want people to be seriously concerned about homelessness, I suggest that you stop burning homes."

"Fair point," I say, sitting on the stairs to the second floor. "Where have you been through all of this?"

Morley sighs and sits on the stairs, too.

"At the station," he says. "Where my name is now mud. I've been assuring everybody for weeks that Solania's intentions were positive and constructive, that we should be supportive and patient with her. You can guess how high my stock is right now. I'm now suspected of being a person of divided loyalties, at best."

He turns sideways on the stair to look at me closely.

"Which I guess is basically true," he continues. "Heaven knows I've wanted to believe in what you guys were doing. I guess I still want to believe in Solania."

I can't think of anything to say. I look out the window beside the front door, watch all the people sitting in quiet vigil outside.

Morley follows my gaze.

"What are you going to do about all of them?" he asks.

"You didn't happen to bring any loaves and fishes, I suppose," I say.

Morley smiles briefly.

"Yeah, I guess I still want to believe in her, I still believe in her. I still care about her. So I'm going to do what maybe I shouldn't do, and give you a heads-up, my friend."

"Thank you," I say.

"We'll be looking to press charges against both you and Solania."

"Yes, I anticipated that."

"We'll be putting together a case against you for the riot itself and the deaths of the bike scum," he says. "Under the law, if you undertake an illegal action that could be expected to result in someone's death, you're culpable. Now, I can convince them that we can't proceed with those charges against you, Perles. I heard you myself, heard you pleading for nonviolence. I'll tell them I'm prepared to testify against our own case. It won't gain me any more friends, but ..."

"I can't allow you to do that, Morley. If you report that exchange, it will be seized upon as proving Solania's guilt. You mustn't try to save me by condemning Solania. I won't cooperate with that. I'll swear to the exact reverse, that I was inciting insurrection while Solania counselled peace."

"Perles, that would probably only result in ..."

"I won't hear of it."

"There's also something more, though, Perles," Morley says ominously. "At the station."

"What?"

"Well, you've got their blood up, Perles. They plan to refocus the investigation into the hooker murders."

"Yes?" I say.

"With you as the prime suspect. They intend to build a case against you, Perles."

"I see." I say. I look out to the people waiting there, I find a reason to worry my thumbnail for a few moment's consideration. "Just on the basis of my tie?"

"That would have been their starting point. I don't know what all they've got. There's something about your known brand of rye bottle broken over one of them. That's not much, but I don't know what else. If the truth be known, I sometimes think those forensic guys can build a case for just about anything. They'll convince themselves that you did it, if they decide to."

I step down the stairs past him, watch the people out there, many of whom watch me, awaiting some word about the state of their Solania.

"What about you, Morley?" I say at last, turning to look at him squarely. "Do you think I killed those poor women?"

Morley studies me momentarily.

"No way, not a chance," he says firmly. "Perles, you vent your spleen publically twice a week for this whole city to read, and then you vent your spleen privately a hundred more times just for good measure. Which means that, if there's a person anywhere who shouldn't have any pent up rage, it's you."

"Hm," I say. "I got the idea that you suspected me at one time."

"Me? Never. That kind of thing just isn't in you, Perles. You're bullheaded, sanctimonious, completely obnoxious, well, I could go on and on; but you're not a murderer."

"No monster lurking inside, you mean?"

"No, no monster, Perles. All that's offensive about you is displayed for all to see."

"I appreciate the glowing praise," I say. "In the spirit of that ringing declaration of your admiration and friendship, I'm going to ask you to do something for me, which I believe you'll find to be difficult; but I must ask that you do it, nevertheless."

"I'll do anything within reason," he says sincerely.

"I want you to let your colleagues proceed with their designs against me without any hindrance from you. Let them aim at me."

He says, "Perles, our guys aren't amateurs, you know. If they make a case against you, it'll be a tight one."

"Morley, if I've given you the impression that I'm feeling all cocky and smart-alecky about this business, I've misled you. But I want you to let them set their sights on me. Will you do that?"

He stands and steps over to the front door.

"I'm not sure you know what you're doing," he says. "If I was to act on the basis of friendship or duty, I wouldn't agree to it. If I try to meet your request, it will be out of respect for the great man you've so surprisingly become since that afternoon in front of the 'God's Right Hand' ministry."

He leaves me to chew on this, makes his way out and into the gathered crowd.

If his last comment was anything more than a generous error, which it isn't, I would definitely be of the 'greatness thrust upon them' variety; and I go to check on the thruster.

I find her sitting on the cellar stairs, leaning against the concrete wall, wan, weak, wrapped in the blanket.

"What are you doing here?" I ask.

"Eavesdropping," she says.

I step below her, bundle her up and carry her back to our bed.

"You can't go to prison," she says, distraught.

I pat her arm.

"Would you like some tea?"

"You can't go to prison."

"That's the problem with eavesdropping; you're liable to hear things you'd rather not," I say. "It seems to me that our greatest risk of going to jail is by being found in contempt of court, when we, of course, refuse to testify against each other."

"Contempt of court?"

"That's where one refuses to obey the direction of the judge. The crown will call us to testify, me against you, you against me, and when we refuse, the judge will direct us to answer the crown's questions, and when we continue to refuse, the judge will send us to jail. No jury, and no limit to the sentence: the judge can keep us in jail until we knuckle under, which, in our case, would be forever. But there's something we can do."

"What?" she asks.

"A spouse can't be required to testify against a spouse. If we were to be married, we couldn't be called upon to testify against each other, and I think that would very much weaken the crown prosecutor's case, particularly against you."

"Are you proposing to me?" she asks tentatively.

"Couldn't you tell from my romantic tone?" I ask. "Yes, I'm proposing. It's my most fervent hope that you'll be my wife, and for every reason you'd like to imagine, besides the one I've just so clinically described to you. Perhaps Pastor Enos would agree to perform the ceremony."

She puts her hands to her temples, looks at me aghast.

"What is it?" I ask.

"O, my love, there's something I have to tell you," she says. "Something I'm so afraid will make you withdraw your proposal."

"No, there's nothing you have to tell me," I say.

"You can't go to prison for those prostitutes," she repeats. "There's something I have to tell you ——."

"No, there isn't," I insist.

" —— about the prostitutes who were killed."

"No," I say. "There's nothing for you to say."

"I'm so frightened," she says, gripping my arm.

"You don't need to be frightened," I say sternly. "There's nothing for you to tell me."

"I'll lose you forever, but you must know!" she cries.

"You won't lose me forever, because you won't tell me anything."

"You didn't kill them!" she cries.

"Be quiet, Solania," I say.

I stand and go across to the sink. I pour myself a cracked mug of water, take a drink. I turn back to her.

"You know, this water really isn't as bad as you said it was," I say.

"You didn't kill them, Perles."

"I know that, darling," I say.

She stares at me like an owlet.

"My mouth is so dry," she says eventually. "May I have some water?"

I sit down beside her and help her lift the mug to her lips.

"Don't you wonder how I know you didn't kill them?" she whispers.

"No, I don't," I say. I help her to drink several sips.

"Have you figured it all out?" she asks timorously.

"Yes, darling, all that I needed to figure out, and then some I wish I hadn't."

"I knew you'd figure it all out in time," she says. "Honestly, my love, I did, and I was going to tell you in time, anyway. But you've no reason to believe that. Why ... why haven't you left me?"

"I'm not particularly stupid," I say, "but I can be awfully slow. The fact is, my innocence enlightened my dim wit only piece by piece. The most convincing evidence was the fact that I didn't murder Rose when I had what would have seemed to be my ideal conditions to do it: I'd drunk myself into a blackout, I was irrationally furious with you, and she was alone, pathetic and defenseless; and I was a perfect gentleman, she said. She said that I'd always been a perfect gentleman whenever she'd seen me in that state. Then I just started putting things together, abnormalities and incongruities, and it became obvious that I wasn't the killer. Unfortunately, it also became obvious who the killer is, which is why I would much prefer to discuss it no further."

She clasps my hand with what I assume to be all her strength, which isn't much.

"Tell me how you figured it out," she says. "I love your brain."

"Do you love me, though? That's what I've had to ask myself, over and over. And how can my answer always be yes, when it flies in the face of all sense?"

She kisses and kisses my hand.

"You'll never know how I love you," she says. "I've loved you harder and longer than you'll ever know."

"My hope has been that I was meant to notice the inconsistencies, that they weren't mistakes at all, but that they were, rather, clues, to relieve me."

"Yes," she says. "Tell me the clues."

"There were the murders themselves: except for the first one, Candy, they didn't seem to be the result of some monstrous rage; one or two sharp blows to the head, they were too efficient and apparently dispassionate in dispatch, there was no gruesome gory savour to them; they seemed too clean and calculated to have been accomplished by an enraged monster, and it would only be as an enraged monster that I would ever kill any poor prostitute. I was fearful for a time that I'd killed them out of some hideously distorted compassion, but if I'd done that, I wouldn't have taken those trophies of each murder.

"After Beth's murder, her bracelet was on my right wrist, and it had a very fiddly little catch; it was all I could do to get it off, left-handed, even when I was sober; it dawned on me that I'd never have attempted, let alone succeeded in, putting it on left-handed while mindlessly drunk.

"Then there was the fact that Layla's scarf was damp around my neck. That's because it was a rainy night that she was killed. But I wasn't wet, my jacket wasn't damp, only the scarf around my neck was wet. I hadn't been out in the rain, so I hadn't killed her.

"And then Carney wanted my help in getting him dressed-up to propose to Velvet. When I was tying his tie on him, I stopped to notice that my hand just naturally ties a windsor knot, the knot I always use. I thought about my tie around Laura's neck, and then I recognized that, in the picture I'd seen of her body, my tie was clearly tied in a basic four-in-hand, the ordinary tie knot that I never use.

"But it was Candy's baby blanket, or, rather, what I was meant to believe was her baby blanket, because I'm sure it was a substitute, that really caused me to review everything. The timing of my discovery of it was altogether too pat, on a night several months after she'd been killed.

"It was all pretty simple, actually."

She waits for me to continue, stares wide-eyed in suspense, but I can't bear to go further.

"May I have more water?" she asks.

I help her to drink more from my mug.

"You're so smart, darling," she says in a hush. "You always amaze me. You're easily smart enough to have deduced who the real killer is."

"Yes, to my grief. I just haven't deduced why I was deliberately led to believe it was me."

"That's because you would naturally be looking for the worst reason, not the best."

"Obviously, it was the killer who put my tie on Laura, who put Beth's bracelet on me, who put Layla's sash on me," I say.

"Obviously," she says.

"And who put Laura's money into my pocket. And therefore, could tell me later that it was there."

"Yes."

"And there was only one person who had the opportunity to do all those things."

"Yes."

"You can see my difficulty, my dilemma, my despair. When I believed that I was it, I at least had the decency to hate the murderer. Now I can't claim even that miserable scrap of decency, for I continue to love the murderer desperately, with all of my heart."

"I didn't murder them," she says limply.

"You sent Buster to murder them," I say impatiently. "That's murder, under common law and under common sense, that's murder."

"In a war, soldiers are often sent to certain death," she says. "Is that murder?"

"Darling, those women didn't sign up to be soldiers

in a war."

"We're all soldiers in a war," she says. "A bizarre war in which their side is free to raid and kill with impunity, and our side is supposed to just die without protest. And no one on our side signed up. We're all draftees. If a captain orders a sergeant to send his privates to their death against an invading force, so that their people, their children, may find liberty, is that murder?"

"I don't know."

"Is the objective of war to save soldiers' lives, or defeat the enemy?"

"I've always been suspicious of the objectives of war," I say. "And I don't know how consigning four of our own women to their doom strikes at our enemy."

She holds my hand, because she knows that she can lead me anywhere, such is my longing to love her and believe in her love for me, so desperate am I to nurture the little green shoot of hope that grew like a miracle from the hidden seed she planted in our cold, coaled corner. She pulls me down beside her, waters the little green shoot with her tears, to lead me through the dark, dank, torchlit serpentine corridors of this subterranean substratum in which we dwell.

Are you lying comfortably, Perles? Is your breathing returning to the deep and steady? Is your hand warm within hers? Is her touch still the conduit through which flows the life that you once so carelessly discarded, yet which she, so sublimely, imparts to you yet again, just so? Is her touch still the charge that beats your heart? Is she still the pacemaker, the peacemaker, the piercemaker? Good. Then the journey on which she guides you may continue. Here is your bedtime story:

Once upon a time there was a beautiful girl of long lustrous clean hair and a clean mind and clean habits, who followed her family into the dirty place that had been prepared for them, where her good mother was destroyed and her beautiful sister was killed by the raiders, marauders and leeches who came to exploit their vulnerabilities. She herself sank into the mire of the place, and also avidly pursued the various anaesthetics available, so reckless was she in her despair. But there was in her a rare and unyielding core of defiance against her exploiters and the future they had designed for her and for her people. When, on hangover doorsteps of the chilly mornings or desultory breakfasts at The Friendship Inn, she began to give voice to her defiance, she soon found that she was collecting a regular audience for her diatribes and denunciations. One day, after holding informal court at The Friendship, Sharon the manager said to her, "Your opinions are very similar to those of a writer in the newspaper. Have you ever read 'The Wisdom of Perles'?" No? Well, there was a copy in her office. And the girl was stunned to read her own thoughts and spirit in his words. By Sharon's assistance, she became a devoted reader of the column, hungrily consumed his eloquence and dark wit in defense of the defenseless, she peered forever at the indistinct little picture of Perles at the top of it, until she felt as though she knew him as her soulmate.

She began to see him from time to time, out on the low-down sidewalks, sometimes in the Inn Continent, so handsome, so romantic in style, she thought, so tragic in some deep consuming sorrow. She wrote to him many times, mailed nothing. A few times he came into The Friendship when she was there, but she was too self-conscious to ever accept Sharon's offer to make an introduction.

Eventually, however, she noticed a softening, a dilution of the column's caustic qualities, a gradual imprecision of its direction. But then, one day, she opened the newspaper to read all about herself, to read of Perles' observation of her in a typical self-destructive self-defilement that predictably drew delicious scorn and hatred from those eastside people who'd made such conduct inescapable. Perles wrote of her, not in celebrative hatred, but in horrified love. From that point on, she believed in their fated unity, and she abandoned herself to unreserved love of him, albeit from afar.

From afar, she watched him sink into the despond that sucked at and slowly smothered her.

She fell very ill with a fever that wouldn't give her up, but The Baron gave her up, for he was able to guess at the diagnosis, and she moved into her tiny debasement room, got it ahead of other less pretty people in consideration of her special arrangement with the slumlord. She lay on the little bed left there by the past tenant who had no means to remove it, lay there in her persistent fever; and there came to her her first vision, of a two-headed firebird that called to the spirits of her people to rise up against the conditions of their oppression. Others might dismiss it as delirium, but to her it was inspiration, and there was no doubt whatsoever in her mind as to who constituted the two heads of the firebird.

She lay on the little bed, day in, day out, and the firebird returned to her mind's eye at her bidding. She subsisted through these fiery days and weeks on water from bad pipes, and by this means she kicked her drug habit. She endlessly debated with Perles on how to proceed, to realize her vision, they would argue with blistering, parching heat and commitment into her dark nights, burning like candles in wine bottles in a 1920s Parisian café, united by their love and compassion.

Her slumlord sullied her quite in excess of their agreement through these days, because he thought she was oblivious to him in her illness.

Through her illness, the pounds poured off her, and her long hair became a matted mess. When her fever finally subsided, she chopped off her hair, and she filed her nails, and then she filed her tooth.

She went back to the street, worked 19th and 21st, and soon was drinking again. But every morning, she would go to wherever there were knots of her people huddled against those harsh swirling winds, and she would recount to them her recurrent visions, and she would liberally quote 'The Wisdom of Perles' when her own descriptive powers of their circumstances failed her, not the new crappy columns about clever ways to silence a neighbour's barking dog without getting caught, but the older ones of passion and pain.

And she discovered that channel that runs from someone's eyes to his heart and back again. When she showed people that she possessed the power to read their hearts, their apprehension of her was elevated from curious respect to devotion.

When she read Perles' heart from a darkened doorway as he staggered by one night, she saw that his fire was burnt out to dull cinders and charcoal, that he would never fulfill their conjoined fate through attraction and passion, that he would deny all desire and would repulse all offers of love, much as he might ache for it. But she was a bright girl who'd learned well how to manipulate men through their revealed needs. She saw the tinder that remained in Perles, knew that it would take her spark; his writing had been the outcry of moral anguish; he would respond to her through the promise of a necessary spiritual redemption. He was past wanting to save his life, but there lingered a longing to save his soul.

She followed him under the cold streetlight to his parked van, saw him just barely lurch into it before passing out. She peered through the window at him, then she opened the side door, climbed into the van, crouched beside him where he'd collapsed onto the middle seat; she took his hand, held it to her cheek, felt the need flickering through fingers like pulsing probes, said "Perles, Perles." And when he did-n't answer, she said "I'm Solania. Fate has given your heart to me. You will tell the world my story, and help me tell our people their destiny. I am your love, you are my love, and you belong to me."

Of her early disciples, the most devoted in his adher-ence was Buster, who responded nobly to her ongoing frailty, and became her staff and attendant by his natural will. She advised him that there were coming into play forces that would surpass his understanding; this was no news to some-one who'd spent his adult life failing furiously to understand why all his own forces rebounded against him, and he accepted her advice faithfully.

And then some eastside john beat to death poor demented Candy. When Solania would speak of this in her little knots, she noted well the smouldering anger in the eyes; she thought she saw first little licks of flame under the smoke, and she waited for the next hooker murder, which would surely come, so that she might fan those flames into a raging fire, her raging fire. But she waited and waited, and no subsequent murder came, and the smoulder diminished and cleared.

She became deeply concerned that her visions had been incorrect, that her gift was really just another curse; she had found no way to draw Perles toward their intertwined destiny, and her followers were falling back into inertia and dissipation.

Then one night, Fate answered her; she looked out from a corner of the Inn Continent barroom where she sat with Buster, and there was Perles sitting in the orange murk of a central table, being unresponsive, in a drunkenly gentle-manly sort of way, to the aroused attentions of sad old Laura.

She knew that Laura, aging too rapidly in her abuses, was soon to be tossed onto The Baron's scrap heap; she was no longer to expect his minimal protections, she was no longer to occupy an advantageous spot on 21st, she was on her own, could look forward to scrabbling ever more desperately for tricks at 20th St. stoplights, lowering her price steadily in the downward-spiralling support of her drug and drinking habits. Everyone knew it but Laura herself.

She saw Perles' drunken concern when he realized he'd spent all his money on his drinking companions, saw Laura pull a folded wad of bills out of her jeans to pay for the last round.

When Laura and Perles staggered out of the bar early that morning, Solania and Buster followed them. Laura was all over Perles, but he'd have none of it. When they got to his van, he turned to her and said "Here is where we say goodnight." When Laura protested and cajoled, Perles said sharply "Whatever charms you may have, I am faithful to my true love."

"And that's me," Solania said to herself.

Perles dove into his van, and Laura swore at him bitterly, and careened down 20th St.

And Solania turned to Buster and reminded him of those forces that he wouldn't understand, explained their unfortunate immediate manifestation.

And moments later, she knelt beside the fallen Perles once again, kissed his hand once again, lovingly undid his tie as though this was a seduction, which it was. She whispered, "Forgive me, my love. But you will come to me only after great suffering."

She held his curled hand to her little chest until Buster came to the van door. She pushed it open slightly, handed him the tie and took from him the folded wad of Laura's twenty dollar bills.

With the second coming of the monster slouching toward the westside from the east to murder our women,

Solania's firebrand condemnations reawakened the flames of outrage in her followers' eyes, and they attended keenly to her assessments and visions.

In the days to come, she singled out Carney for special encouragement of his attentions, as a means of more quickly attracting Perles' attentions. Carney's chivalry in the 'God's Right Hand' entranceway was nothing less than a gift of Fate's right hand. And cavorting obscenely in Fate's left hand was the shameless Beth, fulfilling every mean-spirited stereotype of the character of her people, and soon squatting to spill on the sidewalk between her pink slippers a stinking, swill-soaked baby that would later fulfill every teacher's and cop's mean-spirited stereotype of the intellectual and moral potential of her people.

However, in death Beth was the benefactor of her people, stoking their fires to burn hotter against their oppressors and breaking down Perles' resistance to his destiny, bringing him closer to his ultimate confrontation of his need for his Solania and the redemption she offered, and a sacrificial lamb laid at the altar of their enemies to strike terror into the black sensibilities.

Layla, swaggering and satanic, soldier in service to the traitorous Baron, standing hard against the hope of her people; in war, traitors are dealt with swiftly and surely, and if Layla's execution was the final circumstance to tip the reluctant partner toward the alliance that would serve their people so well, who could mourn it or condemn her executioners?

And for each of the three who fell, a clue was given to Perles, and then finally a fabricated Candy clue, to cause him to recognize his need and its answer, a clue that wouldn't lead the police to him, but would lead him to his Solania.

In war, soldiers die to carry their leaders to their destiny. It's not murder. It's never been called murder.

And all the while, Solania was fighting the war on another front, every night climbing into the shiny cars and pick-up trucks of the exploiters and defilers, the people who maintained the prison brothel to their own convenience and pleasures, who killed her sister, destroyed her mother, broke little girls in two, she looked her youngest and most vulnerable always by the side of the road, and when they stopped for her, told her to pump them free of their little frustrations and meaningless little stresses, took her short hair and thin neck in their fat pink hands, she and her sharp tooth would slice finely, 'Hey, easy, what the —?!', and out the passenger door she would leap, leaving them carrying a time bomb in their veins, carrying it home, tick tick tick tick tick, to their neat orderly homes in the neighborhoods where Solania's people aren't welcome, where ten people don't sleep to a slum cell, where landlords can't demand special arrangements, home to the eastside, there maybe to kill unsuspecting coiffed and tailored mothers and pampered powdered babies, too, the venal mortal sins of the father visited upon them, in its slow, deadly explosion.

Tick, tick, tick, her slumlord, tick, tick, tick, Councillor Rod, tick, tick, tick, and uncounted anonymous casualties in the genocidal imperial war that they so casually declared and carelessly maintained. Solania the Warrior Princess slew them all.

People die in war. If they are of your own, then they are honoured as heroes when they die. If they are of your enemies, their deaths are estimated and celebrated. Solania never asked for war, she never wanted war. She just wanted a job as a secretary. But when she discovered that war was long ago quietly declared and had claimed her family, was killing and crippling those around her, she fought back. And she aroused her people to fight back.

Perles interrupts, says we'll lose the fight.

We're already losing the fight. If we must die, let us die fighting.

Eventually, we have to lash out just to prove that we won't be so very easy to kill. Don't we, Perles?

If that's the only satisfaction left to us, shouldn't we take it?

And are you still lying comfortably, Perles?

No, I'm not, because this is a bed of nails, and as I spin and toss and turn, it tears away at me, strips away all my accumulated barnacles and limed crust, because there can come a time when all I thought I knew is not only inadequate, it's all wrong.

There can come a time when even my hard little acorn core credo is proven to be no more than a meaningless mantra.

She just wanted to be a secretary, isn't that modest enough?

What if I'd found her outside Robert's office, bent over a keyboard? May I help you? O! yes, you may help me, for I've been searching for you everywhere in my darkness, lead me anywhere with the silvered circles of your lamplight, but light my way. By now, we would have bought a house in City Park with enough room for a family to grow into, we'd be checking for canker worms in the garden she'd planted, on the little crab apple trees we'd planted for the shade and blossoms they'd give us twenty years from now, whose fruit we'd pluck 'til time and times are done. She'd have no story for me to tell the world. But when she'd take my tie in her little hand, pull herself in to set her head against my chest, I'd know that I could do anything, anything for the love of her.

She takes my tie in her little hand, pulls herself in to set her head against my chest.

"Have I lost you forever?" she asks.

All I know, absolutely all I know, is that I can do anything, anything for the love of her.

I pull her onto me, shield her against the bed's tormenting upreaching claws.

"I pledged my fate to you," I say. "I am your loyal knight and true. Your vision did not deceive you."

She's as light as a feather on me, but I feel her little form conform to me. She raises her head to study my face.

"And do you still want me as your wife?"

"It's all that I want. It's all that I'll ever want."

She sits up; she lovingly unties my tie, she slowly unbuttons my shirt, spreads it open to bare my chest.

She slowly unbuttons her flannel shirt, lifts it open to bare her chest, then lays herself upon me, settles her beautiful head under my chin.

"Our hearts are beating together as one," she says.

"Yes," I say.

"Now I'm your wife."

I clasp her against me, set my heart to pumping yet harder and harder, so that it might finally suck her soul out through her pores and in through mine, so that she might dwell forever in the care and protection of my strength and health.

She lies like that for a long time without moving, and I can feel her heart against mine. I think maybe she's drifted off to sleep.

But then she says:

"You know, I don't even know your first name."

"Nobody knows my first name," I say.

"Then you'll reveal it to me as your most intimate devotion."

"Yes," I say. "My first name is Aengus."

"Aengus," she says experimentally.

"I don't even know your last name," I say.

"Of course you do," she says. "My last name is Perles. I am what I was meant to become. And we are what we were meant to become."

Chapter Twelve

I f this is to be the end of us," Solania says out to the con-
gregation of her followers arrayed below her on the
slopes of the park, "then let's meet our end with defiance
and disobedience. We must never again assist our enemies
and exploiters by our cooperative self-destruction. If they
really mean to wipe us out, we must make it so that they
have to do it with every obvious intention, not just set up the
conditions for our convenient, compliant self-destructions,
our addictions, our abuses of one another, our deadly self-
indulgences; if they really mean to kill us off, they'll have to
pull the trigger themselves, not merely hand us a loaded gun
with which we'll conveniently blow our own brains out.

"If they really mean to bury us, let their future gener-
ations see that we died while digging our way to the light.

"If they really mean to kill us off, let their history
haunt them forever with the record that we died fighting to
live."

Her voice is surprisingly strong, and her people are
attentive. Marriage seems to agree with her. In the days since
she married us together, she has gained vitality and strength,
and her mood has been apparently optimistic, in spite of the
times she and I have been taken to the police station for inter-
views of the same repeated questions. We are treated there
with rigid courtesy, as though we're the visiting heads of a
hostile state. I suppose it's a balancing act for the police;
Aiken and his party are demanding arrests on a daily basis,
as is the other newspaper, but the police seem to fear our
anger, and hasten to mollify us, at least for the moment,
whenever I show them a flash of mine. I've come to rather
enjoy upsetting them, enjoy the glimpses of their own resentment that they can't quite conceal.

Solania remains very anxious about my design to permit the police to fix me as their primary target. I tell her that the first order of the loyal knight and true is to rescue his lady from captivity, that he is honour-bound to his duty. I reassure her that their hounds will follow my false scent until confounded.

Standing self-consciously amongst our multitude is Pastor Enos, who is here not to spy or subvert, but as a convert. In the riot, he caught his foreshadowing of the coming apocalypse, and it was revealed to him, to his horror, that he was fighting on the wrong side. Twentieth St. was his road to Damascus. At the instant of his greatest peril, when he was certain that his prayers for mercy had been cast back at him in rejection out of God's Right Hand, an angel had appeared, had guided him through the melee to safety. The glowing angel, he later told us, looked exactly like Solania. "Why do you persecute me?" she asked him before evaporating. According to Enos now, the riot was the righteous destruction of Babylon, and our people are the lost tribe of Israel. And our wilderness is paradise, Enos.

Solania sits on a chair at the top of the slope, a chair that Russell placed for her; she sits with her back to Spadina Crescent, and she faces her people spread over the downward slope. As she speaks now, she scans the pale evening sky over the river, as though she's seeking something there. She is bathed in the honeyed light of the sinking sun.

I am standing off to one side of the slope. Ken stands beside me; Buster assigned him to guard me today.

Last night, Solania seemed to suffer a setback, she clung to me through the night in terrors she couldn't or wouldn't describe. It was a very difficult night, but in the morning she was calm and composed, and together we composed her message for this meeting in the park, which she treated as unusually important. She spoke often of the necessary courage to embrace the inevitable.

This afternoon, she'd recovered enough to go for a walk with me, and she held my arm all the way, relied on my strength in her beautiful and gracious way.

"We've broken down the structures of our enemy's exploitation and subjugation," she says to her audience. "Now, what are we going to build in their place? Have we just cleared the ground for new oppressors, or will we fill the gap with structures that really meet our needs? That's the challenge in front of us.

"We must find the frameworks, methods and means of our own progress, and if our enemies and exploiters still mean to oppress us, make it necessary for them to smash our structures. Let the whole world see them doing it, to their shame.

"By our conduct, we must show the world that our oppressors have no excuse, that what they have done is founded entirely on their own hatred and fear and cruelty and greed and wanton lusts, that the place they made for us wasn't justified, wasn't what we deserved by our own deficiencies and degenerations. Never again can we be our enemies' instruments of our destruction. By our conduct, we must prove that we are the victims of our enemy's injustice, not of our own weakness. That's a lot for us to ask of ourselves, I know, but we're beyond choice.

"If we won't fight to live, we will die. And if our enemies really mean to kill us, let the world see that we died fighting to live."

"Listen to me!" she cries suddenly. "I tell you this now because my time with you is drawing to a close."

This arrests everyone's attention, including mine, for this is no part of what we discussed.

She searches out over the river.

"No," people around me say in protest.

The call is taken up, passing from one person to another

like a little grass fire on the slope.

"No, no. No, no."

She raises her hands, closes her deep eyes.

"In my mind, I see our people resisting the design that was decreed for them by the selfish and greedy, those of hatred and perverted passions, I see them fighting to live against the designs of death, I see them struggling to replace the structures that were placed to oppress them, I see the spirits of our people striving to rejoin the path of our progress, smashing the obstacles that were placed on it.

"But I see that I'm not there with my people, their struggle they carry on without me, because our enemies have killed me."

"No!" cries Ken.

"No!" cries Carney.

"No!" cries Velvet.

"No," I say, and I start up toward her.

"Our enemies believe that you will be stopped because I am stopped, but I can see you from where I am flying, from my place up beyond the smoke and the sorrow, I see your struggle, I see that they are wrong," she says. "I see that you will not lie down to die for them again, you won't swallow their poisonous wastes again, you will spit them out, and that if you must die, you will die fighting, just as I died fighting. You will be courageous in the days ahead, I see that."

I step as quickly as I can through the crowd of people who now struggle to their feet in alarm.

She opens her eyes and says, "You all know my husband."

She sets her black eyes on me, stops me where I stand.

"If you would honour me, you will listen to my husband," she says, "because when he speaks, you will hear me. Because I hold —"

And here she stops, and people look from her to me, and back again, but she only looks at me. She waits so long, it would seem that she has forgotten what she was about to say, but then into that frozen instant, she sobs, unable to speak, and her sparkling black eyes, holding mine so hard, overflow.

"Because I will forever hold his heart in my hands," she says at last.

And watching me still, she waves her little birdwing hand in front of her as though she's blessing her people.

"No, please, my love," I say.

She is raising her other hand to wipe her eyes when the shot cracks out, echoes out from somewhere across the street maybe.

She lurches forward, and I reel as though I'm shot.

And dutiful Ken is leaping on me, diving me to the ground. He holds me down amid the uprush of people.

It's not panic that I hear in the screams and cries. How I wish it was. It's the sickening thick-throated wails of grief of the accomplished disaster beyond all urgency, beyond all desperate effort, beyond any course of recovery, not frantic superficial screams skittering across the surface of the moment, but the profound grieving of the final, wrenching death of hope deep inside it.

Ken is over me, but no longer in protection, he's collapsed on me, he pulls at me in abstract affliction, bangs his head beside mine on the ground, growls and wails. I watch the feet around me, worn, torn, poor shoes and boots stepping, scuffling, pivoting, starting, starting back, exploring the futility of a world where all direction is suddenly smashed, where everywhere to go instantly converges upon the one impossible point; where all intention and energy are sucked immediately into its terrible vortex, lost without trace with all vision and light into its black hole.

I try to plot a course through those poor feet, up the slope to my darling, I heave up and crawl out from under Ken, but my legs are tingling, and I seem to have lost my feet altogether, so I crawl, through the feet, through forms doubled over and sinking in pain, through old women banging the sides of their heads with wizened old fists, like there's something they knew just a moment ago that's gone now, women raising their spread hands to heaven as though heaven has ever heard them before, men shuffling limply as in an old dance that might have once invoked a spirit of something they could understand, children dumbfounded or wailing terrified in a terrible world that won't hold itself together, I'm buffeted through worn and torn old shoes and boots and kneeling or falling forms, buffeted through the falling trees and suddenly upsurging quakes of the terrible world wrenching itself apart again, I crawl to my beloved, who lies face down at the only peace at the centre of all pain and beauty, of all existence.

I sit and gather her up into my arms, and she's gossamer, and I speak softly into her glossy black hair.

And over us, as if summoned from the course of the river, the pair of Canada geese wing and cry. They circle over us, wings beating together as one, calling to one another as always, and they seem to be calling to us.

"There we go, my darling, it's time to fly away," I say, as though she can hear me.

Chapter Thirteen

B ut I don't fly away. I can't fly, I have no wings, I can't even walk, I have no legs. I'm just a pale berry grown on the tip of her slender and brittle branch; I guess it's my function to carry the seed, but now I've fallen to the hard ground, to the dirty concrete, I just roll around on it uselessly. I roll and bounce off curbs and walls and fences, I'm channeled by ruts, I'm sent skipping by bumps and stones, bruised and softening in meaningless momentum through these streets as darkness pours into them and into me. And this dirty world spins around me with each of my rotations.

People are milling about everywhere, out on the streets, out on their little lawns, they can't bear to go into their little homes; maybe they're afraid to close their doors on this last day that hope existed.

Me, I have nowhere to go, I have joined the numbers of the homeless, so that's why I roll and bounce around and around and over and over. The people I encounter look away from me. They're kind people, they can't think of anything to say to ease my suffering, they're suffering themselves, after all, so they avoid my eyes, lest they find themselves having to say something certainly wrong.

They talk to each other, I hear them before they fall silent at my approach, I hear them keening and weeping, trying to comfort one another, swapping and confirming rumours of the killer being caught and lynched by our people, it was someone from COIN, it was someone hired by Aiken, it was Aiken himself, it was a police marksman, it was the hooker killer.

And they wonder what will become of them.

They don't ask me. If they believe that they'll hear Solania when I speak, they're not requiring it of me just yet. Maybe they're kindly allowing me time to grieve, unaware that that will take me all eternity.

I don't hear her when I speak, I just hear myself saying that I adore her, but then, I don't feel any legs under me; and that's how I know that I'm rolling like a pale berry. And I can't stop, because I'm always rolling downward.

It must be that she holds my heart in her hands, for nothing else could be causing it to continue to beat, but how she can refuse me the kindness of squeezing the life out of it, I don't know, how she can be so cruel in the face of my love for her, I don't know.

I don't know what all the sirens are for, either. Maybe they're the whoops of official jubilation, of a social order celebrating its rescue, like an all-clear. Squad cars crawl through these streets no faster than I bounce, with no more apparent direction. Sometimes they pull up to me and ask where I'm rolling to, and I have no answer for them, so I just roll, and then they leave me alone. After they interviewed me tonight, the investigating officers told me that I was free to go. I've nowhere to go, and I'll never ever be free.

Maybe I'll happen to be berry tired one day, and I'll roll into a doorway, get caught in a corner, shrivel up like those others who roll homeless and directionless into doorways. It won't be the 'God's Right Hand' doorway, though; that's sacred ground, and no one will sully it with juice stains anymore.

There is a car that is following behind me, its headlights illuminating my route to nowhere; I don't know how long it's been trailing me, I only gradually became aware of it, and I haven't turned to investigate; if she isn't sitting in the back seat waiting for me, I can arouse no interest in it.

But its light bothers me, it stretches out my shadow before me on the cracked and heaving asphalt and gravel like a future I can't consider, and there are the shadows of my legs, anyway, pumping and lifting, I'm not rolling after all,

I'm on my own two feet, which is quite a bit more than I wish to contemplate at the moment.

So I test the resolve of its driver, I turn down the alley between Ave. H and Ave. I, see if he's prepared to make his pursuit so obvious. And the car slowly turns down the alley behind me; so we needn't pretend anything. I assume that it's some guy or group acting on the mistaken belief that it is necessary to kill the firebird's other head. I turn around and confront the headlights squarely, glare into their glare as though they're the eyes of our enemy. Of all the things my love requires of me, dying fighting is the one I'm pretty sure I can do.

The car pulls to a stop right at me, its bumper at my knees, purrs like a panther while I wonder what I can do to maximize its unseen occupants' pain before I go down.

I've no patience.

"What are you waiting for?" I call. "I'm not about to die of old age!"

The driver's door opens in response, and by the automatic interior light, I see that it's Alexi, driving his Baron trophy.

"Perles," he says. "C'mon, man."

"What?" I demand.

"C'mon, man, you've walked it off for now. Get in the car."

"No," I say, turning away. "I'll never walk out from under this."

I start along the alley, and Alexi plays his trump.

"It's what she wants," he says.

I pause.

"What do you mean?"

"She told us, man, before. Now, c'mon, do what she wants. Get in the car."

I'm far from sure that I can sit still in a car, but against my other judgement, I go and get into the passenger seat.

Buster is sort of curled in the corner of the back seat. He looks terrible, tortured, devastated. His brother Russell sits beside him, stoic behind his mirrored glasses. I think I can see myself reflected in them. I look terrible, tortured, devastated.

From somewhere, Alexi has come up with a black tie and black handkerchief to wear with his suit. I should never have sat down, for now I'm instantly exhausted. The gravel of the alley pops under the tires as we drive slowly along it.

At 13th St., Alexi stops and says "Where to now?"

Buster says "Victoria Bridge.", as though he's spitting out his teeth.

"Let's drop Perles off first. We're almost there," Alexi suggests.

"No," Buster says. "Victoria Bridge."

Alexi goes along 13th to the corner of H, drives up H. The shortest route to the bridge would be along Spadina, but he avoids that fatal spot, and no one argues.

Although squad cars still roam the streets, they're no longer stopping everyone, and we travel unhindered to the bridge, to the buffer zone that separates our neighborhood from that other world across the river, where in a hundred lairs, dens and havens of nighttime despoilers and disadvantage advantage-takers, her time bombs tick, tick, tick, all those shop owners and franchisees and business owners and managers who would only ever hire her for that one temporary job.

Alexi steers into the parking lot of the school board building, where of a day they dream up lofty-sounding mission statements and self-congratulations and sort out upon whom else to affix the blame for all the westside children and parents they so blithely consign to the pebble prison of ignorance. Who can parse out that sentence?

Buster lunges forward, grabs my shoulder urgently.

"Me and you," he says. "Let's go."

He reaches down to pick up a rifle from the floor at his feet.

I suppose it's one of the rifles he and Russell used to shoot up the biker gang's clubhouse, but other than that deduction, my brain fails in confusion. I can't figure out why he wants to shoot me, and why Alexi just watches him.

But it makes little difference to me. I get out of the car. I remind myself that I'm supposed to die fighting.

Buster comes up beside me, motions casually with the rifle, says "This way."

We go to the sidewalk and step through an arbour of overreaching bushes, and then walk out on the pedestrian passage of the bridge, to where the deepest channel of the river flows far below us. The black water sparkles with lights from our neighborhood, sparkles like Solania's eyes.

Buster stops there, looks down into the black river, then looks to the rifle in his hands, hefts it before him.

"She was so scared I wouldn't make a clean shot," he says. "But I guess I gave her that, didn't I?"

"Yes, you gave her that," I say. "I guess I ask the same favour of you."

He studies me quizzically while I wonder how exactly I'm supposed to fight someone I don't want to fight.

"I'm not gonna shoot you," he says at last.

He's not going to shoot me. Of course not. Nobody ever shoots me. If I wanted to live, everybody'd be shooting me all over the place.

"Then why are we here?"

"I just wanted a minute with you, man."

He takes a folded piece of paper from his breast pocket and steps toward me, shoves it in mine. Then, on sudden impulse, he hugs me desperately, before stepping back, bowing his head shyly.

"Man," he gasps, "I guess we showed 'em something, didn't we, you, me and her? We showed 'em something, didn't we, Perles?"

"Yes, we sure did."

"I guess nobody's gonna forget about us very soon."

"No."

"You gonna put us all in a story, Perles? She says you're gonna do that."

"Yes."

"So maybe people will remember us forever. Whatya think maybe you'll write about me?"

"I'll write that you're a hero of your people."

He nods, satisfied. He swings his leg up over the metal railing, then the other, so that he's sitting on it, facing out to the river.

I step toward him, but he pivots and points the rifle at me, smiles and wags his finger at me.

"Glad I never learned to swim," he says.

He raises the rifle over his head and gives the long loud high cry of the warrior, he summons up the strength and courage he has developed and refined through ten millennia and more, the traits necessary to his true responsibilities, he shakes his fists into the darkness and cries out, and then he leaps into the waiting embrace of his ancestors.

I don't bother to look down, for I know that the cold water won't weaken his resolve, can't change his mind, that he's steeped in the self-discipline that isn't supposed to exist in our people, that he won't struggle to rise to the rippled sparkling surface.

Behind me, a full moon is rising, I believe that I can feel its light on my back as I stand alone on the bridge. I listen for something of meaning to come for me out of the darkness, I wait a while but it doesn't come.

So I go back to Alexi's car. The door of the back seat is open, and I get in. We three sit in a minute's silence.

"Is Buster coming?" Alexi asks eventually.

"No," I say.

Russell is erect and forward looking. His face is sculpted in stone. But down from behind his dark glasses there flows a tiny river, as though he's a miracle statue.

I turn my eyes away.

Alexi puts his car into gear. He drives us along 19th St., I know not to where, but it doesn't matter to me, not enough to disrupt the solemn silence that is upon us.

In time, he pulls to a stop in front of Rose's house of Solania's Orphans.

He turns around to look at me.

"Here you go," he says.

"Where do I go?" I ask.

"Here," he says. "She said I should take you here. She said you should stay here."

I get out of the car, stand on the sidewalk under the silver circle of the streetlight. Alexi leans over toward the passenger window.

"I'll come 'round in the morning, we'll go get your stuff," he says.

He drives away. I put a hand to the light standard, grip it not for support, but to strain against my restlessness. Across the street, the school looms up like a fortress of darkness against the moonlight, its big old windows black. For no reason at all other than that it's so dark, and that its shadows are reaching out so murkily behind it, I start off toward it.

The front door of the house opens, and Rose steps out onto the stoop. She motions worriedly to me to come to her.

I stop and shake my head, and she motions again, urgently, reaches right into my soft spot for her.

As I approach her, she burps out, "Mr. Perles, aren't

you coming in?"

"Oh, yes, I'm coming in," I say.

She takes my arm lightly and gently steers me inside, as though she's afraid I might bolt.

I step into the house. Around the little entrance area, many girls are gathered, staring at me as though I'm something supernatural. I can think of nothing to say, so I stare back at them.

"Okay, ladies," Rose says, and the girls depart.

She says to me "We fixed up a room for you on the top floor."

She points to the little room to the right of us.

"Maybe this is big enough for an office."

I slump against the wall beside the door.

"Why do you act as though it's not all over?" I ask.

She responds as if she's anticipated the question.

"Oh, no, Mr. Perles," she says as hurriedly as her method of speech will allow. "It's not all over. There's more to do than ever."

"I can't," I say.

"After a rest," she says sympathetically.

"I can't," I say. "I can't even rest."

Rose is strong, but not assertive, and she falls into a perplexed silence.

"Don't you understand? I can't even rest," I say.

And then from the unlit room to our left, little Angela quietly arises from the cot on which she's been lying, stiffly and carefully, she stands and comes to me. Her right arm is encased in a cast.

She looks up at me, and she takes my hand with her little left hand, and without a word she leads me into her room, to her cot.

She sits down and pulls me to sit beside her.

With her eyes, she directs mine to her stained glass

window, which has now been lovingly if roughly repaired, its broken fragments held in place by thin strips of electrical tape like black ribbon.

"Look," she says. "It will help you rest."

I try to look, but all I see is a beer bottle flying through it over and over again.

"You're very sweet, Angela," I say in impatient woe. "I appreciate your kindness, but, you see, everything for me is all broken. There's nothing for me, not even rest."

She looks at me evenly in a moment's critical appraisal.

"Check your pocket," she says.

"What?"

She nods lightly to my breast pocket.

I reach into it, pull out the folded paper that Buster put in on the bridge.

Dumbly, I spread it open. I tilt it into the yellow light from the front hallway.

With stabbing recognition, I see on it my darling's round, generous, careful northern schoolgirl handwriting:

To my beloved husband.

Please forgive me for stealing our last few remaining beautiful moments together. On balance, though, there isn't enough reason to go on. I know that you, my loyal knight and true, would sacrifice yourself to my rescue, but there just isn't any point.

We both know that this place killed me before you and I even met. My martyrdom to the things built against us was going to be too subtle the way it was going, too drawn out, too hard on both of us. Please don't quarrel with me, my dying this way doesn't distort the truth, it just emphasizes it. You know that around here people die for no reason all the time. Dying for a reason is a pretty good way to go. I want you to let my death justify our life together.

Never doubt that I hold your heart in my hands, never doubt that I'm waiting for you in a place where all we need to do is love each other forever.

In this world, though, we do what we have to do, and what we want to do doesn't have anything to do with it. I know that you will do what you have to do, my love, just the way I'm doing what I have to do. I wish they both could have been the same thing. But there's no other way.

Please be kind to Buster, this is going to be really hard on him.

I know that you'll give my life reason, and that you'll give our love reason. As for me, I'll be waiting and waiting in undying love for my own dangerous man.

From your adoring wife.

I fold the page and return it to my pocket. Angela watches me silently, takes my hand when I set it on my knee.

"Now look," she says softly. "It will help you to rest."

I lean back against the wall.

"Just look."

The window has been broken, it displays that it's been broken, and yet the streetlight and the silver moonlight shine through it so beautifully, sparkle so brightly around its repairs, and really, the fragments and fractures seem to take on their own sort of design, almost to the point of apparent intention, and they speak in a sort of eloquence to the beauty of the heart and hands behind its careful repair, and as I gaze at it and gaze at it and gaze at it, my hand in Angela's little warm hand, I begin to think that I feel a fluttering of little warm hands around my own heart, I'm almost sure I feel ... and I'm almost sure I hear a little tapping, something beating softly inside the luminescence ... like little bird wings maybe ... in the rhythm of my own heart, as one with it ...

Maybe I could sit like this forever, while beautiful coloured lights reach into and bathe in illumination any dark doubt still inside me, I would stay like this almost forever, I believe, dwelling in love without regret, my heart nesting in her little birdwing care until my time here is done and I am wholly and holy with my true love again, just stay sitting here, gazing and gazing and gazing, moonlight, sunlight shining in turn through, moonlight, sunlight, but now my eyes seem to be closing. I seem to be falling asleep.